What Readers Say about *Texting Lincoln*

Kudos! *Texting Lincoln* is a unique and delightful read: a clever and witty mystery intertwined with American history! Ettwein crafts a warm friendship between our sixteenth president and the present-day narrator, a history buff with a knack for humor and adventure. Readers will love how the strands of story and history, Lincoln's story, and our story, blend together. A wonderful read!

- David Martin, Milwaukee

A wonderful ride through history with a knowledgeable, insightful and thoughtful guide. I loved learning so much about Kalamazoo, and the life and motivations of our 16th President through this adventure! Beautifully written and thoroughly engaging."

- J. Giles, Michigan

Texting Lincoln

Texting Lincoln

A semi-true tale of an Illinois prairie
lawyer's return to Kalamazoo

Tony Ettwein

Front cover photo: Abraham Lincoln portrait taken by Alexander Gardner on August 9, 1863. Additional image work by Alyssa Scott.

Back cover photo: The Kalamazoo Transportation Center, formerly the Michigan Central Railroad Depot. Photo by Fran Dwight.

Photo inside front: Statue of Abraham Lincoln at Bronson Park in Kalamazoo, Michigan. Designed by sculptor William Wolfe, commissioned by the Kalamazoo Abraham Lincoln Institute and dedicated on August 27, 2023. Photo by the author.

To Molly, Katy, Sam, and the rest of my family and friends

who have encouraged me to write this story.

Introduction

Since his death in 1865, Abraham Lincoln has consistently been regarded as one of America's greatest presidents. A man of contrasts, Lincoln tried whenever possible to find common ground with those he disagreed with, yet he was prepared to do whatever it took to stand on principle, including saving the Union during the Civil War and eradicating slavery. Although he had little formal education, he taught himself law, sciences, history, scripture, and other subjects, and had a great curiosity and love for reading.

Abraham Lincoln was born in LaRue County, Kentucky on February 12, 1809. As a young man, he traveled the Ohio and Mississippi rivers, and as a young lawyer, he traveled the state of Illinois extensively, riding the judicial circuit from town to town on horseback, and later (1858) engaged his friend and political opponent Stephen A. Douglas in a series of seven debates in towns up and down the Illinois countryside. Following the informal rules of presidential campaigning of the day, he traveled very little during the campaign 1860, the year he was nominated by the Republican Party and elected president. He did not even venture from his home in Springfield, Illinois to address the Republican National Convention in Chicago, just 200 miles away.

Lincoln spent much of his adult life pursuing his political interests and preparing himself for the most difficult presidency in this nation's history. But in the summer of 1856, Lincoln, a former congressman and Illinois state representative, was still unknown to most people outside of Illinois. That summer, he received a letter from Kalamazoo, Michigan attorney Hezekiah G. Wells inviting him to speak in Kalamazoo in support of the upstart Republican Party's first presidential candidate, John C. Frémont.

In 1856, Lincoln received invitations to speak in a number of other states. However, he only spoke once outside Illinois that presidential election year: in Kalamazoo's Bronson Park, on August 27.

In the story you're about to read, Abraham Lincoln pays a second visit to Kalamazoo many years later. Imagine if he had returned to this country in the 21st Century, after more than 150 years of technological progress and social changes. What would he think now? What sense would he make of our contemporary world?

Although this book is partly a fictional present-day account of an interaction with Abraham Lincoln, it also includes a non-fictional account of his real life from 1809 to 1865. Every aspect of Abraham Lincoln's life right up to his arrival to see the play *Our American Cousin* that night at Ford's Theater—April 14, 1865, Good Friday night—is depicted as accurately as possible in these pages. That includes the significant events that occurred earlier that fateful day.

Before telling this story, it's important that I mention the Kalamazoo Abraham Lincoln Institute, which is dedicated to sharing the true story of Lincoln's 1856 visit to Kalamazoo; the institute's mission is "to enrich the cultural life of Kalamazoo by creating educational programs that model the example of Abraham Lincoln." Specifically, I need to mention one of the institute's members, Dr. Thomas George, MD, who has spent countless hours researching the life of Abraham Lincoln, particularly his visit to the city in 1856. Without Tom's research and the information he has uncovered, Kalamazoo and historians would know much less about Lincoln's visit to the city. Without that research, this book would have been vastly different, if not unthinkable.

It's my intent to portray Abraham Lincoln as he was in reality: a brilliant, ambitious, good but very human man with legendary physical strength and an equally legendary sense of humor, who gave his life for his country.

Thank you for joining me in this look at our 16th president.

Where to begin?

I've been thinking about where I should start. First of all, thank you for inviting me here and listening to me. I've been sitting on this information for weeks, and it was important to me to finally share it with someone I trust.

What I'm about to tell you took place a few weeks ago. I've thought about it a lot since then, during most of my waking hours. I've wondered whether the best thing for me to do would be to continue to keep it to myself, or to tell the public for the sake of history. I've come to think that the best thing is for me to tell you about it now. But I also need to emphasize that this needs to remain very confidential. I'm scheduled to meet with federal investigators tomorrow and I'll tell them everything—almost everything—I'm telling you now.

Maybe there'll be a time and place to tell the public. After I talk with investigators, someone will determine *how* to make the information public—if that does happen—and how much should actually be revealed. I'm sure there'll be some things that should never be revealed. Like the location of the facility.

If I were you, I'd probably be thinking that this is all a complete fabrication. And I get that. But the fact that you're here, and willing to take time to listen to me, tells me that you're interested. So that makes it worthwhile to me. I want to tell you as much as I can, and let you ask whatever questions you want to. Then, I'm confident that you'll believe that this actually happened. So...

My name is Albert Frey, but most people call me Al. I was born in Kalamazoo, Michigan, and have lived in the area all of my life, about half in Kalamazoo and half in Portage, a smaller city that neighbors Kalamazoo on the south. Even though the Kalamazoo-Portage area has a population of about a quarter-million, the area still has a small-town feel. People there help each other. People volunteer to do things for others, and most of the members of the community who have some degree of wealth were brought up with a strong sense of public service.

If you've never been to the area, I want to give you a picture of what it's like. Native Americans—and this'll be important later—Native Americans of the Hopewell culture around 400-500 A.D. came to the Kalamazoo area and built mounds, for purposes that are still unclear. Some research shows that they were built at a proper height for doing celestial observation. One of these mounds was constructed in downtown Kalamazoo, in Bronson Park. The mound is still there. By the 8th Century, the Hopewell culture began to decline and other people moved into the area. By the time European settlers arrived in the late 1700s, the region was primarily home to the Potawatomi culture. By the War of 1812, the British had established a blacksmith post and a prison camp in the area.

I attended local schools. Soon after graduating from college locally, I worked at a medical supply company, and after doing that for about 10 years, I started work for a pharmaceutical company that's been in town for many years.

I've been married for over 30 years and have two adult kids who live in other parts of the country. I live in Portage now. My wife, Molly, and I enjoy our neighbors, who help each other by doing things like shoveling driveways and mowing lawns when another neighbor is out of town. We like our neighbors, though like many neighbors in today's world, we don't see each other every day, especially during the winter. So pretty typical stuff.

But now, let me tell you about the day that all of this started.

Dad's Farm

My father was born in Kalamazoo and lived most of his life there, but he spent a few of his earlier years in a little town about 15 miles northwest of Kalamazoo called Mentha. Actually, it's now considered a "place" rather than a town. Only a few people live there today. But it used to be a very active little place. Mentha was established by a local chemist and businessman named A.M. Todd, for the purpose of growing mint. In the early 1950s, 90 percent of the world's mint oil was produced within a 90-mile radius of Kalamazoo, much of it in Mentha. With Mentha and another plantation near Fennville in Allegan County called Campania, Todd had 10,000 acres planted with mint. He was known as "the Peppermint King of Kalamazoo." However, a disease called wilt made it harder and harder to grow mint, and by the 1970s, production was virtually ended and most of the country's mint production moved to the Northwest.

My dad's family wasn't directly involved with mint farming, but they did have a farm close to the railroad tracks in Mentha, what used to be the Kalamazoo and South Haven Railroad. They raised some vegetables and other things there, not a big operation. A few decades later, the tracks and ties were pulled up and the rail line was converted to a recreational trail that goes all the way from Kalamazoo to South Haven—now called the Kal-Haven Trail— almost 34 miles long. And the state plans to continue connecting it to other abandoned rail lines around the state.

But back in the 1910s through the 1920s, my dad's farm was just a few hundred feet from the tracks. The house isn't there anymore, and I'd wondered for a long time exactly where it was, and what it was like.

14

My dad died when I was nine, and my mom died about 20 years later, and now I wish that I'd asked my parents more questions about what things were like when they grew up. So finally, one Monday early last October, I drove out there from our house in Portage to find out if there was still anything to be seen. Much of this area has been prairie land for hundreds of years, and is relatively flat, except for downtown Kalamazoo, which is in a valley. When I arrived, I spotted a little overgrown driveway that tractors may have once used, and pulled my car into the spot. This is the kind of country road that might see one car every half-hour, and the place looked very unused.

I got out of my ten-year-old, bright red Buick LaCrosse and walked about 50 feet to where a few parts of an old, weathered wooden fence remained. I leaned up against a fence rail. I just stood and looked around for a while, and not seeing much from that spot, I went to check out the lot where my dad's farm used to be.

It was a beautiful fall day. It had just gotten to be that time of the season when the humidity drops and the comfortable days turn to chilly evenings. The sky was deep blue with a few billowy white clouds, and the leaves were almost at their peak. There was a faint smell of ripening apples in the air. Part of me was just enjoying the weather, and another part thinking about whether it would be appropriate to explore the property that was now owned by …whoever owns it now. Although the area is very flat, you really can't see more than about half a mile in most directions, because of wooded areas and lines of trees that were either planted or left standing between fields, in order to minimize winds damaging crops.

After about 10 minutes of looking around, I walked toward the north, toward the area where my dad's farm used to be. I'd never been here before, but my older sister, Madeleine, had once pointed out the location to me, so I knew where the lot was. The sun was behind me over my right shoulder and my own shadow was in front of me as I crossed the dirt road.

I was struck by the unusual appearance of the place. Everything was overgrown with small trees, bushes, vines, and tall grass. Most of the trees were maple, oak, and black walnut, with orange and yellow leaves. Sumac and Virginia creeper were also growing wild, with their bright red to purple leaves. I'm sure it's very different from the tidy space that would have been an operational farm in its day.

As I approached the old lot and looked through the dense trees and shrubs that grew all around, I saw a large, chain-link fence spanning what appeared to be the whole west edge of the property. The fence was about eight feet tall, a little taller than I'd expect to find in an area like that. When I first saw the fence, I was disappointed: after thinking about visiting this place for so long and finally driving out, my hope of seeing the actual property faded. I knew the fence wasn't here when my dad lived here, around the time of World War I, and I wondered when it had been installed. My guess by its general condition was that it had been here since the 1940s or '50s.

I decided that since I'd made the drive out, I'd at least make an effort to reach my dad's old lot. I searched for an opening, and continued walking from where I'd entered the lot, at the south side, around the southwest corner of the property and north along the west fence line. With every few steps, the brush became heavier and it was more difficult to move forward. But I'd come this far, and I was determined not to turn back, so I kept going, through burrs and briars that were tugging at my shoelaces and sticking to them as well as my shoes, socks, and the bottom of my jeans. As a kid, I used to walk through overgrown woods and lots like this quite a bit, but not much since. Every few minutes, I'd stop for several seconds and check that I was taking the best path. When I stopped, I became more aware of the sounds of birds, squirrels, and other animals, but no cars. It brought back pleasant memories of my youth and made me appreciate that there are still places in this world where natural sounds are more prominent than the sounds of engines, horns, and machinery.

After about 10 minutes, I realized that this lot was much larger than I realized. I hadn't strayed far from the fence at any point, but I had easily gone a few hundred feet from the road. Just as I wondered whether I should turn around and try to find an opening on the opposite fence line on the east side of the property, I saw a large red oak that had fallen on the fence, bending the top rail of one section partway over.

I proceeded to the tree and that section of the fence. We'd had a big wind storm just a few weeks before, and it looked like the wind had snapped this big old tree off a few feet above the ground. Its huge trunk—several thousand pounds of it as it was more than three feet across and at least 80 feet long—had flattened a section of the fence about 15 feet long. Climbing up on the fallen tree and across the fence took some effort, and was definitely harder than in my younger day. But I got up on top of the trunk until I was on the inside of the fence. I hopped down.

In contrast to the area outside the fence, I was surprised to see how free of growth the area inside the fence was. There were some trees that appeared to be 20-30 years old, with trunks only four to six inches across and about 25 to 30 feet high, but no big trees, and nothing really newer than that, either. I wasn't able to account for that...it was like it had been tended to 20-30 years ago but not since. Except for the trees, the entire area inside the fence looked like it might have been a park that hadn't been tended to for some time. It might not have been significant, but having lived in the prairies and woods of southwest Michigan all of my life, I happened to notice.

And this might sound as if I'm off on a tangent, but I remember not just what I was *doing* at the time, but what I was *thinking*. As I kept looking around, I felt...not that I was being watched, but that I felt that I was doing something that I was *supposed to be doing*.

I almost never feel alone. Most of the time, even if I'm in a room by myself, or out on a country road driving alone, or out on a trail going for a walk, I usually feel a presence around me. And I mean that in a good way, not a creepy way. I sense a positive presence. For lack of a better term, I feel that I'm connected to something other than myself, something bigger than me. As I viewed this large lot around me, I had a feeling, not that I was being monitored, just that I was part of a larger presence in this place as I was looking around.

All this time, I continued to glance about periodically to see if anyone else was around. Although I felt a connection to this place, where my dad had spent a few years of his youth, I had no claim to it, and needed to be prepared to tell someone what I was doing. If asked, I was just going to tell them the truth. There weren't any *No Trespassing* signs posted, so although there was some level of risk in being here, I thought I could explain the interest in my dad's old farm to anyone I might encounter.

There was a natural beauty about this whole place, and I started looking for signs of any structure that once stood here. Maybe the foundation of the house. Or a barn. A silo or corn crib. A well. But there were no signs of anything. And it seemed odd, because I thought there should be *something*. Maybe someone had built another house here after my dad's was torn down, and the replacement house was already torn down, as well? It seemed unlikely.

Then, looking back toward the northeast corner of the lot, not far from the eastern run of the tall chain-link fence, I noticed something inside a heavy cluster of trees, really the only cluster on the lot. There appeared to be a building like a shed. I started walking over to it.

The Shed

Just as I'd had to work my way around some brush and trees to get to the opening in the fence, it took me a minute to climb over, under, and around trees to get to the little building. But I got there. It looked like a shed that been there for many years, though probably not as long ago as when my dad lived there. It was about 12 feet east-to-west by 16 feet north-to-south, and had a typical sloped roof with neutral shingles, kind of a grayish green color. In fact, the entire building was painted in neutral colors, almost like you'd expect a small army storage building…or a building that wasn't meant to be seen, but rather to blend into the surroundings.

The only windows in the building were some plain, heavily-frosted rectangular windows up near the top of the walls. That struck me as odd, because I'd think most farmers or home owners would want a little more natural light to find tools or other items inside the building, and to have them low enough that they could reach them to open, close, and clean them.

As I walked around the building, I spotted a single, standard-sized service door. It was slightly ajar, though still closed enough to keep animals from getting in. At this point, I thought to myself that if the door would have been closed, I'd have turned around and gone back. But with the door ajar, I instinctively knocked on it, in the unlikely event that someone was inside. Hearing no response, I carefully opened the door inward and stepped inside, then closed the door behind me.

There wasn't much inside the shed. Other than having a light layer of dust on the floor, there wasn't much to look at. There was a wooden table about six feet square, and on each side of it was a single metal-framed chair with vinyl-covered cushion, much like you

19

might see in an old school gymnasium. I didn't see any leaves, grasses, signs of bird droppings or other animals, so I guessed that the door hadn't been ajar for long. And for being an older building, I didn't notice any mustiness or the stale smell of old, wet wood that I sometimes experience in such structures. The first really odd thing about the inside of the shed was that the ceiling and all four walls were covered with a thick, somewhat shiny metal foil of some kind. Curious, I looked back at the door I'd just stepped through and closed, and saw that its inside surface was covered in the same foil. I thought the foil wouldn't have provided much insulation—even if they needed to insulate the shed for some reason. But I thought—and I know this was a weird thought knowing the little that I did at the time—that whoever worked in this place must not have liked listening to the radio, because the heavy foil would have interfered with any radio signal.

The other strange thing I noticed was that the floor was covered in linoleum tiles, about an eighth of an inch thick and about two-by-two feet across. It wouldn't have surprised me to find this kind of tile inside a nice garage or workshop, but I wouldn't have expected to see it in a little isolated shed in the middle of nowhere, one that had probably been built 70 to 80 years before. Someone over the years had evidently come back and installed them.

I walked around slowly inside the little shed, continually looking around, stopping once in a while to have a better look at things, thinking about how this place might have been used years ago. There was enough light coming in through the windows to see fairly well. I continued to study the foil ceiling and walls, and looked down now and then at the tile floor. I had to laugh at myself…for such a small building, I was spending a lot of time walking around looking at something that most people probably wouldn't care much about.

But this shed stood on the lot where my dad lived more than a century before, and I was determined to find something, anything, to which I might attach some significance.

I stood in the same place for two or three minutes, just looking around and contemplating what would have prompted someone to build this structure. Not finding anything more that was out of the ordinary, I decided that I'd just go outside, take in the beautiful fall weather for a few more minutes and think about my dad playing and doing chores here so long ago, and then I'd go home and do something productive.

But that's when things started to get interesting.

Just as I turned to walk out of the shed, I heard a deep, hollow thud as I stepped on a floor panel. If the floor of the entire structure had the same hollow feel, I might not have noticed, but I immediately sensed that I'd discovered something different in this part of the floor.

Still very aware that I was in a building that belonged to someone other than me, and now feeling uneasy about it for the first time, I stepped outside the door again to see if any friend, foe, or angry farmer was anywhere to be seen. Not seeing or hearing anyone but birds, I stepped back inside to where the tile floor emitted the hollow sound. I got down on one knee to see if I could find a door. I didn't see any signs of a handle. I used the heel of my hand to pound lightly on the tiles in that area, and there was a definite difference in the sound when I struck this one tile. I stood up and carefully stepped on the tile. It supported my weight without giving way. I wasn't going to give up; in fact, I was even more convinced that there was something here worth finding.

Walking to the southeast corner of the room, I moved so that my right foot was on the hollow tile and my left on another tile, so that if

I stepped down on it hard, I wouldn't fall through. I lightly pounded my right foot down onto the square tile. Nothing happened. I did it again, a bit harder this time.

I lost my equilibrium slightly, as if taking a step forward onto a surface that was suddenly a different height than expected. Something had happened.

Moving completely off the rectangle, it popped up about two inches. It was hinged on one side, and I was able to easily open it and flip it over.

Evidently, I had opened a door to something. But what?

I took my cell phone out of my pants pocket and I turned on its flashlight. I then leaned down to look into the dark hole.

But it wasn't dark. There was a room below and it was lit by bluish-white lights.

Down the Hatch (or "the Rabbit Hole"?)

I had driven out to this little rural place called Mentha to take a quick look at where my dad had spent some his early life, and now I was immersed in a puzzle. What was this underground room—evidently hidden—doing in a nondescript shed, out in the middle of this forgotten field? I laughed at myself for envisioning that with my luck, a large white rabbit with a pocket watch would come bounding from out of nowhere, push me out of the way, and disappear down the hatch.

What was down below? And after who-knows-how-many months or years, why did the room down there have lighting when the room upstairs didn't?

Below me, mounted against the wall, was a shiny, sturdy metal ladder leading down about eight feet to a concrete floor.

Then, my focus changed. It's unlike me to go roaming into unknown territory, but that's where my thoughts were heading. And within just a matter of a few seconds, that's where the rest of me was going, too. Down the ladder. I carefully grabbed hold of the ladder and managed to start working my feet down, and then hand-over-hand, one step at a time, I went down to the smooth concrete floor below.

I found myself in the corner of a room about the size of a large living room, where all sorts of electronic equipment was mounted to pale green walls. The room seemed to have several stations for controlling equipment. A table the same size as the one upstairs stood in the middle with four of the padded metal chairs around it, two on the west side and two on the east. Against the north and south walls were metal boxes with buttons, lights, gauges, and switches. About one-quarter of the lights were on in various colors, mostly green, yellow, and red, and some of the gauges were backlit with a soft golden light. So there was still power coming into the building. There was a slight humming sound coming from the boxes, and the faint, unmistakable odor of ozone, so there was a lot of current powering this equipment. Against the north wall next to some electrical panels there was a dark gray metal bookcase, nearly as tall as the wall, looking like something from a military installation. The bookcase had four shelves, with old notebooks on the bottom two shelves. On the top two shelves were plastic containers with labels on them; inside them were what looked like audio cassettes with non-standard dimensions.

Against the west wall, opposite the corner with the ladder, was a large metal door, looking something like the door on a large walk-in freezer. There was no locking mechanism on it that I could see. To the left side of the door was taped a sheet of plain white printer paper with a handwritten message saying "Highway Entrance" with a small, upward-curving line depicting a smile. I took it as a joke. Over the top of the door was a plastic sign, white with red letters, about two feet wide and 18 inches high, saying "Authorized Access Only." To the right side of the door was a heavy pane of glass about two by three feet, something like you might like expect the police to have so they can surreptitiously monitor the interrogation room on the other side.

By the looks of the place, it had been a while since anyone was around to authorize access. I'm sure there was a good reason to restrict access to whatever was on the other side of the door, but I didn't know what it was, so I walked over to the door, grabbed the handle, and pulled it open. This whole visit was turning from a curiosity to a mystery, and I'd gone too far not to check things out.

The Little Bang

On the other side of the big door was another room, which I came to think of as "the Box." (To me, it looked like the interrogation room on *Blue Bloods*.) The room was completely dark, but the light switch was just inside the door at standard height. I flipped it on. Five round recessed ceiling lights came on and gave the room an eerie glow. In contrast to the outer subterranean room from which I'd entered, this room was uncluttered and spare. The walls had a black satin finish, and the only thing in the entire room was a small area in the center that had two gray metal chairs with a dashboard of sorts, about eight feet wide and mounted on three metal posts (left, right, and center) in front of the chairs so that the whole arrangement looked something like the front seats and dashboard of a car. Like the room above, there was the smell of ozone, even stronger here. There was also a humming noise, and when I stood still for about 20 seconds to listen, there was a slight electric crackle every few seconds.

The dashboard had a number of switches and lights on it, all in red, yellow, or green. None of the green ones were lit, and only a few of the yellow ones. There was a series of dials on the dashboard, with four large ones near the center and smaller ones on either side of it. The four large dials were paired, two on the left next to each other and the other two about eight inches to the right. There were no digital readouts here, only dials. This setup had been here for at least 20 years, perhaps 40 or more. All analog…

I heard another crackle, this one louder than the ones before. It was then that I realized that I couldn't see the wall directly in front of the chairs and the dashboard, where the operators would be sitting. Although the room lighting was dimmer than in the entry room next to it, it still seemed very strange that the two side walls seemed to disappear into nowhere.

I took my iPhone out of my jacket pocket, turned on the light and shone it at the wall. No difference. I still couldn't see where the side walls ended. I took a few steps forward, looked back and forth at the two side walls, and remained puzzled. Where did those walls end?

I stepped carefully toward the mysterious black wall, about half the distance that I could still see the side walls before they disappeared. Still not seeing where they ended, I took one more step forward. I heard a low but distinct series of clicking sounds in back of me, and turned around to see that all of the lights on the dashboard had turned to green. Evidently, my stepping toward this black nothingness had automatically activated something.

Turning back, I took yet one more step forward.

That's when my story really started.

As if struck by lightning, I simultaneously felt a tingle throughout my body, saw a bright flash and heard a loud crackle, almost a pop. After an instant, I found myself in complete darkness, and without any sense of sound. Even stranger, I no longer had any sense that my body was still being supported by the floor below. I had the sensation of being suspended. I was in a small building in southwest Michigan, but here in this room, I literally felt as if I were in the middle of nowhere. I didn't feel as if I was falling, but after several seconds passed, my heart began racing and I knew that two things had happened: I had encountered something completely inexplicable, and my life going forward would be very different. I knew that what was happening this moment was something I'd think about for the rest of my days, and that this unique experience would cause other things to happen in my life…though at this moment, I could only guess what those things might be.

After a few more seconds passed, the sensation of the floor below my feet returned as if it had been gently lifted up to meet me, or perhaps more like the nerves in my legs had started working again. Then, the blackest of black to which my eyes had adjusted very slowly began to turn a faint royal blue color. I felt a slight breeze against my face and through my hair, and I once again felt as if I were back in the real world.

For the first time since deciding to drive to this remote location and explore, I felt confronted with the decision of whether to forge ahead or to leave. Although I could see a nondescript room of sorts around me, I no longer had any idea of what reality might be ahead of me, but wasn't sure that I knew how to leave.

The decision was made for me when, suddenly, several feet away, I saw the shadowy figure of a man slowly approaching me within that otherwise dark Void.

"I Knew I Shoulda Made a Left Turn at Albuquerque"

I was at a loss. For the first time in my life, all reason related to the physical world around me was gone. As Grace Slick sang in *White Rabbit*, logic and proportion had fallen sloppy dead. "Fight or flight" took over, and my body knew it was time to fly. I still didn't know what was ahead of me, but a small part of my brain knew that I had come from the place behind me, so I quickly turned on my heel and ran back toward where I'd come from, the entry point in the control room in Mentha.

After just three or four steps, I again felt that electric charge and immediately encountered the same space where I went into the black Void, with no light, sound, or floor. But even though the feeling was just as strange, I knew that I'd already gone through it and was hopeful that I'd find myself back in the Box. Seconds seemed to tick by…it seemed longer than it had going in…but I began to see light and then found my body moving forward onto a solid floor. I narrowly missed hitting something about waist-high and soon realized it was the dashboard in the Box.

I felt my heart beating quickly and hard in my chest and I leaned forward with my hands on my hips to get my breath back. Even after less than a minute, I felt the slight tickle of sweat drops on my forehead and arms. My brain raced to try to figure out what had just happened. As my heart rate and breathing returned to normal, I started to think about driving back home where I could sit peacefully and try to figure out what just happened.

But then I heard a sound behind me. At first it was a light rustling, like someone taking steps in corduroy pants. And before I could turn around, it was accompanied by the unmistakable sound of footsteps.

As much as I was hesitant to look at whoever I'd see when I turned around, I knew I had to do it. I was sure that my uncharacteristic brashness of going into this building would now come back to bite me.

When I turned around, I saw a face and frame that were familiar to me, and I froze. I was looking at someone I'd heard about and seen photos of all my life. But it couldn't be who he looked like; a man who had lived more than 150 years before and had the most profound impact on our nation as any American. I hadn't met him before, but I'd read many books about him and had visited many places that were significant in his life: The log cabin in Kentucky where he was born, the home in Springfield, Illinois where he lived with his family while he practiced law and served in the state legislature, the White House where he lived, aged rapidly, and made painful decisions during America's Civil War, and the tomb in Springfield...where he and his family were buried.

He looked as I'd always envisioned him. A black suit with thin gray stripes, slightly wrinkled and a bit worn at the sleeves and cuffs, covered his 6-foot-4, slender but powerful frame. He wore a similarly wrinkled white shirt with a black bowtie. His face was gaunt with craggy features. He had a beard that matched his hair in color, black and coarse with tinges of gray. His hair wasn't long but was slightly disheveled. Even with these unusual characteristics, the thing that stood out the most to me was his eyes. They were deep-set with slightly heavy, unruly black eyebrows, and his eyes were gray as an overcast winter sky, with no sign of color whatsoever.

He stumbled slightly, as I had done when I tried to get my footing upon reentering the Box. Though I was still trying to adjust from my own reentry, I instinctively raised my arms against his shoulders to make sure he wouldn't fall. Like me a few moments before, he didn't know where he was, but after several seconds his eyes widened slightly and his brows arched, as if to say "Wasn't that something?" Then, unexpectedly, the corners of his mouth turned up slightly into a slight smile.

In the room light, I knew that the tall, shadowy figure I'd seen in the near-complete darkness a few moments before was a man I recognized as a smart, funny, self-taught man who led our nation through its darkest period. Several seconds passed before I shared any words with my fellow Midwesterner, Abraham Lincoln.

Our 16th President

When it comes to presidents, historian and writer Troy Senik says that most Americans know about George Washington, Abraham Lincoln, a few of the most recent presidents, and that's about all. Bipartisan groups of presidential historians as well as the general public perennially rank Washington, Lincoln, and Franklin D. Roosevelt as the three highest-rated presidents. Lincoln's place in American history wasn't the result of accident.

In Jon Meacham's biography *And There Was Light: Abraham Lincoln and the American Struggle,* Meacham focuses on Lincoln's evolving sentiments on equal rights and religion, from Lincoln's time growing up in Kentucky to his time in southern Indiana and Illinois, and finally the Executive Mansion, as the president's home was officially called until it was named the "White House" by Theodore Roosevelt by executive order in 1901. Meacham says "Lincoln was a politician, but he was a politician who ultimately was driven by conscience. If he had solely been a cynical political creature, he would have made radically different decisions at critical points." Historians have said that George Washington led our nation as it was created, and that Lincoln was most responsible for saving that Union.

Lincoln was indeed a politician, but one who used his political capital to achieve objectives that *made a positive difference* in the lives of others. In a famous letter he wrote to *New York Tribune* editor Horace Greeley on August 22, 1862, Lincoln clearly indicated that given a choice between saving the Union or ending slavery, he would save the Union. Lincoln explained "My paramount object in this struggle is to save the Union, and is not either to save or to destroy slavery. If I could save the Union without freeing any slave I would do it, and if I could save it by freeing all the slaves I would do it; and if I could save it by freeing some and leaving others alone, I would also do that." What Lincoln didn't tell Greeley—and very few others knew—was that Lincoln had already drafted the Emancipation Proclamation, which Lincoln announced the following month and would become official by executive order presidential proclamation on New Year's Day 1863. The proclamation changed the legal status of more than 3 million enslaved people in the Confederate States from enslaved to free.

A Meeting of Minds with Abraham Lincoln...and Me???

While my guest gained his bearings for a few seconds, we continued to look at each other. I wondered if his perspective seemed as surreal as mine, not just going through the Void, but also because he was looking at the face of a stranger while I was looking at a man about whose life and presidency we were taught in school, and about whom at least 16,000 books have been written. He was immediately familiar to me.

It was Mr. Lincoln who broke the silence between us.

"I just had the most unusual experience, sir. Do you know what happened?" he asked.

"Not exactly," I responded honestly, shaking my head slightly, "but I did just experience something very unusual, also."

My brain was now going in countless different directions. To the best of my knowledge, my guest and I were the only two people to have had this strange experience. Of course, my uncharacteristic nosiness was largely to blame. (Actually, "uncharacteristic trespassing" would be more accurate...nosiness, or at least curiosity, have always been part of my makeup. On that particular characteristic, curiosity, my guest and I had something in common.)

I reached my right hand out to shake his. "It's nice to meet you. My name is Albert Frey. Al."

His hand met mine in a warm shake as he replied, "The pleasure is mine, sir. My name is Abraham Lincoln."

"Yes, sir. *That* I know," I responded with a smile, which drew a similar expression from my guest. If you've ever experienced a handshake that was very firm but also very gentle, that's exactly what it was like. And his hands were much larger than mine, partly because they were in proportion to his overall frame—he was six inches taller than I—and partly due to his years of splitting fence rails, rowing boats on the Ohio and Mississippi rivers, tending to horses, riding them around the state of Illinois as part of his law work in the circuit court, and doing other manual labor. For the first decades of his life, he was known as the man who could *whup* any other man in wrestling or in splitting rails. His fingers, though strong, looked long and relatively thin but yet rough.

"Do you know where we are, sir?" he asked.

All during this conversation, I was trying to focus on the action of meeting *THE* Abraham Lincoln, but within seconds of meeting him, I was thinking about what had happened and its potential repercussions. Like any good geek I had given due consideration to the warnings of old episodes of *The Twilight Zone*, several *Star Trek* series including the original, *The Time Tunnel*, *The Time Machine*, and dozens of other science fiction stories that cautioned about having contact with people from the past.

People from the past?

That was it, wasn't it? The question and the answer both occurred to me almost simultaneously. There was only one explanation I could think of for what had happened: Because of this facility, Abraham Lincoln had traveled forward in time. And perhaps I'd traveled back halfway to meet him. I still didn't know; I couldn't think fast enough. But from the first minute I met my guest, I began to exercise caution about what I could tell him.

Extending my arm out to the side, hand palm-up, to signal that I was thinking about what I would tell him, I reasoned that it was a worthwhile risk to tell him where we were. Also, I reasoned that it would be tantamount to sin to tell a lie to Abraham Lincoln.

"Yes sir. I was here a short while ago. We're in a small farming community just west of Kalamazoo," thinking he'd likely remember his one visit to Michigan in the few years before he became president, and that it was to Kalamazoo.

"Kalamazoo! I know Kalamazoo! I have very fond memories of Kalamazoo."

His answer confirmed to me that this was the real Abraham Lincoln, not that I needed any more confirmation. With my fondness for the Kalamazoo area, it was a response that I was glad to hear.

Kalamazoo

I'm a fourth-generation Michigander and I've lived in the
Kalamazoo area all of my life. In many ways, Kalamazoo is a typical
Upper Midwest city, with a city center surrounded by businesses,
industries (mostly small) and further out, fields of corn, soybeans,
tomatoes, and other products of the world's greatest breadbasket.
The City of Kalamazoo has a population of about 74,000 people.
Along with neighboring Portage (population 46,000) and other local
communities, the metropolitan area has a population of 262,000.
When the area is enlarged to comprise what's called the *Kalamazoo-
Battle Creek-Portage Combined Statistical Area*, the population
reaches about 524,000; that area includes the "world's cereal capital"
of Battle Creek about 25 miles to the east and St. Joseph and Benton
Harbor, on the shores of Lake Michigan about 50 miles to the west.

Among the top things Kalamazoo and Portage are noted for, I'd nominate something that happened just a few years ago as perhaps the most important. In December 2020, the pharmaceutical company Pfizer's largest global manufacturing facility, in Portage, was the first in the world to manufacture and distribute a COVID-19 vaccination, an event that received global news coverage. COVID-19 has been one of the biggest worldwide health crises of the 21st Century, and the vaccine was a milestone event in bringing the pandemic under control.

Another notable achievement is also related to drugs. If you've ever taken a tablet or pill of any kind—medicinal or vitamin—the concept was essentially invented in Kalamazoo. In 1885, a local physician, Dr. William Erastus Upjohn, developed the first tablet that would consistently reach the stomach and then dissolve. Before that, tablets could be so hard they wouldn't digest, or so soft they'd dissolve in the subject's mouth. The company Dr. Upjohn founded, The Upjohn Company, went on to develop and make well-known products such as Motrin, Rogaine, Halcion, Xanax, Orinase, Unicap vitamins, Cheracol D cough medicine, as well as a number of steroids and other compounds. In addition to human health, Upjohn made medicines for pets and farm animals, as well as seeds through its Asgrow division. Dr. Upjohn's company existed for 110 years, until 1995 when it merged with Sweden's Pharmacia AB. Just eight years later, the resulting Pharmacia & Upjohn company was acquired by Pfizer.

The Kalamazoo-Portage area is also home to one of the world's largest medical device companies, Stryker Medical, which manufactures medical devices, artificial joints, hospital beds, and other medical equipment.

Not long ago, the dominant industry in the Kalamazoo area was paper. Kalamazoo was among the largest paper manufacturing cities in the nation, thanks to an abundant supply of clean water, especially from the Kalamazoo River, as well as the proximity to the railroad lines and its relationship to the large cities of Chicago, 144 miles to the west, and Detroit, 144 miles to the east. Expertise and management skills related to the industry developed, and by the 1930s, one quarter of the population of the Kalamazoo area worked in the paper industry. By 1954, one third of the personal income in the area came from paper. One city of about 2,000 people just northeast of Kalamazoo, Parchment, took its name from the parchment paper company that was once based there. The presence of the industry in town began with the opening of the Kalamazoo Paper Company in 1867, just two years after the end of the Civil War. By the middle of the 20th Century, prominent paper companies that had been based in the Kalamazoo area included Allied, Bardeen, Bradford, Bryant, Hawthorne, King, Lee, Monarch, Plainwell, Rex, Standard, Superior, and Sutherland. Acquisitions and iterations included Georgia-Pacific, Union Camp, Menasha, and Otsego.

Unfortunately, it was later discovered that the process of manufacturing paper discharged toxic compounds such as polychlorinated biphenyls (PCBs) into the rivers. By the 1970s, the movement to clean up the rivers, as well as international market conditions, resulted in the decline of the paper industry in Kalamazoo, and by the early 21st Century, less than two percent of the jobs in the Kalamazoo area were in the paper industry.

Celery was also a huge product in Kalamazoo and neighboring Portage. At one point, the number of rail cars used by Kalamazoo farmers to ship their celery was second in the state of Michigan only to the number of cars used by the Detroit auto manufacturers. The rich, black muck in the area was perfect for growing the crop. Growing celery is very labor-intensive, and the fields were cared for largely by Dutch immigrants who were used to that type of work. As recently as 1939, more than a thousand acres of Kalamazoo's rich earth were dedicated to growing celery. But over time, competitors from other parts of the country, as well as a blight in the 1930s, resulted in a large decline in the industry, and today, little celery is grown here.

In addition to Dr. Upjohn, Dr. Stryker and their families, a number of other notable people have lived in Kalamazoo. New York Yankees shortstop Derek Jeter was raised there, as was NFL running back T.J. Duckett. The Super Bowl champion wide receiver Greg Jennings was born and raised in Kalamazoo, and two-time Olympic soccer gold medalist Lindsay Tarpley was raised in nearby Portage. Dave Thomas, the founder of Wendy's, was inspired to create the international hamburger chain by his trips to Kewpee Hamburgers in Kalamazoo. Thomas spent part of his youth in Kalamazoo, living near the intersection of Kalamazoo and Douglas avenues. Thomas said he was not only impressed by the quality of the burgers, but also by the service. Astronaut Jim McDivitt also grew up in Kalamazoo, and graduated from Kalamazoo Central High School in 1947. In June 1965, McDivitt commanded the Gemini 4 mission, becoming the first astronaut to command a mission on his first spaceflight. He piloted Gemini 4 while his crewmate, Edward White, became the first American to perform a spacewalk. Then in March 1969, McDivitt commanded Apollo 9, the first flight of the entire Apollo spacecraft including the Lunar Module.

In 1942, the first full year of World War II after the United States joined the conflict following Pearl Harbor, the best-selling song in the country for the entire year was "(I've Got a Gal in) Kalamazoo," performed by the Glenn Miller Orchestra. Written by Mack Gordon and Harry Warren, the song was featured in the Hollywood musical *Orchestra Wives* in 1942 and spent 19 weeks on the Billboard charts including eight weeks in the Number 1 position.

Although beauty is indeed in the eye of the beholder, I don't know that a visitor would choose to live in Kalamazoo because of any particular physical feature. The city has a fairly distinct downtown area with defined neighborhoods, business and manufacturing districts, and research parks that are surrounded by countryside with hills and fields where farmers grow corn, soybeans, and many other crops. But despite having good roads and a great linear park system to travel within and around the city, a visitor might not find the city to be visually "beautiful." I could nominate Mackinac Island, Lake of the Clouds or the Pictured Rocks National Lakeshore for that honor.

But what the Kalamazoo area *does* have, in heaps, is generosity. During the Great Depression, if employees of The Upjohn Company fell on hard times, company head Dr. W.E. Upjohn would see that an interest-free loan could be arranged. And if times were slow and drug studies were canceled or postponed, he'd arrange to have scientists equipped with paint and brushes, or hammers and saws, to do other work, to ensure that nobody would be laid off.

Homer Stryker was a local orthopedic surgeon (and businessman and inventor) who founded the Stryker Corporation in 1941. During his career, he made a fortune but remained focused on innovations that would make patients more comfortable during their healing. And he gave much of that fortune away to worthy charitable organizations. His descendants have carried on the tradition.

In 2005, a program called the Kalamazoo Promise was rolled out to provide up to 100% of tuition to most Michigan colleges, universities, apprenticeships and skilled trade programs for any student who graduated from Kalamazoo Public Schools; that amount is pro-rated for students who did not begin their schooling in the Kalamazoo school system. All of the money used to fund their education was donated privately and anonymously. The Kalamazoo

Promise has served as a model for more than two dozen similar "promise" programs in Arkansas, Colorado, Connecticut, and Pennsylvania.

Kalamazoo's Girls on the Run program, which began in 2002, has been one of the most successful such programs in the country. The United Way, Salvation Army and other charitable programs are also great traditions in the Kalamazoo area.

More recently, in a January 2024 event that became a top news story around the country, Ronda Stryker—granddaughter of Homer Stryker—and her husband, Bill Johnston, donated $100 million to Atlanta's Spelman College, a historically Black women's liberal arts college. The couple had previously donated at least $32 million to the college to help maintain its infrastructure and assist talented people with their dreams of attending college. The 2024 donation was the largest single donation ever made to a historically Black college.

That's what I like most about Kalamazoo, the people and their ethos of generosity. As I'll describe later, that was an attribute that was even mentioned during Abraham Lincoln's visit to Kalamazoo in 1856.

Getting Acquainted

We continued to look at each other for a while, disoriented and sizing each other up. I was *clearly* looking at someone who was *clearly* Abraham Lincoln and that was *clearly* taking some getting used to, but I was still pondering what he must be thinking about me. He knew that people in the mid-1860s didn't dress quite like what I was wearing, and I was starting to think about what I should and could say.

Had I really gone partway or fully back to the last days of the Civil War, and had Abraham Lincoln really come back with me? Making a suggestion to Abraham Lincoln seemed like a bold leap in initiative for me at that point, but it seemed to be a day for "firsts."

"Sir, if we're still in the location I believe we're at, we're in the basement of a small building on a farm. If we go upstairs, there'll be more light, and there are also some chairs where we can sit and be comfortable while we work together to figure things out."

"Well sir, that sounds like a very reasonable suggestion. I don't know what happened in that dark place, but I do need to ruminate a spell on how to get back home to Washington." For someone who had just experienced a very disorienting situation, he made the transition to a very composed demeanor remarkably fast. He pointed up to the top of the ladder with his outstretched palm. "After you, sir. Please."

After hearing those few words from Mr. Lincoln, I couldn't help but think about his voice and diction. Had I ever planned to meet him, I'm sure I'd have expected expressions like "ruminate a spell," and I was sure I'd hear more colloquialisms and regional expressions before this odd situation was over. And I already knew I'd love every word of it. In addition to his rough but likeable appearance and expressions, his voice was also much as I expected: Not the deep, booming "stentorian" voice of a man who was 6-foot-4 and probably in the top one percent in terms of physical strength, but a higher-pitched, sometimes almost shrill voice. Journalist and writer Horace White was raised in New Hampshire but was a writer for the *Chicago Tribune* in 1858 when he accompanied Lincoln to all of his debates against Stephen A. Douglas. White described Lincoln as having "a thin tenor, or rather falsetto, voice, almost as high-pitched as a boatswain's whistle." In February 1860, a writer for the *New York Herald* described the future president's voice as "shrill" and "sharp" with "a frequent tendency to dwindle into a shrill and unpleasant sound." However, those same writers, and most others, agreed that once a listener heard the thoughts expressed by Lincoln, the sound of his voice was forgotten.

In addition to the sheer pitch of Mr. Lincoln's voice, his accent reminded me that it wasn't the voice of a man born and raised in the woods and prairies of southern Indiana and Illinois, but rather the twang of a man who spent his first years in Kentucky. Young Abraham was age 7 when his father lost all 200 acres of his land in Sinking Springs, Kentucky, and his father moved the family 122 miles north to Elizabethtown, Indiana. In the process, they left the world where enslaving people was legal and moved into world that was, by law, actually the land of the free.

"Thank you, sir," I responded to his offer to climb the stairs first. "And if you'd prefer, you can call me Al instead of sir. On the other hand, I think I should continue to call you 'sir' because you're the…" I paused slightly while thinking about anything I might say that might affect the timeline.

A broad smile came over his face. "…the president?"

"Yes. Sir. The president," I replied, and couldn't help but reflect his contagious humor.

"Well, I suppose that's true," he continued. "I personally have never been offended by someone calling me by my first name, but I think 'sir' or 'Mr. President' does confirm some degree of respect for the office, and therefore for the nation. But, for whatever value it conveys, I do much prefer 'Abraham' to 'Abe.' I was never fond of the abbreviated form."

"Yes sir, that I know, too," I said, as I put my hand on the rail and slowly made my way up the ladder. I had no sooner reached the top that my guest was right behind me. I began to reach out my hand to help him move from the top step to the main floor, but he took the last step as if he'd done it dozens of times before. He certainly didn't lack for physical strength.

"Well, why don't we have a…" I said, gesturing towards the seats. "Oh, if you don't mind, I wanted to check on one thing down below, if you don't mind. Please have a seat and I'll be right back. I'm just going near the seats and dash below, not near the dark area."

"Certainly. But be careful," cautioned Mr. Lincoln.

"I definitely will," I assured him as I began working way back down the ladder. Without letting my guest know what I was doing, I wanted to check the instruments on that dash before doing anything else, to see if I could gather any clues about what was going on. There were enough implications about him traveling 600 miles in an instant, let alone more than 150 years forward in time. I'd first thought that I'd tell him that I'd forgotten something, but I wanted to avoid—you know—lying to Abraham Lincoln.

Time Has Come Today

Leaving Mr. Lincoln upstairs briefly, I finished my way down the ladder and walked through the "Green Room," into "the Box" and over to the dashboard. I looked at the instruments without Mr. Lincoln in the room so I could inspect them without tipping him off.

The lights and switches on the panel were all labeled, but it was really the four largest dials that I wanted to see. The four dials were about six inches in diameter, as compared to a few others that were closer to three inches. Each of the four dials had three adjacent knurled knobs next to them, which presumably the user would turn to set the destination date and time.

It didn't take more than a few seconds to confirm what I had already gathered, based on the events of the last few minutes. The second dial from the right, which had date settings printed on it, pointed to the word "Current" as did the dial on the far right. The second dial from the left pointed to a time, 8:05 p.m.

As my eyes went to the dial on the far left, under a label saying "Destination," it was difficult to take my eyes off it and the date that it indicated: April 14, 1865. That was the date that President Abraham Lincoln—the man who was upstairs, no more than 25 feet from me—suffered a mortal gunshot wound. Hours after that event, my guest "belonged to the ages," as Secretary of War Edwin Stanton said at 7:22 the next morning, after my guest had taken his last breath.

The historic magnitude of what I was experiencing, and the dichotomy of what seemed to be two separate realities, was hard to process.

Based on the settings of these controls, the man upstairs evidently had come my way about two hours before he became a victim of John Wilkes Booth.

I'd continue to think about this situation, and I knew I'd have to develop some kind of plan. My heart would be involved in my decision-making just as much as my head. In order to avoid changing the timeline of history, I'd need to make sure that I didn't somehow interfere. (And given what had happened in the last few minutes, I didn't know if that was even possible. Perhaps some change had already taken place when my guest suddenly left the box at Ford's Theatre…) But I also felt the need to give my guest all the respect he deserved after all of his personal loss in saving the Union and emancipating millions of Americans, let alone that the People had twice elected him president.

After confirming that the structure we were in was, in fact, a facility that allowed users to travel through time and space, I gave a quick look around. As a sort of science fiction fan, I thought back to some of the stories about time travel I've read or seen in movies or television. Of course, those were all fiction, but I thought they might help me to establish some point of reference. And having grown up in the 1960s, most of my references were from that era: *H.G. Wells' The Time Machine* from 1960. Irwin Allen's *The Time Tunnel* on television in the mid-1960s. Several memorable episodes of Rod Serling's *The Twilight Zone*. The *Star Trek* episode "The City on the Edge of Forever" with its character the Gatekeeper of Forever. That's the episode in which Capt. Kirk and Mr. Spock follow Dr. McCoy back in time to Great Depression-era earth to keep the fictional Edith Keeler from taking an action that would cause Nazi Germany to win World War II.

Then there was the 1980 time-travel romance film *Somewhere in Time,* in which Christopher Reeve wills himself back to 1912 at the

Grand Hotel on Michigan's Mackinac Island so he can meet Jane Seymour, whose picture on the wall at the hotel he has admired. She's under the thumb of her controlling manager, played by Christopher Plummer. It's really a lovely story, and I like the actors and the beauty of Mackinac Island. And if you're a young guy who's going to dismiss every woman in the world to go back to 1912 to meet a woman, and that woman is Jane Seymour, I'm still thinking the story is worth following. But I never really understood the means of time travel in that film. Evidently the power of will is more powerful than the power of time as long as you stay away from pennies, at all costs (so to speak).

Among all the fictional methods of going from one time to another, *The Time Tunnel* is probably closest to the real thing, with *Star Trek*'s "Edge of Forever" portal the next closest. It seems that you physically have to be moving forward to initiate some process, and with the existence of whatever forces existed at the particular location, you can travel in time.

But for now, the 16th president of the United States was waiting for me upstairs, and he had to be even more confused than I was.

Regrouping

"Is everything alright?" asked Mr. Lincoln when I returned upstairs. He was now sitting in his chair, his knees above the level of his hips because of his tall frame, and the bottoms of his trouser legs well up above the tops of his black shoes.

"Oh yes, just fine," I said. "I just wanted to look at something down there. I thought we might just sit here for a while and talk about the situation." In addition to having the opportunity to talk with him, I wanted to pick up on any clues that might determine our course of action.

I started to turn my chair to face him but before I sat down, I rethought and suggested to him that we take our chairs outside to get even more light, and take advantage of the sunshine and nice weather.

"That sounds like a right fine idea. I love the feel of sunshine. I believe that I think better with the sunshine covering me." I offered to carry his chair outside the shed, but he insisted on carrying it himself, and I carried mine. We arranged them next to each other, but before sitting down, we both looked around and took in the beautiful fall day around us.

"Well, here are my thoughts," I started. "We've both come through something unusual. I'm sure that we both want to satisfy our curiosity about what happened, but we should prioritize on using that curiosity to the extent that it helps to achieve our objective…and that objective is to get you back where you belong as soon as possible. Does that make sense?" I continued to look into that well-known face, and at his suit and shirt from another time. I was still in general disbelief that I was talking to him, yet wanted to take advantage of the opportunity, even if it were only for a few minutes before he went back to his own time.

"Indeed, it does make sense," he said in that reedy Kentucky accent, "I agree with you completely. Though as I seem to be farther from home than you, I hope that perhaps you have some ideas about how I may return. I've done a fair amount of study in a number of areas, but what we just experienced is, frankly, beyond anything I know about." As I thought about his words, I continued to notice out of the corner of my eye that he was also evaluating me. I don't think there's anything particularly remarkable about my appearance to others who live around me in the early 21st Century, but to someone traveling from 1865, my clothes, shoes and probably even my choice of words would have seemed unusual.

"I've retired from my regular work," I shared, "and as luck would have it, I have nothing to do this morning, or the rest of the day. My only goal today will be helping you return home. And I do have some thoughts about how to get you back."

"Good, I'm glad to hear this," said my guest. "And I'm most appreciative of your assistance. I humbly consider myself someone who can learn to do a number of things, but as I mentioned, this particular experience is new to me."

His humility was not surprising, though I couldn't help but think about his words "I've done a fair amount of study." Over my years reading and hearing lectures about Lincoln, I'm sure that I couldn't think of anyone who made more of his humble beginnings than Abraham Lincoln. He attended very little school in his life, yet he was a voracious reader who had read several hundred prominent books of the day. That's not bad for a guy who didn't have anything resembling today's public libraries for most of his life. Included among the works that historians are reasonably certain that Lincoln read are at least 14 works by William Shakespeare and multiple versions of *The Bible*. Other works include *Biographical Histories* by Jacob Abbot, *Aesop's Fables, Arabian Nights*, Jane Austen's *Pride and Prejudice*, Francis Bacon essays, Balzac, John Bunyan's *Pilgrim's Progress*, numerous poems by Robert Burns, James Fenimore Cooper's *The Last of the Mohicans*, Darwin's *The Origin of Species*, Daniel Defoe's *Robinson Crusoe*, multiple works by Charles Dickens, and *Orations* by Edward Everett.

Everett was considered one of the greatest orators of his day. He was the featured speaker who delivered a two-hour address at the dedication of Gettysburg National Cemetery, only to be followed by Mr. Lincoln who, in two minutes, gave perhaps the best-known speech in American history.

Lincoln also read *Report of the Exploring Expedition to the Rocky Mountains in the Year 1842*, a definitive exploration journal of the Old West by John C. Frémont. Born in Georgia, Frémont was an abolitionist, and wasn't only an explorer but also the first Republican Party candidate for president in 1856, a major general in the Union army, and a military governor and U.S. senator representing California.

Other works read by Lincoln include *The Iliad* by Homer, works by Jefferson, Longfellow, Milton and Locke, Alexander Pope, Edgar Allen Poe, and Thomas Paine's *Common Sense*. He read Daniel Webster's speeches, and Voltaire. Reportedly, when he met Harriet Beecher Stowe during the Civil War, he remarked "So you are the little woman who wrote the book that started this great war." Mr. Lincoln was referring to *Uncle Tom's Cabin*, the best-selling book of the 19th Century except for *The Bible*.

And that's just a small sample of what he read. He also read numerous law books; numerous people who knew or met him during his days of practicing law in Illinois said that reading was Lincoln's favorite pastime.

But in addition to what one might literally call "book smarts," Abraham Lincoln had a high emotional intelligence. He could read the room, or the legislative chamber, or the Executive Mansion. As Doris Kearns Goodwin described in her best-selling book *Team of Rivals*, Lincoln could read a person and could find a way to work with them, whether that person was a good friend or a political rival.

In brief, I still wasn't sure what I could share with my guest, but even with the state-of-the-art knowledge from some 150+ years ago, I would give serious consideration to any suggestions he may have.

For now, my plan was to go back in the Box and look around to see if it seemed feasible that Mr. Lincoln could simply go back down there, as I had, and step through the Void back to exactly where he was. As I was contemplating how to convey that plan to Mr. Lincoln, he responded with an unexpected question.

"Time?" he asked.

I suddenly got that feeling where my whole body became hot, and also like an electric current had gone through me. For just two or three seconds, I was unable to respond. If he had already picked up on his journey through years as well as miles, I didn't know how I should answer.

"Excuse me?" I was finally able to manage.

"Do you have the time?" he asked. I was relieved, and suddenly realized that I literally had not breathed for that few seconds. So, for now, it seemed I was out of the woods, right? Yeah, no.

I was so relieved at his clarification of his request for the time of day that without thinking, I raised my left arm in front of me at chest level, pulled the left cuff of my tan jacket up with the fingers of my opposite hand, and looked at the time. On my wristwatch. As in, a device that wasn't commercially available until 1904. And further, a digital wristwatch, which wouldn't have been in use until the 1970s.

"It's about 10:15…here in Kalamazoo," I elaborated, knowing that in Mr. Lincoln's day, there were 144 localized time zones in the United States, including regions, states, and even individual towns. In 1865, for example, half of Detroit was in one time zone and the other half in another. Things remained that way until 1883, with the full development of passenger rail service, which allowed people to travel much faster than ever before.

But he saw my watch. My mouth felt like it was stuffed with cotton as I gave the time to Mr. Lincoln, because I now realized what I had just done.

Did he really want to know the time, or was he trying to confirm what I suspected he might be thinking…the truth.

"Thank you, I always like to know the time of day. It helps me to plan things."

"You're welcome," I responded, then started to get out of my chair toward the door, and continued, "I thought I might go back down and take a more thorough look…"

"You're worried about the information I might share with others," Mr. Lincoln interjected.

"I'm sorry?" I asked, wanting to clarify before I jumped to conclusions.

"Oh no, sir, I'm the one that's sorry. Pardon my manners; I didn't mean to interrupt. You're concerned that I might tell others about all of this and that it might change something in the future."

I could feel the blank look on my own face as he added, "It's really not only a matter of *where* I went to as *when* I went to, is it?"

Now it was okay to jump to a conclusion. I knew there was only one.

Revelation

"I haven't been here for a very long spell," continued my guest, "but I can tell from all of that equipment in the building…your clothing…that fine watch on your wrist…that things have advanced from the year Eighteen Hundred and Sixty-Five. That's where I'm from and where I belong. But that's not where I am right now. Am I correct?"

I remained silent for just a few seconds, and realized that there was no other answer, and I wasn't going to start fabricating now.

"Yes. Yes sir, that's right," I said, and added after further gathering my thoughts, "and you're right for my reasoning of not telling you. It's not a matter of trust, certainly, but since I was a boy, I've read fictional stories about people traveling from one time to another. Those stories always remained fiction…most people and even scientists in this day agree that it's not really possible to travel through time. But in those stories, the potential always existed for terrible things to happen if a person went back in time and inadvertently did something, or said something, that changed everything else from that point forward."

"Oh, I quite understand," said Mr. Lincoln. "I'm not blaming you. I'd have done the same thing in your situation. But there's no getting past the reality of this all. And I'm sure you'll agree that the most important thing is for me to get back where I belong…to the right time and place. For anyone…especially the leader of this nation…to suddenly disappear, as I'm sure I must have done back where I came from…would be a great calamity in itself. That's particularly true given how things were when I left. Gen. Lee had surrendered his Army of Northern Virginia to Gen. Grant just five days before. Gen. Joseph Johnston's armies remain fighting in the Carolinas, but I believe they'll surrender to Gen. Sherman soon. When I left so unexpectedly, Americans were already rightfully celebrating the end to the war, but great matters remained on the question of how to return our countrymen from the states in rebellion back into the Union."

As if struck by a realization, he looked at me and added "Ah…my apologies if you might be unaware of some of these events. I know that for you, they happened a very many years ago."

I smiled back at him and assured him, "I think most Americans know what you've just told me. We don't remember all of our history as much as we should, but we do know about the Civil War and your role in it…even though that conflict was well over four score ago, in fact, nearly twice that."

Mr. Lincoln looked down at the ground a few feet in front of him, gave a slight smile, probably bittersweet, remembering full well the sacrifices that were made at Gettysburg, yet knowing that people remember some of his words there. He recognized my reference to "four score ago" from his speech at Gettysburg. That expression was not especially common in 1865; his words were a reference to the Bible, which says regarding the length of a person's life:

> "The days of our lives are threescore years and ten; and if by reason of strength they be fourscore years, yet their strength be labor and sorrow; for it is soon cut off, and we fly away." (Psalm 90:10, King James Version.)

In one of the few instances later in his life on which he would prove to be wrong, he also said, "the world will little note, nor long remember" what he and the other speakers said at the dedication of the national cemetery in Gettysburg that day.

"What I said about you being just west of Kalamazoo is absolutely true," I said. "Also, this has been a very new experience for me as well as you. In fact, I think that everyone else in the world today believes the idea of time travel to be theoretical. Except for whoever built or operated this building. At this point, I have no idea who that was, though some of the paint colors and equipment suggests to me that there was U.S. military involvement…and to me, it looks as if nobody has been here in many years, as if the place were forgotten."

"There have been many stories and shows…plays, so to speak," I continued, "about travelling through time. In addition to being a debated issue among scientists and physicists, it provides an interesting device or means to tell a story, and gives people something to think about…what if Julius Caesar had not been killed, or what if someone gave Gen. Washington advance notice of the location of British troops. Only about 16 years after your time, in 1881, a man named Edward Mitchell wrote a story called 'The Clock that Went Backward'." (I elaborated, thinking there was little risk of sharing a fictional account with Mr. Lincoln).

"Just a few years later," I added, "an author named Mark Twain, who spent part of his youth navigating the Mississippi, like you, wrote an entire novel called *A Connecticut Yankee in King Arthur's Court*. And in 1895, a British Author named H.G. Wells wrote a novel called *The Time Machine*. Those stories are still very popular today."

"Those stories sound wonderful," replied Mr. Lincoln. "There were even some that I read in my day. In the early 1700s, an Irish writer named Samuel Madden wrote a fictional series of letters between British ambassadors, called *Memoirs of the Twentieth Century*, that were supposed to have been written in the late 1990s. And Mr. Dickens told a wonderful Christmas story about characters who moved forward and backward in time. Are you familiar with it?

"Yes! *A Christmas Carol*! Sure. That tale is still told and retold every year around the Holidays," I told him, somewhat excitedly. It was obvious that this man from 1865, though out of place on this sunny fall day in Michigan, had a good idea of the theory of time travel.

"I must confess," he continued, "there were a number of evenings when I had finished reading that I would stretch out in my bed, close my eyes, and imagine what it would be like to go back and meet Gen. Washington, or to stand on the shore in Palos, Spain, and watch Christopher Columbus depart for the New World…or to secretly view his landing at San Salvador Island. To sit in the audience at one of Mr. Shakespeare's plays to hear the words just as he'd written them. Or even, if I may, go back to see Jesus of Nazareth and directly experience how he changed the world." It was easy to see how the substantial amount of reading Mr. Lincoln had done since his youth had affected his thoughts and philosophy.

Other stories, including the Hindu mythology of *Vishnu Parana* and Washington Irving's *Rip Van Winkle* (1819) use literary devices to depict extended periods away from mankind, such as Van Winkle's 20-year "big snooze," (my words) as devices to theorize what it would be like to leap through time.

When it comes to something technical, such as the physics of time travel (or brain surgery, or working on the fuel injection system on my Buick) I tend to trust the experts. During the 20th Century and so far in the 21st, scientists have speculated on the possibility of time travel, with a large majority saying it's not feasible. In fact, the expanded explanation of Albert Einstein's special theory of relativity (summarized as $E=MC^2$) states, or strongly suggests, that it's not possible. And although those scientists certainly have more smarts than I do, and more expertise in that area, one question has kept bugging me: What about the Big Bang?

Sitcoms about physics geeks aside, I mean the original Big Bang theory, which is now the scientific consensus about how the universe first formed. That theory was first expressed in 1927 by Georges Lemaître, a Belgian theoretical physicist, mathematician, astronomer, physics professor…and surprisingly, a Catholic priest. The theory consists of a number of components, including the continuous expansion of the universe.

The dilemma is: Einstein's special theory of relativity and Lemaître's Big Bang Theory are both accepted as probable truths today…but key elements of those theories are partially in conflict with each other.

The consensus throughout my lifetime has been that nothing is able to travel faster than light… except for once: for an instant following the Big Bang. That's the explanation by scientists for how the universe has expanded, and continues to expand, as quickly as it has. So, while Einstein's special theory of relativity holds that nothing can travel faster than light, Lemaître's Big Bang Theory says that it did happen, once.

If it happened once, can it happen again? And if matter can travel faster than light, can time be negative? We've known since Einstein's day that if there are twins and one of the twins goes into space at a high rate of speed and comes back in five years, the twin who remains on earth would literally be older than the one who went into space and traveled at a high rate of speed.

One other explanation for the rapid expanse of the universe was presented in a scientific article in November 2016 in the publication *Physical Review*. That explanation, in an article called "Critical geometry of a thermal big bang," Niayesh Afshordi and João Magueijo, is that the speed of light is *not a constant*, as Einstein theorized, but that it was slower in the early moments of the cosmos. Their theory was determined partly "due to the different maximal speeds of propagation for matter and gravity." Their explanation then continues (far beyond what Mr. Lincoln might have called my "poor power to add or detract": "The cosmological fluctuations start off inside the horizon even without inflation, and will more naturally have a thermal origin (since there is never vacuum domination). The critical model makes an unambiguous, non-tuned prediction for the spectral index of the scalar fluctuations..."

Hey, how 'bout them Tigers?

But now, with Abraham Lincoln sitting next to me, the question of time travel was settled. This was real. As Arthur Conan Doyle's sleuth Sherlock Holmes explained in *The Sign of Four*, "When you have eliminated all which is impossible, then whatever remains, however improbable, must be the truth." For whoever built this place, the question was probably settled decades before.

Of all the time-traveling devices I've read about or seen depicted on TV or in movies, the model that best fits what I saw would be a hybrid of *The Time Tunnel* (our "Void") controlled by a panel much like H.G. Wells described in *The Time Machine*.

Now that I knew what this facility was—with the concurrence of the 16th president of the United States—what would we do?

Working on a Solution

"Thank you for helping me to get back home," began Mr. Lincoln. "I have faith that we'll be able to conceive of a plan that will allow me to return."

"I agree, sir," I responded. "There's some risk in whatever we do, but we need to do *something*. Leaving things as they are is unacceptable to both of us. To me, the solution that makes the most sense is simply returning to the room below, inspecting the controls more carefully, setting them appropriately, and reversing the path. I think it's likely that whoever created this whole machine developed it so people could travel in time in both directions. Again, there's some element of risk by your trying to return. Neither of us has operated the machine or has a real understanding of how it works."

"And there's the matter of…why this facility is here, unattended," he said.

"Yes. Yes, I've been thinking about that, too," I reflected on his thoughts. There was no explanation for why this sensitive machine, very possibly the only one like it ever built, had nobody present to guard it, or to do anything else with it. The power was still on. The door was slightly ajar when I arrived. What happened to the people here? Did they travel somewhere, or some*time*? And if it did happen to them, could it happen to Mr. Lincoln…he was obviously right here in front of me, but could he have been brought here *inadvertently* rather than as part of a plan? Regardless of what happened to those before, the answer in regard to Mr. Lincoln was a somber 'Yes,' he may have come here by accident. In fact, knowing the debates that have taken place between hundreds of scientists and engineers over the decades on numerous innovations, anyone who may have traveled in this machine previously may have had questions about what would actually happen. The scientists who planned the first atomic detonation in July 1945 at Trinity Site in New Mexico weren't absolutely sure that the detonation *would not* destroy the atmosphere of the planet.

"I want to give you the best and most honest information I can," I shared with him. "But I'm not an expert on this machine. I envision going back down, adjusting the controls, and while you return to your original place and time, I'd stay behind to monitor your return. I'm already where I belong. You, obviously, are not.

I elaborated further, "And if we do follow this approach, there's the question of when we do it. Should we do it right away, or should we wait and try it later?"

Mr. Lincoln thought for a short while. When he was deep in thought, he usually stared at that one spot on the ground, perhaps six to eight feet from his well-worn Size 14 ankle-high black leather boots. His gray, deep-set eyes locked onto that spot, likely to help him focus.

"Is there anything to be gained from waiting?" he asked. "Will we have more information if we wait? Will conditions somehow be better?"

I sighed deeply while considering his question, deep in thought like him. "No, probably not. I don't think so." And then I made sure he knew my perspective on how the final decision should be made. "In the end, Mr. President, the risk is really yours. I'll provide my thoughts, but the end decision is yours. Not only are you the one taking the personal risk, but for any impact your presence or absence might have on history. The people of your day elected you to make those kinds of big decisions."

"Thank you for that," he said, raising his voice slightly for emphasis. And then, after no more than a few additional seconds of further consideration, he rendered his decision. "The people of this great nation chose me to lead them, and I belong back there. For the last four years of my life, in my time, young men have chosen the more difficult path, leaving their families, their farms, their trades, and their universities to fight for a greater cause. They took the risk, and in hundreds of thousands of instances, they never returned.

"I'm ready whenever you are, Mr. Frey," said my guest.

"I thought you might be," I replied, and as a smile returned to my face, I continued, "And it's still Al."

Mr. Lincoln smiled again. It meant something to me that he seemed to respect my opinions, but it was also meaningful to me that I could bring a smile to those gray 56-year-old eyes.

Then we both stood up, slowly...he because of his well-worn 6-foot-4 frame, and me because of my 60-some year-old creaky bones that sometimes sounded like somebody pouring cold milk on a bowl full of Kellogg's Rice Krispies, including the snap, crackle, and pop.

And we got ready to send him back home. At least, that was the plan.

Preparing to Send My Guest Home

We went back into the Shed, and then climbed back down the ladder, through the Green Room, and into the Box. This time, both of us would look at the instrument panel, and with some luck, we'd be able to figure out how to make it work. Mr. Lincoln approached the panel first. But before he did, he stood and stared straight ahead into the Void, just as I'd done a short time ago when I first arrived.

"Such a peculiar structure, and such a peculiar experience," said Mr. Lincoln. "Everything was as dark as one could imagine coming through that space, and my body felt as if it had no weight. Everything seemed so still in there." Then he looked at me with slightly raised eyebrows and a slight smile, recognizing that I had experienced the same feeling, "And though I may sound like a half-inebriated man for even saying this, looking back, it might have even seemed pleasant if it weren't for the fact that the darkness and lack of any feeling outside my own body was so…unexpected."

"Yes, I was just thinking the same thing as I was climbing back down here. There was really nothing unpleasant about it. Not hot, not cold…if a person is prepared to go in and then keep their balance and their 'sea legs' coming out the other side, it's almost like a short walk out from the house to the barn." I thought it most expedient to speak in colloquial terms that I knew Mr. Lincoln would understand in his day, but I was also raised on a farm on the south side of Portage.

Mr. Lincoln concurred, saying "Yes, a relatively easy thing to do physically. But such a marvelous idea…to step in and go from one time to another. Well…why don't we look at those controls?" he said, as he was already taking the remaining two or three steps to the dashboard and seats. "We should understand them as much as possible before I try to travel."

"Yes, let's see if we can make sense of those," I replied, stepping about two feet to his right, joining him in looking at the dashboard.

We both looked at the controls for about 20 seconds before either of us said anything. I didn't want to break his focus, and I was guessing that he was doing the same.

"Sir, if I may, let me point out what I think the controls seem to indicate, and let me know if you agree," I said, beginning to point to the dials.

"Yes, please, Al," he said. I probably felt a little like his personal secretaries, John Hay and John Nicolay, must have felt. Hay, from Salem, Indiana, was just 23 when Lincoln became president and Nicolay, from Bavaria, just 29, but the 16th president had given both of them much credit for keeping his administration in order during the secession of 11 Southern states and the calamity of the subsequent four-year American Civil War.

"At top right is the power switch, labeled as such, for supplying power to the controls. And these four dials appear to be the primary controls for time," I said. As I pointed, I described what I had surmised earlier, the two dials on the left for the destination date and time, and the two on the right for the return date and time.

"As you can see, sir, the two dials on the left show the destination time and date. Together, they read April 14, 1865, at 8:05 p.m.," I explained.

"That makes sense," replied Mr. Lincoln. "That's the date on which I left and joined you here." Then he asked, "I left some time after that,

64

a few hours later. Do you think this means that someone from here went back to that evening?"

It was the first time I'd seriously considered that question. The Destination controls were set the same as they were when I made my brief journey into the Void. As I stood there now, I thought it was likely that I would have gone all the way back to April 14, 1865— the evening Mr. Lincoln met his fate—had he not somehow come back with me. I told him that perhaps I had returned without reaching 1865 because of some sort of built-in safety mechanism: that if the system detected someone else in the Void besides the designated traveler, it would automatically return the traveler to this room.

"I think that's a reasonable conclusion," I told him, then telling him my thinking about what my destination would have been had he not somehow gotten into the Void himself. Then I added, "Someone may still be back there, or perhaps something else happened."

"That'll be something for me to ponder," said Mr. Lincoln. "When I return, I'll look for any clues, or anything—or anyone—out of place. I'll find a way of telling them that I know who they are without changing the way things were supposed to be."

Then I looked at two small windows below the Destination dials. I had noticed them before but not looked at them carefully. Each of the two windows had a setting knob to its right, and some writing underneath. The top window said "Washington D.C., USA" and the bottom had numbers in it, which I recognized as latitude and longitude. Evidently when the operator set the knob for gross location (in this case, our nation's capital), they were then able to "fine tune" the location by latitude and longitude using the bottom knob. The numbers for latitude and longitude not only had degrees, minutes, and seconds, but thousands of a second, allowing the traveler to select a very precise location.

"Again, despite the complexity of this all," said Mr. Lincoln, "the controls seem relatively simple." Then, after we both carefully looked over the panel for a few more seconds, he added, "It seems that the first step then is to turn on the power for these controls."

"Yes…" I replied.

"Is something wrong, Al?"

In fact, I had a little chill shoot down my spine when he asked about the power.

"Yes," I said again, "though when I last looked at the panel several minutes ago, while you were upstairs, the power was still on."

We both thought for a moment. "Perhaps the power turns itself off after several minutes if you're not using it?" suggested Mr. Lincoln.

"Yes sir, very good point," I responded. "Electricity is much more commonplace today than it was in your day, and systems turning themselves off to save power is very common today. Even my wristwatch does that." I took a second to show him by moving my wrist to make my watch's display turn on, then waiting about five seconds until it turned off. "That's very possible, and that may well be what happened. But for some reason, the lights on the dials and some of the lights in the room were turned on when I first arrived here…perhaps 20, 30, or even 40 years after anyone was here last."

"When you're ready to go into the Void," I continued, "I'll press this Power switch to turn on the machine."

"Well, Al," as much as I've enjoyed talking with you, I think it's best for me to return home as soon as possible, and now that we seem to have confirmed how the controls work, I believe that I'm ready now."

66

I planned to shake his hand and bid him well in about another minute, just before he'd step into the Void, but for now, I'd go ahead and turn on the Power switch.

"Yes, sir, I think you're right." I then pushed in on the Power switch, a round, bright red toggle button about an inch in diameter under a label that said "Power."

The instant I pressed the button, a loud pop was emitted from the dashboard accompanied by sparks, and soon, the smell of a damaged electrical component. Now I felt not only a chill down my spine, but I felt a lump in my stomach.

"Am I correct that that wasn't supposed to happen?" asked my guest.

"That's correct," I replied. Not wanting to upset him, I looked at him, managed a smile, and said "We'll get it figured out, and we'll get you home. But I think it's going to take a while longer."

Diagnosis

"Yes, that was unexpected," I continued. I'll see if I can open up this dashboard to see what happened. Fortunately, I had seen an electrical breaker box on the wall. When I walked over and opened it, one of the breakers was labeled "Control Panel." After switching the breaker off, I returned to the dashboard to determine how to open it. On the back side of the panel, there were several screws at the corners of a sheet metal panel. There was a small tool cabinet mounted to the end of the panel. I took a Phillips-head screwdriver from the cabinet and removed each of the screws and gently set the panel down on the floor.

"I believe you're aware of some of the of the developments with electricity during the 19th Century?" I asked, knowing that he was an early fan of such developments.

"A number of them, yes," said Mr. Lincoln. "I've read some of Benjamin Franklin's observations and experiments with electricity from the last…from two centuries ago now," he said, adjusting to the perspective of the current year. "Mr. Franklin had such a keen mind and such abilities…though knowing what we do now, I don't think I'd have stood outside in the rain during a storm, trying to attract lightning," he added, laughing. I still remember when I was no more than 13 or 14 years old, first hearing about Mr. Faraday from England, creating an electric motor…a device that could take electricity and convert it to motion, motion that man could then transfer as he wishes.

He continued, "And I've enjoyed reading about the gentlemen from Italy, Mr. Galvani and Mr. Volta, and their research about power…and Mr. Ohm in Germany, who did studies with electrical circuits. But I think I most enjoyed reading about the work of Mr.

Maxwell from Scotland. In the first two years of my presidency, he proposed a link between electricity and magnetic force, two forces that at first seem unrelated." Mr. Lincoln's understanding was even greater than I'd have guessed. Edinburgh native James Clerk Maxwell had indeed correctly theorized about the connection between electricity and magnetism—a force that would become known by the simple combined term *electromagnetic* energy—in what would be called "the second great unification of physics," the first such unification since Sir Isaac Newton proposed the link between gravity and astronomy in 1687, some 174 years earlier.

"Sir, your understanding of science is really remarkable," I said. "And I'm sure that it won't surprise you to know that for the rest of the 19th Century, the ability of humans to control electricity became even more widespread, with everything from lights to communications to travel, and that within a few decades after that, a majority of Americans would have many of these innovations in their homes."

"No, not surprised at all," replied Mr. Lincoln, "and although electricity seems like magic to many people back in my time, having a simple thing like electric lighting in my home would have surely been a blessing," he added with a chuckle. "To be able to push a button and turn lights on would seem so much easier, as well as safer than burning oil or candles."

"Well, although electricity isn't generally considered magic in this day," I explained, "it probably should be. It certainly does many magical things. But like all things, we frequently take it for granted."

"Oh, I understand," said my guest, and I had no doubt that he did indeed understand.

"In this control panel, or dashboard, it seems reasonable that the relatively small currents in here are simply used to control other things, which sometimes consist of electrical energy controlling mechanical devices, and combined are called *electromechanical*. The technology inside this panel is quite outdated by today's standards. Today's electronics have very small circuits, but the inside of this panel is like what I used to see as a boy, when a repairman would come to our house every few years to work on something. Almost 100 years ago, a device was invented called a television. It projects a moving image on a screen and can be thousands of miles away from where the image originated…and it's accompanied by sound…and it's all instantaneous, just like the telegraph in your time. And for many years, devices have been able to record both the moving image and the sound, so events can be used for learning many years later."

"That does indeed sound magic," said Mr. Lincoln as he walked around to the back side of the dashboard so he could see what I was seeing. "I know that I need to return home soon, but I'm just filled with wonder as to the things I'm seeing here. Do any of those parts make sense to you?"

"Not a great deal," I answered. "I know a little about electronics, but I didn't have any special schooling in the subject. Though frankly, what I'm doing right now is looking for anything familiar to me. Fortunately, everything is well laid-out on this panel so I can see things. Instead of using modern circuits, as I'd mentioned, this panel uses vacuum tubes. They were used in electronics for many years, and they generally worked well, except they had to be replaced every so often, unlike modern electronics which frequently outlast the technology itself. Many people today have music on disks or reels of tape that would play just fine, except there's nothing to play them on anymore. It's just a matter of continuous improvement, almost like replacing canals that are less than 10 years old with railroad lines."

While I talked to Mr. Lincoln, I was looking specifically at the 20 or so vacuum tubes inside. Had it been another kind of part, we'd have been out of luck for a while longer because of my lack of expertise, but I did have some idea what a bad vacuum tube could look like, though I didn't have a tester with me, or even know how to use one.

"Here," I said. "This might be it. This old vacuum tube. I'm going to gently pull it out," I said, as I slowly wiggled it a little from side to side as I pulled it upward. The old tube was made of glass with a metal base, out of which several pins extended downward to plug into the chassis of the old-fashioned circuit board. On the side of the glass in fading white paint, the tube had an old RCA logo on the side, and underneath was the number 6L6GC. But it was the contents of the glass tube that suggested the reason this big contraption just sparked, spitted and sputtered. The shiny metal strips in the other tubes, which looked like little metal fins, in this tube were instead a very dark brown or black. The tube was also very warm to the touch.

I explained to my guest what I saw, and why I thought it was the problem.

"Do you think that one tube could cause the whole problem we just saw?" asked Mr. Lincoln.

"It's very possible," I answered. "Despite this being such an advanced piece of machinery with so many parts—not just in this control panel but throughout the building—I'm sure that every piece and part has to work perfectly in order for the whole machine to do its job."

"Is there a possibility that there are more defective tubes or other parts in there?" he asked.

"Yes, that's definitely possible," I responded and was already looking inside the panel for other potential problems. "Yes, in fact, I think this other tube has the same problem," I continued, and pulled this tube in the same way I'd removed the first. It was the same type as the first, a 6L6GC vacuum tube made by RCA.

As I showed it to him, he nodded and said, "Yes, I can see the difference too, as if the old part had done its job well and then just worn out. Like some people I know," he said, jokingly. I couldn't help but laugh along.

After spending another three or four minutes inspecting the rest of the vacuum tubes and components in the panel, I said, "That's all I can see. Again, if there's anything else wrong, it's not evident to my old eyes, but I think this is the way to go."

"And do you have any stores in the Kalamazoo area that sell these vacuum tubes?" asked Mr. Lincoln.

"Umm," I responded, very inarticulately, trying to think of a store in the area who might have them. Probably not Meijer. Or Walmart. Probably not our "big three" big box stores, Lowe's, Home Depot or Menards. Probably not our hardware stores.

"Not that I can think of," I finally said. "Not anymore. There used to be a great chain of stores across the country called Radio Shack. They had every electronic part and small electronic device you could think of. Selling electronic parts and devices was all they did. A little over 20 years ago, they had more than 8,000 stores, but they fell into financial decline and now operate essentially as a mail-order operation. I think the only actual stores they still operate are in the Caribbean and South America."

"It's startin' to sound a little like we're racin' to close the barn door even though the horse is already runnin' down the road," he said with a slight laugh.

"Well, there's always Amazon," I said.

"Amazon? We're going to South America to one of those Radio Shack stores," he said, again smiling, and I knew he already realized that I could provide more explanation about my last remark.

"Not quite," I chuckled. "One of those new communication methods I mentioned earlier is a way of ordering items…umm, sort of like using a telegraph."

"I see. That makes sense. And Amazon is the name of a big company that you can order vacuum tubes from," responded Mr. Lincoln.

"Exactly, as well as thousands of other things" I said, still finding it remarkable how quickly this man with book smarts, street smarts, and emotional smarts from 160 years ago picked up on things. "I'll place an order with Amazon. And if they don't have them available, I'll find another store that does. But now," I hesitated, thinking a little about how I'd tell him this, "if they do have two replacement tubes, they very well may not be delivered tomorrow. It may be three or four days before they're here. Whoever receives the order needs to process it, and then it may have to be shipped hundreds or thousands of miles."

"Thousands of miles? In three days? I think I'm going to have a few more questions for you," he joked.

Answering questions for Abraham Lincoln? I was suddenly looking forward to the next few days. And I'd have a few for him, too.

The Journey Begins

"Shall we straighten the place up and be on our way?" asked the 16th president, who had suddenly appeared here in southwest Michigan, about 10 miles west of Kalamazoo, less than an hour ago.

"Yes!" I responded. "I'll set this back panel on top of the dashboard with the screws in it, and just in case, I'll take one of the vacuum tubes."

"You don't think that anyone will mind that you're taking government property?" cautioned Mr. Lincoln. Although I was looking at the panel and not his face, I already knew that there was a little uplift at the end of his sentence when he was saying something humorous.

"No, I don't think so," I replied in similar mock seriousness. "If anyone shows up for the first time in 40 or 50 years, I'll deal with it then. Also, I think I can claim "Executive Permission" to borrow these tubes. You may not believe it, but I know the president!"

"Well now, I think you have a point there. I like the way you think, Al," he commented and smiled as he began walking toward the ladder.

After we both passed back through the Green Room and climbed back up to the main room in the shed, vacuum tubes in hand, we stepped outside and put the two chairs back inside. Then I ensured that the door wouldn't lock behind us, and closed it.

"Okay," I said to Mr. Lincoln as I joined him a few feet away from the shed."

74

"Okay?" said Mr. Lincoln. "Are we going to talk about the campaign of Martin Van Buren," he said, in another humorous reference, based on the origin of the phrase "okay" or "O.K."

"I don't think so, sir," I replied. "But we're all done with the first step and now comes the next one: getting you to my car without anyone seeing you."

"Car? Are we near a train? Or is that something else?" he asked.

"Yes, something else," I said, and for the first time since soon after Mr. Lincoln appeared behind me coming out of the Void, I was thinking a little more about the whole be-careful-about-something-that-might-change-the-future paradigm. But I was confident that this man, more than anyone else I could think of, would have the wisdom not to act on anything he'd learn here…and now. Besides, I couldn't just leave him here for days, even if I came back with food, water, a cot, pillow, and blankets for him.

"I'm sure that it won't surprise you to know that during the late 1800s and into the 20th Century, technology advanced at an unprecedented rate. In the last few years of the 19th Century, people in Germany and the United States developed the first machines, like carriages, that were powered by motors—instead of horses—which could travel many miles on roads without stopping. In the United States, most of that development would eventually be done right here in Michigan, about 140 miles east of here in Detroit."

"And you have one of those motor-powered cars here?" he asked.

"Yes, I do. In fact, most families in the country now have at least one car, sometimes two or more," I explained.

"Those would doubtless be more expensive than a horse and carriage, but the history of economics would suggest that today, people would earn much more money than during the 1860s," he responded.

"Yes, exactly. Greater earnings help people to afford those improved transportation and communication methods I mentioned earlier, and much more," I said. "At any rate, from now on, you'll see many things that are very new. Perhaps…perhaps just try to treat them as a new display or ride at a county fair. Just try to enjoy them, and I'll answer your questions about them as much as I can."

"That sounds very fair. Very fair indeed. Well, if you would, Al, please lead the way to your car," said Mr. Lincoln, as we began reversing my steps around the tall grass and downed tree limbs back to my Buick.

"Yes, sir. And perhaps…perhaps you could take off your suit coat and I could carry it to my car. Maybe it's just my perception, but I think that would make you a little less recognizable…if that's even possible.

"Alright, very well. I'm inclined to think you're right about that," he said, understanding the need for anonymity, at least *his* anonymity. And his reaction at each point. As I was trying to be careful about divulging too much information—even though I trusted him—he also seemed to be filtering everything I said. He knew he would have control over what he'd say and do when he returned to 1865 Washington, D.C., and we would both be careful about changing anything in the first half of the 21st Century in rural southwest Michigan.

My guest said he'd be happy to carry his own jacket. As we walked to my car side by side, he seemed to be resigned to spending a few days in this new place and time. We engaged in some polite conversation about the trees and plants we were walking past, and not surprisingly, he knew a lot more than I did and I was learning from him. I continued to think about anything I should avoid discussing or showing him, but with him being here for a few days, it was going to be more difficult not to share anything with him.

We continued to attract burrs to our pantlegs and socks. While we were still talking about the plants, he talked a little about when his son Robert was a little boy, and how he'd go out in the woods and get burrs and stick-tights all over his clothing, and would have to spend hours getting them out when he returned home. It brought back memories of when I'd done the same thing growing up on a farm in south Portage. Because of my classes in elementary school through high school, college, many books I'd read and numerous films and documentaries, I already knew something about Mr. Lincoln's youth and his family.

Abraham's Background

Abraham Lincoln was born on February 12, 1809 at the Sinking Spring Farm site near Hodgenville, Kentucky. His father, Thomas, generally had odd jobs through his life, mostly involving farming. His mother, Nancy Hanks Lincoln, took care of Abraham as well as Abraham's older sister, Sarah, and his brother, also named Thomas, who died as an infant. (Mother Nancy was a distant cousin of actor and filmmaker Tom Hanks. Actor George Clooney is also a distant relative of Nancy, as is Camille Cosby, wife of Bill Cosby.) Like George Washington, Thomas Jefferson, John Adams, and many of the statesmen who founded our country 33 years before his birth, Abraham Lincoln did not have a middle name.

Abraham's views on the equality of people began to form early on. Slavery was legal and widely practiced in Kentucky, including his home county of Hardin. In 1811, two years after Abraham was born, there were 1,627 white males in Hardin County and 1,007 slaves. Throughout most of his life, Abraham opposed slavery, though he did not believe in the full equality of African Americans to European Americans. (His views regarding equality advanced much during his four years in the Executive Mansion, largely from his friendships with African Americans including Frederick Douglass.) However, his abolitionist views were not uncommon, even in an area that practiced slavery. For years, Presbyterian minister David Rice, called the "Apostle of Kentucky" by his contemporaries, preached emancipation. And Rev. Jesse Head, who officiated at the marriage of Abraham's parents, and who established the Methodist Episcopal Church in nearby Washington County, Kentucky, spoke out against slavery. Abraham's parents heard many sermons against slavery, and in 1808, 15 members of their church left the church over the issue.

In 1816, when Abraham was seven, his family moved from Kentucky to Spencer County in southern Indiana. Just two years after the move, when Abraham was just nine years old, his mother Nancy died of milk sickness, a poisoning caused by a person drinking milk from a cow that had ingested the white snakeroot plant, which contains the poison tremetol. Her death left Abraham's 11-year-old-sister Sarah to care for Abraham, his father, and his orphaned cousin, 19-year-old Dennis Hanks. Throughout Abraham's life, he had a distant relationship with his father.

In 1828, at age 19, Abraham began a job navigating flatboats between his home in southern Indiana, down the Ohio River to the Mississippi and all the way south to New Orleans. It was there that Abraham first saw markets where enslaved people were bought and sold. His revulsion at seeing the practice grew over time, and he evolved as an individual and as a leader.

At age 21, Lincoln achieved nearly his full adult height of 6-foot-4. The following year, he and his family moved to Macon County, Illinois because of the fear of another outbreak of milk sickness. Young Abraham joined the Illinois Militia and in 1832, at age 23, he volunteered in the battles against Sauk leader Black Hawk. Others who volunteered for service during the Black Hawk War included future U.S. Army general Winfield Scott, future general and president Zachary Taylor, and Jefferson Davis, who would become the only president of the Confederate States of America.

Abraham moved further west to Springfield, Illinois in March 1837, when he was 28. He met fellow Kentucky native Mary Todd there two years later. (In one of the bizarre coincidences of history, one of the other men who courted Mary in Springfield was the 5-foot-4 Stephen A. Douglas, who would meet Lincoln in the famous series of seven U.S. senate campaign debates across Illinois in 1858, and who would be Lincoln's Democratic opponent for the presidency in

1860.) Abraham and Mary were married in 1842 at the Springfield mansion of Mary's sister, Elizabeth Edwards. Together they had four sons: Robert, Eddie, Willie, and Tad, with only Robert living past the age of 18. Abraham's sister, Sarah, who had played a large role in raising him, married at age 19 but died just two years later, at age 21, of complications while giving birth.

After so many deaths among his family and others who were close to him, Lincoln still led the nation during the Civil War.

He experienced more heartache than most of us could possibly imagine in his relatively brief 56 years on Earth.

I looked over at him when my bright red Buick first came into view. His eyebrows rose slightly, and I'm sure he was astounded to imagine all the technology and well over 100 years of learning and improvements that went into creating it. With everything there was to talk about with his travel forward in time as well as hundreds of miles to the west, I somehow chose to talk about cars. Even while I realized the topic was mundane, I thought the creation and development of the automobile was something he would be very interested in, given the many miles he'd ridden in his lifetime on horseback, carriages, trains, barges, and other boats.

"There are a number of different companies that make cars, or *automobiles*," I explained. "When I was growing up, if our family was traveling more than, say, two hours on a drive, my father would check the oil level and the air pressure in all the tires including the spare in back, and fill it up with fuel. Today, we might fill the fuel tank, but other than that, most of us just get in the car and go, even if it's a five- or six-hour drive. Cars have improved that much over my lifetime.

"A vehicle today is comprised of different systems, including the fuel system, the electrical system, and the suspension to absorb the shocks and bumps and keep all four tires on the ground. For someone to look at this today, having never seen one before, I'm sure must seem almost miraculous, but all of these systems have developed over time, with engineers, designers and scientists building on what others have done before, and learning by trial and error."

"It's a beautiful machine," said Mr. Lincoln. "Very sleek, and yet everything with a purpose. I was never an engineer by trade, but I can see that. And how fast does it go?"

"In cities, we normally drive about 30 to 40 miles per hour, and on specially designated highways that have limited access, we frequently cover 70 to 80 miles in an hour. Most cars today are fueled by a very flammable liquid fuel called gasoline, and most cars can travel 300 miles or more before they have to be refueled." He took a few seconds to absorb the information.

"And you have places nearby where you can purchase fuel?" he asked.

"Yes, gas stations," I replied. "They're all over. Most people have at least one within a few miles of their home," I said, and then briefly told him about the current trend toward all-electric and hybrid vehicles.

Now out of the tall grass and within 30 feet of my car, I began reaching for my keys, which of course, were attached to a fob. I took the opportunity to give our 16th president some background on one of the greatest developments in the entire human history of communications: radio signals. Now, some people in undeveloped areas of the world today might think of radio signals as being magic. Those people are right.

"In the next day or two," I began, as we kept walking toward my car, "you'll see and hear a lot of things that really hadn't developed yet in your day. As it turns out, there's energy all around us that comes from different sources. And of course, it's all invisible. A good example is the energy from the sun. It heats the ground and the sea, and lakes, and objects that it strikes. And when it heats the air around us, it heats it unevenly, so it produces wind."

"I *am* familiar with those concepts," replied Mr. Lincoln.

"Yes, I know," I responded. "History shows that you were self-taught, and after more than 150 years since you were president, you're still considered one of the smartest of all the 46 American presidents so far.

He laughed at that one. "You're telling me that there have not been many smart presidents?" continuing to show a slight grin. Then he changed the subject just a bit—from talking about energy and radio waves used for communication—but I knew that anytime he said something, it was worth hearing.

"Well, if I have any ability to think, it was because of the old saw 'Necessity is the mother of invention.' From the time I was very young, there was much work to be done. And to be honest, I didn't like much of it. I wanted to leave my father's home as soon as I could, and at one point when I was older, I told him so. And then…then, if I recall, I just left. But I knew something better was out there. Over time, that sentiment evolved into realizing that I—as president of these United States—was in a better position to change things than anyone else in the country. And it all started with a notion that I've told people over and over: *I will prepare and someday my chance will come.* It didn't come easy. I read hundreds of books, borrowed books and newspapers from friends, visited libraries out on the court circuit any chance I had. But it was well worth it."

"Yes sir, history has shown that." Our history books showed that President Lincoln had his sad appointment with destiny on April 14, 1865, on Good Friday, just five days after Robert E. Lee surrendered to Ulysses S. Grant at Appomattox. President Lincoln was finally aware that the war would probably end soon, but he never fully got to enjoy all that he brought to America, particularly saving the Union and ending the "peculiar practice" of slavery. If I'd have an opportunity here, in the present day, to make sure he was aware of all he'd done, I was going to do it.

Then, it was Mr. Lincoln, not me, who turned the conversation back: "But please, continue with what you'd started to say about energy."

"Oh, yes," I quickly acknowledged. "I mentioned the heat energy that comes from the sun, but there's another kind of energy that we don't see that radiates from its surface. It's called ultraviolet, which means that it's beyond violet in the visible spectrum…it's still there, but we can't see it. Like the sound when someone blows a dog whistle but we can't hear it. Well, that energy radiates millions of miles from the sun to the Earth and we're not aware of it…until, a little later, when our skin turns red as a barn and hurts. That's all from invisible energy."

"Thank you, that makes it easy to understand," said my guest. "And you'd said there are ways that people now can use these kinds of invisible energy?"

"Yes sir, quite a few ways," I replied. "Using the solar energy example, scientists were able to find a way that similar energy can be produced to cook food. And although we still have stoves in most homes, many foods can be heated in a much shorter time by using that energy.

I continued, "And if you take the telegraph as an example, inventors were first able to use very similar technology to transmit human voices rather than just dots and dashes over many miles of wire. And more recently, to use radio energy to transfer those voice signals through the air.

"That's quite remarkable," he said, in a rather joyous tone. "And the way you've explained it reinforces what I've thought my entire life about books, and about people building on the efforts of others who came before. I've been quoted as saying, with reasonable accuracy, 'A capacity, and taste for reading gives access to whatever has already been discovered by others.' Tell me, do you need to go to a certain kind of place to transmit that kind of message?"

"No sir," I said. "Today, we can send a message to someone, in fact, have a complete conversation with them, using a device that I can carry in my pocket."

For all of four or five seconds, he looked at me in near disbelief, and I'm sure he was just processing what the rest of us have processed over a multi-year period that began in 2007 when Steve Jobs introduced the iPhone at MacWorld.

"Do you have such a device?" he asked.

"Yes, I do. Most people in this country today carry one," I replied as I was already starting to remove my iPhone from the pocket inside the left side of my jacket front. "Here it is."

I showed it to him for a few seconds before continuing with my description, turning the phone on by lightly pressing my right index finger against the small indentation at the bottom of the front. Some of my friends have phones that are unlocked with facial recognition rather than pressing a button, but I hadn't updated my model yet.

"It's not only a telephone…a device used for talking with someone miles away, but there's a very accurate clock in it, another

84

component that allows me to research information that's maintained on other machines across the world, and to send people written messages. For longer messages there's a function that sends electronic 'letters' or mail, and another that just sends a brief text message. I can show you later. In a sense, much of this technology is simply a series of improvements on inventions such as the telegraph, but now the function of millions of dots and dashes is performed by microscopic switches that work together to form letters and numbers, and they can be transmitted invisibly through space."

"That's truly amazing, Al," he said. "A remarkable invention that brings together a combination of other inventions."

I handed it to him to look at and touch. He shook his head gently more than once, as if he simply couldn't believe it. Again, I didn't blame him. I find them truly miraculous.

"So Al," he started, "with our task at hand to replace the two vacuum tubes, am I correct that you wanted to show me this remarkable device at this time?"

"Yes sir, there is, for a very important purpose...I need to call my wife."

Of the little bit of joking we'd done since meeting about an hour ago, he thought my response here was the biggest hoot. He laughed out loud, and I gathered that the simple husbandly task of needing to communicate with one's spouse hadn't changed much in over 150 years.

Exchanging Status Reports

"Al, if you need to contact your wife, any subsequent explanation is extraneous. You need to call her!" he said lightheartedly, from one husband to another.

"And Mr. President, I hope you'll understand if I don't tell her who I'm with, or hand my phone over to you so you can say Hi to her."

"Then I guess you don't want her to contact the authorities to have you sent away?" he said with the driest humor imaginable. "Well, I suppose, if you must! Have a good call."

Although the English language and its dialects across the United States have changed over 160 years, I realized that many of the elements of humor remained the same.

"Thank you, I'll just step over here a few feet and I'll call her." Still standing near my Buick, I left my guest standing to look around for a few minutes while he enjoyed Michigan's fall sunshine and cool weather.

I called my wife, Molly. The "routine" call brought me back in my normal reality. She had actually left our house that morning, shortly after I left for Mentha, to spend time at her family's cottage on Pine Lake, about 25 miles north of Kalamazoo. I go there with her sometimes, but today I was on my own. This was just a call to check in; I'd see her either that evening or the next evening, depending on whether or not she decided to stay at the lake overnight. She didn't know yet whether she'd stay, and probably wouldn't until later in the afternoon. I also wanted to confirm that she wasn't going to be home from the lake early: I didn't want her to just walk into our house to find me with Abraham Lincoln.

When I was done talking with Molly, I ended the call and put the phone back in my jacket pocket. I unlocked the doors with my key fob and opened the front passenger door for Mr. Lincoln, who thanked me. I then walked around the front and opened the driver's door, got in, started the car, and fastened my seat belt, showing him so he could do the same.

"At what distance can you talk with someone on a telephone?" asked Mr. Lincoln.

"I've spoken with people in England, Russia, Japan, and China with the other person's voice being as clear as if they were next door," I said. "But the signal from the device itself doesn't have to go nearly that far. There are now towers every few miles, called cell towers, that transmit the signal to a network. I'll point one out as we drive."

Before starting out, I reached between the front seats into the back seat and grabbed my Detroit Tigers cap. I then asked what he thought about wearing it, as the only meager disguise I had available. He agreed, saying it was a good idea. We would come up with something a little better when we got home. The first order of business when we got home would be to order those two vacuum tubes, and once we knew when they'd arrive, we'd plan accordingly.

The drive home was uneventful, but I spent time talking about things like paved roads, which he had never seen. Since we were mainly on country and suburban roads around Kalamazoo, we only drove at 35-45 miles per hour most of the time, which he really seemed to enjoy. He commented about how smooth the roads were.

"Al, it sounds as if you've read much about me and my family," said Mr. Lincoln. Tell me something about yours. Do you and Molly have children?"

"Yes, we have two," I told him. "They're both adults now, Katy and Sam. Katy lives in northern New Jersey and Sam lives in Denver."

"Colorado?" he asked.

"Yes. It takes one long day of driving or two half-days to visit Katy, and about 15 hours of driving over two days to visit Sam. But we enjoy the drive in each direction. We can drive on interstate highways, which have been around for about 70 years. We can average almost 70 miles per hour, and there are places to eat, put fuel in the car, and hotels all along the way. Travel is so much easier today even than it was when I was a young boy.

"But there's now a much faster way of traveling to both places," I said. "In the early 1900s a pair of brothers in Dayton, Ohio, named Orville and Wilbur Wright, performed the first powered flight with a human on board. They piloted a small aircraft a few feet, but over time, companies improved them, and now, people can fly from one place to another with a great degree of safety."

"That's just astounding!" he exclaimed. "As you said, it sounds as if technology really began to accelerate late in my century right into the next! I can't imagine being able to fly in a craft like that. How fast do those 'aircraft' go?"

"Five hundred miles per hour or more," I said. "They only leave from, and return to, the ground at places called airports, which have personnel on hand to control the flights to make sure they don't crash into each other, either on the ground or in the air. When I was a boy, it seemed like about once a week, an airplane would crash into the ground or two airplanes would crash into each other, and always with terrible results. Sometimes dozens or even hundreds of people would be on board. It was almost as if a very bad train accident happened that often, but thousands of feet up in the air.

Today, years typically go by without any large airplanes crashing in our country."

"We began having large number of deaths from train accidents when the railroads became more common," said the president. "I'm glad that safety is so much better now."

"While you're here, you may see something in the sky leaving an exhaust trail behind it. It almost looks like long, narrow cloud. That'll be an airplane."

"I'll look for one of those," replied Mr. Lincoln. He was rightly impressed by advancements in improvements in travel, and he'd seen his share during his time. For hundreds of years, people who came to America from Europe and other places traversed land and water at a relatively slow pace in horse-drawn wagons and carriages, or in sailing ships or steamboats on the Great Lakes or rivers. The Erie Canal was completed in 1825, when Lincoln was 16. The canal connected the Hudson River at the east end with Lake Erie at the west end, for a total of 351 miles. But by virtue of connecting to the Hudson River, the canal for the first time connected the Great Lakes with New York Harbor—and the Atlantic Ocean— allowing much greater numbers of passengers and cargo shipments to come and go between the entire Great Lakes area to the rest of the world. The canal greatly increased accessibility to the entire western part of the United States. Other canals would be built during the period of 1790 to 1855, in a time that is sometimes called "the American Canal Age." Canals were built in parts of Pennsylvania, Delaware, Ohio, Indiana, and other states; some artifacts of those canals, such as bridges and locks, remain. Abraham Lincoln knew much about canals, as he supported the construction of the Illinois and Michigan Canal, which connected Lake Michigan at Chicago to the Illinois River, which in turn empties into the Mississippi. Later, he represented the canal company as their attorney.

Similarly, in Michigan, the success of the Erie Canal inspired businessmen to build a canal connecting Lake Saint Clair on the eastern side of the Lower Peninsula with the little town of Singapore—where the Kalamazoo River empties into Lake Michigan—on the west side, 216 miles away. The Clinton-Kalamazoo Canal, as it was called, was started in 1838 (the year after Michigan became a state) with much fanfare. However, the Great Panic of 1837 led to financial sources drying up, and the canal was never finished. Parts of the Clinton-Kalamazoo Canal are still visible in Oakland and Macomb counties today.

Other canal projects across the country saw work stop before their completion, partly for financial reasons and partly due to new means of transportation. No sooner had the Erie Canal been completed than railroads became the preferred means of mass travel for nearly a century. The Baltimore & Ohio Railroad was incorporated in 1825 (the year the Erie Canal opened) and officially began operations in 1830. Other railroads soon began, with the rail companies being given many priorities and advantages in terms of property rights. For three decades from 1830 to 1860, a railroad boom existed in the United States, especially in Northeast and upper Midwest. And in 1869, four years after the end of the Civil War, the Union Pacific and Central Pacific railroads came together in a massive celebration at Promontory Summit, Utah, completing the first transcontinental railroad.

Beginning in 1830, railroads such as the Michigan Central, Detroit and Pontiac, and Erie & Kalamazoo connected cities, lakes, and rivers across the Michigan Territory, which became a state in 1837.

I told Mr. Lincoln about my father, who was born and lived most of his life in Kalamazoo but spent a few years in Mentha, where he would sometimes hop on a moving train to go into Kalamazoo.

After about 25 minutes of driving, we came to Oakland Drive and Kilgore Road and approached our home. Traffic was relatively light at that time of day, still shortly before noon, but seeing all the vehicles on the roads must have still been quite a sight for my guest. As we approached our first traffic signal, I explained how an automatic mechanism controls whether the signal is red, yellow, or green for both directions, and how the whole invention helps to ensure the safe and efficient flow of traffic.

We finally approached the cul-de-sac where our house is located. Just before pulling into the driveway, I told Mr. Lincoln about the small black button I was pushing just above my windshield to open the garage door. Another use of a radio signal. And as soon as we pulled in and I turned off the ignition, I closed the door behind us.

Escorting him into the house, I showed him the location of the bathroom. At first, I thought I just needed to point to it and keep walking until I remembered that he'd never seen such a thing, so I pointed out the hot and cold-water faucets at the sink, the water tank, the flush handle, how to work the toilet seat (the kind that close slowly if you let go of them) and of course, the toilet paper.

As I left him to use the bathroom, I thought about that last item. Toilet paper. Of all the inventions in the last 150 years, that has to rank among the biggest. Seriously. I pondered that we no longer had any Sears Roebuck or Montgomery Wards catalogs, but realized that those stores didn't yet exist in Mr. Lincoln's time. Centuries ago, people used all sorts of things for the purpose: rocks, shells, sticks, leaves, grass, sponges, whatever. By Mr. Lincoln's day, the two most popular tools for the purpose were corn cobs and newspapers. (For the record, I'd have opted for the latter.) I guess it didn't matter as much when one could just drop the used item down the open seat in the outhouse rather than the twisty glazed pipes and PVC plumbing of a modern house.

I picked up my iPad and sat down on the couch in the living room, opening the Amazon website. Taking one of the tubes out of my pocket, I confirmed the tube type, 6L6GC, and entered it in the Search box. First the good news: I got some hits. None of the tubes that appeared on my screen were made by RCA, but the number was the same and they looked the same. But the not-quite-so-good news: the soonest we could get them was two days. In that annoying way that I know I have, I probably spent 15 minutes checking and double-checking, thinking perhaps I'd missed something that could be shipped sooner (or, miraculously, another company would add an item at the very time I was looking on line), but no such luck. So, I placed the order, closed Amazon and put my iPad away. And began to think about what we'd do for two days.

As my guest walked into our living room, I confirmed to him that I'd ordered them, and that it would be two days before we received them. He nodded as he sat across from me, in my big La-Z-Boy chair, hands on the ends of the arms and feet flat on the floor. I think that anyone in the room with me then would have been struck by the same thing as me: How much he looked like his statue inside the Lincoln Memorial.

When asked what God looks like, some people say they think He looks like Lincoln's statue at the Lincoln Memorial. That's not a coincidence. Like many sculptors and other artists, Daniel Chester French, who designed the statue in 1920, incorporated much symbolism into his work. Depicting Lincoln looking out on the nation with a God-like pose was deemed an appropriate tribute to the man who saved the Union and began the legal process of ending slavery in the United States. In a similar manner, the massive 4,664 square foot fresco *The Apotheosis of Washington* by Constantino Brumidi, painted on the ceiling of the U.S. Capitol Building dome, 180 feet above the rotunda floor, depicts the Father of our Country, George Washington, sitting in the heavens in a godlike pose.

"Thank you, Al. I appreciate your help. It goes without saying that even though only the two of us are sitting here now, your work is very important and will help many people."

"You're very welcome, I'm glad to help," I said. "And frankly, without knowing exactly what happened back there in Mentha, I may have played a role in your being here. What if I hadn't gone into the Void? I mean, would you still be here? I really don't know."

"No, I'm sure these are questions that not many people have had to answer. But either way, I do appreciate your help."

"I'm glad to do it. And if it'll make you feel any better, the federal government can pay me back 150 years after you return home. With interest," I said with the smallest smile I could manage.

"With interest?" he laughed. "Well, that will certainly be a tidy sum after that length of time. I may have to talk with my cabinet about increasing the federal budget!"

"Oh," I replied. No need to do that then. Consider it a contribution. A goodwill gesture!"

"That I'll do. That I'll do," said my guest, nodding slightly.

"It's just past noon here," I said, changing to planning mode. "I'm getting hungry. You must be, too."

"Yes, I could certainly use something to eat," he confirmed. "It's been hours—or should I say years?—since I've eaten. If you're going to eat, I'll be happy to join you."

"Great," I said. "You can either stay here and relax for a while or you can come into the next room and see what today's kitchens look like." Although my family had toured the inside of the White House in July 2001, less than two months before the terrorist attacks of

September 11 of that year, our tour group didn't see the kitchen. But I had seen the kitchen of Mr. Lincoln's home in Springfield, Illinois, in the only home he and Mary ever owned. I knew that he would probably appreciate seeing how things have changed.

"Well, let me join you. I'm thoroughly enjoying seeing these updates in tools and machines that make life so much easier, and I'm enjoying your explanations." He followed me around the corner into our kitchen, which, based on comments from Molly, is as badly in need of modernization as Mr. and Mrs. Lincoln's home in Springfield.

"Well, let's see," I said, wondering where to start. "First, one of the simplest things in here: the lights," I continued, flipping up the switch on the wall. "Nearly all homes and business now have electricity wired into the home from a generator miles away. And it powers many things inside the home, including lights, clocks, radios for listening to news and music, televisions for watching plays and sports, and on and on. Electricity was added to many homes beginning around the turn of the 20th Century, and is part of new homes. Electric lights are much cleaner and safer than oil lamps or other sources like that."

"That's wonderful," he said. "Of everything in your home, I can't imagine any improvement adding more benefit to the family than lights that are so bright, and even, and safe. They light up the entire room!"

"They do," I agreed. "And here is the refrigerator," I said as I opened the big upper door. "This refrigerator will keep food cold for days, weeks, or even months. Most food will still spoil over time, but meats will last a few days, and vegetables and fruits will last for many days inside a refrigerator. For many years, instead of having a motor inside, people in my grandparents' time would put large blocks of ice inside to keep food cold, in fact, until just a few years

94

ago, some of the older people I knew still called their refrigerators 'ice boxes.' And down below," I continued, closing the top door and opening the smaller bottom one, "the freezer. It actually can store things like ice cream, ice, and frozen meats and vegetables for many months."

"That must have been revolutionary for people who first had them. Truly amazing," observed my guest.

I continued to show him the kitchen, including the oven, stovetop burners, and microwave oven. And I went into greater detail about how a pressurized plumbing system can provide hot and cold water at the faucets on demand. I showed him how simple it was to get fresh hot or cold water, just by flipping the lever. Most people I'd known in my life would regard these inventions as second nature, but Mr. Lincoln had never seen them. Many of them were introduced during my parents' day. My mom and dad were both born in the first 15 years of the 20th Century, but they knew men in town who had fought in the Civil War, so it struck me that not so many generations had passed since Abraham Lincoln led our nation.

Looking at the window, I decided to show him one more thing for now. "I want to show you something," I said, walking to the closest window, unlatching and opening it. "Screens. As new inventions and creations come along, we tend to take them for granted, but this is a nice one. You can barely see this metal mesh, but during warm months, it allows air to pass through easily but keeps the bugs outside where they belong." He kept shaking his head. Although this seems like one of the most basic things in a Michigan home today, in his day it would have added a great deal of comfort. I closed and latched the window.

"Now, let's decide what to eat," I said. "We haven't done our grocery shopping for the week yet, but we still have a number of things in the house. One thing I like to make on a cool day like this is a grilled cheese sandwich. I have everything to make that," I added, and then, remembering a book called *Abraham Lincoln in the Kitchen: A Culinary View of Lincoln's Life and Times* by Rae Katherine Eighmey that I'd read years before, I suggested something that Mr. Lincoln evidently enjoyed, corn cakes.

"That sounds *very* good!" said Mr. Lincoln. "Mother...Mary used to make corn cakes a few times a week back in Springfield. She knew how much I enjoyed them. I think we used a barrel of corn meal every month for corn cakes!"

"Great," I told him. The corn cakes won't take long to make, but I'll start making them right now so they can be baking while we're having our sandwiches." The corn cakes were as easy to make as the grilled cheese sandwiches, thanks to the box of Jiffy corn muffin mix we had in the cupboard. One box of Jiffy corn muffin mix, an egg, one-third cup of milk, mix together and put in a greased baking pan and you're all set. Some people like to add bits of bacon, jalapeño, blueberries, strawberries, or other items, but I like the standard mix best. Besides, I hadn't added any of those items before and I wasn't about to try out a new recipe on Abraham Lincoln.

We continued to talk about our house and its mechanicals while I made the corn cakes and then the sandwiches. He was very interested in how the heating system worked, and especially the air conditioning. Although I was still trying to be careful not to give him any history lessons, Willis Haviland Carrier would not invent the first air conditioner until 1902, when he was in Brooklyn, New York to develop a means of controlling humidity in a printing plant. That first application was almost like a heat pump, using a system that pumped cold water through coils to cool the air as well as decreasing the humidity. It wasn't until 1933 that the company named after Carrier first used a system that utilized a condensing unit and evaporating coils as today's units do. That basic concept is still in use across the world today.

After putting the corn cakes in the pre-heated oven and making the grilled cheese sandwiches, I put the sandwiches on plates and took them into the dining room, then poured a glass of milk for each of us. "I've read that you also liked milk. This is nice and cold, but just so you know, this milk has had some of the fat removed at the dairy. In today's world, most people don't expend as much energy as they used to, so the reduced fat helps to ensure that the drinker doesn't have more fat than they need."

As soon as he sat down at the table, he had a taste of the milk and declared that although he could tell that it wasn't as sweet as he was used to, he liked it just fine. And thankfully, he said he enjoyed the sandwich, too.

While we were eating, we talked about the plan for the rest of the day.

"After we're done eating," I began, "we can figure out what we want to do. And I've been thinking. Back in the summer of 1856, you came to Kalamazoo and gave a speech for John C. Frémont, the Republican Party's first presidential candidate."

"I DID?" responded Mr. Lincoln, his eyes getting as big as golf balls.

I literally (yes, *literally*...I really did this) stopped in the middle of a bite of my sandwich. How could I have been wrong about that...or had something changed?

But my guest couldn't feign the surprise long. The corners of his mouth turned upward, bringing his famous beard along for the ride, and then that laugh, almost a cackle, began. I tried to think of something clever to say in response to yank his chain, but decided that the few retorts I came up with may not have been appropriate for the president of the United States, no matter how good a sense of humor he had.

"I'm sorry," he said. "I was just enjoying your history lesson so much that I didn't want it to stop," he continued, while I just smiled and shook my head in relief. "Yes, late in August of eighteen hundred and fifty-six. August 27th, I believe…I recall visiting with a friend the day before my trip began and remarking that I'd be leaving for Kalamazoo."

"Yes, August 27th it was," I confirmed. "Would you like to visit downtown Kalamazoo when we're done here? We can visit Bronson Park, where you made the speech. It didn't officially get the name of Bronson Park in 1899, so you may not have called it that, but that's where you gave the speech."

"Bronson Park. Yes, I remember it. It was a lovely park, right in the middle of the city, with an abundance of trees and flowers. And there were beautiful gravel walkways through the park so visitors wouldn't soil their shoes in bad weather. Yes, as we're not going to see those vacuum tubes for two more days, I would very much like to see the park again, to see what I recognize and what's new. Even in my normal timeline, it would have been…nine years since I visited the park, but I'd enjoy going.

"I'm 56 years old," he continued. I've been a lawyer who's ridden up and down the state of Illinois. I've been on a two-man flatboat crew that made several trips from Indiana down to New Orleans. I've been a member of the Illinois House of Representatives, the U.S. House of Representatives, and I've been president of these United States for four years. But in all that time, that was the only time I've ever been to Michigan.

"Well, that is…until now," he smiled.

"Well, very good. When we're done eating, we'll find some clothes that at least serve as some means of concealing your identity and avoid starting a public disturbance. And then we'll go downtown to the park. It's only three miles from here, so it'll only take 15 minutes to get there."

"Oh, that sounds fine." he said, but with his voice tailing off just a little. There was something a little tentative in his voice. I thought for several seconds about asking him if there was a problem, and decided that, even though I'd never compare myself to Abraham Lincoln, we did have a few things in common: we both grew up without a lot of money in our family, we both did manual labor in our youth, we both loved to read and were curious in nature. I decided it would be wrong if I didn't ask."

"Is everything okay with that plan?" I asked. You don't have to do anything you don't want to do. And you're the president, remember?" I added, trying to keep the discussion light.

"Hmmm," he laughed under his breath. "Yes, everything is fine, Al. I really do want to pay another visit to the downtown area and see what it's like. But I've been thinking, also, though I don't want to put you out…"

I folded my arms and responded, "I once had a manager at work, a very good manager…in fact, he lived in Illinois, in the Chicago area, even though I was able to work from home. He once said 'The answer is always *No* unless you ask.' From then on, I was less concerned about causing people inconvenience. I can say *No* if I don't think we can do it."

"Your manager was wise, Al. Well, I'd like it very much if we went downtown shortly, as you suggest. But even during my first term as president, Mother and I...Mrs. Lincoln and I...had started planning to visit Europe together. Now, I expect that she and I can continue with that planning when I return home. But I had also hoped to return home to Springfield. When Mrs. Lincoln, Robert and I left Springfield for our nation's capital, I bade my friends and neighbors farewell at the train station. I told them that I may not see them again, but I've always longed to return if I could. Now that the terrible conflict between the Union and the states in rebellion is nearly done, I've longed to return, if only for a brief while.

Abraham Lincoln's speech to his fellow citizens of Springfield around 8:00 on the morning of February 11, 1861 is regarded as one of the most heartfelt of his life. A heavy rainstorm had descended on Illinois' capital, and he stood outside his train car at the station, still awaiting the arrival of Mrs. Lincoln from their home, telling his friends and neighbors:

> *My friends, no one, not in my situation, can appreciate my feeling of sadness at this parting. To this place and the kindness of these people, I owe everything. Here I have lived a quarter of a century, and have passed from a young to an old man. Here my children have been born, and one is buried. I now leave, not knowing when, or whether ever, I may return, with a task before me greater than that which rested upon Washington. Without the assistance of that Divine Being who ever attended him, I cannot succeed. With that assistance I cannot fail. Trusting in Him who can go with me, and remain with you, and be everywhere for good, let us confidently hope that all will yet be well. To His care commending you, as I hope in your prayers you will commend me, I bid you an affectionate farewell.*

For President-elect Lincoln, one of the most effective politicians our country has ever known, that speech was more than political lingo.

He was truly saying goodbye to his friends, perhaps forever. Even though it had been less than two months since the first state, South Carolina, seceded from the Union, Mr. Lincoln's life had already been threatened numerous times. Although his trip from Springfield to Baltimore involved a symbolic 12-day, 93-station whistle stop, it was conducted under high security, with Baltimore rather than Washington, D.C. being chosen to reduce the chance of his assassination before he ever took the oath of office.

As he told me about his desire to travel to his hometown, I listened to him and mentally began walking through the steps we'd have to take to travel from Kalamazoo to Springfield, to determine if the trip was feasible. I didn't comment about the plans that he and Mrs. Lincoln had started to make for visiting Europe. The Abraham Lincoln you and I read about in textbooks, who also planned the European trip, never had the option of taking that trip because he didn't finish his second term in office; he was only five weeks into that second term when he and Mrs. Lincoln visited Ford's Theatre to see noted British actress Laura Keene star in the comedy play *Our American Cousin.* John Wilkes Booth heard about Lincoln's attendance at the play and decided to change history. Ever since Mr. Lincoln and I came through the Void together, this was the first time that my own disposition started to turn dark thinking about the fate that would befall him—again.

As I tried to put the inevitable out of my mind for now, I slowly began listing aloud the things we'd need to do in order to travel to Springfield.

"Well, if we go, we'll want to pack some extra clothes," I said. "It takes a little more than five hours to get to Springfield from here in my car, and it would be a bit much to go there and back in the same day. But we could drive there today, arrive early tonight, and spend some time seeing the town tomorrow morning. We'd be back here by a reasonable time tomorrow night. The vacuum tubes aren't supposed to arrive here until the day after tomorrow, so we'd have plenty of time.

"I have an extra toiletries kit, toothbrush and toothpaste," I continued. "The most efficient way to do it would be to go downtown to Bronson Park first and then leave directly for Springfield without returning home first. I can make a hotel reservation along the way, and we'll pass a number of restaurants and gas stations during the drive."

Then I asked him, "So we can do it. Do you want to do it?"

"I would like that very much," he replied. "Even though all of my family and neighbors in Springfield will have departed this world long ago, I always felt a connection with the town itself."

"Great! Then we'll go. After we eat the corn cakes, I'll clean up the dishes a little, then I'll get together all of the things we'll need."

"Do you have maps that show the way to Springfield?" he asked.

"Yes. Sort of electronic maps. One unit called a global positioning system, or GPS. I'll be sure to take ours."

After we ate the corn cakes—which he actually seemed to enjoy—I took care of the dishes by putting them in the dishwasher, to wash in a day or two. I then went downstairs to the basement to get two small suitcases, then brought them upstairs to pack. Although our son and daughter no longer live at home, they both have some extra clothes in their old bedrooms for when they visit. Although my clothes may not be a perfect fit for Mr. Lincoln, our son is over 6 feet, so his shirts would fit Mr. Lincoln better than mine. I packed two long-sleeved shirts for him, two short-sleeved shirts, a jacket, and some other miscellaneous items. I put together a toiletries bag

102

for each of us. And in a rare stroke of luck, I'd bought a package of briefs for myself from Kohl's a few days before, which I hadn't opened yet, and I added it to Mr. Lincoln's suitcase. When I was done, I asked Mr. Lincoln to come upstairs and try on clothes that were more comfortable than the ones he was wearing. He found a shirt he liked, but not surprisingly, decided to wear his own pants, socks, and shoes, lacking anything in our house that fit him well.

We gathered everything together—including GPS, sunglasses, baseball caps (he really liked the Detroit Tigers cap that I gave him to wear)—and some other disguise items, such as a few inexpensive facemasks we had on hand since early in the COVID pandemic. I told him that we were just about ready to go…except for "one more thing I have to do."

"You need to call Molly," he guessed, or knew, without a second's hesitation.

"Yes, sir! You learn quickly!" replied.

"So I've been told, Al," said Mr. Lincoln, with no false humility.

I've Got Some 'Splainin' To Do

I stepped outside onto the front porch to call Molly. The call started with each of us finding out how things were going with the other. Then I sprang my news about going to Springfield on her.

"Hey, I've got an opportunity to do some history research," I said. Some research about Abraham Lincoln. "And the research involves going to Springfield, Illinois later today through tomorrow."

Now, believe it or not, this wasn't the first time I'd been gone for a day or two on a history researching trip. I've gone to Muskegon, Michigan to research two World War II vessels that are now floating museums (the submarine *USS Silversides* and the tank landing ship *USS LST 393*). I've gone to Dearborn, Michigan to research Ford Airport, which no longer exists but was considered the world's first modern airport. I've even gone on an overnight trip to Dayton and Wapakoneta in Ohio to do combined research on the U.S. Air Force Museum and Neil Armstrong's birthplace. But I'd always done so with at least a couple days' notice, not a few minutes.

"Today?!" she exclaimed, not angrily, but rightfully wondering what the big rush suddenly was. And I'm sure you've noted that I didn't lie to her. You noted, right?

"Yes, it's a publishing deadline. I was surprised by it, too. But I should be back by tomorrow night." Then, one of those little chills went up my spine with the precautionary little voice in my head saying "Don't ask me who I'm writing the Lincoln article for, don't ask me who I'm writing the Lincoln article for." I hadn't gotten that far yet, but I knew I'd actually find something to write about while I was gone, and would find a way to write an article about it.

"Okay, well I'm doing fine here. I expect to be home tomorrow night, too. Everything is taken care of at the house, so just drive safely and have a good time. Text me when you get there?" Typical Molly.

"Yes, absolutely. I'll text or call tonight," I reassured her.

We ended the call and I told my guest that I was ready to go. I told him that the call to Molly went well, and that I'd text her when we reached Springfield that night.

"Text? Letters?" said Mr. Lincoln.

"Yes, sir. It's just a written message instead of spoken. I'll show you tonight when we get to our hotel room in Springfield.

We got back into my car as I pushed the button to open the garage door.

Our driveway is about 60 feet long and I've backed out of it and pulled into it thousands of times in the 12 years we've been at the house, and I can't remember a single event of note happening while performing one of those rudimentary functions. Until now.

I had just backed out of the garage and pushed the garage door button to close it behind us, when I decided I'd show him the radio. I explained that at any given time, one could listen to various stations that had music, news shows, and talk shows.

"Radio, or wireless, has been around for just over 100 years," I said. In the early days, in addition to music and news, they essentially did dramas, comedies, and other plays on the radio. Keeping the radio on quietly in the background helps me to stay awake when I drive long distances. If you'll recall what we discussed about frequencies of energy, like that from the sun, that we had when we left the facility where we met, the same applies here. We can't sense most energy waves around us, but thousands of signals are being transmitted right through the air." I pushed a few Channel buttons so he could get a small indication of the variety. (We have SiriusXM on our car radio, but I decided not to take a chance on listening to their comedy channels. Then I'd *really* have some explaining to do!)

"Energy waves with voices and music coming right through the air," he said, then taking a moment to reflect as he listened. "Another very useful invention," he said, "as well as entertaining. I think everyone enjoys listening to some kind of music. Mrs. Lincoln and I love plays. We especially enjoy comedies, and I've seen a number of Shakespeare's plays."

He then continued, "Mrs. Lincoln and I were watching a wonderful play just before I came here. It was at Ford's Theatre in our nation's capital, just a few blocks from the Executive Mansion. I enjoyed the surprise ending very much; it was very funny."

My first physical reaction was to slam on my brake pedal. For a second or two, I couldn't do anything else.

The Abraham Lincoln sitting next to me had attended *Our American Cousin* starring Laura Keene at Ford's Theatre on the night of April 14, 1865. But he did not encounter John Wilkes Booth in Act III, Scene 2. *The Abraham Lincoln sitting next to me had seen the entire play, all the way through to the end.*

This Changes Everything

"Al, is everything alright?" asked my passenger.

After a few seconds while my mind journeyed in multiple directions, I replied, "Yes, I'm sorry. I didn't mean to stop so suddenly. I just thought of something else we might need to do," I replied. My phrase "something else we might need to do," meant my figuring out how and why the entire history of the United States for the last 160 years had just changed. The Abraham Lincoln sitting next to me had sat through the play at Ford's Theatre all the way to the end. His timeline had changed. Had *our* timeline changed as well, and if so, how? Was this something that my presence in the Void had caused? What kind of predicament had been created since I left home this morning? Did we need to somehow set things right? And if so, could we do it without changing the timeline of history? I could only start to ponder the implications.

He didn't say anything in response; I think it was because he knew I wouldn't slam on the brake pedal simply because I'd just thought of something. He was probably already thinking about what he'd said that led to my little driveway panic. I'd let it go for a while, but I knew I'd have to tell him something very soon that was not only feasible but true.

Before I continued backing out of our driveway, I gave myself a few more seconds to recover, to make sure I had my wits about me enough to drive. Then, still mentally occupied, I headed for the nearby east-and-west running Kilgore Road, drove east, and took a left turn onto South Westnedge Avenue. It's a thoroughfare with an unusual name, but one for which the genesis should be remembered.

Westnedge Avenue is the busiest north-and-south running street in Kalamazoo and neighboring Portage. In fact, its north end is more than four miles north of the Kalamazoo city limits in Cooper, and to the south, it only ends where withdrawing glaciers decided to leave Portage's Gourdneck Lake in their wake thousands of years ago. The entire stretch of Westnedge Avenue is about 15 miles long.

When a person is new to the area, you can tell it by the way they pronounce "Westnedge." On some TV commercials, unknowing announcers pronounce it "West Nedge." Our GPS pronounces it "West-a-nedge." Those of us from the area know it's pronounced "WESTnedge," with no pause between syllables.

Westnedge Avenue is named after two brothers who were both born in Kalamazoo, Richard Burchnall Westnedge (born in 1869) and his younger brother Joseph Burchnall Westnedge (born in 1872). They were raised on Portage Street, south of what was then the city limit of Kalamazoo. Both brothers attended Kalamazoo College, where Joseph was a halfback on the K-College football team and led the team to an undefeated season in 1895.

After attending K-College, Richard went on to attend Rush Medical College in Chicago. He married Alice May Gould of Chicago and practiced medicine in Dubuque, Iowa for about a year before joining the U.S. Army. While serving as a surgeon in the Philippines during the Spanish-American War, he died of typhoid fever at age 28, just two years after marrying Alice May.

Richard's younger brother, Joseph Westnedge, also served his country. He was a captain in the Army during the Spanish-American War in 1898, and a lieutenant colonel during the Jackson prison riot of September 1912. In 1916, he was called to duty again with the Michigan National Guard to defend the border with Mexico after a raid by Pancho Villa. His duty on the Mexican border prompted the Army to call him and his unit to serve for a fourth time. By now,

Joseph Westnedge was a colonel in the Red Arrow Division, one of the earliest units to be called up into World War I. The unit sailed to Europe, and after participating in a number of key offensives in the summer and fall of 1918, Joseph Westnedge was a victim of a mustard gas attack and was sent to a hospital in Nantes, France. There, he died on November 29, 1918, just 18 days after the armistice was signed to end World War I.

Two years later, the body of Joseph Westnedge was returned home from France to Kalamazoo. Thousands of people stood along the streets to pay their respects during the funeral procession. Westnedge was posthumously awarded the Distinguished Service Cross and French Croix-de-Guerre. And West Street, which had originally marked the western boundary of the city, was renamed Westnedge.

I drive on Westnedge Avenue almost every day, and I try to remember every time how the name came about.

Driving in Downtown Kalamazoo

We continued north on Westnedge toward downtown Kalamazoo as I was still processing the fact that, unlike the Abraham Lincoln we read about in books and saw in documentaries, the man next to me saw the comedy at Ford's Theatre, *Our American Cousin*, until its conclusion.

History has consistently taught us that instead of that scenario, as the president and Mrs. Lincoln sat in the president's box during Act III, Scene 2, they awaited the delivery of the line that was expected to draw the biggest laugh of the entire play, when the boorish American cousin, played that night by Philadelphia-born Joe Jefferson, proclaims: "Don't know the manners of good society, eh? Well, I guess I know enough to turn you inside out, old gal – you sockdologizing old man-trap!" As the resulting laughter for that line reached its peak, 26-year-old actor John Wilkes Booth, a member of the renowned Booth acting family and Confederate sympathizer, snuck into the box and fired a single .41 caliber bullet from his small derringer into the head of the unsuspecting president. The round struck Mr. Lincoln in the head behind his left ear. A struggle ensued in the box between Booth and the Lincolns' guest at the play, Major Henry Rathbone. As Booth then began a leap down from the box to the stage—a drop of about 12 feet—he became caught, either by a handhold by Major Rathbone or from Booth's own riding spur snagging the American flag decorating the front of the box. He landed awkwardly, probably breaking his ankle in the process.

As "weird history" would have it, the story of that night at Ford's Theatre lived on well into the 20th Century by direct witness. On February 9, 1956, 96-year-old Samuel Seymour was a guest on the CBS game show *I've Got a Secret*. The secret that Mr. Seymour whispered to host Garry Moore before four panelists tried to guess it: As a boy, he was in the audience at Ford's Theatre the night that John Wilkes Booth shot Abraham Lincoln. Panelists guessed Mr. Seymour's secret, possibly in part because when the studio audience saw the secret silently flashed on the studio monitor, they let out an audible gasp. Garry Moore threw all the cards over, thereby awarding Mr. Seymour the maximum cash prize—all of $80. And because the nonagenarian Mr. Seymour smoked a pipe, sponsor R.J. Reynolds Tobacco Company gave him a can of Prince Albert pipe tobacco (yes, they actually did have Prince Albert in the can), instead of the usual prize: a carton of Winston cigarettes.

In follow-up discussion on air, Mr. Seymour shared that he heard the shot and "someone in the president's box screamed. I saw Lincoln slumped forward in his seat." At the time, said Mr. Seymour, his concern was for Booth and his injury, not realizing what the actor had just done.

The game show audience that night was doubly fortunate to be able to see Samuel Seymour: In addition to being blessed in seeing such a witness to history, they would be among the last to enjoy his story in person. Samuel Seymour passed away just two months later, on April 12, 1956, the 95th anniversary of the attack on Fort Sumter that started the Civil War.

Between traffic and signals on Westnedge, I continued pondering the differences between the Abraham Lincoln in my history books and the one sitting in the passenger seat of my Buick. No expert on time travel or quantum physics, I did the best I could, and so far, I came up with two options, keeping in mind that much of my thinking was based on hypothetical scenarios depicted in episodes of *Twilight Zone* and *Star Trek*, as well as some college science classes. Those fictional plots and discussions were based on the premise that we still didn't know whether time travel was possible. After the events of the last couple hours, I knew that such travel *was* possible. I had no doubt that the man sitting in my passenger seat was Abraham Lincoln, but something had seemingly caused a diversion from the timeline you and I know, and that diversion seemed to occur that night at Ford's Theatre.

My thoughts were scattering in multiple directions, possibly in the same manner that multiple timelines might exist once a given event, however small, occurs.

First, the theory of parallel timelines. That theory holds that in order for time travel to be possible, there must be multiple (or even infinite) possible outcomes of any situation. Might it be possible that my passenger came through the Void from a different timeline? Perhaps it was the exact same Abraham Lincoln except that something happened—possibly not long before he stepped into the Void—that resulted in the creation of different timelines. Perhaps the Abraham Lincoln you and I knew from history classes and movies had continued on the same unfortunate path I had learned. Or, perhaps he had gone off on another timeline altogether…

The second possible option had to do with the "time station" in Mentha. Had someone 30 or 40 years ago used the facility to go back and change something, maybe something that I then exacerbated by unexpectedly stepping into the Void? Maybe there was some combination of the two?

A film made in 1998, *Sliding Doors*, kept popping into my head. Near the film's start, the main character, Helen (played by Gwyneth Paltrow) is rushing for her train on the London subway but narrowly misses it when a brief delay allows the train's sliding doors to close in front of her. The film then rewinds, and everything is as it was before, but this time she narrowly manages to board before the doors close. The rest of the film alternates between the two timelines.

Assuming that both timelines were identical before a random event (a dropped earring) caused the delay in the one scenario, the event could have resulted in two different timelines. Go back five minutes and look at another event that caused a change, and there are now four timelines. Another event a few minutes before, and eight timelines. And on an on until there is are more timelines than we can count.

I thought about these scenarios and possibilities for several minutes.

I then began to again discuss the color scheme for the traffic lights with Mr. Lincoln. The three-color system originated in Michigan, having been invented by police officer William Potts in Detroit in 1920.

My guest asked whether the cables strung between poles were still used for telegraph messages, and I explained that the telegraph really wasn't in use anymore, and explained the current purpose of the various cables. He found it interesting that the power to the traffic lights, street lights and some other things came from some overhead power cables, but that some other fixtures had cables that ran underground to feed power to them. Well over 100 years after some of the first power cables in the area were strung, cost remains a factor in putting them all underground.

I periodically looked around to see if anyone happened to be noticing my passenger, but so far, I hadn't seen any staring. He seemed to be similarly checking faces to see if anyone noticed. Again, so far, so good. But we'd only gone about three miles so far, and hadn't gotten out of the car yet. Not surprisingly, when the two of us weren't talking about various things—I sometimes just let him observe and think—he was very attentive and curious. Those were traits that served him well throughout his life, as we learned in school during our youth.

At the top of Westnedge Hill, which looks out over downtown Kalamazoo to the north, the two northbound lanes of traffic branch off into Park Street. I pointed out the view to Mr. Lincoln, and quickly pointed to the right ahead, where we'd see Bronson Park shortly. After passing some construction, we turned right onto South Street, which marked the south side of the city in Mr. Lincoln's day. We were able to find an open parking meter on the south side of the street, just east of the Kalamazoo Civic Theatre. There, on the opposite side of South Street was our first destination, Bronson Park.

"Why don't you stay seated there for just a second?" I told Mr. Lincoln after I'd shut the car off. "I need to come around to your side to put some money in the parking meter. We can also go over just a couple things before we go into the park," I added, taking some coins out of a zip-lock sandwich bag in my console. I used to carry a little change in my pocket, but shortly after the arrival of COVID-19 in March 2020, it became evident that using a debit or credit card was cleaner and easier for most transactions. My few remaining coins had been relegated to my console or a small drawer in my house.

"Certainly, I'll stay right here," Mr. Lincoln replied. "Let me know if you need government help to afford the meter," he joked, and I laughed along with him.

Getting out of the car and coming around the front of it to the passenger side, I opened the door to let him out, with one eye surveying the park across the street. I then stepped over to the meter and put some coins in (meters in town don't take pennies, and I had checked the coins in my zip-lock bag to make sure that I didn't accidentally show any of them to my guest, because I didn't want to have to carefully craft a reason to tell You-Know-Who that our pennies had You-Know-Who memorialized on the obverse of our most common but least valued coin).

"I think luck is on our side. There aren't many people in the park today," I said, looking at perhaps 60 or 70 men, women, children, and a few furry, four-legged family members who were walking, standing, or sitting in the park. "Of course, it's up to you whether you want to wear that cloth mask," I said, referring to the white medical mask I had given him as a potential disguise component, "but I think with a crowd of this size, if you keep the sunglasses and the Tigers hat on, and don't stay in one place or position for very long, you'll be fine without the mask.

I continued, "If anyone does come up to you, or asks who you are, you can say we're planning a movie but we can't talk about it yet. If they think you're an actor who looks like Abraham Lincoln, they'll probably understand. After all, he did speak right here at Bronson Park once, didn't he?" I said, referring to my guest's own speech.

"Yes, *he* did," said Mr. Lincoln, also looking across the street so he could prepare for potential encounters. "And what's a...*movie?*"

"A moving picture," I said. "A series of photographs like Matthew Brady's, but there's a long strip of film that records that series of photos in rapid succession. And when you project light through the moving film onto a surface, you see a *moving* picture...essentially, a play that can be reproduced hundreds of times around the country without the actors ever leaving their hometown. And better yet, the images are in color and are accompanied with the actors' own voices and music. But it's still just a picture. The viewer is never in any danger of being harmed by anything on the projection screen."

"Amazing. Well, that sounds like very good rationale under the circumstances," said Mr. Lincoln. "And are we actually making a movie, or is that just a story we'd be making up to tell people?" he asked.

"We'd tell people we'll be making a movie," I reiterated. "We don't have to say when or about what. We can make a little movie with my phone when we're in the park so we're not lying," I explained, with both of us still looking across the street instead of each other.

"Very well," he acknowledged. "You can be rather devious when you need to be, can't you?" he smiled.

"Yes, but *only* when I need to be," I confirmed. Then, after pondering my guest's own ability to navigate the rivers of veracity in his role as a politician, I added, "Perhaps our movie will mention something about a certain speaker's assurances to Horace Greeley that he would do what he needed to in order to save the Union—regardless of the outcome of slavery—despite the fact that he'd already drafted the Emancipation Proclamation."

"Oh, Albert, Albert, Albert," said my guest, in a mock scolding tone. "Now I fear that you've mistaken your own deviousness as mine. Not to mention your peculiar sense of jocularity."

"Ha-ha," I deadpanned. "At any rate, I believe I'm ready to start our little tour if you are."

"Indeed I am, Al. Indeed I am," ensured Mr. Lincoln.

I told him about waiting for walk/don't walk signs as we approached the intersection of South and Park streets. We were about to cross South Street into Bronson Park. He looked around quickly to make sure he was out of hearing range of anyone else.

"You may find this amusing," he began to share. "In the early stages of the Proclamation in the summer of Eighteen Hundred and Sixty-Two, there were times that I worked alone in drafting it. It was a

116

time when the presidential cook was not on duty, and I realized after working on the proclamation for several hours that I was very hungry. Just then, Mother—Mrs. Lincoln—came in to the office to visit me. I told her that I feared I would have to rename the great document 'the *Emaciation* Proclamation.' She doesn't always appreciate my offbeat sense of humor, but she enjoyed that one."

Given the gravity of the topic at the time and how much he was weighed down by the questions of slavery and the war, I thought that was actually a pretty good joke.

Monday in the Park with Abraham

In 2031, Kalamazoo's Bronson Park will mark its 200th anniversary as a civic property. Its history began in March 1831, when the land was donated to Kalamazoo by the city's founder, Titus Bronson.

By most accounts, Titus Bronson was an "eccentric," even an "oddball," though by today's standards, he may just have been a libertarian of sorts. Born in Middlebury, Connecticut in 1788, Bronson traveled west, first to Ohio, then to Ann Arbor, and on June 21, 1829, he arrived in the town that would become Kalamazoo, where he was the area's first white settler. According to a brief biography about Bronson by the Kalamazoo Valley Museum, Titus Bronson was "a public-spirited, patriotic, and generous man," but "outspoken against intemperance and politics, which frequently put him at odds with his fellow settlers."

The following June, he bought the land where downtown Kalamazoo is now located. After having built a crude house and prepared it for living there, he "returned to Connecticut to retrieve his wife, Sally" and other family members. In March 1831—six years before the Michigan Territory became a state—he and his brother-in-law, Stephen Richardson, requested in court register's office that the settlement be called the Village of Bronson. Just two weeks later, Territorial Governor Lewis Cass chose the spanking-new Village of Bronson as the county seat. That led to the area becoming the focus of future development. Among the beneficiaries were the Potawatomi, who had lived for years in the area that was previously home to Native Americans of the Hopewell tradition since before the First Millennium.

Bronson donated some of his land for public use, including designated locations for a courthouse, a jail, churches, and an

118

academy. (The street that today bounds Bronson Park on the north is still named Academy Street, and the small street that intersects Academy from the north, which remains home to several churches and the Michigan Avenue Courthouse, is still called Church Street.)

But Titus Bronson's contrarian and sometimes "argumentative" behavior eventually led to fellow citizens running him out of the very town he founded. The village was renamed Kalamazoo in 1836, after the Potawatomi word for boiling water, referring to the Kalamazoo River that passes through the city. The surrounding township was renamed Kalamazoo Township in 1837, the year that Michigan became the 26th state in the Union. (Kalamazoo did not become a city until 1884.)

It was within this context that Abraham Lincoln paid a visit to Kalamazoo in August 1856.

Abraham Lincoln arrived at the Kalamazoo train station at 1:30 pm on August 27, 1856 for his speech that began promptly at 2:00. The renovated depot, halfway between Chicago and Detroit, welcomes visitors. Photo by Fran Dwight.

Mr. Lincoln's Visit to Kalamazoo, 1856

Abraham Lincoln, photographed by Alexander Hesler on February 28, 1857, about six months after his visit to Kalamazoo. Lincoln tousled his hair intentionally before the photo, saying he didn't think his friends would recognize him if he would have combed it. Courtesy Library of Congress.

Abraham Lincoln's speech at the Kalamazoo campaign rally in August 1856 didn't go unnoticed. It was a large rally of up to 35,000 people (newspaper accounts varied from 10,000 upward) that drew attendees from across the area and even from outside of Michigan.

In 1856, Abraham Lincoln was practicing law, not having held an elected position for seven years. Some descriptions of his life at that time, including the historical marker in Bronson Park, describe Lincoln as a little-known or "obscure" lawyer by that time. However, he really was on the cusp of being well known, a scant four years before he'd be elected our 16th president. He was known within political circles in Illinois, having served in the state's House of Representatives from 1834 to 1832. And as a member of the U.S. House of Representatives from 1847 to 1849, his name became known to prominent politicians including Jefferson Davis, Lewis Cass, John C. Calhoun, Thomas Hart Benton, Simon Cameron, and Horace Mann. When he left the U.S. House, he stepped away from politics in order to focus on his law practice and family. However, with the passage of the Kansas-Nebraska Act in 1854, he once more became involved in debates and other activities. The bill had been introduced and guided through passage by none other than Lincoln's Illinois rival, Stephen A. Douglas. The law repealed the Missouri Compromise of 1850 (which had prohibited slavery in the Northern states), created the Kansas and Nebraska territories, and gave those territories the authority, or sovereignty, to decide whether they would allow the institution of slavery.

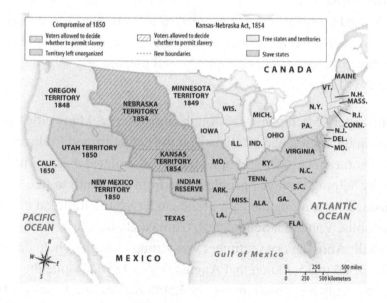

The Kansas-Nebraska Act of 1854 created the new territories of Kansas and Nebraska, and allowed the territories to decide whether to permit slavery. The act caused Abraham Lincoln to return to politics five years after he left Congress, and resulted in his speech in Kalamazoo. Courtesy the Mayhew Cabin Foundation.

Lincoln ran against Douglas in Illinois' 1854 U.S. Senate race that Lincoln knew he had little chance of winning. Two months before visiting Kalamazoo, his name was placed in nomination for vice president of the United States at the very first Republican National Convention in Philadelphia. (The eventual vice-presidential nominee, William L. Dayton of New Jersey, went down in defeat in the general election with his running mate at the head of the Republican ticket, former Western explorer, military officer and politician John C. Frémont.)

As much as anything noted about him, there was the way he spoke. Not a baritone voice that one might expect from a very athletic 6-foot-four man with gaunt cheeks and sunken eyebrows, but a higher voice, the frequency of which might have actually made him easer to hear in a crowd. He had chosen to use simple, sometimes folksy phrases filled with humor rather than the more refined and formal words used by speakers such as Edward Everett, who was thought by many to be the greatest orator of the day. And Lincoln had prepared his whole life to influence people: "I will prepare and someday my chance will come."

Southwestern Michigan was strongly anti-slavery. Many cities and towns in the region had "stations" on the Underground Railroad. Those homes, churches and other buildings violated existing federal laws by helping enslaved people move from the South to free Canada. Towns along the path of the Underground Railroad included Cassopolis, Vandalia, Schoolcraft, Climax, Battle Creek, and Marshall. Anti-slavery sentiment was strong enough to help draw the crowd of up to 35,000 on that August day in 1856, despite the village having a population of only 4,500. Kalamazoo County's first physician, Nathan Thomas, lived in Schoolcraft. He and his wife, Pamela, helped an estimated 1,000 to 1,500 enslaved people on their journey to freedom. Not only did Nathan and Pamela provide a place to stay, but Pamela cooked "hearty meals" and Nathan provided medical treatment.

The Great Lakes region, particularly Wisconsin and Michigan, played a significant role in the formation of the Republican Party, a party formed primarily to stop the spread of slavery into new states, as the Kansas-Nebraska Act would do. Whigs, Free Soilers, and anti-slavery northern Democrats assembled to determine how to best halt the spread of slavery. In February 1854, representatives met at a schoolhouse in Ripon, Wisconsin, about 16 miles west of Lake Winnebago. There, they confirmed their purpose and discussed the formation of a new party. A local attorney named Alvin Bovay suggested the name Republican Party to reflect the republican model proposed by the nation's founders in 1776.

Across "the Big Lake" in Michigan, meetings were held in Kalamazoo, Detroit, and Jackson. A leader of the group in Michigan was Free Soiler Austin Blair, who would become the state's governor in 1860. On July 6, 1854 in Jackson, Michigan, members of the new national party, including some who were in Ripon, gathered. They met outdoors to avoid overheated meeting halls during that summer, and "under the oaks" of downtown Jackson, they formalized the name of the Republican Party and held the party's first meeting. U.S. Representative David S. Walbridge of Kalamazoo presided over that meeting. On the day of Lincoln's speech in Kalamazoo, Walbridge was in the nation's capital, but his wife, Eliza, served tea to a small group that included Lincoln.

Eliza Walbridge was a member of the Kalamazoo Ladies' Library Association, the first women's club in Michigan and the third such club in the nation. The LLA began its meetings in homes in 1852, ostensibly as a sewing group. Books were read aloud during those meetings while women sewed.

Such was the impact of the new party and its message of freedom that just four months after the meeting in Jackson, in the state's gubernatorial election on November 7, 1854, Republican Kinsley S. Bingham of Green Oak Township (in Livingston County, just south of Brighton) was elected Michigan's 11th governor. Bingham was one of the first Republican governors from any state to be elected governor, a full two years before the party fielded its first national ticket with Frémont and Dayton.

Along with David S. Walbridge, Kalamazoo attorney and politician Hezekiah G. Wells served as a delegate at that first national party convention in Philadelphia in June 1856. Wells was born in Steubenville, Ohio, and had lived in Texas Township (in western Kalamazoo County) and Schoolcraft (in south Kalamazoo County) before moving to the village of Kalamazoo. Before Kalamazoo became a city in 1884, Wells served as village president longer than any other person. The location where the Walbridge home once stood is now marked by a Michigan historical marker on the Downtown Kalamazoo Mall. The place where Lincoln stayed overnight in Kalamazoo remains unknown, but it may have been the Walbridge home.

Following the national convention in Philadelphia, it was Wells who wrote to Lincoln, inviting him to attend a rally in downtown Kalamazoo that was being planned by Wells and local hardware merchant Allen Potter. Potter has a number of claims to fame in Kalamazoo. He was the City of Kalamazoo's first mayor (beginning in 1884) and was the first congressman from the district. But perhaps his most forward-thinking act came in 1855, when Potter purchased part of the old "Pioneer Cemetery" at the south end of town (it was being replaced by Mountain Home Cemetery west of town), and on that spot, at 925 South Westnedge, he built an octagon-shaped house. The "octagon house" model was based on an overall notion that people's character evolves somewhat based on the kind of home in which they live. In addition to the eight-sided shape of the house, the octagon houses of the day pioneered the use of family rooms, walkout basements, and a centralized "service core" of utilities including plumbing and heating. The Octagon House still stands and looks very much like it did the day that Abraham Lincoln was in town.

After Lincoln received the invitation from Wells to speak in Kalamazoo, he wrote back to Wells (who Mr. Lincoln addressed as "H.G. Wells") on August 4th, saying:

> *Dear Sir:*
>
> *"It would afford me great pleasure to be with you, and I will do so if possible; but I cannot promise positively–We are having trouble here that needs the attention of all of us– I mean the Fillmore movement– With the Fremont and Fillmore men united here in Illinois, we have Mr. Buchanan in the hollow of our hand; but with us divided, as we now are, he has us– This is the short and simple truth, as I believe.*
>
> *Very respectfully,*
>
> *A. Lincoln*

A little more than two weeks later—on August 21st, six days before the rally—Lincoln wrote to Wells a second time, saying:

> *Dear Sir:*
>
> *At last I am able to say, no accident preventing, I will be with you on the 27th. I suppose I can reach in time,*
> *leaving Chicago the same morning– I shall go to the Matteson House, Chicago, on the evening of the 26th.*
>
> *Yours truly,*
>
> *A. Lincoln*

Bronson Park in Kalamazoo, Michigan, c. 1889-1892, about 33-36 years after Lincoln's speech there. The park has always been noted for its beautiful fountains and many large trees, many of which were felled later by a tornado on May 13, 1980. Photo courtesy Kalamazoo Public Library.

Mr. Lincoln was describing a four-day round-trip from Springfield to Kalamazoo and back. He would make his way from the Illinois state capital of Springfield to Chicago, where he would stay at a hotel called the Matteson House (which stood at the northwest corner of Dearborn and Randolph streets) overnight on August 26th and leave by train for Kalamazoo at 8:30 on the morning of the rally. Following the rally on August 27th, he would remain in Kalamazoo overnight and depart on August 28th. Kalamazoo was a stop on the Michigan Central Railroad; in 1856, the railroad used essentially the same route that Amtrak passenger trains use today. The return trip to Springfield was also a two-day journey.

In addition to Lincoln, a number of other speakers would be on hand at Bronson Park, and the new Republican Party and the local community would have a grand political gathering when they arrived. In addition to the crowd, the *Niles Enquirer* newspaper said there was a five-mile parade through the streets to Bronson Park. It was reported that there were tables full of food and "barrels of ice water." The *Enquirer* also noted about the Kalamazoo people preparing for the rally: "Kalamazoo is but another name for philanthropy and generosity," a trait that would be noted for decades to come in light of the philanthropic and generous work of the aforementioned Dr. Upjohn, Dr. Stryker and others.

In addition to Republican Gov. Kinsley S. Bingham, another nationally prominent politician from Michigan spoke that day, Zachariah Chandler.

Chandler was born in Bedford, New Hampshire in 1813 and at age 20 moved to Detroit, which was then the territorial capital of Michigan. Chandler was a life-long abolitionist and "Radical" Republican—one of the self-proclaimed Republicans who wanted the total and immediate end of slavery. When Lincoln visited Kalamazoo in 1856, Chandler had previously been the mayor of Detroit. The year of Lincoln's visit, he would be elected to the U.S. Senate seat from Michigan, a seat he would hold for 18 years. Following his terms in the Senate, he served as U.S. secretary of the interior under President Grant. During his service in the Grant administration, which was marred by corruption and patronage, Chandler investigated his own department and received approval from Grant to make reforms. Some of the departments that were changed included the Bureau of Indian Affairs, Pension Bureau, Land Office, and the Patent Office. In addition to his government duties, Chandler served as chairman of the Republican National Committee, during which time he managed the successful presidential campaign of Rutherford B. Hayes. After his two years in Interior, he was again elected to the U.S. Senate to fill a vacancy, but died in office in 1879 at age 65.

For nearly 100 years, from 1913 to 2011, a statue of Zachariah Chandler was one of two statues representing the state of Michigan that stood in the National Statuary Hall Collection in the U.S. Capitol Building. In 2011, a statue of President Gerald Ford replaced the statue of Chander, which in turn was moved to Lansing.

One prominent resident of Kalamazoo who represented the loyal opposition to the new Republican Party at the time was Democrat Charles E. Stuart. Stuart was born in 1810 in Waterloo, New York, in the Finger Lakes area and what was then the heart of the Cayuga nation. Stuart studied law and was admitted to the bar at age 22. At age 25 he moved to Michigan, settling in Portage. After briefly serving in the Michigan House of Representatives, he was elected to Michigan's 2nd Congressional District to serve in the U.S. House, to fill the vacancy caused by the death of 39-year-old Edward Bradley from Marshall. Stuart served for two non-consecutive two-year terms between 1847 and 1853.

Stuart was then elected to the U.S. Senate, a position he held at the time of Lincoln's visit to Kalamazoo. He served three two-year terms in the U.S. Senate, during which he was president *pro tempore* for the first of those terms.

Stuart ran unsuccessfully for governor of Michigan in 1858 and returned to Kalamazoo to practice law. He was a delegate to the 1860 Democratic National Convention in Charleston, South Carolina. At about the same time, Stuart built a new home in Kalamazoo, where he lived until 1883. The two-story Italian Villa-style home he built, now officially called the Charles E. Stuart House, is on Stuart Avenue in the Stuart Neighborhood, less than a mile northwest of Bronson Park. In 1972, the house was listed on the National Register of Historic Places.

In a reflection of the relationships that existed then—in contrast to those that generally exist today—although Stuart supported Popular

Sovereignty and Stephen Douglas's Kansas-Nebraska Act, he opposed the more pro-slavery manifesto called the Lecompton Constitution (a document drafted by pro-slavery politicians in Kansas, and named after that territory's capital, which would have flat-out made Kansas a pro-slavery state). Stuart later served in the Union Army during the Civil War. In fact, he used his education and financial means to equip and raise the 13th Michigan Infantry Regiment, in which he rose to the rank of colonel and served until ongoing ill health forced him to resign.

Abraham Lincoln only visited Michigan once in his lifetime, at that big campaign rally in Kalamazoo on August 27, 1856. As luck frequently has it, major components of history including speeches, written records, artifacts, and even buildings are sometimes destroyed or otherwise lost to the ages.

However, such was not to be in the case with Mr. Lincoln's speech in Kalamazoo that day. A reporter for the *Detroit Daily Advertiser* had come to town to cover the rally, and that reporter was skilled at phonography, a phonemic writing system that records sounds of the speaker rather than English spelling. Because of that reporter, we know what the future 16th president said at Bronson Park that day and we know what Hezekiah Wells said when he introduced him. And even that reporter's account of the speech might have been lost to history if not for the efforts of Thomas Starr, an amateur historian and Lincoln researcher from Royal Oak, Michigan. In 1930, Starr discovered a bound volume of 1856 issues of the Detroit Daily Advertiser that included Lincoln's speech at Bronson Park. The volume had fallen behind a shelf at the Detroit Public Library.

With several speakers' platforms having been built in Bronson Park for the rally and a number of speakers on the docket, the reporter from Detroit might have chosen to cover the fiery words of any of them. But he chose to record the words of the tall, perhaps-not-so-obscure-after-all attorney from Springfield, Illinois.

In addition to the big campaign rally in Kalamazoo, August 1856 marked the 80th anniversary of the day that King George III and the rest of the world learned that in an overheated meeting hall in Philadelphia, a group of revolutionary thinkers and leaders had declared independence from Great Britain, establishing a new nation called the United States of America. They told the world that it was "self-evident" that all men are created equal and entitled to "unalienable rights" including life, liberty, and the pursuit of happiness.

We're all fortunate that in 1930, Tom Starr found the record of Lincoln's speech. Diligent detective work has been done for many years by other amateur historians, among them members of the Kalamazoo Abraham Lincoln Institute, in particular, Dr. Thomas George. In addition to being a physician, Dr. George was previously a member of both the Michigan House of Representatives and Senate. Dr. George has spent countless hours and many years reconstructing Abraham's Lincoln's trip to Kalamazoo. He also discovered that, due to a write-over in an actual letter by Abraham Lincoln, historians didn't know for many years exactly why he came to Kalamazoo, while turning down appearances in other states for nearly a three-year period. The answer, which Tom George explains in far more detail: It was an old-fashioned political quid pro quo, "tit for tat." The Illinois lawyer made a four-day speaking trip to Kalamazoo in order to, in turn, obtain support two years hence, when he would make his second bid against Stephen A. Douglas for the U.S. Senate seat from Illinois. Lincoln would lose that election, but in 1860 his message won the presidency.

Back in the Park

I had been to Bronson Park dozens of times before, to hear concerts, have lunch with friends, to get across town while walking or jogging, or to see the park decorated for Christmas complete with colored lights, a manger scene, and Candy Cane Lane. On one occasion, I walked to the park with co-workers on the lunch hour to view an annular eclipse; a homemade projection device captured the light rays in the park and projected the scene onto the front face of City Hall across South Street. On this day, I would enjoy the park again, but this time would be an additional learning experience, listening to the park's most famous visitor ever. (Among others who have spoken in the park were Sen. Robert F. Kennedy in April 1968, during his presidential campaign. Eight years before, in October 1960, the park was filled with people who listened to Sen. John F. Kennedy speak from the steps of City Hall across the street.) To be able to talk with Mr. Lincoln as he returned to a place where he and the city had such a profound impact on each other, and on history, was an experience I'll always remember fondly.

During summer months, Bronson Park hosts events called "Lunchtime Live!" on Fridays around noon. Reminiscent of the day Lincoln spoke here, the events feature live music, food trucks with local vendors, and games. During the Holiday season, the park perennially is the site of the city's Tree Lighting Ceremony.

Even before this rare experience of seeing the park with Mr. Lincoln, I had noticed that my mood rises when I enter the park. As I approach the park, even if I'm just walking by myself, there's always a feeling of excitement and anticipation, as a child might feel on Christmas Eve, with the promise of holiday magic and the coming of Santa. And as I enter the park, there's the feeling that I'm not only observing the experience, but that I'm within it, as a child might feel on Christmas Day while opening presents.

Soon after entering the park at the southwest corner, Mr. Lincoln began looking all around, recalling his previous visit amid those many people who came from all over.

Above, the sky remained the deep blue that comes in autumn. The blue contrasted with the various shades of green of the large trees, particularly the big oaks and sycamores. There were also many smaller trees, including maples and lindens. A few sycamores exposed their beautiful smooth underbark as the top layer of bark peeled away. Between the walkways were extensive flower gardens, well maintained by volunteers. There were flowers of many colors including pink and purple geraniums, and red and pink inpatiens in flower gardens and in hanging baskets in large outdoor flower racks. The celosia was a very deep red on this day. In the northwest corner of the park, within a flower garden, was a small deer carved from vegetation. Other sculptures included a small peacock in one flower garden, a seahorse in another, and an elephant in another. On the south side of the park, adjacent to South Street, were two large peacocks, perhaps 12 feet tall, that looked to have been sculpted from flowering bushes.

One thing that struck me on this day was the number of ongoing changes in the park. Bronson Park is continually changing, with a new tree here, a new bed of flowers there, and a new sculpture across the way. In a sense, the park that you see today will never exist again. The amount of maintenance, much of it by volunteers, keeps the park pristine but also continuously improves it to keep it beautiful. I knew that the flowers required year-round work, from preparing the soil to planting the flowers, to dead-heading them during the summer months, and bidding goodbye to them in the fall (with just a seasonal goodbye for the perennials).

Even some of the smaller monuments had changed locations over time, with the larger ones remaining exactly where they'd been since I could remember. Some monuments commemorated wars, including the Civil War, the "Spanish war and Philippine insurgency" (the Spanish-American War), Korea, and Vietnam. There was a marker to remember those who were lost on 9/11. Others recognized Kalamazoo's sister-city status with Numazu, Japan and Pushkin, Russia. As Mr. Lincoln and I strolled through the park, I thought about the current animosity that existed with Russia following its unprovoked attack on Ukraine. A great friendship had developed over the years between people in Pushkin and Kalamazoo, and I knew that the subject of the Russian invasion was not discussed much between them, in part due to potential retribution against Pushkin people by the Russian government.

I said very few specifics to Mr. Lincoln about the various wars, conflicts, and even the 9/11 attacks. In my mind, I was showing him the memorials as a person might discuss them with a person from another country. I could tell that Mr. Lincoln was touched by the memorials, and that he was all too aware that he was in a Midwestern city—not too different from Springfield in many ways—but also knew that he would prefer not to know more than basic facts about them. We both knew it was likely that within 48 hours, he'd be back in the nation's capital in April 1865 and would want to avoid acting on anything he'd learn here. I also knew that with his voracious appetite for learning history, he wouldn't be surprised a bit that the Civil War would not be America's last conflict. I could have told him how many wars the United States had participated in since the Civil War, but it would have defeated the purpose of the visit. (A subsequent review of information about wars in which the United States has participated shows that the U.S. has been involved in 106 wars and conflicts since the nation's founding; 74 have taken place after the Civil War. This includes numerous conflicts against the peoples who occupied North America before

Europeans, Mexico and countries in South America, and conflicts in the Middle East, Africa, and Eastern Europe over the last 30 years.)

A period of time passed without either of us saying a word. As I stood and looked around at the park, particularly the memorials and the people, I glanced at Mr. Lincoln. His countenance was solemn, his eyes pointing downward and a look of calm on his face, as if he was reflecting on the unchanging nature of war, and of life and death. Then, as if trying to keep from descending too far into a darker place, he quickly raised his eyes and resumed looking around.

"By my calendar, it's been nine years since I was here last," shared Mr. Lincoln. "I've been thinking about my visit here. I remember a few things quite well and some scarcely at all," he said, sharing the sentiment that I've also noticed about recalling events that happened years ago, like celebrating Christmas with my parents and siblings, or attending grade school.

"The atmosphere at that rally was very festive with thousands of people on the walkways and many red, white, and blue banners and other decorations around," he said.

"As I recall," he continued, "there were many more trees at the time." His observation reflected that fact that during my lifetime, on May 13, 1980 (one of those dates that many local residents still remember), an F3 tornado entered the city, causing $50 million in damage, destroying 30 buildings and homes, and devastating trees with trunks three feet and more in diameter. Many of those trees were certainly witness to the rally in 1856. The tornado took the lives of five people and injured 79 more. One man who was killed was driving his motorcycle on Rose Street, adjacent to Bronson Park.

Over the history of Bronson Park, several different fountains served as a central focus of the park. Such a fountain would have been a

134

beautiful and refreshing addition to that warm summer day back in August 1856. However, the first fountain believed to exist in the park—a large, shallow, round fountain that shot a stream of water up from its center—was not installed until the Centennial year of 1876, twenty years after Mr. Lincoln's campaign visit.

"The train ride from Springfield went right on schedule," he explained, "and in that regard, I was fortunate. We left Springfield at half past eight o'clock in the morning of the previous day and arrived at the station in Chicago, where we stayed at the Matteson House. The following day, the day of the rally, the train from Chicago arrived in Kalamazoo at 1:30 in the afternoon. I was scheduled to speak at two o'clock, so we had a nice ride here from the station without it being overly hurried. My speech began promptly at two.

"There were four or five speaker stands around the park," he went on, "and there were times when several people were speaking at a time. Crowds would move from platform to platform to listen to the various speakers. The walkways weren't straight, as they are now. They curved around and were made with a light-colored crushed stone."

"I remember reading that Hezekiah Wells invited you. Did he also introduce you," I asked Mr. Lincoln.

"Yes, he did indeed," responded my guest. "Fortunately, Mr. Wells was familiar with my position against slavery, and of course, that was the primary reason for my being invited here. He was aware of some of the law work I'd done, too. One of the biggest clients I represented was the Illinois Central Railroad, which was seeing a great deal of expansion. It was during my time representing that firm that some well-meaning folks began to call me 'Honest Abe.' I didn't object to it; anytime someone pays a compliment, I think it's good to receive it in the manner it was offered. However, I never called myself Abe. I always used my full first name, in honor of my mother who gave me the name, as well as paying due respect to the man from millennia ago who is the common patriarch of the Christian, Jewish, and Muslim faiths."

"How did he introduce you?" I asked.

A smile came to Mr. Lincoln's face. "Mr. Wells gave me an appropriate introduction to the good people of Michigan," he said. "He called me 'the best lawyer in Illinois,' and after saying a few more kind words, he introduced me with the description 'That tall sucker from Illinois.' The crowd whooped and hollered and enjoyed that description. And I think they enjoyed my speech. I'm honored to say that they cheered a number of times. After the speech was done, I stepped down and walked over to a place where I shook hands with people for quite some time. I have to say that the enjoyment of shaking their hands—the men, women, and even children—and talking with them made the two-day train ride here most worthwhile."

"Do you remember where you spoke?" I asked, a question that local historians had tried to answer for more than a century.

"As I've looked around this beautiful park today, and with all the excitement of the large crowd that day, I've tried to remember, and I regret to say that I do not. I do, however, remember walking toward the Indian Mound at one point, and several speakers did talk from there, in addition to the wooden speaker platforms. I well remember how kind the people were that I met that day."

Abraham Lincoln's speech that day was much longer than many of his speeches, including the Gettysburg Address. His historic address to dedicate the Gettysburg National Cemetery in November 1863 was just 272 words long and took about two minutes to deliver. His

136

historic speech in Kalamazoo was 2,781 words long and took 16.5 minutes.

History showed that Mr. Lincoln stayed in Kalamazoo that night before returning to Chicago the following day, and I had one more question to ask: Where did he stay that night? However, just as I had turned toward my guest to ask him, I noticed a young mother with a dual stroller just on the other side of him; she had stopped and it was clear that one of her kiddos was asking about the tall, gaunt gentleman with the beard. The youngsters were looking attentively and pointing at him.

Rather than waiting for them to ask—or perhaps to not ask, only to take who-knows-what story home to Dad—I looked over and asked "Hi, how are you guys doing today?"

"Hi! I'm sorry, we didn't mean to interrupt," said their mom. "They just thought you looked like somebody," she added, eyeing my guest. My guest looked amused. A smile came on his face as he looked down at the children, a girl of perhaps six years old and her little brother of about four.

"My friend gets those questions a lot," I smiled. "That's actually a good thing. We're here today preparing to make a short movie. Even when he was a young man, people told him that he bore a resemblance to Abraham Lincoln. He has studied Mr. Lincoln for years, and knows a lot about him." Then I took a chance and asked if they had any questions they'd like my guest to answer. Rather than giving me the Scolding Eye of Reprimand, my guest looked over at me briefly and gave me a smile, as if to say "I tried to do what I could in my day, but if I can give these children some good memories early in the 21st Century and help their understanding, I'll be happy to do that, too."

Before asking a question, the little girl told us that her name was Sally and her little brother was named Brian. Then, she pointed to the historical marker on the other side of the park and said "There's a sign over there that says the real Abraham Lincoln spoke right here in the park. Do you know anything about that day?"

"Why, yes, he certainly did speak here," replied my guest. "He had never been to Michigan before, and he spoke to a very big crowd here that day to help a friend be elected president. There were a lot of men and women in the park that day, but also a lot of boys and girls like you, who became our country's leaders years later. One day, you and Brian will be our leaders, too." Sally and Brian's young mom was smiling. Sally and Brian smiled ear to ear, their eyes twinkling. Among all of the virtues I've read about Abraham Lincoln, two of the strongest were that he was a good husband, and a good and involved father.

We've learned many things from our own kids, Katy and Sam, over the years. They're both adults now, but when they were younger, like Sally and Brian at Bronson Park, they'd come with Molly and me on family trips. We'd go to places like Boston, Chicago, South Dakota, the Upper Peninsula of Michigan, Texas, and on a couple occasions, Arizona and Florida. All the while they wanted to do fun rides and see fun things, Dad (and sometimes Mom) wanted to see historic places, like museums, and Jimmy Carter's boyhood school and museum in Georgia, and George Washington's Mount Vernon. We especially made a point to see places associated with Abraham Lincoln, including his Kentucky birthplace, his home and tomb in Springfield, the White House, and Ford's Theatre.

From a young age, I've had a particular interest in Abraham Lincoln, and I've found out that the interest in him is quite common. I think it's partly because of his role on emancipation and leading during the

Civil War, but also because, despite his unusual height and all of the things he achieved, he was somehow a common man.

We were never quite sure if our kids picked up on the historic nature of what they were seeing…until sometimes years later, when they'd ask "Hey Dad, do you remember that time 15 years ago when we went to see the White House, and there were the two Gilbert Sullivan paintings on the wall, and…"

It turned out that our kids were listening all along, whether *they* knew it or not, and whether *we* knew it or not. Somewhere out there today are kids that will try to do what was right based on what they were taught by their parents, and in some cases, by Abraham Lincoln.

My guest and I said goodbye to Sally, Brian, and their mom, and we walked around the park for almost an hour, going around the perimeter once and across both diagonals. A few more people seemed to notice my guest's familiar appearance, and we made it a point to allow ourselves to smile and say hello. Other than that, the visit was uneventful. When we left, we were both "good and tired" from walking and looked forward to the cushioned front seats of my car.

As I walked alongside Mr. Lincoln and noticed his appearance and mannerisms, it occurred to me that some of those characteristics were unlike our current-day perceptions. His face fit the perception: furrowed with sunken eyes and heavy brows. As advertised, his clothes were somewhat ill-fitting, even though he was wearing his own pants and shoes. (Our son Sam's shirt fit him pretty well.) In addition, his eyes focused at somewhat different locations, again, as witnesses had stated. However, his height in our day was not out of place as much as in his day. In 1860, his 6-foot-4 frame was a full nine inches taller than the average male adult height of 5 feet, 7 inches. Although today's average height is only two inches taller than in 1860, the number of males in the 6-foot-4 range is more common. One characteristic that might have thrown people off more than anything was his walk. Films like *Lincoln* with Daniel Day-Lewis (2012), *Young Mr. Lincoln* with Henry Fonda (1939), and *Abe Lincoln in Illinois* with Raymond Massey (1940) tend to depict Mr. Lincoln's walk as being firm and powerful but graceful. In reality, Mr. Lincoln had a slow walk that some people called a "clumsy gait" or "stumbling," which is now thought to be the result of a genetic disorder other than Marfan syndrome; the latter likely caused Lincoln's tall, slender frame and his long, thin fingers, arms, and legs. If it's true that his gait was deceptive, it's a good example of people basing their perceptions on a myth rather than the truth.

By the way, like British actor Daniel Day-Lewis, Toronto native Raymond Massey also had a history of being selected to play prominent Americans. His role in *Abe Lincoln in Illinois* reprised his role in the Broadway play of the same name. The 6-foot-3 Massey played Lincoln at least four times in various television and film productions. Massey also played abolitionist John Brown in two films; Brown was "over six feet tall" and was tall, gaunt, and bearded in his mature years. Brown was executed at age 59 after leading the raid on the federal armory at Harper's Ferry (in the area of Virginia that became West Virginia 11 days before the Battle of Gettysburg). Brown and the other raid survivors were surrounded and captured by U.S. Marines and militia under the command of Col. Robert E. Lee.

John Brown's execution took place less than seven weeks after the raid on Harper's Ferry, following his trial and sentencing.

As we reached my car, I unlocked the doors with my remote key fob, but this time, Mr. Lincoln reached his door and opened it before I got there. However, before he got into the passenger seat, he stood and just looked around for perhaps 20-30 seconds, surely recalling old memories as well as new ones he'd made this day. He didn't get in until he was ready, and I wasn't about to rush him.

Then, one last thing before pulling out of our parking spot: I texted Molly to let her know that I was leaving town for Springfield, and before we reached our first stop light, she signaled a thumbs-up in response.

The upstart Republican Party quickly found a national following, with 1856 being the first year that the party nominated a candidate for president (John C. Frémont). Four years later, Abraham Lincoln led the ticket and won the presidency. As mentioned, during the 1856 election season, Lincoln received a number of invitations to speak outside his home state of Illinois, but he only spoke outside his home state once: On August 27, 1856 in Kalamazoo, Michigan. That visit was also the only time he ever set foot on Michigan soil.

However, in addition to Michigan's connection to the birth of the Republican Party and his historic speech in Kalamazoo, Lincoln had a few more notable connections to Michigan.

In 1848, during Lincoln's two-year term in the U.S. House of Representatives, he referred to Michigan's U.S. Senator Lewis Cass as "the great *Michigander*." It was an early use of the term Michigander, and the gentleman from Illinois didn't mean it in a good way. Cass, who was a former military officer and the Democratic nominee for president in 1848, was regarded as one of the nation's statesmen at the time. He was also a big proponent of "popular sovereignty," which held that it was the right of the states to decide whether it was acceptable for some of its citizens to own other citizens as property. It's obvious that Mr. Lincoln's phrase "the great Michigander" which played on the term for a male goose, was not intended to be a compliment. To be sure, the term "Michigander" was in use before 1848, along with similar demonyms "Michiganian," "Michiganer," "Michiganite," "Michiganese," "Michigene," and in the case of a female, "Michigoose." However, Lincoln's use of the term popularized it, and today it's the most popular term (preferred by 58% of the state's residents) to describe a person from Michigan. Like *me*.

The comments made by Rep. Lincoln mocking Sen. Cass that day, July 27, 1848, accused Cass and other Democrats of exaggerating their military accomplishments. Lincoln said:

> *"In my hurry I was very near closing on the subject of military tales before I was done with it. There is one entire article of the sort I have not discussed yet; I mean the military tale you Democrats are now engaged in dovetailing onto the great Michigander..."*

Thirteen years later, the nation was in the first month of the Civil War following the firing on Fort Sumter by South Carolina Militia artillery on April 12, 1861. On that day, the entire strength of the regular army was just 16,000 officers and soldiers—about the population of the Michigan cities of Caledonia, Grosse Pointe Woods, or Traverse City—hardly enough troops to defend against a massive internal rebellion or an attack by another country. In response, three days later President Lincoln, Secretary of State William Seward, and Secretary of War Simon Cameron issued proclamations to call up 75,000 volunteers, with the number of volunteers from each state based on the state's population. The proclamations went out for volunteers from Southern states as well as Northern states, with predictably negative responses from Southern states including Virginia, Arkansas, Kentucky, North Carolina, Mississippi, and Tennessee.

142

Lincoln subsequently called up an additional 42,000 troops, and when volunteers of the 1st Michigan Infantry marched into Washington, D.C. on May 16, 1861, he is said to have exclaimed "Thank God for Michigan" in recognition of their sacrifice to preserve the Union. By the end of the year, the president and Congress would call up an additional 500,000 volunteers.

Over the course of the war, 90,000 young Michigan men—nearly one in every four recorded in the 1860 census—served in the Civil War, including about 1,600 African American soldiers. Of those 90,000 who served, 14,855 died during the war, about one of every six. And of those 14,855, ten thousand were from disease, the main cause of death among all Union troops.

Again at war's end, Michigan played a key role.

One month after Gen. Lee's surrender to Gen. Grant, Lincoln's Confederate counterpart, Jefferson Davis, was on the run toward the Mexican border in Texas, having dissolved the Confederate government in Richmond, Virginia. On May 10, 1865, Davis and his wife, Varina, were captured by the 4th Michigan Cavalry near Irwinville, Georgia. The capture was regarded as "the most important contribution by the 4th Michigan" because they ended any hope Davis had to attempt reviving the Confederacy in exile, and helped to ensure that some semblance of a peace could be implemented between the former enemies. The soldier who spotted and physically captured Davis, Norway native Pvt. Andrew Bee, is buried at East Martin Cemetery in Martin, Michigan. His commanding officer, Benjamin D. Pritchard, is buried at Oakwood Cemetery in Allegan. Pritchard was a colonel at the time of the capture, and for his role in capturing Davis was promoted to the rank of brigadier general.

An additional link between Abraham Lincoln and Michigan is one that was not completed during his lifetime. That curious story involves Clara Barton in the first days of the important group she founded, the American Red Cross.

The very first place in the United States to ever receive disaster relief from the American Red Cross was Michigan's Thumb region during the Great Thumb Fire of September 1881. By coincidence, the very first meeting of the American Red Cross had taken place just four months earlier at the Washington D.C. home of U.S. Sen. Omar D. Conger, a Republican who hailed from Port Huron and served much of the area that was affected by the fire.

During discussions between Barton, Sen. Conger, and the 13 others at the meeting, it turned out that during the Civil War, Sen. Conger's brother, Lt. Col. Everton Conger, suffered three severe injuries during battle, and for a time, Barton cared for the injured Everton. Barton, "the Angel of the Battlefield," said she had come to know and respect Everton. As a likely result of that connection, Sen. Conger would become Congress's biggest advocate of the Red Cross.

Following Everton's release from medical care, he was reassigned to duty in the nation's capital. It was in that role, following President Lincoln's assassination on April 14, 1865, that Lt. Col. Everton Conger was ordered to accompany a detachment of 25 Union soldiers from the 16th New York Cavalry to pursue and capture John Wilkes Booth. It was Everton who, 12 days after the tragedy, learned of Booth's location in a tobacco barn on the farm of Richard Garrett near Port Royal, Virginia. It was Everton's order to surrender that Booth chose to ignore. It was also Everton who set fire to the barn in order to force Booth out of the barn. When Sgt. Boston Corbett violated orders by shooting Booth through a small opening in the barn's siding, Conger recommended that Sgt. Boston Corbett be punished. Conger recovered Booth's personal effects from his body, including Booth's diary, compass, and the dagger Booth used to escape from the Lincolns' theater box by badly slashing Major Henry Rathbone, who tried to restrain Booth.

Despite Conger's having followed orders and military policy to the letter, it was generally Sgt. Corbett, who shot Booth, who was perceived as a national hero, particularly by people in the North who regarded President Abraham Lincoln as a martyr who had died for his country.

Leaving Kalamazoo

As we left the area of town that was plotted out by Titus Bronson almost two centuries before, Mr. Lincoln told me how much he enjoyed his return visit to Bronson Park and thanked me again for taking him. I told him that it was no effort, and how much I enjoyed visiting with him to get a first-hand account of history. My time spent with him confirmed some things I felt that we had in common. A respect for human rights and for the Constitution and the rule of law. A love of history, books, and the human invention of language.

Starting with Rose Street heading west on South, we had to stop at several traffic lights before even leaving the park area, but it afforded me the opportunity to talk more with him.

Heading west out of town via Stadium Drive, we went south on US-131 to Interstate 94 and from there, it would be a 2.5-hour drive west on I-94 and I-80, then about the same amount of time southwest on I-55. We'd be reaching the southern outskirts of Chicago around four o'clock, during rush hour, but it wouldn't be a problem. And while I didn't want to make Mr. Lincoln conduct a five-hour lecture during our drive to Springfield, I was looking forward to learning a lot over the next several hours.

All during our departure from Kalamazoo, Mr. Lincoln was like an information sponge, taking in the automobiles, traffic flow, signals, larger buildings, and other updates over the last 160+ years; he absorbed the information in much the same way that he undoubtedly had absorbed the English language, Shakespeare, math, science, law, and many other areas of interest.

As we merged from US-131 onto I-94, the highway on which we'd stay for the next 120 miles, I put on my sunglasses clip-ons to shield my eyes from the sun's glare. My son had left his sunglasses in the glove compartment the last time he visited home, and I offered them to Mr. Lincoln. It seemed appropriate to paraphrase Elwood Blues' line about being 106 miles to Chicago with a full tank of gas and we're wearing sunglasses. But since such a comment would have completely missed the mark with my guest, who had never seen a motion picture, I held off. (I didn't say it, but I did think it.)

The Road West

As I spent time with Mr. Lincoln, it continued to occur to me that I was in a unique position. At some point soon after setting out on I-94 toward Springfield via Chicago, I realized that I might have an opportunity to find out more about Lincoln's family life, particularly his time after moving into the White House...which wasn't called the White House yet. Right up until the last few days of his administration, he had been intensely focused on carrying out the Civil War and trying to save the Union. With only five days having passed since Appomattox (in the case of both my historical Lincoln as well as my current passenger), I thought it unlikely that he'd given any meaningful thought to writing his memoirs. And at least in our timeline, much of the story of his family was shared in letters between Abraham and Mary Todd Lincoln, and she methodically burned them in back of their house in Springfield after his death.

Similarly, shortly before Abraham Lincoln's only son who survived past age 18, Robert Todd Lincoln, died in 1926, he burned most of his correspondence including letters between himself and his mother. The exception was a file that he kept of records that he used as evidence of his mother's mental state following the assassination; he used them to have her declared insane and committed to a sanitarium in Batavia, Illinois called Bellevue Place. The few surviving records were lost until they were located in Robert Todd Lincoln's home in Manchester, Vermont by Abraham Lincoln's great grandson, Robert Todd Lincoln Beckwith. Beckwith died on Christmas Eve 1985; he was the 16th president's last living descendant.

Any memoir that Abraham Lincoln might have written following his presidency would have almost certainly been more welcome than that of his predecessor. The first memoir written about a president's actual time in the White House that was published in their lifetime was *Mr. Buchanan's Administration on the Eve of Rebellion,* published in 1866. During Buchanan's presidency, he did not act to solve the worsening situation with slavery, nor did he act to remedy the increasing split between the North and South. Modern presidential historians usually rank James Buchanan near the very bottom of the rankings of Best Presidents, compared with Mr. Lincoln, who is ranked at the very top. And according to presidential historian Craig Fehrman, author of the book *Author in Chief: The Untold Story of Our Presidents and the Books They Wrote,* Buchanan's book wasn't any better than his presidency. Fehrman says, "Buchanan's is definitely the worst presidential memoir I've read. It's mostly just James Buchanan trying to blame everyone except James Buchanan for the war and its aftermath."

"I'm so looking forward to seeing Springfield," said Mr. Lincoln a few miles along I-94. "In addition to the social connections that people have with other people, I've always felt that I had a connection with the city of Springfield itself, the place and the land.

"Well, I've visited Springfield a few times myself," I said. "Because of your presidency, and your connections to the Civil War— fortunately the only civil war we've had—and your role in ending the practice of slavery, the city has paid tributes to you as well as your family. Your house at the corner of 8th Street and Jackson still stands. In fact, I've been inside it. It's a beautiful home."

"I'm glad to hear that! Thank you, Al. I did love that home. Although I did what I felt I had to, in becoming president and moving to our nation's capital, I hated leaving the house, and it broke my heart to leave my neighbors and friends. Almost all of my friends were there at the train station when I left. Almost all of the people who were close to me. Except for Mary and the boys…and my mother and sister, Sarah, who had passed."

"I've read a little about them," I said. "Would you tell me more about them?"

"I'd be happy to," he responded, and then paused for several seconds, as if pondering the best place to start. "It sometimes still brings a tear to my eye to think about both my mother and Sarah. *All that I am, or hope to be, I owe to my angel mother.* I'm also very grateful for Sarah, who looked after my father and me after my mother passed. They both they made sure that I tried to do the right things."

Mr. Lincoln went on to explain that his mother, Nancy, was born in 1784 in Virginia, where her family lived. Just one month after she was born, the family moved to Kentucky. She and Thomas, Abraham's father, were married in 1806. The cabin in which Nancy and Thomas were married is preserved in Old Fort Harrod State Park in Kentucky.

As Mr. Lincoln went on to further describe his mother, he confirmed what I had read about her being both a kind and strong woman. Some who knew the family said that Nancy Hanks Lincoln was "superior" to Thomas, with whom Abraham always had a distant relationship. Lincoln said about his mother "All that I am or hope ever to be, I get from my mother—God bless her." Listening to his descriptions of his mother, I understood why he said that, and why people said that young Abraham took after his mother. She was said to be "a bold, reckless, daredevil kind of woman, stepping on to the very verge of propriety." When I once read this description, my thought was that Abraham's mother had some things in common not only with her son, but also with his future wife, Mary Todd Lincoln, whom Nancy had never met.

William Herndon was Abraham Lincoln's law partner in Springfield, who later wrote one of the first biographies of the 16th president.

Herndon painted a picture of a woman who almost seemed cloned with her son when he said about Lincoln's mother:

> *She was above the ordinary height in stature, weighed about 130 pounds, was slenderly built, and had much the appearance of one inclined to consumption. Her skin was dark; hair dark brown; eyes gray and small; forehead prominent; face sharp and angular, with a marked expression for melancholy which fixed itself in the memory of all who ever saw or knew her. Though her life was clouded by a spirit of sadness, she was in disposition amiable and generally cheerful.*

After the Lincolns moved to Indiana, tragedy struck, beginning a pattern of personal loss that would continue for the rest of Lincoln's life. When Lincoln's mother died rather suddenly from milk sickness, Sarah, then just 11 years old, had the strength to immediately do what needed to be done. The day that her mother died, "Sarah helped the neighbor women prepare, dress, and place her mother's body into the casket." Like her brother Abraham, two years her junior, Sarah felt she was "raised in an environment of love, trust, and understanding." She used this upbringing as the basis with which to treat others after the death of their mother. Like Abraham, Sarah was heartbroken at the loss of their mother, but Sarah knew that she was being relied on to care for others. In addition to Abraham and their father, Sarah was also charged with taking care of Abraham's older cousin, Dennis Hanks, after the loss of mother Nancy. Dennis had been orphaned when both of his guardians died from milk sickness. In Indiana, Dennis and Abraham would share the loft space in their small cabin. Photographs of Dennis Hanks taken late in the 19th Century show a man with a full head of hair, a gaunt face with sunken cheeks, prominent cheekbones, and prominent eyebrows above his gray, sunken eyes…someone who had more than a passing resemblance to his younger cousin Abraham. During Lincoln's presidency, Dennis helped to care for Abraham's stepmother, also named Sarah, who Thomas married about 14 months after Nancy's death. Sarah and Abraham's stepmother was 73 and ailing when Lincoln left Springfield for Washington.

My passenger still felt loss for his sister.

"My sister, like me, had difficulty adjusting to the death of our mother," said my passenger. "My sister's situation was further complicated when our father remarried, because our stepmother brought three children of her own into the house. However, when our father married our stepmother, it did allow Sarah more time to spend playing with Dennis and me as siblings, and our three step-siblings as playmates."

Abraham's sister was described as "short of stature and somewhat plump in build, her hair was dark brown and her eyes were gray," the gray eyes that people also noted about Abraham and Dennis. Cousin John Hanks said of Sarah "She was kind, tender, and good-natured and is said to have been a smart woman." Her future brother-in-law, Nathan Grigsby, also spoke of her virtues, which he compared to those of her brother, saying "she was a woman of extraordinary mind. Her good-humored laugh I can hear now, is as fresh in my mind as if it were yesterday. She could, like her brother, meet and greet a person with the kindest greeting in the world, make you easy at the touch of a word, an intellectual and intelligent woman."

Around the age of 13, Sarah attended a "subscription school," a school that her parents had to pay for her to attend. She brought her younger brother along with her. Both Sarah and Abraham had Andrew Crawford as their teacher. Their first teacher in Kentucky, Zachariah Riney, first taught Abraham to read aloud. Andrew Crawford not only taught Sarah and Abraham "The Three Rs," but also taught them manners and other socially important lessons. But during the entire time, Sarah was also there, helping her younger brother to learn his letters, and no doubt contributing to his love of reading and learning.

However, like many of Abraham Lincoln's family and friends, his sister would leave this world too early, making the world a darker place for Abraham and others. In April 1826, Sarah joined the Little Pigeon Baptist Church in southern Indiana, and just four months later married Aaron Grigsby. Almost exactly nine months after their marriage, Sarah announced to her family that she was pregnant. But on January 20, 1828, unexpected complications arose during childbirth. Sarah died along with her child. Sarah is buried at Old Pigeon Cemetery near the Little Pigeon Baptist Church in Lincoln State Park.

Before Sarah's death, Abraham had spent a great deal of time at the Grigsby home, a few miles from the Lincoln cabin. The Abraham Lincoln Library says that Abraham partly blamed the Grigsby family for his sister's death.

As we continued west on I-94 toward the Indiana state line, I was still thinking about my surprise fast-stop in our driveway before heading to Bronson Park. It had taken me a while to process how I wanted to bring up the subject, namely that the President Lincoln sitting next to me had seen *Our American Cousin* all the way through. I also wanted to be sure he realized that it had been many years since anyone he knew in Springfield was still alive.

"I've been thinking about what to say about my sudden stop in our driveway," I began.

"I appreciate that you want to be careful about the information that you share," Mr. Lincoln replied. "If you'd like to talk about it, I'll be happy to do the same. But if you don't, I understand why."

"Well, without getting into too many details," I answered, "we're heading to Springfield, Illinois, a place you first saw…nearly 200 years ago, by the current timeline. None of the friends and neighbors you knew so well will be there. And the Abraham Lincoln who was born in LaRue County, Kentucky in 1809…"

"…is not living in Springfield anymore, either," said Mr. Lincoln, letting out an unexpected laugh. "Yes, I've been thinking about that, as well. My guess is that somewhere in Springfield, in a very quiet piece of land with many oak trees, there's a block of granite with my name on it. Yes, that doesn't bother me. I do have a somewhat peculiar feeling thinking about Mary, the boys, and my mother. But I'm 56 years old now…not so old as some men I've known, but I'm certainly not a young man anymore. I'm well past that age when I fully realized that I won't be on this earth forever, and I'm old enough, and have been through enough with my own family and friends, that I know the same fate has awaited them all, and every soul who has had the pleasure of living on this planet. I've accepted that part."

"I appreciate that," I said. "I think that could cause confusion when you get back. Obviously, there are cemeteries in Springfield…"

"Certainly," replied Mr. Lincoln, "and I've thought about them. There's a time and place for everything, including visiting cemeteries to pay respect to those who have gone on. That time will come. But it isn't now. If all goes as we plan, I'll be back in my own time two days from now. When that happens, I'll have plenty of time to pay any respects. But for now, I'll just be happy that I still have those people in my life, back where I'll return. And let me add again how thankful I am that you're taking me back to my hometown, even though the good people I know won't be there. I know that in a real sense, they're still alive somewhere...in some time. And I'm thankful for your efforts to get me back home." It was a relief to hear him say that.

On the question of timelines, the dilemma raised by my passenger having seen the end of *Our American Cousin* raised questions that I still didn't have enough information to answer. I didn't know that I'd ever have enough information to explain it.

One topic that I would have liked to know more about, but which I decided to avoid, was his children. Abraham and Mary Todd Lincoln had four children by 1865, all sons. By that time, two of them had already died, and a third would die six years after the end of the Civil War.

Eddie Baker Lincoln, named after a close friend of Mr. Lincoln, was born in 1846 and died of tuberculosis at the age of 3. William "Willie" Lincoln was born in 1850 and died at the age of 11, probably from typhoid fever, while the Lincolns were in the Executive Mansion. The deaths of Eddie and Willie both had a heartbreaking impact on Mr. and Mrs. Lincoln, both of whom had already suffered from the loss of family members. Abraham and Mary both despaired about the dissolution of the Union and the toll of the war. In addition, the two were subject to what we would now call clinical depression.

The Lincolns' last-born son, Thomas "Tad" Lincoln, was born in 1853 and was 12 years old the night his parents attended the play in Ford's Theatre. That night, while his parents attended the play, Tad was at Grover's Theatre (now called the National Theatre, just a few blocks from the Executive Mansion and about one-quarter mile from Ford's Theatre) to see the play *Aladdin and His Wonderful Lamp*. While Tad was enjoying the play, the performance was stopped while the manager took the stage and announced to the entire audience that the president had been shot.

Tad, like much of the nation, was devastated, with the impact on the lad's future, of course, being much more pronounced than for most Americans. Tad soon acknowledged:

> *"Pa is dead. I can hardly believe that I shall never see him again. I must learn to take care of myself now. Yes, Pa is dead, and I am only Tad Lincoln now, little Tad, like other little boys. I am not a president's son now."*

The only child of Abraham and Mary Todd Lincoln to live past age 18 was Robert Todd Lincoln. In an odd twist of history, late in the Civil War, Robert served in the Union Army and while he was at the train station in Baltimore, his life was saved when he began to fall between the train platform and a train that had just started moving. He was pulled up to safety by his collar by the man standing next to him. That man was Edwin Booth, recognized by many to be the greatest American actor of the 19th Century. The older brother of John Wilkes Booth, Edwin was a strong supporter of the Union and of Abraham Lincoln.

In another twist related to the Lincoln family, Robert Lincoln had a connection, either directly or indirectly, to three presidential assassinations. In addition, two presidential assassins once lived in Michigan.

On the night of April 14, 1865, Robert had been invited to attend the play with his parents, but he was still fatigued after being on the battle front, so he stayed home to rest. However, when word of the shooting arrived at the Executive Mansion, Robert hurried there and met his mother across the street at the Petersen House within 45 minutes, and he attended his father's deathbed.

On July 2, 1881, Robert Lincoln, who at the time was secretary of war, was present at Washington D.C.'s Sixth Street Train Station when long-time political worker Charles J. Guiteau shot President James A. Garfield. Garfield, who had been a major general in the Union Army during the Civil War, was in office less than seven months when he was shot. Garfield died two months after the shooting. Guiteau was angered that Garfield did not appoint him to a position in his administration. Born in Freeport, Illinois—one of the cities in which Abraham Lincoln had debated Stephen A. Douglas in 1858—Guiteau moved to Ann Arbor, where he attended high school and later, the University of Michigan.

On September 6, 1901, Robert Lincoln was just outside the Temple of Music at the Pan-American Exposition in Buffalo when anarchist Leon Czolgosz fatally shot President William McKinley. Czolgosz was born in Detroit in 1873, and his family later moved to the Michigan cities of Alpena and Posen before moving to Pennsylvania.

On May 30, 1922, Robert Lincoln was on hand in the nation's capital to dedicate the Lincoln Memorial. He spoke along with President Warren G. Harding and Chief Justice William Howard Taft.

They Loved Lucy

History is stranger than fiction. That's because history consists of real events, and in the case of many events related to Abraham Lincoln, a Hollywood script writer wouldn't dare create some of those strange twists because they wouldn't seem believable. But they happened.

We've talked about how Mary Todd was courted by both Abraham Lincoln and his cross-town adversary, Stephen A. Douglas. We know the two ran against each other in Illinois' U.S. Senate race in 1858. And then, improbable as it seems, the two represented the nation's two major political parties when they ran against each other for president in 1860.

We talked about how Abraham and Mary Todd Lincoln's son, Robert, was nearly killed on that train platform in Baltimore when the train began to pull out and he started to fall between the train and the platform, only to have his life saved by Edwin Booth.

We talked about how, in addition to rushing to see his father in his final hours at Petersen House, Robert Lincoln was an eyewitness to the assassination of President James Garfield 18 years later, and was at the building where President William McKinley was killed 20 years after that.

We'll see more odd coincidences in the rest of this story.

But for now, it's time to meet Lucy.

Lucy Hale was born on New Year's Day 1841 in Dover, New Hampshire. Lucy's parents were U.S. Senator John P. Hale of New Hampshire and his wife, Lucy Hill Lambert. Growing up, she was described as "pretty, precocious, sweet, and good," and by the time she was 12, she was the recipient of poems from a Harvard student. By the time she was 17, she was described as having "dark hair, blue eyes, clear skin, and a stunning figure." She was seen at many parties and was considered a Washington belle.

Now, you've probably noted that I'm describing Lucy's physical characteristics in more flowery language than I've used with most of the other characters in the Abraham Lincoln story. But that's sort of important in order to convey the fact that Lucy was somewhat of a heartbreaker, a notion that's supported by her occupation, which is listed in Wikipedia as "socialite." (To be fair, Lucy and Lucy—Lucy Hale and her mother, also named Lucy—were also frequently present at the front lines aiding Union troops when there were breaks in the fighting.)

Although Lucy didn't have a keen interest in politics, her parents were noted abolitionists and supporters of Abraham Lincoln and the Union.

It should be no surprise that with her father's political connections (remember, he was a U.S. senator from New Hampshire), her parents fancied that she might develop a romantic relationship with the president's son, Robert Todd Lincoln. Robert was handsome, Harvard-educated, a captain in the Union Army late in the Civil War, and of course, he had heaps of his own political connections. Friends said that Robert was very fond of Lucy, and in fact, Lucy's parents actually entertained thoughts of marriage between their daughter and Robert.

But that wasn't going to happen. She was already engaged.

To John Wilkes Booth.

By the day of Abraham Lincoln's second inaugural, March 4, 1865, Booth and Lucy were engaged, in a relationship that was secret except to a very few others. In fact, Booth attended Lincoln's second inaugural with a ticket Lucy had obtained from her father.

John Wilkes Booth and Lucy Hale saw each other frequently by early 1865, and from all evidence, she was completely unaware of Booth's plan to kidnap Lincoln, a plot that changed from kidnapping to assassination just three days before the play at Ford's Theatre. The plan changed when Booth heard a speech by Lincoln in which the president discussed Reconstruction and said the government should not only end slavery, but also consider giving African Americans the right to vote.

That turned out to be Abraham Lincoln's last speech, and it was more than Booth could tolerate. He made his decision then and there to end the lives of Lincoln and other top members of the federal government.

On the day of the assassination, Good Friday 1865, Booth and Lucy spent time together in the morning and then again in the evening, with Booth excusing himself from dinner at 8:00 p.m. That afternoon, Lucy spent studying Spanish…with Robert Lincoln.

Even more improbable, but true, was that in addition to Lucy seeing both Robert Lincoln and John Wilkes Booth on that fateful day, Lucy's father visited President Lincoln in his office that morning shortly after 10:00. John Hale, the former U.S. senator, was giving his regards to the president before he left for his new assignment as minister to Spain.

When Lucy was told about Lincoln's assassination and Booth's role in it, she was devastated, and by all accounts, could not believe her fiancé had committed the crime.

Twelve days later, as Lt. Col. Everton Conger—brother of U.S. Sen. Omar Conger of Michigan—recovered John Wilkes Booth's possessions from his body outside the tobacco barn in Port Royal, Virginia, he found photographs of five women in Booth's pocket, one of which was of Lucy.

Soon after that tragic Good Friday, Lucy accompanied her parents to Spain. She remained in Europe for five years, during which time she received but declined numerous offers of marriage from continental aristocrats.

When Lucy returned home in 1870, she renewed her relationship with successful corporate lawyer William E. Chandler—the guy who, as a Harvard student, sent poems to Lucy when she was 12. They were married, and in 1882, William "Bill" Chandler became secretary of the Navy. In 1887, he became a U.S. senator from New Hampshire, the same position Lucy's father had held.

Lucy passed away in 1915 and William in 1917. Their grandson, Theodore Chandler, was a highly decorated admiral in the U.S. Navy during World War II.

More than 150 years later, so many questions remain. Why did Booth—a champion of the Confederacy and hater of Lincoln, the Union, and African Americans—propose marriage to Lucy, a member of a family of abolitionists who supported Lincoln and the Union? And how aware was Booth of Lucy's friendship with Robert? How much did Robert know about Lucy's engagement to Booth?

No evidence was ever uncovered that Lucy knew about Booth's plans, or the extent to which he despised Lincoln.

Mary and Her Family

Even though I was still doing a balancing act in terms of what information I could share with Mr. Lincoln, I could still ask him questions, and I did that freely.

Mr. Lincoln's law partner in Springfield, William Herndon, later became one of the 16th president's most prominent biographers. Soon after the night at Ford's Theatre, Herndon began collecting information and interviewing others who knew Lincoln, then co-authoring, with Jesse W. Weik, the biography *Herndon's Lincoln: The True Story of a Great Life*. Herndon writes in the book that Lincoln "usually had but little to say of himself, the lives of his parents, or the history of the family before their removal to Indiana. If he mentioned the subject at all, it was with great reluctance and significant reserve. There was something about his origin he never cared to dwell upon." According to Herndon's account, it was clear that Lincoln was much more at ease talking about his life in Springfield than how things had been in Kentucky or southern Indiana. Accordingly, I generally tried to focus any discussion we might have on his time in Springfield.

"Who were some of the people in Springfield that you remember most?" I asked.

"Well, my family, of course," said Mr. Lincoln. "I had a good relationship with Mary's older sister, Elizabeth. Mary and I met at a gathering at Elizabeth's home in Springfield in 1839, and we were married in Elizabeth's house three years later. Elizabeth was born in Kentucky, as were Mary and many others I knew in Springfield. Ten years before Mary and I took our vows, Elizabeth and her husband, Ninian Edwards, were married. Ninian's father, whose name was also Ninian, was a territorial governor of Illinois, and then became the first governor of the state. The elder Mr. Edwards was actually born in 1775, a year before our nation's independence.

"Elizabeth's husband—my brother-in-law—was a very capable man indeed. He served as Illinois' attorney general, was a member of the state house of representatives and the state senate, and then was the Illinois superintendent of public instruction at the time I visited Kalamazoo in 1856. Elizabeth lived with us in the Executive Mansion for a period after we moved to Washington. Elizabeth was five years older than Mary, and Ninian was nine years older than Mary. Ninian served for a time as Mary's guardian."

History shows that Elizabeth and Robert Todd Lincoln were at odds with each other over Mary being institutionalized after the night at Ford's Theatre. Robert had Mary committed to the asylum in Batavia, Illinois in 1875 over Elizabeth's objections, and Elizabeth cared for Mary after Mary was released from the asylum.

Mr. Lincoln told me about the talks he had with Mary while they were in the Executive Mansion. They talked about visiting Europe and Jerusalem after their days in Washington were done. (Mr. and Mrs. Lincoln would have been the first sitting president and First Lady to visit another country. Instead, that distinction wouldn't take place until November 1906, when Theodore Roosevelt inspected construction of the Panama Canal, which was controlled by the United States until 1977).

The Abraham Lincoln we read about in school and saw in movies was the third president to die in office, and the first to die from a cause other than illness. William Henry Harrison, who was in office only 31 days, died eight days after becoming ill, and Zachary Taylor died five days after he became sick while laying the cornerstone to the Washington Monument. At the request of Robert Lincoln, who wrote a letter to Lincoln's successor, Andrew Johnson, Mary Todd Lincoln was allowed to remain in the Executive Mansion for almost six weeks after she lost her husband. Upon leaving, she traveled to Chicago, where she settled and found herself in financial difficulties in the days before presidents or their widows received pensions.

Two years later, in 1867, Mary traveled to New York City to sell her best dresses. During her days in the Executive Mansion, she had been criticized for her lavish spending habits, and she was criticized again for attempting to sell her dresses.

In October of the following year, 1868, Mary realized the dream that she and Abraham would not be able to realize together, by making her first of two extended trips to Europe. On her first visit, she spent two and a half years in Europe with her son Tad, who was 15 when the first voyage set out. Mary and Tad departed Baltimore aboard the steamer *City of Baltimore* on October 1 and arrived in Southampton, England on October 15.

Mary and Tad arrived in Bremen, Germany two weeks later, and then traveled to Frankfurt, where they moved into a relatively expensive hotel near the center of town, the Hotel d'Angleterre. Tad attended and boarded at an educational institute there. He studied English, French, German, as well as drawing and dancing. While Tad continued at the institute, Mary moved for a while to Nice, France. She returned to Frankfurt and this time checked into the less expensive Hotel de Holland.

During the summer of 1869, Tad was on break from his schooling. He and his mother used the time to their advantage by visiting much of Scotland, including Glasgow, Edinburgh, and Balmoral. Of all the places she'd been in Europe, Mary especially liked Edinburgh and the beauty of Scotland.

In May 1871, Mary and Tad returned to the States. They sailed from Liverpool to New York aboard the Cunard liner *Russia*, which at the time held the transatlantic crossing speed record of eight days and 25 minutes. Gen. Philip Sheridan happened to be aboard the ship. (President Lincoln, one of the greatest practitioners of the English language prior to Yogi Berra, once described the 5-foot-5 Sheridan, whose nickname was "Little Phil," as "A brown, chunky little chap, with a long body, short legs, not enough neck to hang him, and such long arms that if his ankles itch, he can scratch them without stooping.") Soon after their arrival in New York, Mary and Tad traveled to Chicago, checking in at the Clinton House. Tad had become ill during the voyage home and, sadly, his condition worsened. He became very sick by the end of the month, and after rallying somewhat by the end of June, he worsened again and died on July 15, 1871, leaving only Mary and Robert left among the former First Family.

Mary's second trip to Europe came five years later. In the years between trips, she was institutionalized in Batavia on Robert's legal filing. On October 1, 1876, she left New York for Le Havre, France aboard the steamer *Labrador*. She spent much of this trip living in the commune of Pau in the French Pyrenees, which French statesman Alphonse de Lamartine described as having "the world's most beautiful view of the earth just as Naples has the most beautiful view of the sea." While on the continent she visited Bordeaux, Marseilles, Avignon, Naples, Rome, and Sorrento. During her stay in Pau, Mary fell from a stepladder, injuring her spinal cord. In October 1880, Mary returned to the States, sailing from Le Havre to New York City aboard the *Amerique*. During that voyage, the *Amerique* passed through several storms. Mary was about to fall again, down a flight of stairs, but was caught by another passenger, Sarah Bernhardt. Like the Booth family and Laura Keene, Bernhart was one of the most noted actors of the day. Sarah told Mary that the former First Lady could have been killed, to which Mary promptly replied "Yes, but it was not God's will."

Mary stayed in New York City for a time, then returned to Springfield, where she lived with her sister's family. There, she began to lose her vision and general health. Robert came to visit her the following year. In 1882, Mary Todd Lincoln died at Elizabeth's home at age 63. Elizabeth died six years later at age 74. Mary and Elizabeth are both buried at Oak Ridge Cemetery in Springfield; Mary is interred in the family tomb there.

At five o'clock in the afternoon on that Good Friday of 1865 when Abraham and Mary Lincoln rode around our nation's capital in a carriage, they discussed those post-presidential plans including a trip together to Jerusalem in addition to Europe. One quote attributed to the president on that day—probably spoken during his rides with Mary rather than in the box at Ford's Theatre—was "After the war we shall go to Jerusalem." A friend and neighbor of the Lincolns in Springfield, Rev. Noyes Miner, said that Mary had told him that the two planned to visit the Holy Land as well as Europe after their time in Washington. Although Mary realized the trip to Europe, twice, neither ever realized the trip to the Holy Land. I asked my passenger whether he and his wife had indeed planned to visit Europe and the Holy Land, post-presidency, and he confirmed that it was all true, then adding that he was surprised that people today even knew about those plans.

Over his lifetime, Abraham Lincoln's views on religion evolved, somewhat in parallel with his views on equal rights for African Americans. Although Lincoln was always opposed to slavery, over much of his lifetime he did not advocate total equality in matters such as voting rights and equal pay. However, those views were somewhat influenced by his study of the Bible and with his relationship with members of the clergy. Friends and family said he was also very much changed by the many hardships in his life, including the deaths of two of his sons and the terrible loss of life during the war, for which he felt partly responsible.

Lincoln's knowledge of the Bible was such that he certainly recognized the Jewish origins of the book, and the Jewishness of Jesus Christ. And although one would be hard-pressed to find a valid religious connection to the motivation behind John Wilkes Booth's terrible act that night, the Abraham Lincoln in our history was assassinated not only on Good Friday, but also during Passover.

As we drove on, everything my passenger said and did confirmed that he was, in fact, the President Abraham Lincoln that we'd all read about, but that something quite recent in his timeline—perhaps immediately before his jump from 1865 Washington to today's Michigan—changed his ability to see the end of *Our American Cousin*.

I had asked him about the *planning* he and Mary had done to visit Europe and the Holy Land after his presidency, and I wondered whether this version of Abraham Lincoln, unlike the one you and I learned about, would actually make the trip.

1864: Reelection During Wartime

It was clear that visiting Europe and Jerusalem after his time in the Executive Mansion had been on Mr. Lincoln's mind. Although he was only seven weeks into his second term when he and Mary visited Ford's Theatre, there was likely an extended period during his first term when he and Mary thought that trip might be possible much earlier.

The 1864 presidential election was like no other in American history, the only election to take place while the country was literally at war with itself. Michael Burlingame of the nonpartisan Miller Center of Public Affairs in Virginia wrote in 2023:

> The amazing fact about the election of 1864 is that it occurred in the first place. In the middle of a devastating civil war, the United States held its presidential election almost without discussion about any alternatives. No other democratic nation had ever conducted a national election during times of war. And while there was some talk of postponing the election, it was never given serious consideration, even when Lincoln thought that he would lose.

I found the topic intriguing, and I was excited to find that Mr. Lincoln was very willing to discuss the subject, as he seemed to find the result to be a very positive thing, as well as vindication for his policies and his deep-held beliefs.

"I was quite pessimistic about my chances for reelection in 1864. My closest advisers told me not to expect to be returned to office. Despite Union victories at Gettysburg and Vicksburg in July of 1863, the war continued to exact lives and national treasure, and there was dissatisfaction with my presidency across the political spectrum. Those who were dedicated to the continuation of slavery continued to criticize my policies, and those at the other end of the spectrum, who had continued to support a complete and immediate end to slavery—the Radical Republicans, who would later be called the Stalwarts—thought that I was not acting quickly enough to end the practice.

"Further, many citizens did not like the draft. In New York City, just 10 days after the end of the terrible battle at Gettysburg, workers rioted. No more had the smoke cleared from those fields and valleys in the farmland of Pennsylvania that I had to order several regiments of militia and volunteers to travel from Gettysburg directly to New York City. They fought alongside the city's police department. Much of the violence was directed against Black men, who some blamed for the very need for the draft...the need to draft for a war to preserve the Union and to end slavery. By the end, at least 120 people, and perhaps more than one thousand, had been killed in the riots.

"The reunification of the nation we'd worked for so earnestly actually began in late 1863," Mr. Lincoln continued. "In December of that year, I issued the Proclamation of Amnesty and Reconstruction. It became known informally as the '10 percent plan' or policy. That policy said that when a state which had been in rebellion wanted to rejoin the Union, it could do so if 10 percent of its voters took an oath of allegiance to the Union and pledged to honor the principles I'd put forth in the Emancipation Proclamation."

Of course, in America in the 1860s, that meant 10 percent of *white males* had to make those vows.

"By the end of Eighteen Hundred and Sixty-Three," said Mr. Lincoln, "most of us, including our counterparts in the so-called Confederacy, had our bellies more than full of war. The Amnesty portion of the proclamation stated that except for high-ranking officers of the states in rebellion, officials, junior officers, and citizens would be granted pardons by me as president. I thought—and continue to think—that we'd had enough bloodshed and retribution. I felt it was time to apply the bandage, heal the wound, and move forward.

"But many of my fellow Republicans did not agree with me. They felt that I was too lenient on the states in rebellion. For that, I received much criticism and outcry in the press, on Capitol Hill and in our state capitals. My friends in Congress responded by passing the Wade-Davis Bill, which required fully *50 percent* of a state's voters to pledge allegiance to the Union and swear to the enforcement of emancipation. I trusted that the day of achieving that majority would come one day, but not likely in the immediate future. I 'pocket vetoed' the bill—I neither signed it nor formally vetoed it—after which time it failed, to the exasperation of those friends in Congress, and to a large extent, to their supporters back in their districts. In early 1864, by executive order I decreed the reconstruction of the seceded states beginning with Louisiana, in which there were actually many pro-Union and anti-slavery supporters. I felt it would be the right thing to do, but all of those problems resulted in the very distinct likelihood that my tenure as president would not continue past four years." A parish (county) in northern Louisiana is named after Lincoln.

"However, one thing we may not have fully appreciated at the time was the resolve of the People," said Mr. Lincoln. "That may come with some degree of astonishment, particularly given my remarks about sacrifice and commitment that I made at the dedication of the Gettysburg National Cemetery in November of Eighteen Hundred and Sixty-Three, but it was not the only such underestimate. It was true that by the end of that year, Americans on both sides of the question were weary of the conflict. But that weariness was overshadowed by the steadfastness of doing what was right, and of ensuring that all that had been given by our young men and their families had not been in vain."

"In addition to that dedication, and I say this with all humility," he added, "is the loyalty and confidence that so many Americans continued to express for this weary and imperfect old lawyer from the farm country of Illinois. During the campaign of that reelection year, I had told voters on several occasions 'Be cautious about swapping horses in the middle of a stream.' The war created great turbulence, and I honestly felt that it was not in the nation's best interest to select a new leader until the war was over—until the nation was no longer at risk from the fast-moving currents of that stream."

Today, the world is full of famous quotes, fake quotes, and memes all attributed to Abraham Lincoln, but as far as I can tell, the phrase about not changing horses in the middle of the stream was really his.

One of the many things that continued to impress me about Mr. Lincoln was how he analyzed problems and solutions. He regretted the war and its losses, but he maintained that the cause was just.

There were two additional events that likely contributed to President Lincoln's reelection in 1864, which neither of us brought up.

First, in 1864, Abraham Lincoln—the first Republican ever elected president—did *not* run on the Republican Party ticket. Instead, Lincoln attempted to appeal not only to Republicans but also to "War Democrats," those Democrats who supported the Union as well as the continuation of the war in order to preserve that Union. The ticket itself, for the 1864 election only, was renamed the National Union Party ticket. In the general election, the ticket would go up against Democratic Party candidate George McClellan. That's the very same George McClellan who President Lincoln appointed general-in-chief of the Union armies in November 1861, only to have Lincoln fire McClellan a year later when it became evident that McClellan was completely unwilling and/or unable to perform the very army-like duty of waging war against an enemy.

In January 1862, Lincoln remarked to other Union generals, "If Gen. McClellan does not want to use the army, I would like to borrow it for a time."

The second major change made during the 1864 campaign—a change that would likely affect the country for the rest of its history—was changing Mr. Lincoln's vice-presidential nominee from 1860.

In the 1860 election, Lincoln and the Republican Party nominated Sen. Hannibal Hamlin as Lincoln's running mate. Hamlin was born in 1809 in Paris, Massachusetts, in the northern part of the state that would become Maine in 1820 as part of the Missouri Compromise. That year, Missouri was admitted to the Union as a state in which slavery was legal, in exchange for the addition of Maine, where slavery was prohibited.

From early in his life, Hamlin was staunchly anti-slavery, more so than Lincoln. In Congress, he strongly opposed any measures that would allow the expansion of slavery. He supported the Wilmot Proviso and opposed the Compromise of 1850 and the Kansas-Nebraska Act, both of which had the effect of allowing the proliferation of slavery. The nomination of Hamlin to the ticket with Lincoln was done largely to balance the ticket, Hamlin being from New England in contrast to Lincoln's Midwestern background in Illinois, and Hamlin's Radical Republican approach to abolition compared to Lincoln's more moderate approach. Lincoln and Hamlin were not personally close during the first four years of the Lincoln administration (and Hamlin and Mary Todd Lincoln did not get along, a situation that was common with those who came in contract with the First Lady); however, Lincoln and Hamlin had a good working relationship.

But the same objective that led to Hamlin's selection in 1860, balancing the ticket, led to his exclusion and replacement in 1864. As Lincoln, the Republicans, and the War Democrats formed the National Union ticket, they determined that pro-Union Southerner Andrew Johnson would give the ticket much wider appeal. Johnson, a Democrat, had been governor of Tennessee (officially called "Military Governor of Tennessee" beginning in March 1862) who looked forward to reestablishing civilian government in Tennessee and restoring the other seceded states to the Union.

Andrew Johnson was born in Raleigh, North Carolina. Raised in poverty, Johnson never attended school. Instead, he apprenticed as a tailor and went into that business in several towns before settling in Tennessee. A political cartoon from early 1865, following the 1864 election, showed an uncoordinated-looking Andrew Johnson, scissors and thread nearby, sitting atop a five-foot globe of the earth, which in turn was being moved by President Lincoln using a large wooden fence rail. The caption was "The 'Rail Splitter' at work repairing the Union." Obviously, the pair would have their work "cut out" for them, so to speak, though the cartoon was in quite good humor compared to some of Mr. Lincoln that continued to depict him in racist terms due to his passion for abolishing slavery.

As a result of those three things: making progress in the war, the support of Lincoln's cause by Union soldiers and their friends and families, and the larger appeal of the National Union Party ticket that now included Andrew Johnson, the ticket overwhelmed the Democratic ticket of George McClellan and Ohio's George H. Pendleton on November 8, 1864. The Lincoln-Johnson ticket won the popular vote by 55%-45%, but more importantly won the electoral vote 212-21, a win that today would almost be considered a Soviet-style victory.

And though we all know now that Lincoln's victory bode well for the Union, the inclusion of Johnson on the ticket instead of Hamlin did not. Following the tragedy at Ford's Theatre and Johnson becoming the 17th president, Johnson pushed to return the seceded states to the Union with very little regard for the African Americans for whom Lincoln and many others had struggled, including the millions of Americans who had either died or lost family members during the Civil War.

As president, Johnson tried to remove any resistance to his goals, and that included Secretary of War Edwin Stanton. That move was the last in a long line of actions that would have angered Lincoln, and in 1868, the House of Representatives impeached Johnson. The vote by the U.S. Senate to remove him from office failed by only one vote.

Had the waves of history flowed slightly differently, Andrew Johnson might have been removed from office on Good Friday 1865. The plan by John Wilkes Booth and his co-conspirators included not only the assassination of Abraham Lincoln, but also of Vice President Andrew Johnson and Secretary of State William Seward that same night. Seward was badly injured in a knife attack by Lewis Powell, and he probably would have been killed if he hadn't been wearing a heavy splint around his jaw that was broken in a carriage accident 10 days earlier. Would-be assassin George Atzerodt, who Booth had assigned to kill Johnson, lost his courage, went to his hotel bar and got drunk, and threw away the knife he was supposed to use to kill Johnson.

By the 1870s, in spite of (or partly because of) the losses during the Civil War, weariness and avoidance of additional conflict settled in, and likely played a part in determining who our 19th president would be—as well as setting the stage for laws in the South well into the following century.

The 1876 presidential election was a race between the Democrat, Gov. Samuel Tilden of New York, and the Republican, Gov. Rutherford B. Hayes of Ohio. After the votes were counted on November 7, Democrat Tilden had about 252,000 more popular votes than Republican Hayes, and in the more important electoral vote, Tilden led 184-165. However, that left Tilden one electoral vote short of the 185 needed to give him the presidency because three states remained contested: South Carolina, Louisiana and…yup, Florida. Florida, Florida, Florida. There were allegations of voter fraud and election violence, as well as disenfranchisement of African American voters. Emotions ran high during the election, and to date, the 1876 election remains the highest voter turnout percentage among eligible voters in American history, at 82.6%. By contrast, 59.2% of eligible Americans voted in 2016, and 66.9% in 2020.

Faced with an unprecedented constitutional crisis and pressure from the American public, Congress, for the only time in its history, appointed a 15-member bipartisan commission comprised of five senators, five U.S. representatives, and five Supreme Court members to settle the issue. After deliberations, the commission awarded the presidency to Rutherford B. Hayes. But in order to ensure that Democrats nationally would accept the ruling after Tilden's plurality in both electoral and popular votes, new president Hayes agreed to remove all remaining federal troops from the South, leaving the local governments to create new laws, frequently at the expense of African Americans who thought they had attained equality.

As a result of the ruling, 1877 is recognized as the beginning of the Nadir, the worst period of race relations in the United States. Legislators in the South began to pass the Jim Crow laws, lynchings increased, and the Ku Klux Klan became more active and accepted by public officials. In many cases, those officials were actually part of the Klan.

Before the Nadir, during the period of Reconstruction, African Americans occupied positions they'd never held before. Between 1867 and 1872, sixty-nine African Americans served in the Georgia state legislature or as delegates to the state's constitutional convention. Tennessee, Mississippi, Alabama, and South Carolina all elected a number of African American state legislators. Republican Hiram Revels of Mississippi, an African American legislator, was elected to the U.S. Senate. Robert Smalls served five terms as a U.S. representative and Jonathan Jasper Wright was elected to the South Carolina Supreme Court.

In major league baseball prior to 1885, at least three African Americans were among its ranks: William Edward White, Moses Fleetwood Walker and his brother, Weldy Walker. Late in 1884, the league imposed its color barrier, and no other African American played in the major leagues until Jackie Robinson in 1947.

Republicans in former slave-holding states passed laws to fund schools for African American children, with the intent of making them as good as schools for white children.

Rights that came about as the result of the 13th, 14th, and 15th Amendments, and four years of devastating civil war, were largely lost following the Compromise of 1877 and the end of Reconstruction.

The Need for (Joshua) Speed

The year 1837 was a big one in Abraham Lincoln's life. At the age of 28, he left his home of six years in New Salem, Illinois and moved to Springfield, which would be his home until he left for Washington, D.C. as president-elect with his family 24 years later. In February of the same year, Illinois' state capital also moved to Springfield. The Illinois legislature voted to move it there from Vandalia, where it had been located for 17 years.

Overall, there would also be setbacks for Illinois and the country in 1837. The financial panic of 1837 was in full force by the end of the year, and it worsened and lasted until the mid-1840s. Michigan became a state on January 26 of that year with reason for optimism, but due to the financial crisis, many new railroads and businesses that had already been planned were put on hold or canceled altogether. A number of small banks collapsed, dashing many people's plans to create or expand businesses. The previously mentioned Clinton-Kalamazoo Canal, which would have completely changed transportation across lower Michigan by connecting Lake Michigan at the west terminus with Lake Saint Clair at the east, was also among the canceled projects and dreams.

Mr. Lincoln told me about his arrival in Springfield and his first friendship there, with Joshua Speed.

"When I arrived in Springfield, I was already a member of the Illinois House of Representatives, to which the people of Sangamon County had elected me about two years earlier. With the move of the state capital to Springfield in February of Eighteen Hundred and Thirty-Seven, I desired to live closer to my work there. Accordingly, in April, I rode—on a borrowed horse, by the way—to Springfield, about 25 miles to the southeast. I brought very little along with me, so the first two items of business were to purchase some sundries for living, and then to find a place to live.

"I occasioned to visit a general store on Washington Street, between 4th and 5th Streets, in Springfield. I knew that it was co-owned by an old friend of mine from New Salem, a gentleman by the name of Abner Ellis. I met Abner in 1833 after I returned to New Salem from fighting in the Black Hawk War. After I was elected as a state representative in 1834, I sometimes visited Springfield, and Abner allowed me to stay in his home there. He also guided me around town so I could become acquainted with Springfield, as well as getting to know some of the prominent Whig politicians in town, who had similar views on halting the spread of slavery. Abner knew that I was moving to Springfield. Well, when I walked into the store that day, Abner was not present, but his business partner, Joshua Speed, greeted me as soon as I walked into the store."

Years later, when Lincoln's law partner William Herndon wrote his biography of Lincoln, he obtained a good deal of information from Abner Ellis, especially about Lincoln's time in New Salem.

"Like Mary and me, and many of those we knew in Springfield, Speed first lived in Kentucky. Speed's grandfather, Capt. James Speed, originally lived in Virginia. He and six of his brothers served in the Continental Army under Gen. Washington. In recognition of his service, the Continental Congress awarded him a land grant of 7,500 acres in Kentucky. Capt. Speed's son, Judge John Speed— Joshua's father—built the Farmington Plantation in Louisville.

Although Speed and Lincoln had never met before, Speed had attended a campaign speech given by Lincoln during the latter's run for state representative. Speed had arrived in Springfield two years earlier from Louisville, thinking that the Midwest would be a better place to start a business. In addition to his partnership running the general store, Speed assisted in editing a local newspaper.

Springfield, which today has a population of well over 110,000 people, then had just 1,500 residents.

The 28-year-old Lincoln told the 22-year-old Joshua Speed about some food items he needed, as well as his need to have a roof over his head. (Throughout his adult life, Lincoln almost always referred to his friends by only their last name, and almost immediately he began calling his new friend "Speed".) Lincoln also shared with Speed that, although he needed those things, he did not have money to pay for them. Speed later described Lincoln's appearance and bearing, saying "I looked up at him and thought…I never saw so gloomy and melancholy a face." It had been only 20 months since the death in New Salem of Ann Rutledge, who many acquaintances of Lincoln would say was the true love of his life. Ann died at the age of 22 when an outbreak of typhoid fever spread through New Salem. Lincoln was subject to bouts of depression, and this period was one of the low points of his life.

"Well, my friend," said Mr. Lincoln, "it may have been his altruism or his perspicacity, or some combination of the two, but with no hesitation Speed told me that he lived in a room above the store, and he offered to share the room and his double bed with me while I settled into my new home town of Springfield." I resolved that when I returned home, I'd read more information about the generous Mr. Joshua Speed. I'd also blow the dust off my Funk & Wagnall's Dictionary so I could look up the word "perspicacity."

According to later accounts by Speed himself, when he made the offer to the new Springfield resident, Lincoln grabbed his saddlebags and "trudged upstairs" without saying a word. Speed could literally hear Lincoln drop his saddlebags on the floor above.

"When I returned downstairs to Speed a few minutes later," said Mr. Lincoln, "my disposition was much changed. Having a comfortable place to stay and a source of food, I was much cheerier, and he had a smile on his face, which I quickly realized was a reflection of my own. I think we both took a shine to each other and that was the beginning of a great friendship and professional partnership that has continued. Evenings in our room together, we talked about matters of the day, and both being young single men, we shared tribulations and consulted with each other on matters of the fairer sex.

"Speed told me that with Illinois moving its capital to Springfield, there was a shortage of housing," said Mr. Lincoln. "I was therefore most relieved to have a place to stay. He also told me, incidentally, that because most of the legislators and others working at the capital would be males, men outnumbered women in Springfield. This made it somewhat more difficult to develop meaningful relationships, but Speed and I each met someone over time, of course."

Mr. Lincoln went on to tell me that he, Speed, and several other young Springfield men gathered and frequently had dinners and discussions together. In addition to discussion of the events of the day in Springfield and across the nation, they sometimes discussed music, poetry, and philosophy, in part to enhance their respectability.

In March 1840, Joshua Speed's father died and Joshua decided to sell the store and return to his parents' plantation near Louisville. Lincoln had recently become engaged to Mary, but before the planned wedding date of January 1, 1841, Lincoln called off the wedding. When Speed left for Louisville, Lincoln was once again depressed.

"By the middle of that year, in July 1841," explained Mr. Lincoln to me, "I was feeling quite sad and guilty for canceling our wedding plans and decided to visit my friend in Louisville so I could make sense of things. Joshua's brother, James, was an attorney and he lent me law books from his library. There were many books that I hadn't seen before and it occupied my mind greatly." Lincoln stayed at the

Farmington plantation for a month, and his mental health was improved when he returned to Springfield.

"When I arrived in Washington in 1861 to serve as president, I offered Speed several positions in my government but he felt he was not the right person for the task. I felt that was unfortunate because I knew how capable he was. But when the war began, he helped our cause greatly by coordinating Union activities in Kentucky. And in November of Eighteen Hundred and Sixty-Four, the month that I was reelected, I nominated his brother James to be the attorney general. The entire family served me and the country well."

In the timeline you and I know, after that tragic night in Ford's Theatre, Joshua Speed organized a memorial service in Louisville for his good friend. In preparation for writing his biography of Lincoln, Speed wrote a number of long letters to William Herndon, hoping that the world would better know about Lincoln by hearing the true story from his friends. Sixty members of the Speed family donated money for Lincoln's monument in Springfield.

The Speed family estate near Louisville, Farmington, is today on the National List of Historic Places. The house is used for local events and open periodically to the public.

Joshua Speed and Abraham Lincoln had a lifelong friendship. Despite all of the things they had in common, they had one particular difference: the issue of slavery. Lincoln was an opponent of the practice, whereas Speed, like many residents of Kentucky, thought it was the right of the states to allow it. But the two remained friends, and when Lincoln needed assistance "on the ground" in Kentucky organizing activities for the Union—the very establishment that was in the process of abolishing the institution—Joshua speed was there working on behalf of Lincoln. At least to some extent, some minds about slavery were changed through Joshua Speed.

I was grateful to hear about Abraham Lincoln's friends and acquaintances, and some great looks into history, from the man himself.

First Rest Stop

"We've been driving a little less than an hour and a half," I told Mr. Lincoln, "But we've gone almost 80 miles. When I drive anywhere for more than about two hours, I like to stop periodically to stretch my legs and use the toilet facilities. We'll be passing into Indiana in just a few minutes and there's a rest stop about three miles past that. I thought we could stop there if it's okay." My passenger was only 56 years old, but he was also six inches taller than me, and I thought he might like to unwind those long stems, and probably use the rest room, too.

"Of course, that's a fine idea," he agreed. "When I rode the court circuit in Illinois on horseback as a lawyer, I always looked forward to the next stop and changing position, and relieving my *own seat* from some pressure for a few minutes." His voice rose up in a humorous expression when he referred to his "own seat."

"Good," I acknowledged. "There'll probably be a number of people there, so you probably want to keep your sunglasses and cap on. Now, of course it's possible that someone will recognize you and will ask you questions. Do you want to answer them or would you like me to do that?"

There was silence for perhaps ten seconds, and I was already anticipating his response. And though I'd only been in the presence of this man for a few hours, I was starting to tune into his sense of humor. I had a good idea that his response wouldn't be so much an answer as a clever retort.

"Well Albert," he began dryly, calling me by my full given name for the first time, "I'd be happy to have you answer for me. But I'm confident that if I were to take a fine survey of people who report to me, perhaps Generals Grant, Sherman, Sheridan, and Meade, or members of my cabinet such as Secretary Seward, or Blair, or Chase, or Wells, they might agree that I'm very quick on my feet in terms of making decisions. I suspect that Jeff Davis, or generals Lee or McClellan might also concur." He was able to complete his response without any hint of humor, even though I was obviously laughing and probably blushing in the driver's seat.

"So…you're comfortable responding on your own?" I said, in mock clarification.

"Yes," he said, then after several seconds passed, he added, "though I do appreciate your rhetorical question as a courtesy."

"Very good," I chuckled, just as we passed a large royal blue sign with a red silhouette of Indiana, saying "*Welcome to Indiana: Crossroads of America.*" Like many expressions, the origin of "Crossroads of America" as Indiana's state motto is lost to many today. The expression originally referred to a particular intersection of roads in Terre Haute, in western Indiana. An east-west thoroughfare passing through Terra Haute was called the National Road, sometimes called the Cumberland Road, and it was the first major improved highway in the United States. When it was completed in 1837, it spanned from Maryland to Illinois and was a major path to the West. In 1926, it was renamed US Highway 40. At the same time, the north-south running highway, US Highway 41, was commissioned to run from Chicago to Miami, Florida. Where the two highways intersected became known as "The Crossroads of America." Today, the term better applies to Indianapolis, smack-dab in the center of the state.

In 1820, the Indiana state legislature authorized a committee to select a site near the center of the state to serve as its capital. The location and name Indianapolis (taken from the name of the state, *Indiana*, and the Greek word for city, *polis*) in 1821. Today, Indy serves as a hub for the state with the "wheel spokes" leading inward

184

and intersecting at its center, Indianapolis. The spokes are the four major interstate highways: I-65, I-69, I-70, and I-74). The wheel-and-hub theme repeats within the city itself, with the major roads coming together at the city's center with the central point being the 284-foot-tall Soldiers and Sailors Monument, dedicated in 1902. The monument was built to honor those who served in the Civil War and America's other wars, and was the first monument in the United States to be dedicated to the common soldier. A 342-foot-diameter town-center ring road with sidewalks called Monument Circle encircles the monument, and the buildings that face the monument have curved, concave building fronts. The buildings include retail shops, churches, radio stations, a theater, and financial institutions.

About three-tenths of a mile from the exit for the rest stop, I lightly tapped my brake pedal to disengage the cruise control and let my car start to coast onto the offramp. We slowed down to the point that we could stop directly in front of the building. There were several semi-trucks on the other side of the rest stop's median, but I only saw three vehicles on our side, a newer gray Cadillac and two compact SUVs. It was a smaller number of cars than I expected, but I attributed it to the time of day and light traffic on I-94. Not everybody notices those the kinds of cars in a parking lot, but with the smaller number of vehicles I took more notice. In addition, I grew up in the 1950s and 1960s and my dad and brother were car guys, and I took after them in that interest. Living less than 140 miles from the world headquarters for Ford, General Motors, Chrysler, and American Motors (and Studebaker in South Bend for the first the first eight years of my life) we probably tended to notice those things more than most.

We got out of my car, and my weary old bones definitely had more difficulty getting out than Mr. Lincoln's. I immediately walked over next to him as we approached the building so I could quietly tell him about things like the urinals and the blow driers. I suggested that if he couldn't figure anything out right away, he could stand at the sink and wash his hands and he could observe me or others using the equipment. After he was done washing his hands, we smiled at each other as I watched him watching me dry my hands under the blow dryer. He stood at the next dryer and did the same. The sound and the entire idea of an electric hand dryer both probably seemed crazy to him, and seemed a little crazy to me when I thought about them. I didn't see anyone else in the men's room, and quietly mentioned that paper towels were also available.

As we exited the men's room and walked toward the exit doors, we started to pass the vending machines. This rest stop had a soft drink machine with Pepsi products and bottled water, a candy vending machine, and an ice cream vending machine.

"Would you like something to drink, or a snack?" I asked Mr. Lincoln. "Some of the drinks may come in flavors that you may or may not like, but they also have cold water. I have to say that I'm somewhat addicted to this one," I said, pointing to the Diet Mountain Dew. "I picked up the habit from some co-workers years ago, but I still like it. Too much. And by the way, none of these drinks have alcohol in them." I'd read that in his youth, Abraham partook of beer and hard cider with his friends, but that as an adult, he generally refrained from drinks with alcohol, and did not use tobacco of any kind.

Coca-Cola, Pepsi-Cola, and Dr. Pepper would not be introduced to the public for 20 to 30 years after the end of the Civil War. One carbonated beverage (called "pop" in Michigan) that was available prior to those beverages was Vernor's ginger ale. Vernor's, a mixture of ginger, vanilla, sugar, and other ingredients aged in oak casks, was developed by Detroit pharmacist James Vernor, who first

186

developed and marketed the beverage in 1866. Contrary to a marketing story shared by the company, Vernor first developed his spicy, effervescent beverage after he returned home from the Civil War (with the rank of lieutenant colonel in the 4th Michigan Cavalry); he did not accidentally discover a brew that had aged since he left for the war.

"Well, if you don't mind, cold water would just hit the spot," replied my passenger. "Riding the circuit as a lawyer, I frequently developed a thirst between towns, and I found that water mitigated that thirst better than beer or anything else."

"Here you are," I said to Mr. Lincoln, handing him the cold bottle of Dasani spring water I'd purchased from the machine. "You might have noticed that there are holders in my car to hold cups of coffee, water, or whatever." He thanked me for the water. I then bought a 20-ounce plastic bottle of Diet Dew from the machine. But before we left, I couldn't take my eyes off the peanut butter M&Ms in the candy machine. I thought he might enjoy a package, and I knew I would. I bought a small package for each of us.

"Peanut butter M&Ms," I said, as I handed him a package and we stepped out the door to the car. "Some people might say they're a bit decadent, but I prefer to think of them as an all-American food. On the outside is a layer of chocolate, which were first cultivated and used in southern Mexico and Central America almost two thousand years ago. Inside them is a product called peanut butter. It's a thick paste made from peanuts. In fact, that paste also first originated with the people in the Aztec and Inca civilizations. The first commercial use of peanut butter, which was more uniform than the original paste, was by a scientist and pharmacist named Marcellus Gilmore Edson in Montreal, Canada about 20 years in your future."

"That's truly interesting," said Mr. Lincoln. "I think you and I share a curiosity about things around us. Do you also know a lot about other foods?" he asked.

"No, just things I like!" I said, smiling.

Back on the Road

About halfway to the car, I noticed that there was only one vehicle remaining in our part of the lot, a newer black Chevy Suburban. I hadn't seen anybody entering the building, so the occupant(s) were either still inside the SUV, or perhaps were out toward the back of the lot walking a dog. This Suburban had smoke-colored plastic deflectors over the side windows, and a long antenna on the roof, as if the owner might be a HAM radio operator. Someone obviously gave some thought to how they wanted to equip their SUV. I've sometimes thought that a bigger SUV like a Suburban would be a great car for taking longer trips: big, lots of room to move around, room to carry a number of suitcases, or to keep books, iPads and other things around you without feeling crowded. But I enjoyed my smaller Buick, which is relatively comfortable and quiet on good roads and gets good fuel economy.

I unlocked my car and we got in. After starting the car, I carefully pulled through the parking lot, onto the onramp and back out onto westbound I-94. I continued sharing a few thoughts about the M&Ms...perhaps not a particularly notable topic, but my passenger seemed interested. (Also, once I begin telling story, no matter when or where, I feel the need to finish it. Sorry.)

"So, peanut butter M&Ms. Chocolate was originally used in Mexico and Central America, and the Aztecs and Incas used a crude form of peanut butter centuries ago, which was refined by the scientist Edson in Canada. And not many years later, a professor named George Washington Carver wrote a paper about how there were "105 ways to prepare it—peanut butter—for human consumption. Professor Carver was born in Missouri in 1864, attended college in Iowa, and taught science classes in Alabama.

"And here's a connection I think you'll be interested in. For ten years, George Washington Carver worked for someone you knew in Springfield."

"Is that right?" replied Mr. Lincoln. "It is indeed a small world. I'm trying to recall who Professor Carver might…what was the name of my acquaintance in Springfield for whom Professor Carver worked?"

"Moses Carver," I said, and then remained quiet while those well-developed wheels in the mind of my passenger whirled and spun.

"Oh, certainly, I knew Moses Carver!" said Mr. Lincoln. "He lived in Springfield the first two or three years I was in Springfield. But the last name…was Professor Carver related to Moses?"

"No, Professor Carver took the family name of the people who lived there," I replied. I again became silent, and by now he knew I was playing a serious guessing game with him. After a short delay, my passenger's eye brows arched in realization.

"Oh!" he exclaimed. "Professor Carver was a Negro?" asked Mr. Lincoln.

"Yes, he sure was," I replied, "or, as people generally say today, an African American. But George Washington Carver never lived in Springfield. As you may recall, Moses moved to Diamond, Missouri where he 'acquired' George's parents in 1855; 'acquired' being my nice word for 'purchased.' And like your friend, Frederick Douglass, Professor Carver was extremely intelligent and extremely accomplished. At the time, people in much of society weren't accustomed to seeing an African American in an elevated position—laws and customs were intentionally put in place to keep them from achieving their goals. So well-intentioned people referred to Mr. Douglass, Professor Carver and others as being an 'intelligent' or

190

'accomplished' Negro, though both of them have said they'd have preferred to be called just an 'intelligent' or 'accomplished' *man*, or even *person*."

I could tell that it was a lot for my passenger to process, even though his thinking on racial equality was so advanced for the day. Reality in his day hadn't caught up with the thinking of abolitionists and human rights activists.

"Yes," he replied after several seconds, "and I have to say that, unfortunately, I've been somewhat guilty of that myself. I was always opposed to slavery—always—but I have to say that it has only been in the last several years, and seeing accomplished men like Frederick Douglass, and brave young men like those who have fought for the Union, that I really appreciated that abolishing the terrible institution of slavery was just one step in achieving what our Creator intended."

Libraries are full of books about Abraham Lincoln and how his views on equality had evolved over time, and his comments to me— as well as knowing what he actually did in the last decade of his life—showed the changes in his philosophy and in his heart.

His first public speech in which he raised the possibility of African Americans voting was made just three days before he and Mrs. Lincoln attended the play at Ford's Theatre.

Unfortunately, John Wilkes Booth was in that crowd that day to hear the speech.

The Biographers: Herndon, Nicolay, and Hay

William Herndon's biography of his former Springfield law partner is still considered a definitive account. But another biography of our 16th president was written by two other men who knew him very well: his two personal secretaries, John G. Nicolay and John Hay. Herndon published his biography, *Herndon's Lincoln: The True Story of a Great Life*, in 1889. Nicolay and Hay published their version, *Abraham Lincoln, A History* the following year. Nicolay and Hay's version was published as a ten-volume work that was more than 4,000 pages long, and the account by Nicolay and Hay was very different from the one by Herndon.

Herndon was another native of Kentucky, and his family moved to Illinois in 1820, and then in 1823, to the German Prairie settlement just north of Springfield, when William was age five.

I wanted to find out more about Mr. Lincoln's biographers, Herndon, Nicolay, and Hay. I asked Mr. Lincoln about Herndon, who would posthumously write the best-known biography of our 16th president. Accounts from people who knew both Lincoln and Herndon, and even by their own accounts, said their relationship was a symbiotic pairing of very different individuals.

"I couldn't have asked for a better law partner than Herndon," said Mr. Lincoln. "He was very dependable, and our clients appreciated the manner in which he provided his services. The way we referred to each other might say something about the differences in our personalities. He called me 'Abraham,' which I preferred to 'Abe,' and I usually called him 'Billy,' though to others, I usually referred to him by his last name. I'm nine years older than him, and we practically had a father-son relationship. Herndon, I have to say, was more…exuberant than I, and I tended to be more reserved. But I

192

believe my more reserved manner had a steadying influence on him. And in the same way, his energy had a positive effect on me when I needed it. Herndon once said 'Mr. Lincoln is the great big man in our firm and I was the little one. The little one naturally looked up to the big one.' Humor aside, I was flattered that he looked up to me, but I looked up to him, as well.

"Billy came from Kentucky, as I had," said my passenger, "but his family had greater means, and he had a much stronger formal education. That education and his knowledge of the law gave our clients the comfort in knowing he provided sound advice, and was a very fair man. And not to tell tales out of school, but the only complaint I ever heard about Billy was that he sometimes indulged in the bottle more than he should have. But that was infrequent, and I sometimes felt that his outgoing personality was sometimes mistaken for being inebriated."

After Mr. Lincoln left Springfield for Washington, Herndon became partners with Charles Zane, a New Jersey native who to a farm in Sangamon County, Illinois in 1850, and moved to Springfield in July 1856, the month before Lincoln visited Kalamazoo. When Zane later sent his thoughts to Herndon for Herndon's own biography of Lincoln, he agreed with Mr. Lincoln's assessment about Herndon:

> He (Herndon) was a rapid thinker, writer and speaker, and usually reached his conclusions quickly and expressed them forcibly and positively. His clients usually went away perfectly satisfied with his advice. He examined witnesses rapidly, and was not unfair, persistent, or tedious. He was always courteous and respectful to the court, and to his professional brethren. He was popular as a man, as a lawyer, and as a public speaker. It was easy to follow the thread of his argument. He was interesting and always secured the attention of his hearers. He was not always sufficiently careful as to his

premises and his data. In this he was unlike his famous partner.

"At first, I hired Billy to be my partner as a favor to his father, who helped me countless times as I set up a new life in Springfield," said my passenger. "I had two law partners before Billy: John Todd Stuart and Stephen T. Logan. They were both older than me, and more experienced than either Billy or me. But Billy had the ability to find the point in any analysis, and to quickly come up with the exact words to sum that up to a judge and jury. That made up for any lack of experience, and made him a valuable partner. I enjoyed working with him, and he was a valued friend.

Historian David H. Donald, author of *Abraham Lincoln and His Friends*, said of Lincoln's last law partner "Herndon idealized his partner. He not merely felt grateful to Lincoln; he considered him his mentor, an older man who was a friendly, safe counselor. A man of extremes – indeed, a man who sometimes fell off the edge – Herndon found a steadying influence in his relationship with Lincoln."

Like a number of key people in Lincoln's life—including Secretary of State William H. Seward, Chief Justice Salmon P. Chase, Vice President Hannibal Hamlin, social reformer and orator Frederick Douglass, and Gen. Ulysses S. Grant—William Herdon was a stronger opponent of slavery and proponent of equal rights than the more moderate Abraham Lincoln. And like the others, Herndon was partly responsible for changing Lincoln's views in those areas. Herndon, truly a Radical Republican, thought that Lincoln did not act quickly enough to end slavery and felt that slavery could only be ended "through bloody revolution." Herndon was among the first members of the Republican Party in the United States.

Like many friends, neighbors, and business associates of Abraham Lincoln, William Herndon had a "contentious relationship" with

Mary Todd Lincoln. Despite a business partnership that lasted 17 years and a friendship that lasted even longer than that, Herndon was never invited to the Lincoln's home for dinner. I didn't ask Mr. Lincoln about anyone's relationship with his wife, but he offered a few words in a very guarded manner.

"I regret that Mary and Herndon didn't always see eye-to-eye on matters," said my passenger. "Though Herndon and I were friends and had a very good working relationship, I felt that having the two of them in the same room would be tantamount to storing nitroglycerin and a burning flare in the same room," he said, surprising me by mentioning the explosive that had been discovered by an Italian chemist in 1847 and first used commercially by Alfred Nobel during the last year of America's Civil War. "Later, after we had moved to Washington, Herndon paid a visit to the Executive Mansion in 1862. He and I greeted each other warmly, but I determined not to invite him into the family quarters in order to ensure that things remained on a civil basis."

Herndon also stated that he was uncomfortable with his friend's permissive parenting. Although Abraham Lincoln was said by everyone to be a loving father, Mr. Lincoln sometimes permitted the boys to run about the office and be disruptive. Herndon's pleas to his friend to control the behavior resulted in some of the few harsh words between the two.

Not long after Good Friday and the events at Ford's Theater, William Herndon decided to write "a faithful portrait" about his good friend and former business partner. He and a co-author, Jesse Weik, began to have conversations and write hundreds of letters to others who knew Lincoln in order to achieve their purpose. He contacted acquaintances from Lincoln's earlier life in Kentucky and Indiana as well as Illinois. Herndon decided that he would author an unvarnished and subjective account of his friend, with all the nicks and dings revealed to posterity along with Mr. Lincoln's many positive attributes. Such an account was controversial and went against the Victorian principles of the day which avoided the unveiling of "dirty laundry." The approach would also be contrary to much of the literary and artwork of the day following Lincoln's death; some of the accounts essentially depicted Lincoln as being saintly.

One of the more controversial topics mentioned by Herndon in his book was his contention that Ann Rutledge, to whom Lincoln evidently proposed and who died back in New Salem at age 22 during the typhoid outbreak, was the one true love of Lincoln's life, a claim that had some supporting evidence but did not go over well with the Lincoln family. Other topics included Lincoln's depression, and the fact that Lincoln confided to Herndon that Lincoln's mother, Nancy Hanks, was not the biological daughter of the man who married Nancy's mother. (The latter claim is supported by DNA evidence from a 2015 study.)

Of course, with Herndon's attempt to paint a balanced picture of Lincoln, reactions were mixed. Among the detractors was Robert Todd Lincoln, the eldest surviving son of the president and First Lady, who denounced the negative aspects mentioned by Herndon. Even Herndon's co-author, 32-year-old Jesse Weik, thought the way that Herndon depicted Mary Todd Lincoln and Nancy Hanks was "especially hurtful" to the family.

Although Weik had started out as a supporter of Herndon who wanted to help him in his effort to write Lincoln's biography, by the end he felt that Herndon's ultimate depiction was unfair, so Weik, who had saved the notes from his interviews and correspondence, wrote a follow-up book, *The Real Lincoln: A Portrait*, which he published in 1922, the year Robert Lincoln helped dedicate the Lincoln Memorial. Weik's book included photographic images of

Lincoln family documents and artifacts including the family Bible. Although Weik recognized Herndon's work and generosity of spirit, he made clear that he felt Herndon's biography left an unnecessarily negative image and that the record needed to be set straight. At the time, the manner in which Herndon wrote his book (i.e., a balanced description based on interviews, letters, and other records), was considered ground-breaking in the Victorian late 19th Century.

Because of Herndon's significance in Lincoln's life and the resulting impact on our country, a number of biographies have been written about Herndon himself, including *Lincoln's Herndon* (1989) by David Herbert Donald. One particular book, *Herndon's Informants: Letters, Interviews, and Statements about Abraham Lincoln* (1997) edited by Douglas L. Wilson and Rodney O. Davis, provides substantial supporting evidence about Herndon's biography of Lincoln as well as details about how Herndon's book was written.

Herndon began researching his book in 1865. Soon after traveling to Indiana to interview people for the book, Herndon's father died and William returned to Kentucky to manage the property. Inheriting the property led to Herndon becoming something of a gentleman farmer, and not being proficient at it, he fell on hard times. With the many distractions, Herdon did not publish the book until 1889.

The following year, Nicolay and Hay published their biography, *Abraham Lincoln: A History.* Early in his presidency, Lincoln specifically granted his two personal secretaries permission to publish his official biography, so they were able to take notes, access and retain information during his time in the Executive Mansion, the years during which the Civil War took place. However, within the first two years after the events at Ford's Theatre, a Chicago-based U.S. representative named Isaac N. Arnold worked quickly to complete a biography of the 16th president, which he did in 1867. Following the publishing of that book, the public was evidently not in a hurry to purchase another biography. Accordingly, Nicolay and Hay took the time to thoroughly research and write a biography that ultimately would not be published until 25 years after Lincoln's death.

Two notes about Rep. Issac N. Arnold. First, although he published the first major biography of Lincoln, the consensus about that work is that it "suffered from not having sufficient research." Second, although Arnold's name is generally lost to history today, in 1864 he was the first congressman to propose a new constitutional amendment to prohibit slavery. The resulting amendment, the Thirteenth, was passed by the Senate in April 1864, by the House in January 1865, and was certified as ratified in December 1865.

I asked my passenger about his two trusted secretaries, both of whom came with him from Springfield to serve him in Washington, D.C. It was evident that he felt blessed to have both of them on his staff. During our discussion, we were coming from two different perspectives: Mine viewing the two men through the lens of history, knowing they had been gone for well over 100 years, and his from a perspective of the man who had hired them, brought them along to Washington during his presidency, who had seen them within the last 24 hours, and who he expected to see again in a few short days. I was also talking with a man whose thoughts were those of the leader of a great nation in the last days of the greatest internal conflict in its history.

"Nicolay and Hay," he began. "I was so fortunate to be associated with both of those young men. I hope that generations will know about their service to the nation. The victory to preserve the Union and our efforts to emancipate those who were held in slavery may not have happened if not for their work. It certainly would have been more difficult for me.

"They have two very different and distinct personalities," said my passenger. "Sometimes when Hay steps into my office, we joke about things including family and friends, or news of the day. I have to say that, particularly in the absence of our son Robert much of the time, Hay has probably been as close to a son as I could have without actually being of the same blood. Nicolay, on the other hand, seems like many people might expect, being descended from German aristocracy. Although he is very efficient and capable, he can be brusque and perhaps does not find much in common with the common citizen. And although I've tried to keep my pledge of restoring the seceded states to the Union, I resolved that once the conflict has ended, we would again be brothers and sisters. Nicolay definitely has a harsher attitude toward the South. I listen to his suggestions, of course, but as the elected leader of the republic, the final decisions will belong to me and the Congress.

"John Nicolay…born Johannes Nicolai in Bavaria," he continued, "moved to these United States with his family when he was six years old. John's father died when John was a teenager, and knowing that his mother was not able to properly care for John, he was adopted by neighbors, the Garbutts. Nicolay attended school in Cincinnati and then moved to Pittsfield, Illinois, about 70 miles west of Springfield and not far from the Mississippi River town of Hannibal. Well, John was very bright and capable, and it was there in Pittsfield that Nicolay became editor of the *Pike County Free Press*. That particular newspaper was among the first in the country to contain an editorial suggesting that the Republican Party might nominate me as their presidential candidate.

"Nicolay sold the Pittsfield newspaper in 1856 and became more and more involved in politics. It wasn't long before he was noticed by the right people in the state capital, and he was hired as an assistant to the secretary of state of Illinois. It was in that position that I first met Nicolay. We struck up a great friendship as well as a great professional relationship. When I was elected to the presidency, I appointed Nicolay as my private secretary, to come with me to Washington. He worked in a position in which I could place a great deal of trust in him. Shortly before my magical trip here to this time and place, I named Nicolay the United States Consul to Paris. As I came here, one of the things I needed to tend to was his transition into that position. When I return to my own time in Washington, that shall be one of my first areas of business."

I told Mr. Lincoln that I'd read about Nicolay and Hay, who both had the title of "private secretary" when they worked for Lincoln in the Executive Mansion, and asked if he could clarify the differences in their roles.

"John Hay was really the assistant to John Nicolay," replied my passenger. "I mentioned that Nicolay was very capable when he came to Washington with me at the very mild age of 29. Well, John Hay was only 23. But again, very capable, and very loyal.

"Hay was born in Salem, Indiana, and his family, which was very much opposed to slavery, moved to the Illinois town of Warsaw, not far from Pittsfield. And as chance would have it, Hay and Nicolay met and became friends when they were boys. Hay's family sent him to Brown University, from which he graduated at age 20.

"Hay did not initially support me politically until I was nominated by the Republican Party in 1860, at which time he got on board quickly and enthusiastically, writing letters and speeches and working hard for our cause.

"Following my election, Nicolay, who was then my only private secretary, recommended that I also hire Hay, primarily due to the large amount of correspondence that required responses. I was initially reluctant, telling Nicolay '*We can't take all of Illinois with us down to Washington!*' However, after pondering on the matter, I knew that he didn't make the recommendation lightly, and I yielded, saying '*Very well, let Hay come.*' Well, it didn't take long to realize that Nicolay was right, and their assistance to me and their country was immeasurable."

The ten-volume biography by Nicolay and Hay written following the White House years, *Abraham Lincoln, A History* remains one of the most authoritative biographies ever written about the 16th president, supported of course by the fact that they both knew him well for years. Although Lincoln himself authorized Nicolay and Hay to write the biography soon after moving to Washington, following the tragedy at Ford's Theatre the pair required permission from Robert Todd Lincoln to access a number of important records. Not surprisingly, the biography by Nicolay and Hay steers clear of some of the controversial topics that were addressed in William Herndon's version.

Nicolay and Hay both had other government positions after leaving the Executive Mansion, and their biography of Lincoln sat on the back burner for years. However, negative events of the 1870s and '80s came along, including the end of Reconstruction and the removal of federal authorities from the South, allowing local white authorities to keep suppressing the rights of African Americans. Other sources had begun telling a distorted picture of the 16th president.

In 1872, Hay told Nicolay and Robert Lincoln he thought that "we ought to be at work on *our* 'Lincoln,'" using official records and their first-hand experiences as references. "I don't think the time for publication has come," he added, "but the time for preparation is slipping away." Hay was the first to begin writing the biography, getting started in 1876. Work on writing was completed in 1885, and they were then submitted to Robert Lincoln for review and approval. Their 10-volume biography was initially published in serial format in *The Century Magazine* from 1886 to 1890, an then it was published in book form in 1890.

John Nicolay and John Hay both remained very active as writers and editors, working together again on the two-volume work *Complete Works of Abraham Lincoln*.

From 1872 to 1887, John Nicolay served as Marshal of the United States Supreme Court. He lived the rest of his life in Washington D.C., died in September 1901, and is buried in Oak Hill Cemetery in Springfield, not far from Abraham Lincoln. As an interesting footnote, a 1992 TV movie entitled *Lincoln* featured a number of prominent actors who provided voices of main characters. The series was narrated by James Earl Jones, with Jason Robards as Lincoln, Glenn Close as Mary Todd Lincoln, Burgess Meredith as Winfield Scott and Oprah Winfrey as Elizabeth Keckly. The voice of John Nicolay—who grew up in Cincinnati, Ohio—was provided by Arnold Schwarzenegger.

John Hay, the capable young man who graduated from Brown at age 20 and began working for President Lincoln at age 23, then had a career of nearly half a century in government. Following Lincoln's presidency, Hay served in several diplomatic positions and then for the *New York Tribune*. From 1879 to 1881, he served as assistant secretary of state. Hay then returned to the private sector until President William McKinley appointed him ambassador to the United Kingdom. Hay then served for seven years as U.S. secretary of state under presidents McKinley and Theodore Roosevelt. It was Hay who negotiated the Open Door Policy which called for keeping China open to all potential trading partners on an equal basis. In 1903, he negotiated with Colombia to establish the Hay–Bunau-Varilla Treaty, which established Panama as a Republic and gave the United States the authority to govern the Panama Canal Zone.

Historian Doris Kearns Goodwin wrote that by the middle of Lincoln's first term, Hay was, "Smart, energetic, and amusing," and that "the twenty-five-year-old Hay had become far more intimately connected to the president than his own eldest son. Their conversation moved easily from linguistics to reconstruction, from Shakespeare to Artemus Ward," the latter being a Maine humorist whose real name was Charles Farrar Browne, and who is credited as being America's first stand-up comedian.

As Mr. Lincoln and I continued to drive toward Springfield, I thought about April 14, 1865, and all those events I would not share with my passenger, who was very much alive. John Nicolay and John Hay, Lincoln's trusted secretaries and future biographers, were both preparing to move on to new jobs, driven mainly by worsening relationships with Mrs. Lincoln. John Nicolay was preparing to become the U.S. ambassador to France. That evening, John Hay sat in the Executive Mansion with Robert Lincoln, the two of them drinking whiskey in celebration of the pending end of the Civil War. It was there that they were informed that Robert's father had been shot. They rushed to Petersen's boarding house across from Ford's Theatre, where the president had been taken, and both remained there through the night.

Hay and Robert were both there when the president took his last breath, at which time John Hay observed "a look of unspeakable peace came upon his worn features." It was Hay who then recalled Secretary of War Edwin Stanton's solemn proclamation "Now he belongs to the ages."

Lincoln's death had a profound impact on all of his friends and staff, including Nicolay and Hay. Hay, who was still only 27 at the time of the death, felt "a personal sense of loss, like the loss of a father." In a personal letter that Hay wrote the following year, he called his former boss "the greatest character since Christ." In 2013, historian

John Taliaferro said that "Hay would spend the rest of his life mourning Lincoln... wherever Hay went and whatever he did, Lincoln would *always* be watching."

Despite Lincoln's initial half-hearted protestations about bringing Hay along to Washington, it became evident talking with my passenger that he had developed a warm relationship with both Nicolay and Hay, if not a sort of father-son relationship. And with his former law partner Herndon, for whom he still had great regard, he had a similar warm working relationship and perhaps more of an older brother-younger brother relationship.

Although the nature of their biographies was different—Herndon's with warts and all, Nicolay and Hay's with a more reverent tone—their relationships and their biographies continue to reflect, to this day, the respect they had for Abraham Lincoln.

One final note about Pittsfield, Illinois, the town in which John Nicolay and John Hay both lived before moving to Springfield. As the county seat of Pike County, Pittsfield was frequently visited by Abraham Lincoln during his days on the circuit court. He worked on 34 cases there between 1839 and 1852. Today, Pittsfield has the distinction of having the most buildings in the country that have a documented connection with Abraham Lincoln. In addition to the Pike County Courthouse, there are nine homes still in existence that have a connection to the 16th president. A number of documents that he signed at the courthouse have been stolen, and a number of people in Pike County know that they still exist. The general public is on alert to look for them in case they ever come up for sale or auction.

And one additional note about the relationship between Abraham and Mary Todd Lincoln, knowing that the president's relationship with William Herndon, John Nicolay, John Hay, and many others was affected by the First Lady. Friends who knew both Abraham and

Mary said that, despite occasional bickering between the two, they loved each other and were attracted to each other. However, the same organizations that periodically rank all of America's presidents and consistently rate Abraham Lincoln at or near the top also rate Mary Todd Lincoln at or near the bottom.

The District of Columbia: 1847-1849

"It could probably be shown by facts and figures that there is no distinctly native American criminal class except Congress."

-       Mark Twain

Photograph of the U.S. Capitol Building in 1846, much as it looked when Abraham Lincoln arrived the following year to serve his first term in Congress. Construction of the Capitol began on September 18, 1793, when President George Washington and eight other Freemasons laid the cornerstone. Photo courtesy Library of Congress.

Mr. Lincoln and I were having a great discussion, interspersed with times of quiet reflection. Although I could have asked enough questions to keep Mr. Lincoln talking non-stop, I sensed that he enjoyed periods of rest and quiet thought, during which he looked around to see the scenery as well as buildings that were taller than any he'd ever seen, many different types of vehicles, signs, power poles, and many other things that are common in 21st Century America that would have only been dreams in his day.

We couldn't have had a better day for the drive. When we woke up that morning (he in the Executive Mansion and me in Michigan), neither of us expected to drive from Kalamazoo to Springfield, but the weather remained great and the traffic was not heavy. The deep blue fall sky was interspersed with some billowy white clouds, with some darker gray clouds many miles away, but nothing that looked like there'd be rain.

We had passed most of the heavy traffic south of Chicago on I-94, I-80 and I-90. We ran into some heavier traffic from merging highways going past Joliet and were now heading southwest on I-55.

As we drove along, my mind was occupied with thoughts of what it must have been like for him to be a prairie lawyer one day, and a few months later to be the president of the United States, as well as the leader of a nation that most people expected to be at war with itself in the near future.

I've visited Washington, D.C. about ten times, either with my family or for work-related conferences and meetings, and the feeling of grandeur, magnificence, and history that strikes me in that city is almost overwhelming. Flying or driving into the city, to first see the Washington Monument in the distance, then the Capitol Building, then the Lincoln Memorial, Jefferson Memorial, and other structures is, to me, beyond a meaningful description. And the new monuments and structures have only added to the city's magnificence. In addition to the aforementioned structures and the White House, I grew up thinking that our nation's capital was a fairly static place with few changes of note. But the Pentagon, the largest office building in the world, was built during my parents' lives at the height of World War II. With its ground breaking taking place on September 11, 1941—sixty years to the day before American

Airlines Flight 77 was flown into its west side by an al-Qaeda terrorist hijacker—the 6.5 million square foot building was completed in just 16 months in anticipation of a major conflict. And during my time, the FDR Memorial, MLK Memorial, World War II Memorial, and memorials to those who sacrificed in Korea and Vietnam were all built and have changed the city greatly. Along with the National Museum of African American History and Culture, which was dedicated in 2016, many have wondered why it took so long to build those structures that honor those who did so much to make America great.

I asked Mr. Lincoln about his time in Washington. He began by talking about his first years spent there, in the U.S. House of Representatives. The 30th Congress, which met from March 1847 to March 1849, seemed to be an unusually active period for our federal legislators.

"Before I was elected president," he said, "two years in Congress comprised my only government service at the federal level. That was in addition to eight years that I served in the Illinois House. Over my political career, I lost two elections for state house and two elections for U.S. Senate. I also lost the nomination for the vice presidency in 1856, though that nomination was an unexpected occurrence, and didn't involve any campaigning. Believe me, I remember the losses every bit as much as the victories, and more.

"The period of Eighteen Hundred Forty-Seven through Eighteen Hundred Forty-Nine coincided with the last two years of the Polk administration," said my passenger. "We had a Whig majority in the House of Representatives, but the Democrats held a majority in the Senate. The Speaker of the House, from our party, was Robert Winthrop from Massachusetts.

"I do, in fact, agree that the two-year period was one of great change, and perhaps nothing reflects those changes more than our friend and colleague during that time, John Quincy Adams," said Mr. Lincoln.

"I forgot that John Quincy Adams was in Congress," I replied.

"Yes, indeed he was," he responded enthusiastically, "and of course, his time in Congress was unusual in that he served in the House of Representatives for nearly 17 years after having already served as the sixth president of the United States.

"Over his time in politics," continued Mr. Lincoln, "President Adams was a member of five different political parties, starting with Alexander Hamilton's Federalist Party in 1792, then Jefferson and Madison's Democratic-Republican Party, then the National Republican Party, which is not to be confused with today's Republican Party, but was an anti-Jacksonian party that Adams himself led when he ran for president in 1824. Then he was a member of the Anti-Masonic Party, and finally a fellow Whig.

"Adams' education and abilities were most impressive," said Mr. Lincoln, with no reluctance to mention it due to his own modest formal education. "He attended school in France and the Netherlands, and spoke several languages to some degree including French, Dutch, German, Italian, Russian, and classical Greek. By the way, our eighth president, President Martin Van Buren, did not speak English as his first language. He was born in the Dutch town of Kinderhook, New York, and spoke Dutch at home for most of his life. He learned English in school.

"But above all," said Mr. Lincoln, returning to a discussion about John Quincy, "Adams was vehemently opposed to the expansion of slavery, and all that would accommodate that expansion, including the addition of Texas to the Union." Adams opposed the Mexican

War but supported the use of federal funds for building roads and other infrastructure when they were for the common good.

"After Adams lost the presidential election to Andrew Jackson in 1828," he explained, "he thought his days in public life were over. The following year, his son, George Washington Adams, took his own life during a voyage from Boston to Washington, D.C. George was very bright and had himself been elected to the Massachusetts House of Representatives, but his problems with alcohol caused his outlook to become dark. George's death served as confirmation to me that the problems of using alcohol can easily outweigh any benefits. But John Quincy had become increasingly upset at actions of the Jackson administration, and decided that his service could still have meaning. He won election to the House in 1830 and continued to be reelected through 1848."

Mr. Lincoln described how John Quincy Adams served in the House through the Jackson, Van Buren, Harrison, Tyler, and Polk administrations—five administrations—with an emphasis on opposing the expansion of slavery, *after he had already served as president, U.S. senator and U.S. secretary of state.* On February 21, 1848, the House of Representatives was discussing how it might honor returning U.S. Army officers who had served in the Mexican-American War, which had ended 18 days earlier, and of which Adams had remained a vocal opponent. When the vote took place, nearly all members of the House rose up to say "Aye," Adams rose up and yelled "No!" Seconds later, Adams collapsed with what turned out to be a cerebral hemorrhage. He was moved to the chambers of Speaker Winthrop, and he died there two days later. Among those present at the deathbed of John Quincy Adams was the freshman representative from Illinois, Abraham Lincoln.

The U.S. Capitol Building where Lincoln worked for those two years was very much under construction during that time—as it had been since September 1793, when nine local Freemasons, among them George Washington, laid the cornerstone for the building. When Abraham Lincoln took his first presidential oath in March 1861, the 8.9-million-pound cast iron dome had not yet been placed atop the Rotunda; it wouldn't be placed there until 1865.

"Questions regarding that terrible institution of slavery became much more common by the time we arrived," said Mr. Lincoln, mindful of the fact that the Founders had approved the U.S. Constitution even with its clauses allowing slavery. Even in his own life, Mr. Lincoln's view had changed from one that regarded the banning of slavery as unconstitutional to an institution that was evil and would tear the Union apart. "Before and during my time in Congress, many countries that had allowed slavery abolished it. Great Britain, France and Greece had banned it years before. During my first year in Congress, the Ottoman Empire and several countries in Africa abolished the practice. The number of people around the world who realized that the practice was wrong was increasing, as it was in the United States. And yet a dozen more years lapsed—when I was elected to go to Washington again, this time as president—before any real meaningful benefits came to Black Americans.

"And of course," Mr. Lincoln continued, "only 18 months after I left Congress, in September 1850, the Compromise of 1850 was passed by Congress, which had the net effect of extending the duration of slavery. Rather than face the issue head-on, and to ease tension between the regions, Congress passed five separate but related laws that were intended to ease such tensions.

"The most notable of the five was Fugitive Slave Act," he said, "which required that people who had escaped from the bonds of slavery would have to be returned to their so-called 'owners' even if they were captured in a free state. After that law was passed, good people in Michigan played a big role in helping people travel to Canada, from which they couldn't be returned.

"To offset the first act," he explained, "Congress passed two other acts: It admitted California to the Union as a free state, and banned the trade of enslaved people in Washington, D.C. Note that the bill did not ban the practice of slavery itself, it just kept people from being bought and sold there. Imagine. Human beings being bought and sold.

"The remaining two acts unquestionably were favored by the Southern states and those who supported slavery. The first defined the northern and western borders of Texas, which had become a state a few years earlier; that act also established the Territory of New Mexico. The second act established the Territory of Utah. However, neither of those two acts specified whether Texas, New Mexico, or Utah would allow slavery. To me, it was like...I don't know if today you have an analogy for it, but for us it was like walking down the road and kicking a rock ahead of you to get it out of the way, only to have to kick it again because you never dealt with the actual problem."

"Oh, we've become much more advanced in our modern world, Mr. President," I joked. "We began to use cans. When we don't deal with a problem at the beginning but rather leave it to ourselves, or our children or grandchildren to deal with that problem, we say 'it's like kicking a can down the road.'"

"A can?" he responded, smiling in kind. "That actually makes more sense. A can implies that you're procrastinating when it comes to something of value, not just a rock. I like it. I may use that expression the next time," he concluded, with a little chuckle.

"Careful," I mock-cautioned. "If you use that expression when you get back, it may be like a stone causing a ripple in a pond and change the world."

He laughed at that, adding, "Well, you're right. I certainly wouldn't want to do that. I do, however, like your last analogy as well, about the stone causing the ripples in the pond. I expect I'll be using that analogy in a big future speech," he deadpanned. "The future be damned!" we both laughed at that one.

"When I return to my place and time," Mr. Lincoln began again, "the first item of action will be in healing the Union. I very much look forward to working with old friends to do that. When I served in Congress, I had a very good working relationship with Alexander Stephens of Georgia. When I became president, of course, he became vice president of the so-called Confederate states. To be sure, he and I saw the issue of slavery very differently. The fact that Georgia and some of the other Southern states were much more agricultural than the Northern states makes it more understandable that he would support the institution of slavery. Understandable, but not justifiable. He came from generations who thought it was acceptable to have free labor to do the work. But somewhere, sometime, one needs to have the strength and integrity to break that chain of poor decisions. Stephens and I saw eye-to-eye on many things. We were both strongly against the Mexican War. We were both pro-Union, in fact, he opposed the secession of Georgia right up to the time the state's legislature voted to withdraw from the Union. Like me, he was a Whig. And like me, he spent much of his early life farming. He's a very smart man; I've never heard anyone question his intellect. But that one divisive issue of slavery has always been between us. Now that the law will be on our side, I trust that I can make him, and other friends like him, see the benefits of putting an end to slavery once and for all.

"Regarding California, one very important thing happened in January of Eighteen Hundred and Forty-Eight," he went on. "More than two years before California became a state, a construction worker named James Marshall discovered gold while building a sawmill for the property owner, John Sutter. Well of course, we had known for years about the wonderful climate in that part of the country and the abundant vegetables and other crops that could be grown, but finding gold led to more than 300,000 people moving to that state in a seven-year period, from 1848 to 1855. That's roughly the total population of Pennsylvania at our nation's founding, some 72 years earlier."

I knew that there was a lot of money to be made after the gold rush. Many of those who traveled to the Golden State, of course, went to make claims for gold. Many made money growing or cooking food for the prospectors. A 25-year-old German-born wholesale dry goods businessman named Levi Strauss traveled to his family's San Francisco outlet in 1854 during the rush, where he later formed a business partnership with Jacob W. Davis, who had developed riveted denim pants that were extremely long-wearing. Levi jeans became one of the most ubiquitous clothing items in the world.

Early in the gold rush, while brothers Henry and Clem Studebaker owned and managed a blacksmith shop in Gettysburg, Pennsylvania, their younger brother John traveled to Placerville, California seeking riches. He soon realized that claims were nearly tapped out, but that prospectors and others needed a way to move their gold, tools, and other equipment. So he started building and selling wheelbarrows, making a small fortune and earning the name "Wheelbarrow Johnny." In 1852, Henry and Clem moved their blacksmith shop to South Bend, Indiana, and John rejoined them there, funded largely by John's wheelbarrow proceeds. In 1857 (the year after Lincoln spoke in Kalamazoo), the brothers began making wagons and carriages, and the same year landed a contract to supply the U.S.

Army with supply wagons. Many of those wagons were used by the Union Army during the Civil War, and by 1865, Studebaker had supplied the Army with over 5,000 wagons as well as supplying President Lincoln with carriages (including the one he and Mary used to ride to Ford's Theatre). Future presidents Ulysses S. Grant, Rutherford B. Hayes, and Benjamin Harrison also rode in Studebaker carriages. In 1902, the company began making automobiles. Their first vehicles, from 1902 to 1911, were electric, and they also began making gasoline-powered automobiles late in that period. In 1952, Studebaker became the first American automobile company to celebrate its 100th anniversary. However, by the late 1950s, the company was doing poorly financially and it manufactured its last vehicle, a Studebaker Cruiser four-door sedan, in 1966.

In yet another connection, Abraham Lincoln's mother, Nancy Hanks Lincoln, was buried in a small cemetery near her home in Spencer County, Indiana. By the 1870s, her gravestone had fallen into disrepair, and the current stone marker was purchased by Peter Everst Studebaker, who served as treasurer and chairman of his brothers' wagon business.

As we continued driving southwest on I-55, Mr. Lincoln continued to share with me the accomplishments of the 30th Congress, of which he was a member between March 1847 and March 1849.

"In July 1847, the United States issued its first postage stamps," he explained, "following the passage of the Postage Stamp Act in March. To people during the Civil War days, using postage stamps seemed like a natural thing, the only way that mailing a letter could be done. But before 1847, the recipient of the letter would usually pay the postman directly. In 1855, postage stamps on U.S. mail became mandatory."

That method of paying for postage certainly wouldn't have worked well a few years later, during the Civil War; it would have required soldiers to pay postage for letters from their families and sweethearts. Interestingly, though, most letters delivered between soldiers and their families during the Civil War were delivered within 10 days, even to and from men in battle. However, mail *between* states in the North and those in the South were banned by both sides.

On February 2, 1848, Mexico and the United States signed the Treaty of Guadalupe Hidalgo, ending the Mexican-American War and ceding 55 percent of Mexican territory to the United States, including California, Nevada, Utah, and most of New Mexico, Colorado, and Arizona, and a small portion of Utah. Mexico also ended any claims it had to Texas. Essentially, the southwestern quarter of the United States that had belonged to Mexico belonged to the United States after that treaty.

"As I alluded to earlier," Mr. Lincoln continued, "there was much opposition to the war, largely along partisan political lines. The Whig Party, of which I was a member at the time, tended to be opposed to the war, while Mr. Polk and the Democrats tended to support it. Part of that had to do with the spread of slavery."

Although opposition to the Mexican-American War was widespread, many of the members of the military who felt obligated to follow orders fought in the conflict. Those who participated included future leaders Winfield Scott, Zachary Taylor, Franklin Pierce, Commodore Matthew C. Perry, future presidential candidate and California governor John C. Frémont, future Confederate president Jefferson Davis, and future Civil War generals Robert E. Lee and Ulysses S. Grant.

"Wisconsin became the 30th state during my time in Congress," said Mr. Lincoln, "and the Oregon and Minnesota territories were established. Congress also approved the building of the Washington Monument."

About halfway between Joliet and Springfield, traffic slowed way down for construction, as several signs going back a few miles cautioned. I was used to driving through construction zones from the last few years in Michigan where so many roads, highways and bridges had been repaired, and I knew we'd be driving between 20 and 30 miles per hour for a little while. Those huge black-and-white barricades, round black burning smudge pots and flares of my youth had been replaced by orange plastic barrels and cones over the last 25 years, and the sunshine made the orange look like it was almost glowing, and in places matched the orange of the fall leaves.

Traffic that had been so spread out slowed to half speed condensed in less than a minute. Unfortunately, even though the traffic had been light, we had the poor fortune of having the last vehicle in back of us be a big semi-truck with a bright red-orange cab, which was now no more than five feet from our rear bumper. Definitely not enough room to stop if I had to slam on the brakes, and I just hoped that he would back off a bit. Behind the semi was a silver Honda CR-V, and behind that a big black SUV; I would have preferred to have one of those directly behind us, but when you're on the highway, you take what you can get. I couldn't see the end of the construction zone, but the signs said the zone was three miles long, so we wouldn't be in the construction zone for much time.

I knew that my passenger was used to seeing the construction of new and big things, and he seemed interested in just watching for a while, so I turned my car radio volume up slightly. I turned on the '40s Channel, which didn't play the music of my passenger's day, but I thought it might be more tolerable for him than AC/DC, Hendrix, or even the Beatles or Moody Blues. I think it's fair to say the look on his face was one of amusement more than anything else, but I did notice his fingers tapping to Duke Ellington and Glenn Miller.

The District of Columbia: 1861-1865

The U.S. Capitol on March 4, 1861, the day Abraham Lincoln became president. Crowds gather on the Capitol grounds and steps and soldiers guard the building. The dome was completed in 1866, the year after the Civil War ended. Photo courtesy Library of Congress.

During the 1790s, the District of Columbia was drawn up as a big diamond, 10 miles long on each side, from land donated by Maryland and Virginia. However, prior to the creation of the District—during the American Revolution and its aftermath—our nation's capital was moved several times. It was located in Philadelphia (five different times!), York, Pennsylvania; Princeton, New Jersey; Annapolis, Maryland; Trenton, New Jersey, and New York City.

But during the Civil War, Washington, D.C. remained our nation's capital. It has always fascinated me what the city would have been like during those years.

The city had grown and developed a lot during the mere dozen years that Mr. Lincoln had been absent. When he was there as part of the 30th Congress, the city had a population of 50,000. When he returned on February 23, 1861—twelve days after leaving Springfield and nine days before being sworn in as 16th president—the population had grown 61 percent, to more than 80,000 people, a little larger than the population of Kalamazoo during the 2020 census. (In the decade during which the Civil War took place, 1860-1870, the population would double to 131,000.) Part of the increase during both the 1860 and 1870 censuses was due to the expansion of the federal government during the war, the additional protection that had been brought in to defend the nation's capital, and an influx of people who were formerly enslaved. In a very real sense, between Lincoln's term in Congress and the end of Reconstruction in 1876, our nation's capital went from being a small town to a world capital with substantial infrastructure.

During that same 12-year period, the population of the United States increased about 70 percent, from about 22.5 million to 38.5 million. The population of Michigan increased from about 358,000 to 793,000, an increase of 121%. That increase seems huge by today's standards, but it's paltry compared to the decade of 1830-1840, the decade that Michigan became a state, when the population increased by 658%. (Except for the decade of the 1930s, Michigan experienced at least double-digit population growth every decade until 1970.

For the states in the South, the election of Republican Abraham Lincoln on November 6, 1860 was a source of outrage, and the beginning of their secession followed soon thereafter. By the time Lincoln arrived in the nation's capital, seven states had already

220

seceded (South Carolina, Mississippi, Florida, Alabama, Georgia, Louisiana, and Texas). Starting about five weeks after his inauguration, four more (Virginia, Arkansas, North Carolina, and Tennessee), followed, with the last of those, Tennessee, leaving the Union on June 8, 1861, making the group of 11 Confederate states complete. In addition, pro-Confederate governments in Missouri and Kentucky declared secession, but those governmental divorces could not be consummated because of pro-Union citizens there.

Ironically, exactly one month after Lincoln's inauguration, the legislature of the most populous Southern state at the time, Virginia, voted *against* secession. However, following the Battle of Fort Sumter one week later and President Lincoln calling for volunteers from all states to help put down the rebellion three days after Sumter, the Virginia legislature voted to secede.

Two years later, the far more pro-Union and more mountainous northwest Virginia split off from the rest of the state to form our 35th state, West Virginia. It became a key border state during the war.

As soon as Abraham Lincoln was elected president on November 6, 1860, he began to dread the job ahead in our nation's capital, including the added security risk posed by his position on abolition. He didn't always listen to the experts when it came to his physical security, but law enforcement authorities did keep him informed of plots and potential plots they knew about. The conspiracy by John Wilkes Booth and his cohorts was at least the sixth such plot. The first serious plot following his election, the so-called Baltimore Plot, had the potential of ending his presidency before it even began, so Lincoln cooperated with Allan Pinkerton and his national detective agency on his journey from Springfield to Washington, D.C.

Pinkerton had become involved in protecting the president-elect almost by happenstance. Just prior to Lincoln's trip from Springfield to Washington, D.C., Pinkerton's company was hired by Samuel H. Felton, president of the Philadelphia, Wilmington & Baltimore Railroad, to investigate threats to his company's equipment by secessionists. Pinkerton himself was able to ingratiate himself into a group of his conspirators, and although he personally heard viable threats to Lincoln's life, evidence was primarily gathered by one of Pinkerton's most trusted agents, a 28-year-old woman named Kate Warne. Five years earlier, Warne had persuaded Pinkerton to hire her because she felt women "had an eye for detail and were excellent observers." Warne uncovered not only the plan to kill Lincoln, but for secessionists to blow up bridges, cut telegraph cables and damage rail lines in the Washington, D.C. area, and for troops to surround and capture the nation's capital. At first, Lincoln did not take rumors of plots against him seriously, but Pinkerton and Warne were able to provide credible evidence to him.

Lincoln's train was re-routed several times, including the last leg which ended in Baltimore instead of Washington, D.C. as publicly announced. Warne was present during the entire last leg of the trip and personally provided Lincoln with a disguise. Lincoln was then taken under cover of darkness to the District of Columbia, where he was inaugurated nine days later.

Allan Pinkerton, police, and other law enforcement agencies were used to protect the president because no federal agency had been assigned to do so. In one of those strange twists of American history of things that couldn't possibly happen—but did—the United States Secret Service was authorized on April 14, 1865 by President Lincoln, just a few hours before he and Mary Todd Lincoln left for Ford's Theatre. The original purpose of the agency was to combat counterfeiting of currency at a time when an estimated one-third of U.S. currency was counterfeit. Two years later, the agency's scope expanded to include investigations of the Ku Klux Klan, smugglers, and illegal alcohol distillers. In 1901, following the deaths of presidents Abraham Lincoln, James A. Garfield, and William McKinley over a 36-year span, Congress requested that the Secret Service protect the president. It wasn't until shortly after the attempted assassination of President Harry Truman in November 1950 by two Puerto Rican pro-independence activists that Congress permanently charged the Secret Service with protecting the president, the vice president, and their families. In 1968, following the assassination of Sen. Robert F. Kennedy, Congress also authorized the protection of major presidential and vice-presidential candidates and nominees.

In addition to the assassination plots against Lincoln, a separate plot was uncovered which involved insurrection, taking over the U.S. government and installing the outgoing vice president, John C. Breckinridge, as president. Among those warning Lincoln of the plot—a "widespread and intricate conspiracy"—was none other than his political rival and fellow Springfield attorney, Stephen A. Douglas, who had defeated Lincoln for U.S. Senate in 1858, and who Lincoln defeated for the presidency in 1860. It's quite possible that advanced knowledge of the plot kept the insurrection from taking place.

As mentioned, the enormous U.S. Capitol dome had not yet been installed when Abraham Lincoln first took the oath of office on its steps, and many other expansions and improvements were taking place to the U.S. Capitol Building. Photographs taken that day show the framework of a large tower protruding high above the unfinished

Rotunda, and scaffolding outside the Rotunda and other parts of the building.

President Lincoln was sworn into office on the steps of the building by Roger B. Taney, the U.S. Supreme Court chief justice whose 28-year tenure as chief justice of the court was tarnished irreparably by the Dred Scott decision, which ruled that African Americans could not be considered U.S. citizens and that Congress could not prohibit the expansion of slavery. Taney, whose own family held people in slavery in Maryland, delivered the ruling, which is still rated by constitutional scholars as being one of the worst (if not *the* worst) ever issued by the high court. Taney tried to be a burr under President Lincoln's saddle during Lincoln's administration, but the former prairie lawyer from Illinois more than held his own against Taney.

One of Lincoln's first acts as president was to order construction of the Capitol Building to continue. Lincoln felt that it was more important than ever for the Congress representing the growing nation to have sufficient space to conduct its business; in addition, Lincoln felt that construction on the Capitol Building would demonstrate to the North and South alike that the Union would continue to conduct its business as usual despite the looming war.

The Washington Monument, which had been approved by Lincoln and the rest of the 30th Congress 13 years earlier, would have to wait to be completed, but that delay had already begun. Construction on the monument, which had started almost immediately after it was established by Congress in 1848 (on the 4th of July, not by coincidence), was suspended for a 23-year period from 1854 to 1877 due to funding issues, as well as a power struggle within the monument's management, and lastly because of the war. Visitors to the monument today can see the differences in shading of the marble at a point about 150 feet up on the 555-foot monument. Construction resumed in 1877 and was completed in 1884, at which time it became the tallest human-made structure in the world.

Before the Washington Monument was completed, the tallest human-made structure in the world was the Lincoln Cathedral (really…you can't make this stuff up) in Lincolnshire, England. Completed in 1311, the Lincoln Cathedral (also called the Cathedral Church of the Blessed Virgin Mary of Lincoln) held the record for tallest human-made structure for 573 years. The Washington Monument's record, however, wouldn't last so long. Just five years later, in 1889, Gustave Eiffel's 984-foot tower was completed and would become the centerpiece of that year's Paris World's Fair. It remains a world landmark. (But don't feel bad, Washington Monument! The Chrysler Building in New York City, which surpassed the Eiffel Tower as the world's tallest human-made structure in 1930, held the record for just 11 months, when it was surpassed by the Empire State Building, a little more than half a mile away. But the Washington Monument and Chrysler Building can both find comfort in the fact that they remain among the most beautiful structures ever built by our species).

When President Lincoln took office, very few people, the president included, had any idea that the war would be so bad or so long. Although Union defenses were built up around the city, their number wasn't nearly sufficient to defend it against forces of the Southern states.

The first major battle of the war, the First Battle of Bull Run (called the "Battle of First Manassas" by the Confederates) was fought on July 21, 1861, just over three months after President Lincoln's inauguration. The battle took place only 30 miles west-southwest from the capital, with both sides having roughly 18,000 new and poorly-trained troops.

The battle was a major loss for the Union, and Lincoln's retreated troops were said to have wandered the streets of Washington, which caused him to increase the city's defenses. He also ordered the construction of additional forts and military hospitals. As a result of those actions, the nation's capital was untouched by Confederate troops during the entire war.

Because of the war, and Lincoln himself, the Washington, D.C. that Abraham Lincoln arrived in in 1861 was much different from the one he left in 1849.

ButterBurgers® and Olive Burgers

The drive from Kalamazoo to Springfield had gone well so far, but the construction zone outside Peoria, another construction area north of Bloomington, and some heavier truck traffic over the last hour had added a little more than an hour to our drive. Whenever I drive longer distances, I've developed three rules: first, when in doubt about whether or not to stop to use a rest room, stop and use the rest room. Otherwise, as soon as I pass one, my need to use one increases. Second, get my wallet out of my back pocket and move it to a front pocket. Sitting unevenly on a wallet can cause back pain and leg fatigue while driving. And third, similar to the first rule above and all other things being equal, eat sooner than later. I wasn't really hungry yet, but like a good marathon runner who starts drinking water before he or she gets thirsty, eating early can keep one from getting overly hungry. In addition, traffic had lightened up over the last few miles, and because it was well before the regular dinner hour, I thought we could go into a restaurant and sit down without a full dining room having the chance to get a good look at my passenger.

I explained the situation to my passenger, who agreed that he wouldn't mind eating a little earlier, nor mind avoiding curious eyes. And since crossing from the Eastern to Central time zones when we passed into Indiana, our stomachs were actually an hour ahead of us.

"I have an idea for dinner," I told my passenger. "There's a chain of restaurants throughout the Midwestern states called Culver's. They make great hamburgers. Have you ever had a hamburger?" I asked, not remembering whether the ubiquitous American sandwich was around in the mid-1860s.

"I think so. I've heard of *hamburgs*," he replied. "Perhaps they're the same thing? I've heard people talk of them. The Hamburg ship line served them to passengers…a piece of cooked steak between slices of bread?"

"It's usually a variation of that today," I said, "but it's the same basic thing. The beef is ground and formed into a patty before it's cooked, and they use special bread that are called hamburger buns. They're pretty good."

"It sounds very good," he said. "We didn't have beef very often when I grew up, but we sometimes now have it in the Executive Mansion. I like mine cooked for a long time, even charred on the outside." I thought that perhaps in the mid-19th Century, it would be a good idea to cook any meats longer than we might today, from a perspective of potential bacteria as well as flavor.

"Me too," I said. "Well done. It makes the beef taste completely different. And today, you can get any number of ingredients put on it. Catsup, mustard, mayonnaise, cheese, onions, lettuce, steak sauce, mushrooms, and on and on.

"I love olive burgers," I continued. "It's a hamburger with a mayonnaise sauce, and sliced or chopped green olives. They're delicious. We used to have a drive-in restaurant near our house in Portage. A drive-in restaurant is one where you pull up in your car, and place your order and eat right in your car. And at the restaurant we used to go to, West Lake Drive-In, you could look out over the lake while eating and talking with your family or friends in the car. Well, that restaurant no longer exists, but I love burgers at Culver's restaurants. Their best-known burger is called the ButterBurger. It's named that because they actually butter the bun before they toast it.

"But…" I continued, "you can't get olive burgers at the Culver's restaurants in Illinois. Or most other states. It's a Michigan thing.

We can order them at our Michigan Culver's restaurants, even though they're not usually listed on the menu, and they know exactly how to make 'em. But in Illinois, Wisconsin, and other states, they don't know what you mean. In Michigan's state capital of Lansing, they had an olive burger festival last June to celebrate olive burgers, which are difficult to find outside of Michigan. Whether or not they were created in Michigan, they became very popular there. So…while we're here in Illinois, we'll have ButterBurgers…which are also delicious."

"Well, when I return to the Executive Mansion," said Mr. Lincoln, "I'll be careful about anything that might change history. But I just might ask our cook to make a hamburg with olives on it."

"You won't be sorry," I assured him.

We were still about 40 minutes north of Springfield, but we were coming up on the little town of… Lincoln, Illinois. When we began to see highway signs pointing out how far ahead it was, my passenger smiled knowingly.

"I practiced law in this little place occasionally from 1847 to 1859," explained my passenger. "When it first became a city, in 1853, a small group of townspeople led by an industrious man named Virgil Hickox named it, and they happened to name it in my honor. Mr. Hickox and others knew me from my days as a lawyer working for the Chicago and Mississippi Railroad Company." The city of Lincoln, which today has a population of 13,288, was located on Route 66 during that highway's heyday. Among the people who once lived there are writer Langston Hughes and theologians Reinhold and H. Richard Niebuhr.

I steered onto the offramp closest to the Culver's. My thinking that the traffic would be relatively light was correct, and we pulled into the Culver's. I had thought about going through the drive-through, but on a five-hour drive I like to get out of the car once in a while and sit in a real seat.

I again checked that my guest was wearing his baseball cap and sunglasses, and we got out, locked the car doors, and went into Culver's. As I've come to expect from Culver's, a young lady behind the counter greeted us as soon as we stepped through the door. She continued to smile but her eyes remained on my guest for what I thought was an extra-long time. However, we came armed with our explanation that we were "researching a movie."

When she asked what we'd like, just for the heck of it I tried to order an olive burger. After a few seconds of silence during which I received a "you must be from out-of-state" look from the young lady, I ordered the combo of a ButterBurger with cheese, a medium order of fries and a drink. I then told the young lady that I'd also be paying for my friend's order. I watched her face as he ordered the same thing as me. I had no doubt: She thought he looked familiar to her. After paying and getting the blue, triangular order marker for our table, we walked into the dining area and had a seat near a row of windows.

After sitting for several minutes, another Culver's "team member" brought a tray with our meals and took the blue marker.

I unwrapped my ButterBurger but didn't take a bite until my guest took one, and I watched his face for his reaction. It was worth waiting for. After it was in his mouth for a few seconds, he stopped chewing altogether and closed his eyes. He then verified its flavor by telling me it was delicious. The corn cakes we'd had earlier in the day were for sustenance, though he seemed to like them. The ButterBurger seemed to give him a new taste sensation. It's always good to introduce a friend to something new that they like a lot.

Nobody was sitting close to us, so we continued to talk about the people he knew, and he also asked about my own wife, kids, and friends. He asked what Molly and the kids were like, what they did, and what they liked to do. But again, we didn't talk continuously. I was guessing that he was thinking about the city of Lincoln that we were in, as well as his hometown of Springfield, where we'd be in less than an hour of leaving Culver's.

With our unusual circumstances involving time and location, my mind was working in multiple streams. While we continued to sit and enjoy our meals, I used my iPhone to make hotel reservations for that night in Springfield. And of course, my thoughts occasionally went back to the fact that my guest was every bit the same Abraham Lincoln we'd heard about in history class, read dozens of books about, and seen documentaries such as *Ken Burns' The Civil War*—I had no doubt that this was the same person—except, of course, that I knew that something, somehow, had changed on that Good Friday of 1865 that allowed him to see the end of the play, and then allowed him to be here at my table at Culver's.

I thought about shows and stories that dealt with time travel, particularly those that were based on real theories of reputable scientists. Was the man at my table the exact Abraham Lincoln up to some point on that day of the visit to Ford's Theatre, or was he an exact copy? Might there be an infinite number of Albert Freys in multiple universes?

I tended to think that reality was closer to the former, that this was the very Abraham Lincoln who had ridden around our nation's capital with his wife on April 14, 1865, signed the Secret Service Act into law that same day, taken the 10-minute ride to Ford's Theatre with Mary Todd Lincoln in the Studebaker carriage, and entered the theatre, taking his place in the Presidential Box behind the American flag bunting that was draped over the front of the box.

Then I began to think about a man named Kurt Gödel and his theory of how a rotating universe could allow time travel.

Kurt Gödel was born in the Austro-Hungarian Empire in 1906 in a region that is now part of the Czech Republic. He possessed a rare combination of skills as a logician, mathematician, and philosopher that resulted in him developing theories that left other brilliant physicists and scientists of the day pondering his thoughts. He studied with the best professors and the greatest minds in Europe until March 1938, when Nazi Germany annexed his homeland of Austria. Soon thereafter, Gödel and his wife, Adele, left Vienna for Princeton, where he accepted a position at the Institute for Advanced Study, where his work frequently brought him into discussions with others at the school, including Albert Einstein and J. Robert Oppenheimer.

Gödel's theory, which he developed to help explain questions about Einstein's general theory of relativity, was that if the universe itself is in motion and if it rotates like most solar systems and galaxies, then setting a particular path across the universe can result in the traveler going back into his or her own past. In theory, an alternate diversion might result in the traveler taking another path and returning to another time in the past. Gödel's colleagues generally reacted to his theory with skepticism. Gödel himself did not say he was sure the theory was correct; he merely offered it as a means to explain parts of Einstein's theory that didn't seem clear.

I was about halfway through my burger when I noticed a particular man sitting at the opposite end of the dining area, about 30 feet behind Mr. Lincoln. There wasn't really anything unusual about the man physically; the only reason I noticed him was that every time I happened to look at him, his eyes went from my guest and me and then quickly darted away. In my young adulthood and bachelor days, that sometimes happened with females I saw—by accident, of course—but this was the first time it happened under such different circumstances. It seemed likely that the reason for his glances was that the guy sitting at my table had more than a passing resemblance to a local favorite son, Abraham Lincoln.

The man looked a lot like Christopher Walken in his early-40s, except with very dark eyes. He had very short hair, almost a buzz-cut, dark brown and just starting to turn gray at the temples. It looked like he hadn't shaved in two or three days. But he wasn't threatening and I didn't have any reason to worry about him. If he thought my guest was, in fact, that local favorite son, my guest and I would initiate our "preparing for a movie" scenario. Also, if he thought the guy sitting at my table in the 21st Century was really Abraham Lincoln, he'd have to be pretty peculiar. Right?

The man was wearing a sport shirt with a brown cloth jacket over it, and blue jeans. The only thing on his table in front of him was a large drink, which he seemed to be nursing slowly. I noticed all of this in my quick glances. (Was he also thinking that *I was staring at him* but glancing away when he looked over?)

After Mr. Lincoln and I finished our ButterBurgers and fries, we continued sipping our drinks while we engaged in some talk about things he observed. We looked at cars going through the parking lot and I described different aspects of them: SUVs, vans, trucks, sedans, convertibles, and a couple motorcycles. Not surprisingly, he was very observant, and retained and understood my simplistic explanations of design and technology. On the drive from Kalamazoo, he had already noticed the name on the rear of several vehicles: LINCOLN. I told him that it was named after him because of his role in emancipation and preserving the Union, which was a true statement. I still hadn't discussed the events of the evening of April 14, 1865, the ones you and I learned about in school.

After we finished our drinks, I took one more glance at the wannabe Walken. One more time, we diverted our glances from each other.

My guest and I prepared to leave, putting our jackets back on. I used the rest room and I met him just inside the door leading to the parking lot.

As we stepped back out into the cool, crisp autumn air and walked to the car, I confirmed to my passenger that we'd be at our hotel in Springfield in about 40 minutes.

"That's wonderful. I'm so looking forward to it. Thank you again for your hospitality. This obviously isn't anything that either of us had planned to do, but I'm enjoying our discussions very much."

I told him that it was no problem, and that I was enjoying his company, as well, something I'm sure he'd have known even if I wouldn't have told him. Among our 16th president's greatest abilities was his emotional intelligence. He could read people so well, and then react accordingly.

As we were about 20 feet away from my car and I grabbed my key fob to unlock the doors, my guest offhandedly said, "You were telling me about the larger SUVs and some of their features. Those big Chevy SUVs with the long antennas must be very popular for some reason."

For a second, I thought he was making a general observation, but as I looked at him, he was pointing to the rear parking lot. There, next to the big waste dumpsters behind Culver's was a shiny black Chevy Suburban. It did, in fact, have the long whip antenna on top like the kind that two-way radio operators use.

And it had smoke-gray wind deflectors over the side windows. Like the one we'd seen back at the rest stop a couple hours ago.

Am I Paranoid...Enough?

I experienced that funny chill up and down my spine and arms while I looked at the black Chevy Suburban. It had the whip antenna and the smoke-gray plastic wind deflectors over the side windows; it also had blacked-out side windows like the one back at the rest stop. The entire windshield was tinted dark, although not as much as the side and rear windows. The Suburban had been backed into a parking space, so it was in a position to view the restaurant...or us.

But was it the same Suburban? It certainly looked the same, but I wasn't sure. If it would have had the whip antenna *or* the wind deflectors *or* the blacked-out windows it wouldn't have seemed too much of a coincidence. But it had all three of those features.

After a few seconds, without thinking I unlocked the doors with my fob while we were still approaching my car. I was focusing so intently on the question of whether this was the same Suburban we'd seen at the rest stop. But I had stopped talking as we approached my car. And for just a few seconds, I just stopped motionless and looked down, thinking, while my passenger got into the passenger seat.

When I got into the driver's seat and closed the door, Mr. Lincoln was looking at me. I knew that he realized I had suddenly become quiet, and after a few seconds, it occurred to me that he hadn't said anything since pointing out the Suburban, either.

"Do you think it's the same one?" asked my passenger.

"I don't know," I said, shaking my head slightly. "If it is the same one, it certainly might be that another driver heading in the same direction just happened to stop at both the rest stop and here. That happens sometimes on Interstate highways...people from many miles around might take the same highways to go in the same general direction. And it could be a completely different vehicle."

After perhaps 20-25 seconds during which we both did some thinking, he asked, "If somebody is following us, do you have any ideas about who it might be, or *why* they're following us?"

After thinking for a few seconds, I replied, "No. I'm not sure who it might be...or if they *are* following us. When we were in the restaurant, there was a man sitting near the back who seemed to glance at me every once in a while, and when I'd return the look, he would glance away. But that happens sometimes, and the people never see each other again. Other than that, I never saw anyone all morning long while we were in Mentha. Nobody that I could see before I arrived at the shed, or inside, or down below in the room or in 'the Void'. And nobody after we left, or on the way home, or around Bronson Park. If anyone had an issue with me being there, it seems they would have approached me by now."

"Do we want to walk over there and look around?" my passenger asked.

After thinking for a minute, I replied "I don't think so. If it is the same Chevy SUV, I think our best bet at this point is not letting them know that we know...or that we suspect."

As Mr. Lincoln responded, I noted that little rise in his voice again. "Aha!" he said. Then your approach is *we* don't want them to know that *we* know that *they* know that *we* know that *they* know."

I let my head drop and I nodded slightly, and I almost kept from smiling. "I think you took it a few steps too far, but that's the general idea." Then I got things back on a more serious track, adding "Let's go ahead and head to Springfield and check into our hotel for the night. We'll keep an eye open for the Suburban. You can let me know if you see anything, and I'll do the same. Are you all set?"

"Yes, I remember how to buckle my seat belt and how to sit in the seat and everything," he half-joked again. "And be assured that I'll look around for the Suburban."

"Very good. Let's be on our way, then."

I started my car and slowly drove toward the street. After traffic cleared, I turned right onto Woodlawn Road toward Springfield, following the instructions of my GPS. Interstate 55 was just ahead of us, and I was making sure I was in the far-right lane to get back on the highway to head south. I kept looking in my rear-view and side-view mirrors to be sure traffic was clear. All the while I was getting ready to leave town, my passenger was looking over his left shoulder, back in the direction of Culver's.

"Is everything okay?" I asked, almost rhetorically.

"It's gone," he replied.

"What?!" I asked, hearing something that didn't seem feasible, given that we had been looking at the Suburban no more than 30 seconds ago.

"The Suburban is gone," replied my passenger.

The Last Leg to Springfield

"Do you see it anywhere in back of us on the road?" I asked him.

"I haven't seen it, no. I've been looking for it, but I don't see any sign of it."

After thinking for a short time, I replied "Okay, maybe that's a good thing. If you don't see it in back of us, it might be that it went in the opposite direction on Woodlawn Road after leaving Culver's."

"And we never did look inside the vehicle," he added, "so it might be that the driver was already in it when we were getting into yours. Or…it could be that the city of Lincoln was their destination. It might even be that whoever drives the Suburban lives right here in the city of Lincoln."

"Yes, to all of those," I concurred. "We should exercise due caution, but at this point there's no reason to think that anyone means us any harm," I finished my thought as I brought our car onto the cloverleaf and back onto I-55 south toward Springfield.

It would still be daylight when we reached Springfield in about 35-40 minutes. The traffic was starting to pick up for the afternoon rush hour and I'm glad we'd be at our destination soon. For the first part of the last leg, we were both a little quieter than we'd been. I was thinking about what-ifs, and I thought my passenger might be, too.

Mr. Douglas

If you haven't heard me talk about enough of those strange coincidences in American history while I've been telling this story, here's another one. You may already know some of these things, but it still just makes me shake my head.

Picture a growing nation, one that began only 84 years before, but that had expanded by leaps and bounds every decade, with regular population increases of 33-36 percent every decade since its founding, with a total increase of more than 340 percent since its founding. Yup, that was us back then, folks.

Fact: In 1860, that very same nation chose its leader from the eligible candidates among a population of 31.4 million people.

Also a fact: The nation's two leading candidates came from the same prairie town in Illinois, which had a population of about 3,500 when they lived there. Both were lawyers, both had courted the same woman several years before, and they used to hang out together telling stories with their buddies.

Those two men were Abraham Lincoln and Stephen A. Douglas. Telling the story of our 16th president would be incomplete without discussing his relationship with Douglas.

I asked my passenger about Douglas and that relationship.

"Douglas spent time in Springfield," my passenger confirmed, referring to his senatorial and presidential opponent by only his last name. "But we met before he moved to Springfield, and he moved to Chicago by the time I left Springfield for Washington.

"Douglas and I actually had many important things in common," he reminisced. "And, of course, we had a few distinct disagreements. The most of important of those differences was the question of slavery.

"During the 1840s and 1850s," he explained, "there were two issues debated by politicians in the United States that far outweighed all the others. The first was whether we'd preserve the Union or allow states to leave it. And the second, on which the first issue was based entirely, was whether new states admitted to the Union would allow slavery. The two questions were inexorably connected. Without exception, those 11 states that left the Union stated in their articles of secession that the reason for their departure was slavery.

"Just as with my friend from Georgia, Alexander Stephens," he continued, "we had strongly agreed about preserving the Union, but had strong disagreement about the proliferation of the practice of allowing one person to own another. Stephens gave a major speech in Savannah just days after I became president. He said that, in contrast to the United States, their new government 'is founded upon exactly the opposite ideas; its foundations are laid, its cornerstone rests, upon the great truth that the negro is not equal to the white man; that slavery, subordination to the superior race, is his natural and normal condition.'

"Until that time," he continued, "I had always been of the mind that the U.S. Constitution kept us from preventing individual States from determining whether slavery would be allowed within their sovereign territory. But now, Stephens—and others—were proclaiming that the new land would literally reverse the Constitutional guarantee that all men were created equal. People wanted to break the bond to *mandate* that slavery would be legal.

"Regarding Douglas," my passenger half-joked, "he seems to be an exception from most of the people I've told you about who I met in

240

Illinois: he wasn't originally from Kentucky! He was from out East, born in Vermont, and came to Illinois after many stops along the way. I met Douglas in the Illinois House of Representatives in early 1837. We had both just been elected to that body, he was a Democrat and I was a Whig. At the time, Douglas lived in Jacksonville, Illinois, about 35 miles due west of Springfield.

"Douglas was an ardent proponent of Andrew Jackson," he continued, "Douglas and others who supported Jackson to such an extent called themselves '*Whole Hog* Democrats.'

"Douglas was a very accomplished man, I always gave him that," continued my passenger. "Even while he was serving in the Illinois legislature, he concurrently served as a judge, secretary of state for Illinois, and for the state land office. It was during his first term in the state house that President Martin Van Buren appointed him to that position in the land office in Springfield, and that was when he first arrived in Springfield."

Stephen Douglas was indeed an accomplished man, a man who had experienced much during his 48 years on earth. That life began in 1813 in Brandon, Vermont when he was born—a very substantial 14 pounds, according to his nurse—to a physician (also named Stephen) and his wife, Sarah Fisk Douglass, with two S's.

That's right. Ironically, Stephen's family name was spelled with two S's, the same as that of abolitionist and orator Frederick Douglass. However, in 1846, Stephen Douglas dropped the second S from his last name. The previous year, Frederick published his first biography, *Narrative of the Life of Frederick Douglass, an American Slave*. Also in 1846, Stephen Douglas won his first election to the U.S. Senate from Illinois, so one can now only guess as to the reason for the name change.

Perhaps impacting Douglas later in life, even subconsciously, was his father's death, and the manner of that death. According to the August 1865 issue of *The Atlantic*, Stephen was first mentioned in the newspaper at the age of two months, upon the death of his father, who at the time was playing with Stephen and his sister in front of an open fireplace. According to the *Atlantic* article, little Stephen "had the misfortune to lose his father, who, holding the baby boy in his arms, fell back in his chair and died, while Stephen, dropping from his embrace, was caught from the fire, and thus from early death, by a neighbor, John Conant, who opportunely entered the room at the moment."

My passenger resumed, "Douglas received a respectable elementary education as a youngster, and a teenager, he left home and apprenticed with a cabinetmaker. He had several other jobs, as well, and attended an academy to learn some advanced skills. One of those skills was debating, and let me tell you, right here and now, that few excelled in that skill as much as Douglas.

"At the age of 20," my passenger continued, "Douglas left New York for the west, where he thought, like millions of other Americans, that there was a great deal of opportunity. He spent some time in western New York, Buffalo and Niagara. From there, he lived briefly in the Ohio cities of Cleveland, then Portsmouth, and Cincinnati. From there, he headed west, living briefly in—you've probably guessed, Louisville, Kentucky—and then St. Louis before arriving in Jacksonville, Illinois.

"It was in Eighteen Hundred and Thirty-Nine," my passenger continued, "while Douglas and I were both serving in the state legislature that we both met Mary Todd, to whom I now have the great honor of being married. She came to town in October of that year and began living with her sister, Elizabeth, who was already married to Ninian Wirt Edwards. And for a short time, Douglas himself courted Mary. The two of them got along quite well, though I think it was the same question of slavery that made any long-term relationship between the two of them an impossibility. But I won't complain; I remain very satisfied with the outcome.

"We spent a great many hours together," he said, "in one combination or another, Mary and Douglas and me. In gatherings at Elizabeth's house, we tried to follow the social graces as much as possible, in part because it was mixed company, and in part because even though we gentlemen could be a little rough around the edges, we wanted to improve our manner and our lot. In contrast, it was only the men who gathered at Joshua Speed's store. And although we acted as only men will act at times, we also discussed books, poetry, and philosophy. Politics, however, was normally avoided. I recall one very cold December evening when our discussion wandered from philosophy to politics, and it became evident why the subject is sometimes avoided in social gatherings. Emotions became somewhat heated, and it was Douglas who rose his voice, saying 'Gentlemen, this is no place to talk politics!' Although most everyone on the room engaged in politics to some extent—Douglas and me certainly being guilty as charged—we realized he was right and the discussion returned to literature and other less heated topics."

All told, Stephen A. Douglas served as an Illinois state representative, registrar at the state land office in Springfield, Illinois, and secretary of state. At the age of 28, he was elected to the Illinois Supreme Court. At the age of 33, he was elected to the U.S. Senate from Illinois, an office that he held until 1861.

Lincoln and Douglas saw a great deal of each other across the state of Illinois in 1858. That year, two years after Lincoln's visit to Kalamazoo, Abraham Lincoln decided to challenge Stephen Douglas for his U.S. Senate seat. Long-time political adversaries but friends,

Lincoln and Douglas planned and conducted a series of debates. Between August and October, the two conducted debates in seven Illinois cities: Ottawa, Freeport, Jonesboro, Charleston, Galesburg, Quincy, and Alton. In addition to trying to spread out the debates geographically, the two agreed to the locations partly based on the location of state legislators. Until the 17th Amendment to the U.S. Constitution was ratified in 1913, U.S. senators were elected by state legislators, rather than by popular vote.

Although Illinois remained with the Union during the Civil War, the state was not without its violence over the matter of abolition. On November 7, 1837, the Reverend Elijah P. Lovejoy, an abolitionist who owned a printing press in Alton, was murdered by a pro-slavery mob while trying to keep his printing press from being destroyed for a third time. Alton is just across the Mississippi River from Missouri, where slavery was legal until abolished by Missouri's legislature in January 1865. Blood was spilled numerous times in that state over the issue. In addition, in January 1859, John Brown led a group into the state where they liberated 11 people from enslavement, took two white men captive, and looted wagons and horses in an event called "The Battle of the Spurs." Nine months later, Brown led a group of 18 followers on a raid of the federal armory at Harper's Ferry, Virginia (in the part that's now West Virginia), where the raiders were killed or captured by federal troops led by U.S. Army Col. Robert E. Lee and First Lieutenant J.E.B. Stuart. Ten of Brown's raiders were killed including two of his sons. Brown and seven others were captured. They stood trial, were found guilty, and were executed, all within just seven weeks.

The main topic at all seven Lincoln-Douglas debates was slavery, including the potential proliferation of the practice. Each debate took about three hours, with one candidate speaking for 90 minutes, then the other candidate speaking for one hour, and then the first candidate speaking for the final 30 minutes. The order of speaking was switched between the sites. Several of the debates were attended by more than 15,000 people, and the three debates that were held in cities near Illinois' borders—Freeport, Quincy, and Alton—saw large numbers of attendees from the neighboring states.

When the votes were counted, Abraham Lincoln had won the popular vote with 190,468 votes to Douglas's 166,374. However, the state was sufficiently gerrymandered that Douglas won the vote that counted, in the Illinois legislature, 54-46. It was another electoral defeat for Lincoln. But although Douglas won the election, Abraham Lincoln had taken a big step in bolstering his national recognition. Just two years later, during a presidential election in which armed conflict between the states was a very real possibility, the results were reversed with Lincoln winning.

Despite the reverence with which the 1858 Lincoln-Douglas senate debates are regarded today, the two did not engage in debates during their 1860 presidential campaigns. In fact, no presidential candidates agreed to debate each other until 100 years later, when Richard M. Nixon and John F. Kennedy conducted a series of four televised debates against each other. Representatives of the two major parties did not debate each other again until 1976, when Gerald R. Ford and Jimmy Carter debated each other. Since then, every presidential election year has seen debates between representatives of the two major parties, with third-party candidates also being included in 1980 (Rep. John Anderson) and 1992 (businessman Ross Perot).

Each of the presidential debates held since 1960 has had its stories, its backstories, and its sound bites. However, what may have been the most interesting and meaningful debate never took place due to another tragic event in history.

In 1963, it was widely expected that the incumbent Democratic president, John F. Kennedy, and Republican Sen. Barry Goldwater from Arizona would be the presidential nominees of their respective parties in November 1964. Like Lincoln and Douglas, Goldwater and Kennedy had a relationship that would be considered unusual or even remarkable today.

Despite differences in political ideology, Goldwater and Kennedy developed a strong friendship and mutual respect soon after they were both elected to the U.S. Senate in 1952. Both had served with distinction during World War II and supported a strong but fiscally sound military. Both were strongly anti-communist, and both had a distrust for Richard Nixon, with a mutual skepticism toward Vice President Lyndon Johnson not far behind that for Nixon.

Goldwater and Kennedy looked forward to campaigning against each other in 1964, from a personal perspective as well as political. They agreed that they would have a series of whistle-stop debates against each other, in which they would both arrive in a city by train or airplane, debate each other, and then move on to another city.

Of course, those plans became moot when President Kennedy was assassinated in Dallas in November 1963.

"When Jack Kennedy died, I lost all interest in running," said Goldwater in an interview with the *Chicago Sun-Times* in the late 1970s. "The country wasn't ready for three presidents in three-and-a-half years. And I knew Johnson would not run an honest campaign like Kennedy."

About 10 miles before our exit to Springfield, my passenger shared some additional history about his friend and political adversary, Stephen Douglas, and some thoughts about him following Douglas's departure from Springfield.

"Douglas actually left Springfield in the summer of Nineteen Hundred Forty-Seven. By that time, Chicago was becoming one of the fastest-growing cities in all of the West. He actually lived in that city all through his service in the U.S. Senate, including the time of our debates."

Mr. Lincoln recalled a particular story about Douglas. "One evening during the debates in Illinois, I was talking with Mrs. Lincoln about how Douglas and I presented ourselves on a platform during the debate. Mrs. Lincoln made the observation 'You're six-foot-four and he's five-foot-four. You should find a way to take advantage of that foot.' I responded, saying, 'With Douglas during the debates, I'd sometimes like to take my foot and put it where he has no doubts about its location.' But honestly, despite our diametrically opposed views on slavery, we seldom raised our voices to one another, and certainly never thought about laying a hand on the other in anger. And that included times during which there were—may I say—some very enthusiastic things said about the other during three long hours of debate."

Mr. Lincoln's tone lowered when he said, "Douglas married a young lady named Martha in 1847, and they were very well suited to each other. They had two sons, Robert and Stephen. In 1853, Martha was with child once more, but unfortunately, Martha passed during childbirth. She was only 27 years old. Their infant girl died just a few weeks later. As you might imagine, although Douglas and I sometimes fought like cats and dogs, the news about both Martha and their little girl pained both Mrs. Lincoln and me greatly. Douglas needed time to account for their loss, so he visited Europe for some time. He visited London, St. Petersburg, Paris, and Turkey. During that trip, he met Czar Nicholas I and Napoleon III. Never having been to Europe and desiring to go there one day with Mrs. Lincoln, I would have been somewhat envious, except with Douglas, the tragic events that prompted the trip were something I would not wish upon anyone.

"One might think that the slings and arrows that befell Douglas's marriage to Martha would depart and allow the sun to shine again," added my passenger, "but as in a Shakespearian play, such was not the case. In November of 1856, Douglas remarried, to another young lady, Adele Cutts. Adele's father was a nephew of President James Madison. They tried to have more children, but Adele suffered a miscarriage in 1858, the year of our debates, and then in 1859 gave birth to a daughter, Rachel, who lived for just a few weeks. Again, Douglas and I were sometimes adversarial, but that is not an outcome I would wish upon my worst enemy."

Despite Douglas's consistent support of the institution of slavery— he authored the Kansas-Nebraska Act of 1850 and frequently used the N-word when referring to African Americans, Lincoln valued some of Douglas's actions, and perhaps wanted to change his friend's mind about the practice. In that way, was Lincoln demonstrating his ability to use a combination of logic, humor, and friendship to bring adversaries over to his side, as Doris Kearns Goodwin wrote in her best-selling 2005 book *Team of Rivals: The Political Genius of Abraham Lincoln*?

"One of the most important things that Douglas did was to advocate for Chicago as a railroad hub," explained my passenger. "As soon as he and his family moved to Chicago, he began to picture Chicago, not as the small town but as a city of several hundred thousand people, or even more in the future. From what I saw as you and I drove miles south of the city, it must be a city of several million today. And the way Douglas envisioned doing that, in addition to taking advantage of the city's location at the south end of Lake Michigan, was the railroads.

248

"In September of 1850," continued Mr. Lincoln, "Douglas authored and passed the Illinois Central Railroad Tax Act, which granted rights of way to railroads not just in Illinois, but also in Mississippi and Alabama. The act almost immediately created the longest railroad in the country, the Illinois Central, which spanned from Galena in the northwest corner of Illinois to Cairo at the south. That network expanded into the South—and by the time my presidency was interrupted by this mysterious journey from Washington to Kalamazoo earlier today—that network was approaching a point where there would be interconnected railroads from East to West and from North to South."

He further explained, "That work by Douglas not only expanded Chicago, but interconnected the country. To Douglas, the importance of the railroad wasn't just moving cargo, or even people, from one place to another. It was interconnecting all of us...as a union."

Mr. Lincoln's appraisal of Chicago was certainly correct. Just 17 years before Douglas's rail bill, in 1833, the village of Chicago had only 200 people. By the year he authored and passed his bill, 1850, there were about 30,000 citizens there. That increased to 112,000 just 10 years later, the year that Lincoln defeated Douglas for president. As I tell you this, more than 2.7 million people live in Chicago, the third-most populous city in the United States.

"The railroad was, I believe, one of the four things Douglas did that will make a lasting change to the country. I think the second of the four things was the work he did for the Mormons," said Mr. Lincoln. He actually performed work on two separate but linked issues. The first was during the brief time that he served in the Illinois Supreme Court, from November 1840 to February 1841. Douglas saw that there was a great deal of anger from the community at large towards the Mormons, which was no doubt emphasized one evening when he had dinner with the founder of the faith, Joseph Smith, in the early

1840s. Douglas told Smith that he sympathized with the right of the Mormons to express their own faith. Douglas soon drew up a charter for the Mormons who had then their settlement in Nauvoo, Illinois. And it was in his role as judge that Douglas ruled that members of the Nauvoo Legion, which was the Mormon militia, were exempt from military service. His ruling clarified that the Mormons were independent from the state.

"The third thing that Douglas did," continued my passenger, "which will have a lasting effect, was to advocate for popular sovereignty, a concept that was established earlier by Lewis Cass…from Michigan. That concept turned out to be a two-edged sword for Douglas. He actually verified his support for that concept during our debate in Freeport, Illinois, which led to his idea sometimes being called the "Freeport Doctrine." His tenet of popular sovereignty held that each state had the right to determine whether slavery would be legal on its soil. Some people called this position "state's rights." Douglas's opinion was actually in contrast to the Supreme Court's terrible Dred Scott ruling, which said that Negroes could not be citizens of the United States. Naturally, those of us who were against the practice of slavery still felt that Douglas's proposal was unacceptable. However, the states in the South remained firmly opposed to Douglas's proposal just as they did to the idea of free states. They felt that under their so-called Confederate constitution, slavery *must be allowed* throughout their union.

"And that position did two things," said Mr. Lincoln. "First, it led to Douglas being an even more adamant supporter of the Union—a union of all the states—than he was before. Even before I arrived in Washington from Springfield, he was spending long days and nights working with people from both parties to keep the Southern states from leaving the Union. He continued that work after I arrived, and was one of my biggest supporters. He did everything I could have asked, and more.

250

"And the other impact of Douglas's popular sovereignty," he said, "was the 1860 election. May our nation never have another one like it."

My passenger explained that even though Douglas was a Democrat—like most of the state leaders in the South—and even though he supported the ability of states to allow slavery, that wasn't enough for those Southern states. Accordingly, they didn't support him. Instead, the Southern states ran their own ticket called the Southern Democratic Party. Their presidential nominee was John Cabell Breckenridge, the pro-slavery sitting vice president of the United States from—here we go again—Louisville, Kentucky. During the war, Breckenridge was commissioned a major general in the Confederate army. In the last four months of the Civil War, he served as secretary of war for the Confederate states.

Added to the major candidate list, in addition to Lincoln (Republican), Douglas (Democrat) and Breckenridge (Southern Democrat) was a Southern former U.S. senator from Tennessee named John Bell. So it was a four-way race for the presidency.

When the vote counting was done, the Republican ticket of Lincoln and Hannibal Hamlin won comfortably, despite the fact that they were not even on the ballot in 10 of the 11 Southern states. The final electoral map was highly regionalized, with Lincoln winning all the Northern states as well as Kentucky, Tennessee, California and Oregon; Breckenridge winning all of the other Southern states; and Douglas winning the Western border state of Missouri.

According to some of Lincoln's neighbors, he was playing a game of ball (perhaps baseball) when he heard about his victory. It was a bittersweet victory for him because he knew that, even if the Southern states didn't secede, they would still make governing very difficult. Six states would leave the Union before he arrived in his new residence on Pennsylvania Avenue in Washington, D.C. and five more would follow soon after.

Ironically, Abraham Lincoln's reelection in 1864 made him the first president to be elected to a second term since Andrew Jackson some 28 years earlier. Lincoln only served six weeks of his second term before the night at Ford's Theatre.

One other area in which Lincoln and Douglas had contact was during Douglas's term as an associate justice on the Illinois Supreme Court. Over the two short years that Douglas served on that court, Lincoln argued before the court 24 times, and he found Douglas to be knowledgeable and fair.

"Many leaders throughout history are noted as being complex," explained my passenger, who had obviously given the whole matter of his friend, Stephen Douglas, considerable thought. "Julius Caesar is generally regarded as a great leader, but he became a dictator and was assassinated by a conspiracy that comprised more than 60 men. George Washington is called "the father of his country" but he held slaves. Stephen A. Douglas would not become a national leader in the same way, though he was considered the predominant advocate of popular sovereignty in the nation.

"After becoming the youngest associate justice and secretary of state in Illinois history, and serving in the state legislature, Congress, and representing his party as a presidential candidate, Douglas was a tremendous advocate for the Union in his final months, executing every trick in the book to keep the nation together. In February of Eighteen Hundred Sixty-One, days before I took office, 131 leading American politicians and statesmen attended a so-called Peace Conference at the Willard Hotel in Washington. The states that had left the Union did not send representatives, and I could not in good conscience support a conference that would end in slavery still in existence.

252

"Then," he added, "in May of 1861, just two months after he'd have become president of these United States had the election gone differently, he contracted typhoid fever and was confined to bed. After less than a month, he passed away, at just 48 years old. By coincidence, that was the third of June, the same day as the Battle of Philippi, the first skirmish of that awful war. I asked Secretary of War Simon Cameron to send a message to all Union armies, announcing the loss of Douglas. Secretary Cameron's message described the loss as "the death of a great statesman...a man who nobly discarded party for his country.""

"Days later," my passenger reflected thoughtfully, "someone asked me whether Douglas actually supported the institution of slavery or, based on his interpretation of the Constitution, supported what he thought was the right of legislatures to allow it. The result was the same, I suppose, and either way, the result was four years of war and the loss of hundreds of thousands of young men."

Coming into Springfield

After five hours on Interstate highways and our early dinner in the city of Lincoln, we got off at the North Peoria Road exit, taking the business loop due south into Springfield. Neither of us saw the black Chevy Suburban since leaving Culver's about 35 minutes before. No Christopher Walken doppelganger, either. Though we'd still be mindful of it, it was no longer the source of unspoken terror. (Mine, not his, I'm sure.)

Destination: DoubleTree Hotel, which happened to be less than a quarter-mile north of my passenger's Springfield home. I had planned to drive directly to the hotel, but on the last leg of our trip I had started thinking about the rest of the evening and how my guest and I would communicate if needed. I had reserved two rooms at the DoubleTree. (Fortunately, I had enough Hilton Honors points to get both rooms for one night at no charge. Sometimes we get lucky.)

As we had approached Springfield, I thought about the fact that we'd be in separate rooms, or that we might get separated for one reason or another. I thought of a better way to communicate than one of us having to go out into the hall and knock on the door of the other.

Driving along Peoria Road, I saw what I was looking for just ahead on the left: a Best Buy. I began to describe my communication plan to my passenger as I slowly pulled into the left-turn lane and into the Best Buy parking lot.

"Are you going to buy a phone for me?" asked Mr. Lincoln, half-jokingly.

"As a matter of fact, I am!" I confirmed.

After parking and going into the store, we went inside and I found just what I wanted: a burner phone. Low-cost, low-functionality phones were something I had always associated with "perps" on *Law & Order*, *NCIS*, and *Blue Bloods*, but I suddenly had a new appreciation for these little 21st Century versions of tin cans and string. The phone was relatively cheap (*relatively*, compared to newer phones that are well over a grand) and I'd find a use for it when my guest was finished with it.

We went back out and got into my car, and as we started up and began heading for the DoubleTree, I explained my ideas for the evening and to get his thoughts. My idea was that we'd just go to our respective rooms and if either of us had a question, we'd just text the other. We'd already eaten dinner, so we wouldn't need to do that again. I told him that when we got to the hotel, I'd show him how he could get a beverage, snack, or even a full meal if he so desired. He agreed with my plans. Later, I'd show him how to text a message with his newfangled phone.

Whenever I go on a trip of any distance, arriving at the destination hotel is always a highlight of the trip. We'd be able to see what that evening's base camp would be like, and we'd have comfortable places to sit and sleep. Coming into downtown Springfield, after a slight veer from Peoria Road onto North 9th Street, we turned right onto East Adams Street, and there on the right was the DoubleTree.

"Now, sir," I explained, "we get to deal with one of the great challenges of the 21st Century: finding a place to park the car in a strange city." Fortunately, the hotel had an easy-to-use parking ramp. When we pulled in, a very friendly machine provided us with a ticket that would be used the next day to determine how much our parking would cost for our stay.

We were able to find a parking space with no difficulty, and we unloaded the suitcases from our trunk. I put the new burner phone in an inside pocket of my jacket so I wouldn't forget it. As we wheeled our small suitcases from the car to the hotel door, Mr. Lincoln pointed out how handy it was to have wheels on a suitcase. I had thought the same thing in the past: All through my youth and early adulthood, we carried big, fabric-covered suitcases around. Though some of them may have weighed 40 pounds or more full, sometimes it seemed easier to carry one in each hand in order to keep our spines in balance.

We passed through a short hallway then into the lobby, which looked very clean and well-decorated. It had some nice, big, padded armchairs for people who might want to wait for the rest of their group before going out together, or to read. We approached the check-in desk, where well before we got there, we were welcomed by a pleasant young man, about college age, whose name tag said "Srinivas" and just under that "Trainee." An older man, probably early 40s, in a yellow shirt and blue tie next to him was tending to some paperwork but also seemed to be monitoring how Srinivas checked us in.

"Hi. We're checking in," I said, stopping in front of the desk with my tall passenger and two suitcases. Srinivas didn't say "Duh," so maybe walking up to the desk from the parking ramp with two suitcases wasn't always a 100%, sure-fire way of knowing that a guest was checking in.

"Certainly. Name?" asked Srinivas.

"Albert Frey," I responded.

"Yes, I see your reservation here," he said, looking at his computer monitor. "Two guests, two rooms, for one night?" he asked.

"Yes, that's right," I said.

"Very good," said Srinivas. "And I see that you're a Hilton Honors member, and that you're paying for both rooms using points; is that correct?" he asked.

"Yes, that's right," I confirmed.

"Very good," said Srinivas. "And if I could please see your identification and a credit card to pay for any incidental expenses."

"Sure, here they are," I said, seemingly fumbling, as always, to take out my wallet and then remove my driver's license and credit card.

Srinivas began to take my credit card as he spent several seconds looking at my driver's license, to make sure that I was me.

"Thank you," Srinivas said. Then, looking at my traveling partner, he said, "and sir, if I could also see your identification."

His identification.

Well, let me tell ya'. We hadn't expected that. At least I hadn't, and I didn't need to ask my traveling partner to know that he didn't expect it. And while some of the previous "surprises" I'd had since stepping into a big, black hole that morning caused chills to go up and down my spine and arms, this last request probably stopped me from breathing and definitely caused my poor heart to shift into a higher gear. I was just hoping that Srinivas wouldn't notice that I was having a sudden panic attack.

"Oh," said the older man behind the desk, still handling some paperwork, but now looking directly at me. "You're using *your* points to pay for both rooms, is that correct, sir?"

"YES!!! YES!!! What you said! What he said!" my brain told itself very loudly and clearly. Outwardly, however, in that far more meaningful act that we call human speech, I managed to quietly mutter "yes" and nod my head, and that was about it.

He looked at Srinivas and politely said, "Mr. Frey is paying for both rooms. So we don't need to see the other gentleman's ID."

"Oh, certainly," replied Srinivas. "My apologies."

We all make mistakes, and any other time, I would have told the mistake maker, Srinivas "Oh, that's not a problem," or similar assurance. However, at this particular time, I was trying to resume my breathing, my heartrate was just starting to return to normal, and my lips weighed roughly 30 pounds and were drier than the surface of Death Valley late on a July afternoon.

Relative silence resumed while Srinivas processed my credit card. It appeared that their computer network was running a little slowly, and it looked like Srinivas was trying to hide some frustration. It may have been my imagination at this point, but I also thought I saw the older man, probably a more senior manager, looking several times out of the corner of his eye at Mr. Lincoln. But then it looked like he had a little smile, as if to say "Yeah, right, that's the guy that used to live down the street about 160 years ago."

Srinivas finished his transaction and returned my credit card to me, again with a polite "Thank you." This time, I was able to manage aloud a relatively cheerful "You're welcome," which, of course, was accompanied in my brain by a very silent "and for that thing asking for my traveling partner's ID, that's not a problem. We all make mistakes."

"Mr. Frey, have you stayed at this DoubleTree before?" asked Srinivas, starting to wrap up the check-in.

"Not at this one, no," I answered.

"Very good," he said again, as he explained the hotel's hours for dinner that night, and hours and location for breakfast the next morning. He then handed us me a small folder, slightly larger than my room key, which held my key; the envelope with the room number 232 written in the upper right of the inside. He handed my traveling partner a similar folder and key for room 233 across the hall, and gestured just down the hallway to where the elevators were.

And then came the best DoubleTree part.

"And gentlemen, here you are," said Srinivas, reaching into a cabinet under the counter, "your cookies." Srinivas then handed both my guest and me a big, warm, chocolate chip cookie. And they smelled like warm chocolate chip cookies. It may take all of 50 cents to make them, but when you're traveling for several hours and finally arrive at your hotel, it's something to look forward to. I looked over at my guest and he had a smile on his face, as did I. We then started down the hall toward the elevators.

During our time together, Mr. Lincoln and I had both developed a habit of looking around, slowly and inconspicuously, before saying anything that might have tipped people off to his identity. We were both doing so as we approached the elevators.

Some of the things that seem the most commonplace to us today were completely foreign to people of the mid-19th Century, even people of means or political power.

The first passenger elevator in the world was installed in March 1857 by Elisha Otis. Because Mr. Lincoln came to present-day Michigan from 1865, I thought it was unlikely that he would have been in an elevator. The look on his eyes...not concerned, but rather wide open, taking everything in...told me that he had not. When I asked him, he confirmed that although he had heard about elevators, he had never been in one.

But his wife had.

That first Otis elevator was installed in the E.V. Haughwout Building, a five-story commercial building at the corner of Broadway and Broome Street in the SoHo neighborhood in Manhattan. It was nearly razed in 1941 to make space for a planned Lower Manhattan Expressway, a major highway that would have connected New Jersey with Long Island via lower Manhattan. The project that was under discussion in various iterations for almost 30 years until it was canceled by Mayor John Lindsay in 1969. But the building is still there, and in 1973 was added to the National Register of Historic Places.

In January 1861, between the time Lincoln was elected to the presidency and the time he was sworn in, Mary Todd Lincoln—then just 42 years old—went on a shopping trip to Manhattan looking for new clothes. While there, she became acquainted with the city's merchants for fine clothing, furniture, and other household goods.

When the Lincolns moved into the Executive Mansion two months later, they found much of the home and its contents to be in disrepair. President James Buchanan was a bachelor, and Mrs. Lincoln did not feel that preserving fine dinnerware, furniture and other articles was among Buchanan's skills or list of priorities. So in May 1861, the First Lady returned to Manhattan with a small entourage to shop for items to refurbish the home. (One of the members of her party, Col. Robert Anderson, was the commander at Fort Sumter one month before when he defied Gen. P.G.T. Beauregard's demand to surrender the fort, resulting in the beginning of the Civil War.)

Mrs. Lincoln returned to E.V. Haughwout & Co., where she carefully selected replacement china, 666 pieces in all. The china was cream color with banding of a reddish-purple color called *solferino*. It was manufactured in France with E.V. Haughwout adding additional ornamentation. (Mr. Haughwout had added engravers, designers, artists, and glass cutters to his staff to become somewhat of a full-service store for fine items.) It was the first set of china ever to be completely selected by a First Lady. She also ordered silver-gilded and gold flatware. The cost of the order was $3,195, the equivalent of $111,471 today, for which the president gladly paid the bill from U.S coffers.

While Mrs. Lincoln was in the store, she rode on the world's first passenger elevator, and she reported her experience back to her husband. She ordered china twice more while she was in the Executive Mansion.

The Lincoln presidential china, also called the solferino china, is still considered among the most beautiful ever to grace dinners and other functions at the Executive Mansion. A number of presidents have ordered variations of the Lincoln china. In the early 1960s, First Lady Jacqueline Kennedy frequently used the set. In 2009, President Barack Obama used reproductions of the Lincoln solferino china at his inaugural luncheon.

Over the years, much of the original set has been damaged or disappeared, but collections of remaining pieces can be found at the Smithsonian in Washington, The Henry Ford in Dearborn, Michigan, the Chicago Historical Society, and the Philadelphia Museum of Art. Some pieces are in the hands of private collectors, and those have sold for more than $14,000 each.

Mr. Lincoln and I arrived at the second floor in a few seconds and walked to our rooms. First, I opened my door briefly to put my suitcase inside, and then, after checking around to make sure nobody was nearby in the hallway, showed my guest how to use his electronic room key. In this hotel, the room doors used proximity readers, so one just needed to hold the key next to the reader on the door to open it. Then we went into Mr. Lincoln's room, where I showed him a few things, including the television, the thermostat, and the bathroom. Since he'd seen the bathroom in our house, there wasn't much new, but I wanted to be sure he knew where all the towels were, and what was shampoo for hair and what was soap. I showed him how to turn on the shower and regulate water temperature, making sure he knew that he might have to wait a while for the water to warm to the proper temperature.

He continued to catch on quickly, and as soon as I was done making sure he knew about everything in the bathroom, I was going to show him how to send a text message with the new phone. But with everything else, he seemed most interested in the toilet paper. It's another simple invention that most Americans and people around the world take for granted.

Although toilet paper was used in China as early as 589 A.D., it seems to be one of those inventions that remained unknown in other parts of the world for centuries. The first patent in the United States for "toilet papers and dispensers" was issued in 1883, with the Scott Paper Company beginning to market T.P. in rolls in 1890. Catalogs, like those published and distributed by Montgomery Ward and Sears, Roebuck and Co. weren't available until 1872 and 1888, respectively. Before that, people of substantial means could use cloth. Some people used pages of old books, and before that, leaves or whatever was available. My guest seemed mesmerized by the product.

I removed the phone from my jacket pocket and took a seat near the desk in Mr. Lincoln's room, asking him to sit down across from me so I could demonstrate its use. I took the phone out of its small box, receiving a slight but painful cut on my right index finger while trying to get the phone out of its clear plastic bubble inside the box. As I removed the power cord and plug from the box and plugged it into a wall outlet above the desk, I began explaining, step-by-step, what I was doing to Mr. Lincoln. I tried to be thorough in my explanations, but he still had questions, all of which I found insightful. I left the phone plugged in to ensure that it had sufficient charge, and turned on the phone. When prompted by a start-up menu, programmed some basic information into it. (I registered it under my name, having originally thought I'd register it under the name of my guest, but then laughed at myself for even thinking it, realizing that it might raise questions.)

I programmed my own phone number into the burner phone and then programmed its number into my own. Then I handed the phone to him and told him to be ready for me to call him. I intentionally didn't tell him what to say when he answered, just to see what he'd do and say. After pressing the number of his phone, his rang after a delay of just a second or two. He put it to his ear, as I was doing with my own by that point.

"Yes? Good evening! It's me! It's great to hear from you after so long" he said with a grin on his face. His grin stretched into a full smile when he heard my voice on the other end. I then told him how to end the call and I showed him how to text. I opened my text messaging app, found his name, and texted "Hello, Mr. President! Voilà!" and then pressed the *Send* button. No more than two seconds passed when his phone signaled. He opened his text messaging app, and then after I confirmed what to do next, he opened my message. He quickly burst into a brief laugh.

"Now, don't go introducing me to many more French words or I may not know what you're saying!" he joked.

I asked him if he had questions about anything. I didn't need to remind him that he had a large flat-screen TV in his room, but I wanted to double-check whether he thought he might like to see anything on it. I knew there was some risk about his finding out about darker past events as they happened in my timeline, but I thought it was small.

"No, I don't believe I'll watch anything on the television," he confirmed. "It would be a great experience to see those moving pictures in such bright colors and admire the whole apparatus, but I won't have that opportunity when I get back. And frankly, if I don't see it, I won't miss it."

Although he'd been in the 21st Century for less than 12 hours, his philosophy about "If I don't see it, I won't miss it" still seemed to ring pretty true, given the choices available today.

"Yes sir, I understand," I said.

I made sure that he didn't need anything else, and then assured him that if he needed anything at all, he could text me. I also made sure he knew about the snack and beverage area near the check-in desk, and told him that if he became hungry or thirsty, he could simply go down, pick up whatever he wanted, and tell the clerk his room number so it could be added to our bill. I reminded him to take his room key. I also noticed two bottles of water in a little basket on the desk. He said he thought that would probably be plenty, but he thanked me in advance in case he did go down for a snack or beverage.

We agreed to meet at 8:15 in the morning. We thought that would give us a good night's sleep, especially since we'd gained an hour since crossing from Michigan into Indiana. In the morning, I'd drive him around Springfield, especially his old neighborhood. It had been more than 160 years since he'd been there, but by his reality, it had only been four. And he had ruled out any trips to the museum, to the cemetery, or other locations that would seem out of place in his reality. It was one thing for him to see modern inventions, electronics, buildings, roads, and other developments from the last century and a half, but another to experience artifacts related to one's own mortality—or the mortality of one's family members or friends.

My guest reiterated how much he appreciated my help driving him to Springfield and helping him with meals and things. He said his current thinking was that if we spent perhaps four or five hours driving around Springfield the next morning, that should allow him to see the things he'd hoped to see. That would mean we'd start driving back to Kalamazoo around mid-afternoon, and put us at my house before 9:00 the next evening.

As I stood up and headed toward the door, we said good night to each other and agreed that unless he needed anything, we'd meet up in the hotel lobby at 8:15 the next morning.

"And you're going to do two things when you get back into your room," said Mr. Lincoln.

"Which two things?" I asked, smiling slightly, not knowing if he'd be joking or not.

"First, and probably several times during the evening, you're going to go to the window while your room lights are out and look down below to see if there's a black Chevy…"

"…Suburban SUV," I filled in, the smile turning into a slight nod and look of acknowledgement.

"Yes. A black Chevy Suburban down there," he continued. "I'm fixin' on doing the same thing myself, and I knew you would be."

"Yeah. That's right," I confirmed. "Just to be on the safe side."

"Indeed," he concurred. "And second…you're going to call Molly and let her know you arrived safely."

"Yes…I…am!" I confirmed. And with that, I headed out his door and closed it behind me, then stepped across the hallway and opened my own. I called Molly and found out how her day went, and told her that my day had been without incident. She asked about the hotel, and I told her how much I liked it. We talked for perhaps 15 minutes and said good-night to each other. I then decided to take a quick shower before going to bed. The shower had the pump shampoo, body wash, and conditioner that I like, and the big 10-inch diameter Speakman shower head that I frequently see in hotel rooms but never at my local Lowe's or Home Depot.

After drying off, putting on a t-shirt and long gym shorts and brushing my teeth, I settled into bed, looking for what I hoped would be an uneventful and restful evening.

Things that Never Were

True story…

In 2006, when our kids were young teenagers, Molly and I took them on a trip to Springfield, Illinois. We left our house on a Sunday afternoon, checked into a hotel in Springfield, and did our sightseeing the following day, which was Martin Luther King Jr. Day. It was a very cold day; on the drive to Springfield and back, the thermometer in our Pontiac minivan showed an outside temperature of just 3 degrees above zero.

We drove to Oak Ridge Cemetery northwest of the center of town and followed the signs to the Lincoln Tomb.

The tomb is made of Maine granite and is a story-and-a-half high, with stairways and railings leading to the top platform. Atop the center of the tomb is a 117-foot obelisk, and on small circular platforms around its base are statues of civil war soldiers in various poses; the statues have darkened patinas, almost black.

On the front side of the tomb is a must-see for children of all ages. The bronze head of Lincoln, about three feet in height and mounted atop a five-foot granite pillar, was cast by Gutson Borglum, who would later design Mount Rushmore. The face depicts Lincoln in 1860 before he grew his famous beard, and is actually based on a life mask he had made that year. The bust is about the same dark color as the soldiers—except for one part: the nose. His nose is shiny bronze, and if the sun is out, it reflects brightly. Of the 200,000 visitors to the tomb each year, many of them rub Mr. Lincoln's nose because they consider it lucky, and/or as a way of paying their respects.

Inside the tomb are several rooms including an entrance and the burial room. Mary Todd Lincoln and three of the four sons are interred in crypts inside in a burial room. (Robert is buried at Arlington National Cemetery.) And of course, most people, including our family, come to pay respects to the 16th president. Opposite their crypts is a seven-ton block of dark reddish-brown marble which serves as the Memorial Marker to Mr. Lincoln. In that simple block is carved his name, Abraham Lincoln, and his years of birth and death, 1809 – 1865. Nothing else. Nothing about the Civil War, saving the Union, emancipating millions of our fellow American who were once held in slavery.

Near the top of the wall behind the monument are the words expressed by Secretary of War Edwin Stanton upon Lincoln's last breath at the Petersen boarding house: "Now he belongs to the ages."

But while we were in the entrance corridor, before we visited the burial room, we had the opportunity to talk with a National Park Service Ranger who was an expert on the tomb, who tells visitors about the tomb and the people who are buried there, and answers their questions. Having visited a number of history-oriented national parks, I've always thought the National Park Service Rangers were the absolute best. He appeared to be happy to have our small family of four visit on this cold January morning, and we were thrilled to have a ranger all to ourselves.

We asked him several questions. Then he mentioned that just a few days before, actor Liam Neeson had visited the tomb, and he was standing right where we were standing now.

"He came to research a movie in which he's going to play Lincoln. He stood right where you are, and he asked some of the same questions."

Liam Neeson as Lincoln. Interesting call, and I thought a good one. I was impressed. Neeson is from Northern Ireland, but I knew he was capable of very good regional American accents, and of course, he was and is a very good actor. He's 6-foot-4, the same height as Lincoln, also physically strong, and known for portraying strong, straightforward characters.

After we thanked the ranger for his time, we spent another hour or so at the tomb. We then drove into downtown Springfield and visited the family's home as well as the new museum.

After our family returned home from Springfield, I got online and spent perhaps 45 minutes before I found anything about the film, even using search engines. I found that there was indeed a movie about Lincoln in the works, and that Liam Neeson had agreed to play Lincoln. I didn't find much more.

Well, the years went by and every once in a while, I'd search to see if there was any news about the film. Finally, in 2012, the movie came out. But it wasn't Liam Neeson playing Lincoln. It was another respected actor from the other side of the pond, Daniel Day-Lewis. The film, called simply *Lincoln*, was directed by Steven Spielberg and based largely on the book *Team of Rivals* by Doris Kearns Goodwin.

As it turned out, Liam Neeson was formally cast in the role of Lincoln in 2005 and researched Abraham Lincoln extensively. However, by 2010 when all was ready to start shooting, Neeson, by then 58 years old, told Spielberg that he was too old to play Lincoln.

If you've seen photos of President Lincoln in 1865, when he was 56 years old, the irony will probably strike you as it did me. By age 56, Abraham Lincoln looked like a much older man, probably in part due to heredity, perhaps physical conditions such as Marfan syndrome, and largely due to the loss of a beloved mother and sister at a young age, the loss of a beloved woman, Ann Rutledge, the loss of two beloved young sons, the raging fight over the abolition of slavery, and the deaths of nearly a million Americans and untold injuries of 1.5 million more.

As I'm telling you this story, Liam Neeson is in his early 70s. To me, he still looks younger than Abraham Lincoln did at 56 in the last year of the war. I'm sure that Liam Neeson would have made a great Abraham Lincoln.

Daniel Day-Lewis gave one of the great performances in the history of film. In addition to a Golden Globe, British Academy, Screen Actors Guild and almost 40 more awards won by the film, Daniel Day-Lewis won his third Academy Award, making him the only male actor ever to do so.

Visitors

I woke up in my room at the Springfield DoubleTree at 6:30 the morning after showing Abraham Lincoln how to send me a text message. Shortly after waking up, I checked my text messages. There was nothing from my traveling partner across the hall, which I took as a good sign. I texted Molly to say "Good morning" and find out how her day was going so far. She has always gone to bed an hour or two before me and woken up at some crazy hour like 5:00 in the morning. I then shaved with my cordless razor, brushed my teeth, got dressed, packed my few possessions, and went downstairs.

Mr. Lincoln and I met in the hotel lobby shortly before 8:15 as agreed. Actually, I arrived 10 minutes early in order to check out and make sure I arrived first. But he was already there. We nodded to each other as I checked out and then I walked over to him as he sat in a large chair near a fireplace. Repeating the scene from my house, he was once more sitting up very straight with his arms extending forward, flat on the chair arms, his fingers curled over the front over the arms. I was once more struck by the resemblance between my guest and the 19-foot-tall Georgia granite statue of him that looks out on Washington, D.C. from the Lincoln Memorial. Thinking about that resemblance again, I had a slight grin on my face by the time I reached him in his chair, where he remained seated.

"Either you want to share a joke, or an amusing event, or both," said my guest, noticing the grin that I wasn't aware of until then.

"Oh…time just became compressed for me. A face I'd seen in Matthew Brady photographs all my life suddenly had a real person to compare them to," I said.

"I see," he said, smiling a little more broadly. "I'm sure I'm seeing a similar phenomenon, just from the opposite perspective.

"But if I have the wisdom for which American people of my day seem to give me credit," he said, continuing with a light tone in his voice, and looking around to make sure nobody else was within earshot, "as much as I'm enjoying the great developments that took place since I was here the first time, I need to forget these things when I return home, and act as if I've never seen them. It may seem sad, but truth be told, I have the opportunity to see the best of both worlds...or of both *times*. I do wonder how many other people, if any, may ever be able to do that. But keeping from changing the intended timeline is an objective that deserves my utmost care."

"I can appreciate it. I appreciate your insight," I replied. Then I added "How did you sleep?"

"Oh, I slept very well, thank you," he replied. "My bed was comfortable beyond my ability to describe it. Despite all these marvelous new inventions that help people to do their work, it's simple things, like mattresses...and toilet paper...and toothbrushes and toothpaste...that seem to...that seem to allow people to focus more on what they really *want* to do, instead of things they *have to do*."

I thought about something I call *the Jetsons effect*. In the old animated cartoon series, George and Jane Jetson and their children (i.e., his boy Elroy and daughter, Judy) had all of the imagined conveniences of the future including Rosie the robot maid and a DE-luxe apartment in the sky. When I watched it as a kid, I always thought that as humans developed all of these wonderful, new time-saving inventions to perform their labor, adults would be working 20-hour weeks and spending the rest of their time traveling, reading, and watching good movies. But it didn't turn out like that. Most adults continue to work 40-hours a week, or more, either because our employers expect it or because we expect it of ourselves.

"The weather was very pleasant last night," my guest said. "Nice weather for sleeping. From the time I was a boy, I found that I liked cool sleeping weather. If it's too warm, I have difficulty sleeping. If it's too cool, a blanket can make me very comfortable indeed. Last night, it was a bit warm in my room, and just as I was ready to retire, I discovered that I could slide my window open. I opened it just two or three inches. My windows had screens, like those screens you showed me at your house, and being up on the second floor, I didn't have to worry about anybody climbing in through the open window. And no more than four or five minutes after I settled into that comfortable bed, I heard a whip-poor-will, in some woods no more than a few hundred feet away. I enjoy their call. It called for perhaps 10 minutes, and then stopped for about a minute, and then started again. I don't know how long it called the second time because its call helped to put me to sleep.

"And how did *you* sleep, my friend?" he asked.

"I slept very well, too," I responded. "Straight through the night. And I've realized that, as much as I've become accustomed to some of these inventions that are very new to you, many of them are no more than…well, it's only been about 20 years since people have widely used these portable phones. And I remember when I was young, even simple things like mattresses and pillows were not as comfortable as they are today."

"I suppose we've both seen a lot of changes in our respective times," he posited.

"I sure think that's right," I agreed.

Then, during a brief time while I was putting my paper receipt (I still like paper receipts) in an outer compartment of my small suitcase, he looked around again briefly, smiled slightly, and asked "Did you see it?"

I looked at him and thought for just a few seconds before responding, making sure that I knew what he meant, but there was only one thing.

"No, I didn't," I replied. "I looked down in the parking lot just before I went to bed, and then just after I woke up, but no black Suburban. I take it that you didn't see it, either?"

"No, I did not," he confirmed. "I did the same as you, although I did wake up once during the night and looked then. But the conveyance in question was not there," he said, speaking just slightly in lawyer-ese. "And I haven't seen anybody or anything unusual inside the hotel, either," he added.

We hadn't yet talked about breakfast. Probably by force of habit, it's difficult for me to start the day without something to eat, and usually a bowl of cereal with milk is just the ticket. With Mr. Lincoln, however, he didn't seem to need much. His secretary, John Hay, had written that my guest usually just had an egg and a cup of coffee, or a biscuit and a glass of milk, or a plate of fruit in season to feel satisfied before doing his tasks. I asked my guest, and he confirmed that was correct.

In addition to big, warm chocolate chip cookies, I noticed that this DoubleTree had "On the Go" breakfast bags. In order to minimize the likelihood that someone would recognize my traveling partner—I felt there would be a greater likelihood of that here in his hometown, just a few blocks from where he and his family lived for 17 years—I asked him if he minded if we each grabbed one of the bags and then found a quiet place to eat down the street. He agreed that that was a good idea, and we each picked up a bag o' breakfast.

We gathered our things, walked out of the DoubleTree, and loaded our suitcases in the trunk of my car. The temperature was in the lower 40s, a bit cooler than when we had arrived late the previous

274

afternoon. The cars in the parking lot all had a fine, whitish coating of dew on them, including mine, and there was a very light fog in the air. We climbed into the front seats, started up and headed south on South 7th Street, in the direction of my guest's Springfield home.

Less than five minutes later, we drove to the Lincoln Home National Historic Site Visitor Center and arrived at the parking lot just north of it. I was prepared to take a ticket from a machine to pay for parking, but was pleasantly surprised to find that there was no charge for it.

The four blocks closest to the Lincolns' home are blocked off to vehicles, so stopping at the Visitor Center first is the way to go. I pulled my Buick into a parking space. It was just a few minutes before opening and there were only six other vehicles there. I took a quick look and saw they were from all over: Illinois, Georgia, Wyoming, Massachusetts, New Mexico, and Wisconsin. Mr. Lincoln suggested this would be as good a place as any to eat our breakfasts, and I agreed.

We opened up our breakfast bags and were both pleased at the contents, light but tasty and nutritious. The contents of both bags were identical and included a Nature Valley apple granola bar, a blueberry muffin in a sealed plastic bag, an apple, a sealed plastic cup of orange juice, a cup of yogurt, along with a plastic spork and two paper napkins. As my guest took a good-looking apple with a small sticker saying Honeycrisp on it, he remarked how large it was, and I realized that in his time, it would have been an enormous piece of fruit. We started eating as we developed a little more detailed approach for our visit.

The main thing Mr. Lincoln wanted to see was the home that he and his family left in February 1861.

"I've thought about our home in Springfield a great deal since leaving this city," he told me thoughtfully. "In the first few years of the war, I never felt I could harbor a realistic hope for returning. The first glimmers of hope came in early July of Eighteen Hundred Sixty-Three, when our boys fought so bravely at Gettysburg under Gen. Meade at the very time that others finally ended the Siege of Vicksburg under Gen. Grant. With the newfound momentum and hope for ending the war, I felt that Mary and I, and perhaps Tad, could safely make the trip back by rail and visit my extended family and good friends here in town." He then described the other homes in the area and their relative locations. It sounded as if we might be able to see all of them while leaving my car parked right in this space.

As he finished chewing a bite of his apple, my passenger looked over at me and said, "I know that most people never have an opportunity to do what I'm doing, and I'm grateful. Thank you."

I told him that I was the one who should be grateful, without going into details about the Good Friday night play at Ford's Theatre or the subsequent events. I then asked him how he liked his breakfast, and he said he was enjoying it very much.

As my watch displayed 8:30 a.m., people began to step out of their vehicles to head toward the front door of the Visitor Center about 100 feet to the north. A few folks hobbled a bit, as if they had been sitting for a while during long drives. My guest and I stayed in the car for another couple minutes while we finished our breakfasts. A few minutes after opening, we took our bags, now full of used sporks, napkins, and apple cores, and headed toward the Visitor Center. We could see a staff member inside coming to unlock the door. We deposited our bags in a large green waste container that was several feet away.

Once inside, we got in line at the front desk to purchase tickets. Most of the people who'd walked in ahead of us were already looking around at photographs and displays around the room, and we came to the front of the line after less than a minute. There is no charge to visit Lincoln's home and neighborhood, but they issue tickets to control foot traffic on the streets and in the homes. Visitors must be accompanied by a park ranger when they enter the Lincoln home, and no more than 15 people are allowed into the house at a time.

A staff member in a dark green National Park Service t-shirt—who saw my familiar-looking guest and gave him a big smile—asked for my zip code and gave me two tickets. I took them and handed one to my guest, then proceeded to walk around inside the Visitor Center to look at the photos of the local homes and stories about President Lincoln, his family, and their neighbors. Until this time, we had both avoided references to the manner of my guest's passing, and I continued to hope that we would not encounter any reference to it. I thought it was reasonable to expect that in the Visitor Center, the focus would not be on the last day of President Lincoln's life, but rather on his growing up, his life in Springfield, and his presidency including the Civil War and the end of legal slavery in the United States.

As we entered one room of displays, there stood a life-size cardboard cutout with an actual photograph of President Lincoln attached to it. My guest noticed it at the same time that I did, and he walked up to it. A small smile appeared on his face. And, as happenstance would have it, during the few seconds he stood there in his rudimentary disguise, a young mother and father and their two young kids appeared from behind us and stared. In an echo from our encounter at Bronson Park, a little boy, about four years old, mouth wide open, pointed at my guest. At that point, my guest's little smile turned into a big one.

"A movie," we both responded at the same time, even jinx-ishly, which resulted in the mom and dad, my guest, and me all laughing. "PBS," I added. "A local documentary for another market. Did we pick the right guy for the role, or what?" I asked the young couple.

"Oh, yes!" they replied. "Very believable."

"Well, thank you," replied my guest in that surprisingly light Kentucky accent.

"Oh," replied the young woman. "Well…you may not sound like him, but you look just like him."

I smiled and looked over at my guest, who still had the smile on his face, but whose eyebrows were now arched halfway up his forehead in a look of complete amusement.

"Well, I'll keep working on the voice," he said.

We engaged in some brief talk with the children as well as the parents, then said goodbye. I knew that my guest would remember that encounter.

After spending about 30 minutes in the Visitor Center, we decided that we'd be on our way to see the homes. Prioritizing, we decided to visit my guest's home before the others. We found a sign next to a side door of the Visitor Center that pointed toward the home, and we stepped out the door.

The cool, early fall morning was already turning into a warmer mid-morning and it was becoming quite pleasant. Remembering the encounter with the young family, my guest laughed again, and he assured me that he'd keep working on that voice.

You Can't Go Home Again?

The home of Abraham and Mary Todd Lincoln in Springfield, Illinois. The house, where the family lived from 1844 to 1861, was the only house the Lincolns ever owned. Photo courtesy National Park Service.

Although changes were made on some neighborhood homes after 1865, the National Park Service restored them to how they looked when the Lincoln family lived there. After the Lincolns left their home at the corner of Jackson and 8th streets, the home was rented to a number of tenants who charged visitors to visit the house and who frequently left the home in disrepair. As a result, in 1887 Robert Todd Lincoln donated the house to the State of Illinois on the condition that it would be well maintained and would be open to the public free of charge.

But that all happened after the Lincolns left Springfield for Washington in February 1861. Fortunately, it was restored to a state where it could be proudly shown to visitors, and even its proud former owner, who was now walking alongside me toward the house.

The four-block area, now blocked off from vehicular traffic, still had gravel roads as it had when Mr. Lincoln lived there. In order to keep shoes from getting dusty or muddy in his time, wooden-plank sidewalks lined both sides of the east-and-west running Jackson Street and the north-and-south running 8th Street. During our visit, the sidewalks were gray from exposure to the sun and weather but in good condition, and enjoyable to walk on. I liked the clonk-clonk-clonk sound as our feet took steps on them.

We had only walked about 40 feet when Mr. Lincoln's home came into view, and from the instant he saw it, he barely took his eyes off it.

"Does it look like you remembered it?" I asked him.

"Yes, it does indeed," he responded. "Frankly, I never imagined that it would look so much as it did when we left." The house was a two-story Greek Revival style, dark mustard color with green shutters aside each of its many windows. On the front side from which we approached at an angle, the upstairs had five windows and the bottom had four, with the front door directly under the center upstairs window. On the side, there were four windows—two upstairs and two downstairs—on the main section, with additional windows on an addition that was visible in back. As we continued to walk toward it, he continued to occasionally check around that nobody else could hear him, and he began to tell me about his family's house.

One of the most notable features of the Lincoln home was that it sat about three feet up above the sidewalk with a brick retaining wall surrounding the yard. Because the house was so close to the street on both the Jackson and 8th Street sides, there really was no room to slope the yard down to the sidewalk, so the Lincolns had the wall built.

Although the house today looks almost exactly as it did when the family left, it's very different from how it looked when the Lincolns first moved in, both inside and out.

"I'm so happy they preserved it so well," he said. "It reflects the way it looked after Mary and I had work done on it, which was a big change from when we first saw it. The house was built in 1837 by the Rev. Charles Dresser, who performed our marriage ceremony in 1842. It was much smaller than you see it now. It was just one-and-a-half stories high, and the entire house was the height and width that the main front section is now. The house was white then; it had green shutters, about the same color they are now. When we first saw it, it was small and very comfortable and Mary loved it from the start. We purchased it, along with the lot, from Rev. Dresser for $1,500 in May of 1844. Mary and I moved in along with Robert, who was less than a year old then.

"During the evenings," he continued, "after I came home from working, Mary and I talked occasionally about the house, and it soon became evident that our little home would serve us better if it weren't quite so little. So in 1846, we began the first remodeling. We added a bedroom and a pantry to the back and moved the kitchen.

"Our son Eddie was born while we did that first remodeling," he said, and then sighed. Not surprisingly, thoughts about his young son, who was born just 19 years before by his calendar, did not come easily.

"Then, three years later, we performed additional work," he said. "That's when we built the retaining wall, bricked over the sidewalk, and installed stoves in the parlor." Mr. Lincoln then explained that it was during that period, in December 1849, that Eddie died, less than two months after contracting what was likely tuberculosis. Mr. Lincoln was then silent for a short while, and I thought the best thing was to just allow him to be with his thoughts for a minute.

"By my internal reckoning," he finally explained, "Eddie left us just 16 years ago. The sadness is different, but it's still there." I replied that I was sorry for his loss, and I had some idea what he was going through, as Molly and I lost a son about three years after we were married, and his memory and presence are still with us. Mr. Lincoln went on to tell me how Willie was born in 1850 and Tad in 1853. It was Willie who died in February 1862, when the Lincolns had been in the Executive Mansion less than a year, just three years ago in my Mr. Lincoln's reality. And Tad would die six years after the end of the Civil War.

It was during 1855-56, the general period of Mr. Lincoln's visit to Kalamazoo, that the height of the house was increased from one-and-a-half stories to two stories. The bedroom that had been downstairs was moved upstairs, allowing for a true parlor to be created downstairs. It was that parlor where, for a brief period after his election, Mr. Lincoln would see visitors and well-wishers before he departed for our nation's capital.

We approached the front of the Lincoln home, where a group of about eight people were gathered with a male park ranger whose name tag said "Jonathan." He was engaged in a friendly conversation with the other visitors; when we approached the group, he was asking visitors where they were from. Jonathan was roughly college age—about the same age that Robert Todd Lincoln was when he served as an assistant adjutant in the U.S. Army in 1865, and was present in the McLean farmhouse in Appomattox Courthouse, Virginia when Gen. Lee surrendered to Gen. Grant. Jonathan actually had a slight resemblance to young Robert except

Jonathan had blond hair. He wore the light olive shirt and dark olive slacks of a park ranger and was wearing a dark olive insulated jacket, something that I thought he'd probably be removing soon because the day was getting warmer.

Jonathan looked at everyone in the group and literally did a double-take when he saw my guest, and a smile came to his face as he continued to look at the 6-foot-4 tourist in front of him wearing sunglasses and a Tigers baseball cap.

"Hi, how ya' doing today?" asked Jonathan in the enthusiastic voice of someone who enjoyed their work.

"Oh, very fine, very fine indeed," responded my guest. "I'm looking forward to seeing this home and the others here." By now, others in the group were looking at my guest, trying politely not to stare but stealing a glance now and then. Invariably, their faces were smiling and their eyes were wide, taking in how much my guest looked like the former occupant of the home we were about to visit.

"Well, something about you tells me you know a little bit about Lincoln," Jonathan said, with a slight laugh.

"Oh, well, I do know something about this area and the people who lived here," responded my tall guest with a slight chuckle. "I've done some research."

"Oh, wow. That's great," responded Jonathan with an interested laugh. "Where are you folks from?"

"We drove from Kalamazoo," replied my guest, "though I'm originally from Kentucky, and spent some time in this area when I was younger."

"Oh, is that right?" responded Jonathan. "I graduated from the University of Illinois this spring and one of my roommates was from

Kalamazoo. He says it's a great place. I never got to visit, but I may still do that, maybe get together for a football game in Kalamazoo or Ann Arbor. You probably know that President Lincoln was originally from Kentucky, and spent some time in Indiana before coming here to Springfield."

"Yes, I did know that," responded my guest, with no attempt to be condescending. "I know something about his time he spent in New Orleans and navigating the Ohio and the Mississippi as a young man, also."

"That's right," answered Jonathan. "I've read a number of books about President Lincoln, and it was my interest in him that brought me here. He was a great man whose views evolved over time, and he's really unique among Americans."

"Thank you," replied my guest, "…for sharing that with us."

As a few more people gathered for the tour, Jonathan welcomed them in a slightly louder voice as they approached, and I took the opportunity to give my guest a good-natured elbow to the arm, whispering "Nice recovery."

"Once again, thank you," he replied.

As all of the group was now present, Jonathan welcomed us, thanked us for coming, acknowledged the president for whom the site is dedicated, and then took about five minutes to tell us about the house. Virtually everything he said about the house was a restatement of what my guest had told me a few minutes before, as well as a confirmation of what I had read previously and our family's previous tour of the house. He added a description of some of the repairs and maintenance that paid and volunteer craft experts had performed over the summer, and told the group about Robert Lincoln's requirement that the house remain both free to visitors and well maintained, two promises that our National Parks staff had made good on. Jonathan's remarks demonstrated that both his training and interest in the subject matter had served him well for this position.

Then it was on to tour my guest's house, and we filed up the short front walk.

After passing through the brown front door, we passed through the entryway and into the front parlor with its muted wallpaper, dark red rug and rust-and-gold-colored curtains with gold cornice. There were a number of paintings of flowers and people on the walls, including portraits of George and Martha Washington, in round or oval picture frames. The frames hung from the walls with yarn that was suspended from the crown molding at the top of the wall. It was in that parlor where Mr. Lincoln received his formal offer to be the Republican nominee for president in May 1860, and where he received guests in November 1860 after winning the presidential election.

From the front parlor we moved along, like a big centipede, to the rear parlor, with similar wallpaper, carpet and curtains. Like the front parlor, there were many items that showed the natural browns and grain of the wood from which they were made, including the fireplace, mantel, and furniture. The fireplace, mantel and larger pieces of furniture tended to be made of lighter woods, with chairs and similar smaller items made of darker woods. In both parlors there were candles on the mantel; they would have been very functional in their day. The front parlor had a large black stove next to the fireplace and the rear parlor had two large world globes on wooden stands.

As we entered each room, Jonathan described the room and how the Lincoln family would have used it. My guest continued to look at the contents of each room closely and smile, no doubt pleased with how well they had been maintained over 150-plus years. I'm sure that many items brought back memories, which for him were created as recently as four years earlier.

We entered the sitting room, which had cream-colored wallpaper with a rose-colored design. The curtains again were green with a gold cornice. After Jonathan had finished describing the room and its purpose, and asking for questions, he and the other visitors moved on to the next room. I stayed back with my guest, who explained that the boys were not allowed in the parlors but that they had the run of the sitting room. He said he played with them for hours in this room, and I could tell that he wanted to spend a little more time there.

The dining room, like the parlors, had wallpaper that was generally muted, but the dining room wallpaper had clusters of colorful flowers about every two feet. The curtains here, too, were green with a gold cornice. Plates and other dishes sat on a hutch made of wood that was quite dark. Jonathan said Mrs. Lincoln had the dining room built separate from the kitchen so the boys would know the two different functions (cooking and eating) and that they were taught etiquette in the dining room.

The kitchen was at the back of the house, behind the dining room. It looked very utilitarian, with light tan walls, just one window, and a few kitchen tools hanging on the wall or sitting on a dark wooden table about 10 feet long on which meals were prepared. There was a black cast iron cooking stove but, of course, no refrigerator or microwave oven. There was a wooden cabinet with a small metal basin. The floorboards, which were about five inches wide, were painted dark green. On the wall behind the stove, several cooking tools hung from hooks on a dark wooden four-inch-wide wooden strip. I recognized the rolling pin, funnel, a strainer, and a spatula used for a griddle, along with a few older tools that I didn't recognize.

Later, after we left the house to visit other homes at the site, my guest told me that when the Lincolns first purchased the home, Mrs. Lincoln didn't cook much. Having been raised in a family of means in Kentucky, the Todd family had staff to do all the cooking, cleaning and other chores. But she learned how to cook, did much of the family cooking, and Mr. Lincoln found her dishes to be very tasty.

I went along with the visitors' group when they went upstairs to view the foyer near the top of the stairs, and my guest followed along shortly after. We viewed the guest room, Mr. Lincoln's bedroom, and Mrs. Lincoln's bedroom. For families that were upper-middle-class or outright wealthy at the time, it was common to have separate bedrooms for the husband and wife.

When I think about homes of the average citizen in early America, I tend to think of their décor as being very Puritan with many shades of black, white, and gray. But the wallpaper in Mr. Lincoln's bedroom, which has been reproduced as it was when he left, consists of a wild pattern in cream and dark taupe, and irregular shapes of deep purple that would do Prince and Donny Osmond proud. Similarly, the carpeting was alternating strips about 12 inches wide each of intricate green and red designs. His spindle bed, in a medium-dark grain that looked like walnut, was very similar to some of the beds we had in our house growing up. A small writing desk in the corner had some letters and other items in its compartments, with a few books sitting on top...not a surprise given Mr. Lincoln's enjoyment of reading. There was also an armoire and a dresser.

Mrs. Lincoln's bedroom had the same wallpaper, but a smaller bed, an armoire in a corner, a commode and wash basin, and a potbelly stove for heat against an exterior wall. Her curtains were plain white.

The boys' bedroom was close in size to Mrs. Lincoln's but it didn't have any wallpaper and it was more sparsely furnished, with just a double bed and two small chairs and tables. A game board was set up to show visitors where the boys would have played checkers or marble games. The walls were painted a cream color, and the curtains were white. When the Lincoln family left the home in 1861, Robert—who was born 18 years earlier—was already studying at Harvard, so the room was shared by nine-year-old Willie and seven-year-old Tad. I could only imagine the boyish mischief they must have gotten into, particularly with their permissive father. And I could only imagine the excitement they must have had when they learned they'd get to move from the small Midwestern town of Springfield, Illinois, to the rapidly growing Washington, D.C., where they'd live in the sprawling Executive Mansion with their mother and father, the president and First Lady.

Except for the "trunk room," essentially a single large closet near the back of the second floor, the last room remaining upstairs was the maid's room, also called the "hired girl's room." The "hired girl" would have been a teenager with a lot of responsibility, including cleaning, cooking, and helping to take care of a couple rambunctious young boys. Her bedroom was similar to the boys' bedroom except smaller. The room had no carpeting or rugs, with the floorboards painted a rust color.

After we all stood in the crowded upstairs hallway looking at the rooms, we turned in place to head down the stairs and stepped back outside. The group gathered again, and Jonathan answered a few more questions. Then the group disbanded and we went in our separate directions. My guest told me that he thought Jonathan did a "commendable job" of leading the tour, and also said he enjoyed interacting with the other visitors, all of whom expressed an evident interest in our 16th president, his family and neighbors.

The two of us strolled around the area and walked past some of the homes that were there when the Lincolns lived in the home we just left. Those houses included the Dean House, the Charles Arnold House, and the Henson Robinson House. All of them were well maintained and helped to show visitors what the neighborhood looked like when Mr. Lincoln walked to and from his law office each day.

My guest told me a number of stories about the neighbors and changes to the neighborhood that he remembered during his 17 years there. After we had both satiated our desire to see these beautiful old homes, including the Lincolns', we walked back to my car and drove to the Old State Capitol Building about a half-mile to the north.

Man About Town

When we arrived at the Old State Capitol Building about four blocks away, we parked in the underground parking garage located directly under the building.

On the short drive to the old building, my passenger told me about his role in making the city of Springfield what it still is to this day.

"For a few years, a motley caucus of nine Whigs, including yours truly—I was the one whose presence ensured that we were particularly motley—tried to bring the state capital here from Vandalia. Vandalia was selected as the state's capital in 1820, when I was a confident eleven-year-old, because it was close to the center of the state, and also to the state's waterways, primarily the Ohio River, from which the state was settled. However, over time, the population of the state increased substantially more in the northern part of the state, particularly in Chicago and its surrounding communities, so there was strong sentiment for moving the capital north. Finally, in 1837, the legislature voted to move the state capital here.

"Construction was begun that same year," he said, "and completed three years later. Immediately, the legislature began using the new building." The building served as the state house from 1840 until 1876, when it was already evident that a larger building would be needed to serve a growing state of Illinois.

Built in the Greek Revival style, the Old State Capitol Building was constructed from yellow limestone from the town of Cotton Hill, Illinois, less than 10 miles southeast of Springfield. Although it's called "yellow limestone," it's actually variegated shades of tan and brown. A dark red dome tops off the building, supported by bright white columns.

After we finished parking my car, we climbed the steps up to the grounds outside the old building. When we arrived at ground level, we were perhaps 100 feet away from the building, and we took a few minutes to stop and just look at it.

"It still looks good," said Mr. Lincoln, "very good for a building that's nearly 200 years old. The limestone has become darker and browner, but that's to be expected. Overall, it's in marvelous shape.

"I only worked for one two-year term as a state legislator here," continued my guest. "Eighteen Hundred Forty and Forty-One. But after that, for almost 20 years, from 1841 to 1860—the last year of which I campaigned for the presidency—I pleaded cases before the Illinois Supreme Court here. Many cases. Mr. Douglas was a justice on the court for some of those cases. I also gave a number of speeches here while in the legislature.

"Now, whether a politician admits to it or not," said my guest, "their actions are partly dictated by how the public reacts to them. By 'the public,' I mean both the voters and the press. If I were asked which of my speeches, prior to my assuming the presidency, were most important, I'd mention three. The first—and this may or may not surprise you—was my speech in Kalamazoo in 1856. That speech produced a great deal of recognition, not only to my thoughts about the issue of slavery, but also opened the minds of many and generated much discussion about the question itself. After that speech, the general public, particularly in the Midwestern states, no longer relied on the so-called 'statesmen' to solve the question, but rather made it clear that *all* citizens could and should have a say in the matter.

"The second speech," he said, "which I gave almost four years later, in early 1860, was the Cooper Union Address in New York City. I had been invited to give that speech five months earlier, and spent a great deal of time researching it. My friend, Mr. Herndon, told me he observed that 'no former effort in the line of speech-making' had 'cost me so much time and thought as this one.' In preparing for the Cooper Union Address, which I gave at Henry Ward Beecher's church in Brooklyn, I examined the views of 39 signers of our Constitution. I found, and the speech detailed, the fact that of the 39 signers, a majority of them—21—specifically stated that slavery should be controlled by Congress, not allowed to expand. Therefore, my overall position on the topic was close to the consensus of the Founders, although, as you know, it was causing consternation among many in the South.

"The third speech," he explained, "occurred midway in the time span between the other two. It was my speech at the Republican State Convention in this very building on June 16, 1858, accepting their nomination for the U.S. Senate. At about five o'clock that afternoon, more than 1,000 delegates from the party selected me as their nominee for that position, and I had a speech sufficiently prepared to present it at eight o'clock that evening. Although I thought the address was exactly the right one to give at the time, some in my party as well as Democrats questioned whether it was the right time to give that address. Soon after, people started calling it the 'House Divided Speech'."

The consensus of Mr. Lincoln's contemporaries, including close friends and colleagues, was that the speech cost Mr. Lincoln the seat in the U.S. Senate, but did much to gain him the presidency two years later. (Mr. Lincoln lost the senate seat to Democrat Stephen A. Douglas by a 54-46 vote of the state legislature.) Mr. Lincoln's friend and law partner, William Herndon, thought the speech was "morally courageous but politically incorrect." Herndon thought the speech would be fodder for Lincoln's political opponents, saying "when I saw Senator Douglas making such headway against Mr. Lincoln's 'house divided' speech I was nettled and irritable." But later, after Mr. Lincoln's election to the presidency, Herndon thought the speech contributed significantly to his winning the office."

Another colleague of Mr. Lincoln, Maine native Leonard Swett, gave Lincoln advice and assistance throughout his political career. In an 1866 letter to Herndon, Swett reflected on the idea of short-term cost but long-term gain as a result of the House Divided Speech. Swett wrote to Herndon, noting that "Nothing could have been more unfortunate or inappropriate; it was saying first the wrong thing, yet he saw it was an abstract truth, but standing by the speech would ultimately find him in the right place."

Mr. Lincoln's words, all 3,209 of them, were thought to be quite logical and straight-forward by his supporters, but the following few sentences stood out to those who heard it that day or later:

> *"A house divided against itself cannot stand. I believe this government cannot endure, permanently half slave and half free. I do not expect the Union to be dissolved—I do not expect the house to fall—but I do expect it will cease to be divided. It will become all one thing or all the other."*

Mr. Lincoln and I entered the front doors of the building and were both very impressed by its architecture. The discussions that took place here more than a century and a half before had given shape to the state, and because of Lincoln and Douglas, the shape of the nation was formed, as well.

One hundred sixty-five years after Mr. Lincoln's memorable speech, another historic speech took place on the front steps of the Old State Capitol Building, when U.S. Senator Barack Obama announced his candidacy for the presidency.

In all likelihood, the building was in better condition when we toured it than when my guest originally spent time here. Originally, fireplaces kept the building warm, and the walls and ceilings, now bright white, where covered in soot. Round columns about a foot in diameter helped to support the upper story and roof, and actually added to the "old building charm" of the place. Desks similar to the ones that Mr. Lincoln and his colleagues used still remained.

Signs around the building described the building's history and its remarkable renovation that took place in the late 1960s.

Shortly after the end of the Civil War, officials realized that the building, which had only stood for about 30 years, was no longer large enough to serve a state that was growing in population and also financially—growth that was largely caused, ironically, by the war. So in the 1870s, the sixth and current Illinois State Capitol building was constructed, about a quarter-mile west of the old building. From 1876 to 1966, the old building served as the courthouse of Sangamon County and was altered substantially.

Then, in the early 1960s, renewed interest in the Civil War prompted by the centennial of the conflict led to discussions about restoring and preserving the old building. Prior to the 1960s, dedicated preservation of historic structures in the United States was a relatively rare thing, with one exception being the restoration of George Washington's home in Mount Vernon, Virginia, which began to fall into disrepair as early as the 1850s.

Another notable exception is the previously mentioned Ladies' Library Association (LLA) Building on South Park Street in Kalamazoo, of which Eliza Walbridge was a member. The LLA formed in 1852 and was the first women's club in Michigan, and just the third in the United States. One of their members, Ruth Webster, donated the property on which the beautiful building still stands, but before the LLA could build there, they had to change Michigan law, which stated that a woman could not own property unless she inherited it from her husband. The law was changed with the help of State Representative Jonathan Parsons, and the LLA building was constructed in 1878-79. Designed by Chicago architect Henry L. Gay, the Venetian Gothic style building is a testament to Kalamazoo's women who were ahead of their time.

During the renovation planning in the early 1960s, local Springfield architects were brought in to manage the project with financial support from the state. In addition, they consulted with other architects across the country. Their conclusion was that due to changes that were made over time, the best way to restore the building would be to dismantle it, piece by piece—including its 3,300 limestone blocks—and start anew.

And that's what they did. As each piece was removed, it was numbered, cataloged, and moved to the Illinois State Fairgrounds about three miles north of downtown Springfield. Then, while the building was temporarily gone, a 400-vehicle, two-story subterranean parking garage was built directly under where the old building had once existed, and where it would exist again.

The restoration project began in 1966 and completed in 1969. The process was described and acclaimed in newspapers and architectural journals across the country. The project served as a model for other restorations, including, to a much smaller extent, Mr. Lincoln's home a few blocks to the south.

We spent about an hour visiting the Old State Capitol Building. There was one remaining building he wanted to see, and it was literally right across the street from where we were.

The early 1840s were a time of extreme growth and change for the area. In addition to the completion of the brand-new state capitol building (now the Old State Capitol Building) in 1840, a local businessman named Seth M. Tinsley built an office building on North 6th Street south of Adams Street. In 1843, Lincoln moved in with Herndon's predecessor in the firm, Stephen T. Logan, one of Mary's cousins. Lincoln and Logan rented space on the third floor, which was considered excellent office space. The federal government rented the first floor as a post office, and the second floor served as a district courtroom, a judge's chamber, and a clerk's office. The entire building, especially the spaces allocated to district court work, were critical because at the time, the entire state of Illinois was a single district.

In this very building, in addition to carrying out his practice of law, Lincoln appeared before U.S. District Court Judge Nathaniel Pope in resolving 112 cases including 72 bankruptcy proceedings.

After being in business together for about a year, Lincoln and Logan dissolved their partnership and Herndon joined Lincoln as a new junior partner. A year after that, Gibson Harris joined as a clerk and student; he later described the office as having little furniture, and the few pieces they did have were usually in disrepair.

In Herndon's biography of Lincoln, he described an interesting habit that Mr. Lincoln had, the knowledge of which didn't reach our classrooms. According to Herndon "When he [Lincoln] reached the office, about nine o'clock in the morning, the first thing he did was to pick up a newspaper, spread himself out on an old sofa, one leg on a chair, and read aloud, much to my discomfort. Singularly enough Lincoln never read any other way but aloud." When we were there in Springfield together, I felt it would be untactful to ask my guest whether, during all those nights reading by candlelight as a boy, he read out loud while others slept.

When Abraham Lincoln left Springfield for our nation's capital in early 1861, people said Herndon already felt a piece of his life missing, and after the night at Ford's Theatre, they said the professional and well-organized Herndon's life lost direction. The legal partnership between Lincoln and Herndon was never dissolved until after that tragic night.

Before Lincoln left Springfield to become president he said to Herndon, "If I live, I'm coming back some time, and then we'll go right on practicing law as if nothing had ever happened."

Pre-Return Check

"Anything else you'd like to see?" I asked my passenger. We were once again sitting in the front seats of my Buick. He hadn't mentioned other places he wanted to go, but I wanted to check in case he'd thought of someplace else or had a change of heart.

A few seconds went by before he said "Well…" as I could tell he was thinking with that great mind and just wanted to let me know that he'd heard me, and was pondering the issue.

"No," he said softly, with a slight nod. "No, I don't need to. If we had an unlimited amount of time, it might be different. I still agree with you that it's not a good idea for me to visit the cemetery here. And I'm sure that there would have been many interesting things at the museum, but there undoubtedly would have been too much information about major events after my time. I had thought about visiting the train depot, but when I envisioned actually returning, I thought it would make me sad more than anything, thinking about all of my friends and neighbors who said farewell to me and my family there. I think I'll just let that particular location have a very special place in my memories."

I allowed a few more seconds to pass in silence in case he had *second* thoughts about visiting another place. Then he then looked over at me, and a slight smile appeared on his face.

"No," he said again. "But thank you for your time and effort, and for footing the cost of everything for your traveling partner. This has meant a lot to me. For the last four years, through many events, good and bad—mostly bad, I'm afraid—I thought about returning to Springfield. You made it possible for me to do that."

When I told him "The pleasure is all mine," it wasn't just a polite response, but reflected how I actually felt about the journey home with the 16th president of my country, a man responsible for profound positive changes in the country.

Before we got underway on our return trip, I told my passenger that I had some news: I'd talked with my wife on the phone and she asked if I'd mind if she spent another night at the lake. He and I agreed that it was unfortunate that he and Molly couldn't meet, but if I ever told her the full story about this unusual trip, to give her Mr. Lincoln's regards.

I inserted my key into the ignition and started the car. I decided that I wouldn't even need my GPS on the way home, as the signs and my memory of the few roads we'd taken would be enough. We pulled out of the parking structure and onto East Washington Street, and after only three blocks turned left on 9th Street, which would become North Peoria Road just north of town and take us to I-55, then I-94 south of Chicago.

On Our Way Back Home

"Two of us riding nowhere, spending someone's hard-earned pay."

- John Lennon and Paul McCartney, "Two of Us"

Not five minutes after leaving the parking structure underneath the Old State Capitol Building in Springfield, we were settling in for the ride, heading north on I-55 toward Chicago, then up and across into southwest Michigan. It was about two o'clock in the afternoon, and it would be at least partially dark by the time we got home.

Mr. Lincoln provided some bonus educational information to me by recalling some of the things we'd seen, then expanding on them. A few of his stories were based on subsequent thoughts he'd had since leaving the individual sites, but more of them were simply delayed to avoid having others overhear him talking about "having dinner with Mary and the boys" and the like.

I didn't expect there to be a constant banter between the two of us on the way back to Kalamazoo, but it was great to hear more stories.

At one point, Mr. Lincoln sighed and said, "I keep thinking about two days ago…my two days ago, my last day in Washington. Even before Mrs. Lincoln and I attended the theater, it was such a wonderful day. It was unusually warm for mid-April. We awoke to a chill much like the one here today, but by noon it had warmed to 63 degrees, and by five o'clock, it was 71. Mrs. Lincoln and I enjoyed our carriage ride around the city that afternoon. And I was happier than I had been since the beginning of the war four years earlier."

300

Indeed, before the president and Mrs. Lincoln left for Ford's Theatre, it had been an unusual and even historic day in a number of respects.

Although Gen. Grant had received Gen. Lee's surrender five days earlier with Robert Lincoln in attendance, the war was still not over. There was still fighting in the Carolinas as Confederate Gen. Joseph E. Johnston reluctantly ordered his troops to keep fighting—at least for now—at the insistence of Jefferson Davis.

Today, for the first time ever, Gen. Grant attended the cabinet meeting in the Executive Mansion. The meeting began at eleven o'clock in the morning. President Lincoln and Gen. Grant both felt that this might be the day they received news from Gen. Sherman that Johnston had surrendered and the war was over. Sherman's troops entered Raleigh that day, and Southern troops were falling back. However, Sherman was still preparing to follow Johnston, whose troops continued to head west, delaying an end to the conflict.

The cabinet meeting that day, like most, took place in President Lincoln's office. When Gen. Grant first entered the office, those present said that the president's face lit up. It was the first time the two had seen each other since Gen. Lee's surrender to Grant at Appomattox, and Lincoln soon asked Grant about the conditions of surrender. Grant replied that "I told them to go back to their homes and families, and they would not be molested, if they did nothing more…Kindly feeling toward the vanquished, and hearty desire to restore peace and safety at the South, with as little harm as possible to the feelings or the property of the inhabitants, pervaded the whole discussion." The two wanted the hostilities to end amicably, and seemingly the last thing on their mind was the actions of a person like John Wilkes Booth, or months later, the actions of new president Andrew Johnson which set back many of the gains made by brave men and women during the war.

Unlike other cabinet meetings for the last four years, the primary purpose of this meeting was to discuss not war, but peace, particularly the reentry of the Southern states into the Union. The president's office was usually large enough for cabinet meetings because his cabinet only had seven department heads, and even with Vice President Hamlin (recently replaced by Vice President Johnson), President Lincoln, and sometimes the First Lady in attendance, that would only be 10 people.

The American flag at the Executive Mansion that day was raised by Gen. Robert Anderson on the fourth anniversary of his surrender of Fort Sumter at the start of the war.

The president also described to me the dreams, or premonitions, he'd been having recently. Lincoln had long been known for attaching meaning to his dreams, and he frequently described those dreams to friends and family. He had also described those dreams to his cabinet at that last meeting on Good Friday.

Lincoln told his cabinet that he had recently dreamed of being on a "singular and indescribable vessel that was moving with great rapidity toward a dark and indefinite shore." The president said he'd had that same dream "before nearly every great and important event of the War" including the Union victories at Antietam, Gettysburg, and Vicksburg.

In those final days, Lincoln shared another dream with his friend Ward Hill Lamon, who frequently "took it upon himself" during much of Lincoln's administration to act as the president's bodyguard. Like Lincoln, Lamon stood out in a crowd. Lamon was also 6-foot-4, but unlike the lean 6-foot-4 Lincoln, Lamon weighed 260 pounds and was more physically imposing, a good size for a modern NFL linebacker. He was usually heavily armed, with two Colt .44 pistols, two Bowie knives, and an eight-inch dagger in the handle of his cane. Unfortunately, before the Lincolns' visit to

Ford's Theatre on Good Friday night, the president had asked Lamon to tend to matters in the former Confederate capital of Richmond, which had been occupied by federal troops for less than two weeks.

Lincoln told Lamon about the dream he'd had just three nights before his trip to Ford's Theatre. Lincoln said that in the dream, he had "wandered the Executive Mansion searching for the source of mournful sounds. I kept on until I arrived at the East Room, which I entered. There I met with a sickening surprise. Before me was a catafalque, on which rested a corpse wrapped in funeral vestments. Around it were stationed soldiers who were acting as guards; and there was a throng of people, gazing mournfully upon the corpse, whose face was covered, others weeping pitifully. 'Who is dead in the White House?' I demanded of one of the soldiers. 'The President,' was his answer. 'He was killed by an assassin.'" The president went on to tell Lamon that in this dream, the victim really wasn't himself, but rather "some other fellow" that the "ghostly assassin had tried his hand on."

After there had been a lull in the conversation for several minutes, I told my passenger that I had begun thinking again about the next leg of his journey, the one that would take him not only to our nation's capital, but back to his own time. Compared to the ten-hour round-trip we were on our way to finishing, it would seem like a few moments to him, but would be a monumental leap.

"Yes, I continue to give some thought to that impending event, as well," replied my passenger. "As I understand it, our required actions will be fairly simple. The vacuum tubes should be delivered directly to your house. We'll take them to the building where you and I met and install them. We'll make sure that the controls are set to the right return time and location. We'll turn on the machine, I'll bid you adieu and step through the dark Void. And then I should be back from whence I came."

"Yes, everything we've seen points to exactly those steps," I replied quickly, still astounded at how he processed information and how simply he shared it with others, in straightforward, logical terms. "But we're dealing with something that even in my time, few people know about. The general consensus in this day is still that traveling through time is not possible. And yet, here you are."

"Yes, there's no debating that," he responded, lightheartedly. "Here most certainly is where I am."

"We've both been careful about you not seeing anything here that you might act upon when you return," I said. "We avoided visiting the cemetery, and tried to avoid any information that might reflect the future of your administration. But there are still a lot of things we don't know. We know you're here, but we don't know *why* you're here. What made you come to this time? I think it's safe to assume you wound up in Mentha, near Kalamazoo, because that's where the entrance to the Void is. But did someone set a control to bring you here? Or…was there some series of events that took place that automatically brought you here when your own time or events reached a certain point?

"Did I trigger your unexpected journey here?" I continued. "And if that's the case, was it just an enormous blunder on my part, or did my entrance into the Void trigger something that was supposed to happen anyway?

"And then," I wondered aloud, "What'll happen when you return? Can we be sure that there's not already another Abraham Lincoln there, who will be surprised to find another one of himself when you show up at the front door of the Executive Mansion?"

"Two of me?" he said, with exaggerated shock. "I'm sure that my contemporaries won't be ready for that. Except perhaps for Mary. She might like one Abraham Lincoln to continue being president while the other Abraham Lincoln helps her when she goes shopping. Of course, I'd let her be the arbiter in terms of which Abraham Lincoln does which. If I followed the method I used as a young man, I'd wrestle any man in the Executive Mansion, including the other Abraham Lincoln, with the winner being the president. And I assure you, in my somewhat advanced years, I'd still the strongest man in the Executive Mansion…well, of course, except for me."

We both laughed a bit at his string of logic, and I also shook my head a bit, though my own reaction remained impressed that he had such a sense of humor after all he'd been through in his 56 years.

"And of course, I have to think about what happens to my own timeline when you return," I said, bringing things back to a conversation of wonder but seriousness. "Of course, if everything goes as expected, I won't notice any difference in this timeline at all. I know it won't surprise you to know that the population of this nation has increased several times over since your day, as has the population of the planet. A very small event could cause a large change in this day, like the ripples on a pond or the flutter of butterfly wings multiplied many thousands of times over."

"Well, be assured that I'm well aware of the need to avoid changing the way that things are supposed to be," said my passenger. "And I'll exercise my very best judgement in that matter."

"I know you will," I assured him.

We had good conversations during the five-hour drive back to Kalamazoo, and I'm sure we both checked periodically, when we remembered to, to see if there was a certain black Suburban around.

Back in Kalamazoo

We had a good drive back home. We stopped at two rest stops but we both decided it would be preferable to forego dinner in order to get home earlier and minimize driving in the dark to avoid deer. It was shortly before nine o'clock when we pulled into my driveway. My passenger was again amazed to see the garage door raise after I pushed the overhead button in my car, and then lower when I pushed it again.

After taking the suitcases out of the trunk, we went inside and collapsed in chairs in the family room in back. After confirming my guest's preference for a beverage, I went into the kitchen and poured a glass of milk for both of us. We were both a little tired but neither of us felt like going to bed yet. We started to talk about what we might do the next day until the vacuum tubes arrived. After coming up with a list of several options, he came up with the simplest one: reading a selection from my Shakespeare books. I bought a used set of Shakespeare's complete works at a local Kalamazoo bookstore a few years ago but had still not read them. I told my guest that when we were done with our glasses of milk, I'd show him into my office so he could select which book he'd like to read.

But first, I excused myself so I could go out to the mailbox at the street and get the mail. I grabbed the four or five pieces of mail that were in the mailbox and started back to the front door when I first noticed the Amazon box on our front porch. I stopped for a second, immediately thinking what Molly or I might have ordered other than the vacuum tubes. I couldn't think of anything, but either way, I picked up the box from the porch and took it inside with me.

I set the mail down on the small end table next to my chair in the living room, then took the box through our short entry hallway and across the front corner of the kitchen. I grabbed a small box cutter from our junk drawer in the kitchen and then walked into the family room where my guest was still sitting quietly.

"Let's see what we have here," I said.

He turned to me and asked "That wouldn't be the two tubes, would it?"

"I don't know," I said as I cut the tape on the top of the box, being careful not to go too deep. "I can't think of anything else we've ordered, but let's find out…" I continued as I finished opening the box.

There, in two smaller cardboard boxes, were two RCA 6L6GC vacuum tubes.

"Well, that sometimes happens. Items sometimes arrive before the planned date. Better that way than the other way around most of the time. They wouldn't want to disappoint customers by promising one date and then having it come days or weeks later. Well, at least we won't have to spend any time tonight or tomorrow wondering if we'll get 'em on time."

"Yes, that *is* a positive thing," he replied.

"That would have made two of us," I said. It was true, although my lack of patience would have been tempered by the fact that I'm living in my own place and time, and even if I don't watch the television or listen to news stories on the radio or drive around town in my car, I'm refraining from doing those things by choice; I could do any of them if I wanted to. My guest was a visitor not only in place, but in time.

Seeing that he'd finished his glass of milk, I asked if he'd like to go into my office to select a book or two to read.

"Umm…yes. Yes, I would, thank you," he said in a seemingly distracted manner as he got up out of his chair. We went into my office together and I showed him where the books were. All of my Shakespeare books, all 22 volumes, were on the same shelf of my bookcase. They all have similar covers, dark brown with gold lettering, with the name of the work and Shakespeare's name on the cover and spine.

After taking a minute or two to look at them, he selected two: *Macbeth* and *The Life and Death of King John*. I was sure that he'd read both, probably multiple times, but on this night, these two particular books by the Bard had an appeal for him.

"You must also be fond of Shakespeare, as I am," he asked.

"Yes, I am," I responded, "but honestly, you and some of my friends have developed quite a deep fondness for his work. I always felt that fully appreciating Shakespeare is like a light bulb…or a lantern…that for some people the connection lights up suddenly and brightly. That light probably isn't as bright for me, at this time in my life, but I do enjoy his work, and hundreds of years after he practiced his work, he's still regarded by most experts as the greatest practitioner of the English language. What do you like about those two particular works?"

"When I was a young lawyer riding the court circuit in Illinois, I had the good fortune of having friends and acquaintances from whom I could borrow various works, including Shakespeare. Of all the works I borrowed, and all the works I read, it was *Macbeth* that appealed to me most. It's about political ambition and the cost of power. As fortune would have it, of course, for the last four years I've found myself at the very center of both of those questions: political ambition and political power. But the tale has a lot to say to anyone.

"*The Life and Death of King John* is a lesser-known work, at least in my time. But it, too, has a message that shouldn't be ignored. History has recorded that of all the things John should have been, king of England wasn't among them. He was regarded as very impious and he fathered a number of children with wives of noblemen, which even in his day was considered unacceptable. His reign was marred by war, and he lost Normandy and other parts of France.

"The darker aspects of his reign are memorialized by the fact that in English history, there has only been one King John," said my guest. "The story goes that his reign was so ruinous and immoral that no subsequent king wanted to use the name. There have been several Henrys, Charles, Georges and Edwards, but only one John."

However," he said with the grin of someone about to deliver a punchline, "it should be noted that there have not been any subsequent Eadreds or Eadwig All-Fairs, either, or multiple adopters of several other appellations, but those individuals are generally not prominent in the annals of history.

"But for all the scandalous and appalling behaviors and malfeasance of King John, his rule led to one significant advancement for mankind. The Archbishop of Canterbury, Cardinal Stephen Langton, drafted the *Magna Carta Libertatum*, or as we generally abbreviate it, the *Magna Carta*, which was a revolutionary document in terms of declaring rights of the common man, even within the context of a monarchy. Of course, the *Magna Carta* led to the *Declaration of Independence*, *Constitution*, and similar documents created by democracies around the world.

I decided that this would be just the right time for me to start a systematic reading of the Bard's works. I began by selecting *The Two Gentlemen of Verona*, considered by some Shakespeare experts to be his first play. I didn't know how late we would be staying up that night, but for all those days and late nights that my guest sat somewhere reading alone, I thought he might enjoy having another person in the room, also reading the classic works of Shakespeare. (And I'd find out whether or not he actually read aloud all the time!)

We went back into the family room and each took a seat. I instructed our little Alexa unit to play music from Mozart's *Magic Flute* in the background at a low volume, knowing that Lincoln had attended a performance of it one month before he and Mrs. Lincoln saw *Our American Cousin*. He marveled at the seeming magic of small device that could play music upon verbal command, but also smiled in recognition of music he knew and enjoyed.

I wanted to minimize interrupting my guest's reading, but I no sooner opened my book when I noticed that one of the characters listed on the very first page of *The Two Gentlemen of Verona* was named Speed, "a clownish servant to Valentine." I mentioned that fact to my guest who chuckled, "Oh, that's right. I had forgotten. Perhaps Mr. Shakespeare was familiar with the inner workings of Springfield."

He and I sat for perhaps five minutes when I noticed him fidgeting a bit and occasionally looking away from his book, as if in the distance. He went back to reading his book and then, five or six minutes later, quietly tapped his fingers on the side of the book, and then looked away again. His reading style may have been situational: He didn't read aloud as his law partner William Herndon said that he did without fail, but then, he probably felt like a guest in someone's house and didn't think that appropriate. Perhaps he was just thinking about something he'd just read? I didn't think it likely.

By the third time he mentally took leave of his reading, I was now thinking about his seeming disengagement more than I was thinking about my own reading. Even before I noticed his actions, I was already having a little difficulty focusing myself. I was preoccupied

310

with my guest's absence from his rightful time and place—and wondered what might be happening then and there. I was thinking about the unlikely scenario that someone in the neighborhood back on that country road in Mentha might have seen me going in, or seen the two of us coming out—Mr. Lincoln without any disguise until we arrived at my car—and then gone into the shed, then found the hidden hatch and climbed down the ladder, and either vandalized the place or somehow rendered it useless. Although I was thinking about these potential disasters, I knew that the likelihood of any of them actually happening was very low.

But then, in satisfying my interest in researching history over decades, I realized that much stranger things have happened. The last 48 hours had proved that: I was certainly among a very few people in the world who knew that moving from one point in time to another was really possible.

And then it hit me.

Like Ray Romano's character of Ray Barone, who was perpetually unable to "read the room" in *Everybody Loves Raymond*, I'd failed to recognize what my guest was concerned about, and failed to realize that he was processing the same difficulties that I was.

"Do you want to go now?" I asked him.

He looked up, away from his book and at me, with those famous deep-set, dark-circled gray eyes and a growing smile on his face.

"I didn't know what *you* were thinking," he replied, "but I was beginning to think I was daft for imagining what might happen between now and when we return to the time station tomorrow morning. Am I daft?"

"Yes, I think so," I tried to deadpan, "but I am, too. In fact, I may be even dafter than you. And I was starting to realize that your imagination was starting to make you miserable, and misery loves company."

"I didn't feel I could ask you to drive us back to the time station after the hours of driving you did today," he confided, "but I'd be much obliged if you're willing to do it. Are you capable of making that drive?"

"Oh sure," I told him, "It's not more than 25 minutes away. We'll be there before we know it. I'll be happy to drive. Unless you want to."

"Hah!" he exclaimed in a burst of laughter. "Oh, no, no, that won't be necessary. I'll leave that job to daredevils such as you!"

My guest didn't really have any possessions to speak of, and I had unloaded our suitcases from the trunk, so within five minutes, we were in my car with our two RCA 6L6GC vacuum tubes. I left them in the shipping box and then placed them inside a small black and gray Swissgear computer backpack and gently set it down on the floor behind the driver's seat. My passenger again marveled at the invisible signal my car conveyed to the overhead garage door opener, causing it to open and then to close. Then we were off toward the shed, to the place where my dad's old farm house used to be when he was a boy. That place would now be the location where history would be set back to where it should be.

Reflections in the Dark

We drove back to Mentha on the dark, rural roads, a few miles per hour below the speed limit, knowing that deer were out in force on Fall evenings such as this one. About a half-mile before reaching the shed, I turned off my headlights and slowed down even further to minimize the chance of detection. This time, I pulled further off the road when we parked. We stepped out of my car and I grabbed the backpack from behind the driver's seat. I put it on my back and then locked the car. We both checked around to be sure that nobody was watching. The temperature had dropped into the low 40s.

Unlike the bright blue fall sky under which we left the day before, it was now very dark, with only the slightest crescent moon to light our way. The closest streetlight was more than a quarter-mile away. Some light came from windows and porch lights nearby. My guest and I still happened to be dressed in the darker clothes we were wearing when we returned from Springfield. That made us more difficult to see, which was good. I had my iPhone with me, but in order to avoid being seen, we'd only use its flashlight function if absolutely necessary.

"It's going to be a little bit of a challenge in the dark, isn't it?" I said to Mr. Lincoln. "But I have my eyeglasses and you don't, so why don't I lead the way? You can follow right behind me."

"That makes sense, I agree. My vision isn't dreadful without my spectacles, but since your vision is better, I'll follow your lead."

"Very good," I said. "I think the moon is giving just enough light to see where I'm going, and I think I remember the way pretty well."

We began making our way into the tall grass that started a few feet from the edge of the road. The dew had already been forming on every surface for the last hour or two, and the grass and everything else was quite damp. There was also a thin, fine fall haze in the air.

As we walked along slowly, we occasionally heard small rustling sounds around us from squirrels, raccoons, cats, and whatever other animals heard us coming. It didn't bother me too much, but if a garter snake happened to take the opportunity to find me and crawl up my pantleg, I didn't want my guest to see or hear my response.

After a few minutes, we were both startled when a barred owl in a tree less than 30 feet away suddenly let out a cry, sounding like "Who cooks for you? Who cooks for you all?"

As I turned around to look at Mr. Lincoln with my eyes wide, as if to say "That's not something I'm particularly used to happening," he replied "It's nice to know we have friends out here looking after us." Maybe it was due to his upbringing in the wilderness, but at any rate, it just goes to show how perspectives differ. But I liked his perspective more than mine.

It took about 10 minutes for us to reach the shed. I turned the handle, opened the door, and went inside with Mr. Lincoln right behind me.

After I closed the door behind us, I took my iPhone out of my pocket and turned on the flashlight, keeping it at a low level and pointing it downward to minimize the chance that it would be seen through the windows. We walked over to the hatch in the floor with me leading the way. When I opened the hatch, the room below gave enough light so we could see where we were going, so I turned off my flashlight. I started down the ladder and Mr. Lincoln followed right behind me. I headed through the Green Room and into the Control Room, then walked toward the back of the control panel to install the tubes.

"That backpack," he said, unprompted. "For me, that may be even more brilliant than your telephone." Curious at his remark, I smiled at him and asked him what he meant. Whatever his thoughts were, I knew they were in the context of a man who was relieved to be going home. I'd also be happy after he left, glad that he was back where he should be, but knowing I wouldn't be hearing his jokes or his accounts of one of the most important times in American history.

"Your telephone is a miraculous thing," he replied. "I've seen you use it, and I know that you can talk with other people with it, send and receive written messages, determine the temperature and weather forecast, find out the title of a song you used to listen to, take photographs—beautiful photographs with color—and you can carry all of that with you in your pocket.

"That miraculous device is the result of many hours, many years of technical advancements, which should not come as a surprise to anyone. It was just a matter of time before that was to happen. But your backpack..."

"Your backpack is such a simple idea, but they didn't have them in my time. I had a small, heavy canvas bag with a strap so I could carry it over my shoulder while riding the circuit. But its capacity was limited, and every hour or so, I'd have to switch sides because it made my one shoulder tired. But your backpack takes no such effort, and you could carry four or five books in it without any effort, or having to stop occasionally to switch it. And it's made from such a lightweight material. It's an example of something so simple that it seems it should have existed many years before.

"And going to the hotel in Springfield...wheels on our suitcases!" he exclaimed. "Our family never had them on our suitcases, and I'm sure that nobody I knew had them. And I'd reckon that none of us even thought about putting them on suitcases. But I'm sure that once companies began to put them on suitcases—what, 70 or 80 years ago???—they became commonplace, perhaps more common than suitcases that did not have them."

My guest made a great observation. The backpack and rolling suitcases both seemed so simple. I had to give some thought about his time estimate about the invention of the rolling suitcase. At first, I thought he might be off by several decades, but he was closer than I thought. In 1970, the year after Project Apollo with its 450,000 participants landed Neil and Buzz on the moon and returned them safely to the earth, an American named Bernard Sadow, owner of a small company called U.S. Luggage, removed four casters from his wardrobe and attached them to a suitcase. The idea was refined and patented two years later. However, many Americans didn't begin to replace their old, tried and true suitcases for years after that.

"I also appreciate your showing so many things to me," he said "the many inventions. Your descriptions have allowed me to use what knowledge I have and apply it to actually understand how these things work…perhaps not so well that I could have invented them myself, but well enough so I know they're not some sort of…black magic," he said, chuckling again.

"Our discussions and what you've shown me have made clear the differences between knowledge that's processed by the brain and knowledge that's processed by the heart," he said. "Knowledge that's processed by the brain involves "the three Rs": reading, writing, and 'rithmetic, as well as the sciences like chemistry, astronomy, and physics. All of these areas are best practiced by people with the appropriate education. People such as Isaac Newton and Galileo. Lacking the education, an ordinary citizen would likely have great difficulty understanding the inner workings of things such as your car or your phone.

"But knowledge processed by the heart is different. That knowledge involves things such as philosophy and how to treat others. You said

316

earlier tonight that you don't consider yourself an expert on Shakespeare, but nevertheless, you or I could have a discussion with one of these artists from hundreds or even thousands of years ago…Aristotle, Socrates, Plato…or old Will Shakespeare…and we could understand each other, differences in language notwithstanding. Those men could discuss poetry, love, hate, life and death, or political power, and we would understand them."

I had come here to install the tubes and get Mr. Lincoln back home, but for some time, I just continued to look back at him over my shoulder and admire both his wisdom as well as the truth he had just spoken.

"And though our Founders were among the most learned citizens of their day in the areas of sciences, languages, and the like," I added, "it was their knowledge of human behavior and philosophies of how people behave that left their legacy."

"Yes, exactly," he replied, nodding, and obviously excited. "And a tremendous legacy it was…and continues to be."

Prep for the Trip

"Every morning brings a new day, and every night, that day is through."

- Paul McCartney, "Every Night"

Our concerns about someone detecting our presence and changing something in the facility seemed unfounded. All of the equipment in the control room was just as we'd left it the previous morning. The rear panel was still removed from the dashboard and the screws and screwdriver were right where I'd put them. It was really no surprise: Before our presence the day before, the place seemingly hadn't witnessed any human visitors in a few decades. I set the backpack down to the side, far enough away that we wouldn't step on it or drop something on it. I then knelt down next to the chassis where the tubes would go.

Before I started my task, I looked at my watch and saw that it was shortly past10:30 at night. It hadn't been a particularly rough day, in fact, it had been a very enjoyable day. But 10 hours of driving over nearly 700 miles and changing time zones twice (once there and once back) had made me pleasantly sleepy. It didn't seem like it was the very same day that we had toured Mr. Lincoln's home, his neighbors' homes, his law office and the Old State Capitol Building in Springfield. And it certainly didn't seem like it had been only 36 hours since we had been at this place, and that I'd meet our nation's president from more than 160 years before. But I had no doubt that I had my wits about me enough to complete this task.

"Let me know if you need any help," said Mr. Lincoln, stepping over near where I was working.

"I will, thank you," I replied. "Stand by…I can easily replace these vacuum tubes, but when I put this panel on the back of the dashboard, I may need some help aligning it. It looks like it may go back on just a bit harder than it came off."

"I was wondering that, also," he said. "I'll be ready when you need me."

I thanked him and picked up the backpack, taking out one of the new vacuum tubes. I briefly described each step I was taking so Mr. Lincoln would know exactly what I was doing. It took me no more than a minute to take the first one out of the box and plug it into the socket. I did the same thing with the second tube and they were all set to use.

"There," I said. "Those are ready to go," I continued, reaching back for just a few seconds and wiggling each tube slightly to make sure that all of the pins in the tube were making good contact with the contacts in the respective sockets.

"What do the vacuum tubes do, exactly?" he asked.

A feeling of humility came over me as I realized, over the course of about two full seconds, that I had absolutely no idea. I turned around and looked at him and gave an exaggerated shrug of my shoulders. He started to laugh and realized that I wasn't joking.

"Well," he suggested, still laughing, "perhaps sometimes it's enough to know that something works without knowing *how* it works."

"I think you're right," I replied slowly. "In this case, I have no other option. Maybe it's like some people. I may not know how a vacuum tube works, but I know a bad one when I see it." He thought that was funny.

I then stood up and told him I was ready to reinstall the rear panel on the dashboard. When we lifted it up together, it took a bit of jockeying to get it into the exact position, but once it was there, a small lip on the top of the panel mated with a lip on the opening of the dashboard and held it in place while I reinstalled the screws.

I could feel myself taking a big sigh when I said, "I think that's it. We're ready to power up."

Does Anybody Really Know What Time it Was?

After we made the repair, I walked over to the breaker box on the wall, opened it, and turned on the power to the control panel. Then I walked over to the control panel while Mr. Lincoln joined me. We looked down and checked the controls. Like everything else, they remained as we'd left them 36 hours earlier. Destination date: April 14, 1865. Time: 8:05 p.m.

Wait. Time: 8:05 p.m.

After thinking about this critical moment for the last 36 hours, it wasn't until this instant, when I looked at the destination time, that I realized that we had a dilemma.

"Oh…" I said.

"Is there a problem?" replied Mr. Lincoln.

"This is the first time this has struck me," I replied, still looking at the dashboard setting. "The time on the control panel says 8:05 p.m. But…" I said, now looking directly at him. "You saw the end of the play. *Our American Cousin.* That would have been well after 10 p.m. At 8:05, you and Mrs. Lincoln probably would have been on your way to the theater. If we keep the control set for 8:05, there might be two Abraham Lincolns at Ford's Theatre that night. I can't believe I didn't think of this earlier."

"Of course," he said, shaking his head slightly. "I should have realized that, too. Having two of me at Ford's Theatre could be confusing for those in attendance," he said, joking but not laughing.

"To say the least," I replied. We looked at each other for a while, as if that connection might bring the answer.

"Well…it was obviously someone from this station who set the destination time to 8:05. We don't know who it was, and we can only speculate as to why they did it."

"Perhaps they sent someone here to Washington to observe something happening that night, or even to change something," he replied.

"Yes, I think that's a very reasonable assumption," I concurred, without going into additional details about what happened that night in our timeline.

"What time did you arrive at the theatre?" I asked.

"Mrs. Lincoln and I arrived at the theatre shortly after 8:25 that night," he responded, adding details that he thought might be helpful. "The play had begun some minutes before. We were late in arriving because of an important meeting that took place in my office. As soon as we stepped through the theater's doors, the play was halted, the performers and audience stood, and the orchestra played 'Hail to the Chief.'

"We had guests there to accompany us," he added. "A Major Henry Rathbone and his fiancée, Clara Harris. Miss Harris is the daughter of Sen. Ira Harris of New York. We knew the major and Miss Harris for some time. We had asked some others to attend, including Gen. Grant and his wife, Julia, but none were able to."

History shows that Major Henry Rathbone, a native of Albany, New York who fought at Antietam and Fredericksburg, acted heroically that night, as did his fiancée, Clara Harris. Subsequently, life did not go well for either of them.

By the time Major Rathbone noticed John Wilkes Booth surreptitiously enter the presidential box at 10:14 p.m. through a rear door, Booth already had his .41 caliber Philadelphia Deringer drawn; Booth pulled the trigger an instant later. Rathbone jumped up and tried to restrain Booth. However, Booth was also armed with a dagger—the one that was recovered by Lt. Col. Everton Conger 12 days later—which had a blade about six inches long and a handle made of animal bone. When Rathbone grabbed Booth, the assassin used the dagger to slash Rathbone's left arm from the elbow to the shoulder, nearly bone-deep. As Booth assaulted Rathbone, the major was looking Booth in the eye, and said he was "horrified" by the look of anger on Booth's face.

As the 5-foot-8, 160-pound Booth prepared to leap down onto the stage from the president's box, Rathbone again grabbed for Booth. It was very possibly that action—or Booth catching his riding spur on the bunting that draped the box—that threw Booth off-balance, causing him to break his left fibula when he landed. According to several witnesses, Booth shouted out the state motto adopted by Virginia in 1776, "Sic semper tyrannis" ("thus always to tyrants"), then quickly left the theater, riding away on this awaiting horse.

The atmosphere in the theater box was surreal: The president badly wounded, Mrs. Lincoln crying and shouting uncontrollably, Clara Harris stunned, and people now rushing into the box. On more than one occasion, Mrs. Lincoln looked at Clara and cried remarks about "my dear husband's blood," not realizing that much of that blood was Rathbone's. The badly injured Rathbone had fallen to the floor, but moments after the president was picked up and carried from the box and across the street to Petersen's boarding house, Rathbone tried to calm Mrs. Lincoln and escorted the First Lady across the street so she could be with her husband.

Once Rathbone completed escorting the First Lady, he passed out due to loss of blood. Clara arrived shortly thereafter and cradled Rathbone's head during his periods in and out of consciousness. Dr.

Charles Leale, who had been caring for the president, then saw Rathbone and realized that the major's injury was much more serious that originally thought.

Rathbone was driven home to recover while Clara remained at the Petersen boarding house to comfort the traumatized Mrs. Lincoln. Over the next eight hours, the president's body functions would gradually shut down until 7:22 the next morning, when they would stop altogether.

As with hundreds or perhaps thousands of people whose paths have carried them into the disturbed lives of assassins, the event changed the lives of Henry Rathbone and Clara Harris, and not for the better.

Even before U.S. Army Major Henry Reed Rathbone left the presidential box that night to escort Mrs. Lincoln, he began to blame himself for the president's death. He felt that of all the people in this world, he was the one individual who could have stopped the assassination, but that he failed.

Rathbone and Clara were married two years later and had three children, but Rathbone's behavior became less stable, and he resigned from the Army five years after the end of the war. He was unable to keep a job. He drank heavily and gambled. Every year on April 14-15, he had to deal with questions from the press about the assassination and his inability to defend the president. In addition, he became convinced that Clara was having an affair, and was also resentful of the attention she paid to their children.

In 1882—the year after President James Garfield's presidency ended prematurely as he lingered for six months after being shot— Rathbone was appointed consul to the Province of Hanover, Prussia by President Chester A. Arthur. But Rathbone's mental state only continued to decline.

On December 23, 1883 in a state of madness, Rathbone physically attacked their children. When Clara defended them, Rathbone shot her in the head, killing her. She was just 49 years old. Rathbone then continued trying to hurt the children, but the subsequent attacks were thwarted by their groundskeeper. Rathbone stabbed himself in the chest in an unsuccessful attempt to take his own life.

Rathbone was charged with his wife's murder but was declared insane; he spent the rest of his days in an asylum in Hildesheim, Germany, where he died in 1911. The children were sent home to live with their uncle, William Harris, in the States.

In an action that would be echoed 98 years later by First Lady Jacqueline Kennedy after the tragedy in Dallas, Clara Harris Rathbone saved the bloodied white dress she was wearing that night at Ford's Theatre without washing it first. She eventually stored the dress in a family home in Albany, New York. She later had the closet faced over with bricks after she claimed to have seen the ghost of President Lincoln.

In 1910, the couple's oldest child, Henry Riggs Rathbone, had the bricks removed and the dress destroyed, reportedly thinking that it had cursed the family.

The younger Rathbone later became involved in politics, and like the man his father had unsuccessfully tried to defend at Ford's Theatre, he became involved in politics, and was chosen a delegate at the Republican National Convention in 1916. Then, as if closing a loop, in 1923, he was elected to the U.S. House of Representatives, becoming a congressman—from Illinois. More than 60 years after that Good Friday night, Clara and Henry Rathbone's son held the same position as the man his father risked his life to defend.

Henry Riggs Rathbone served for just five years, until 1928, when he died in office at age 58.

"You saw the end of the play," I said, "That might give us a general idea of the time we should target. "What was the name of the play again?" I asked, knowing the title of the play full well, but not wanting to hint at the historical importance of the event, at least in our timeline.

"*Our American Cousin*," he replied. "It truly was an enjoyable play, especially coming during the beginning of the end of the war. It was an English play…a comedy about an English family whose American cousin, Asa Trenchard, goes to England to claim their estate." Mr. Lincoln continued to provide details about the play to me. I knew he was very eager to begin his return trip, but he also knew it would be helpful for both of us to know the events of the evening as well as possible so we could pinpoint the time of his return, and perhaps the exact location, presumably within the theater.

"The play starred a delightful British actress named Laura Keene. Miss Keene is…*was* not only a talented actress, but she became the first person of her sex to be a powerful manager of theaters and productions in New York City."

Laura Keene eventually had to transition away from owning her own theater due to poor health, but for a short period in 1869-70, she managed the Chestnut Street Theatre in Philadelphia. She died of tuberculosis in November 1873, at age 47, less than nine years after her most famous performance in front of the president and First Lady.

"So…it must have been…what…at least 10:30?" I followed up. "You don't happen to know the exact time," I asked as a question, but knowing there was no way of his knowing.

"Yes, it was 10:36."

At this point, I was aware that Mr. Lincoln had become amused by how big my eyes had become and how open my mouth was.

"Ten thirty-six?" I asked. "You know the exact minute? I didn't think to ask earlier because I didn't think you'd know. I don't imagine the theater had any clocks on the wall at that time."

"Clocks? Oh, not that I recall," he responded. "But I do try to keep my watch set as accurately as possible," he said, reaching into his top vest pocket and taking out a beautiful gold pocket watch.

"I'm not given to wearing jewelry or expensive clothes," said Mr. Lincoln, "but I purchased this watch from a jeweler in Springfield, and, in general, a fine watch will keep more accurate time than an inexpensive one. The U.S. Naval Observatory is about three miles northwest of the Executive Mansion, and that's where the nation's exact time is maintained. Occasionally, if I'm in the area, I'll make a brief stop there and set my watch to it."

"That's remarkable," I responded. "Even though you have the resources to do that, I'm sure that not many people would keep their timepieces set so accurately. Do you typically note things such as the time that a play ends?"

"Well...not always," he said, squinting his eyes just a little, as if he just remembered something that he'd forgotten that he remembered. (You know what I mean, right?) "If someone were to ask me the question about the time a few days from now, I might not recall. But in my timeline, it was less than 48 hours ago.

"As I just happened to remember," he continued, "I looked at my watch more frequently near the end of the play. Between 10:12 and when the play ended at 10:36, I looked at my watch perhaps every three or four minutes because at 10:12, there was a bit of a commotion just outside the presidential box. I mentally noted the time each time I glanced, but nothing became of it."

Wait…what???

I Repeat: Wait…What???

I'm sure that by this point I was staring at him, and this time, there was no sense of jocularity on my part. I was unable to process the correct response to him. There was a commotion outside the rear of the presidential box at 10:12? In our timeline, the nation and the world changed at 10:14 that night. But in his timeline, "nothing became of it." It wasn't much of a stretch of the imagination to think that in his timeline, that commotion involved one particular actor who had performed in front of Mr. and Mrs. Lincoln in that very theater. And almost certainly at least one other person, as well.

In their final plans, Booth and his conspirators agreed to execute their respective parts of the plan at 10:15 p.m. At that time, Booth was to kill Lincoln, George Atzerodt was to kill Vice President Andrew Johnson, and Lewis Powell was to kill Secretary of State William H. Seward. The leader, Booth, was the only conspirator to succeed in his goal. George Atzerodt lost his nerve, went to the hotel bar and became "heavily intoxicated," and spent the evening walking the streets of the District of Columbia. Lewis Powell badly injured Secretary Seward but did not succeed in killing him, thanks to Seward's two gutsy adult children and, ironically, an injury from a few weeks before.

Secretary Seward was at his home in bed that Good Friday evening, recovering from a severe injury suffered in a carriage accident nine days earlier. Would-be assassin Powell showed up at the front door and managed to talk his way into the house, but Seward's 35-year-old son Frederick—who had been at the president's cabinet meeting earlier, acting on behalf of his father—sensed that something was wrong and blocked Powell when Powell began heading for the stairway. Powell drew and pointed a handgun at Frederick's head at point-blank range but the pistol misfired. Powell then slammed the gun down on Frederick's head, causing skull injuries. Co-conspirator David Herold, who led Powell to the house and was to help Powell in carrying out the deed, left Powell on his own and fled the house as soon as people started getting hurt. (Four years earlier, it was Frederick Seward who actually delivered the letter from Allen Pinkerton to President-elect Lincoln warning of the Baltimore Plot.)

At the top of the stairs, Seward's 20-year-old daughter Fanny heard the angry voices and closed and blocked the door. Powell managed to get past Fanny but her blocking of the door may have given Seward's other son, Augustus, and an Army sergeant time enough to arrive and keep Powell from killing Seward. Powell reached Seward with a knife and hacked away at his head and neck, but Seward's life was probably saved because of a metal and canvas splint that had been applied to help him recover after the carriage accident. Powell managed to escape and hide out in the city for three days. But late on the evening of April 17, Powell had the poor fortune of showing up at Mary Surratt's boarding house just as military investigators were about to leave after questioning Surratt.

The trials of the four surviving primary conspirators—Powell, Atzerodt, Herold, and Surratt—were carried out by military tribunal instead of civilian court on the orders of the attorney general, Kentucky native James Speed, brother of Abraham Lincoln's old partner at Springfield's general store, Joshua Speed. James Speed had held the position for only four months, having replaced Edward Bates of Missouri, who disagreed with Lincoln's increasingly "radical" position on emancipation. In contrast, James, who had met Lincoln in 1841, had long been vehemently anti-slavery and successfully advocated to keep Kentucky from joining the Confederacy.

The trial of the four began three weeks after their crimes and lasted seven weeks. The four were executed together one week after that, on July 7, 1865, at Fort McNair in Washington, D.C.

You may find the ages of the assassins to be of interest. With the exception of Mary Surratt (42), who owned the boarding house where the conspirators met, the average age of the conspirators was 24 years and 3 months (Booth, 26; Powell, 20; Atzerodt, 29; and Herold, 22). That pattern fits with ages of other assassins. James Garfield's assassin was 39, but William McKinley's was 28 and John F. Kennedy's was 24. Gavrilo Princip, the Bosnian Serb who killed Archduke Franz Ferdinand and his wife, Sophie, in June 1914 was just 19 when he committed the act.

In the absence of any words coming out of my mouth, Mr. Lincoln continued with details about the unexpected noises near the end of *Our American Cousin*: "There were a few loud bumps just outside the door at the back of the box. I thought someone might be having a problem. I nearly went to see if someone needed help or was trying to get in, but then thought better of it. As president, I didn't want to raise any consternation among the audience who, like Mother and me, came to the play to hasten the day that the war wasn't our primary thought, day in and day out."

"That's good to know," I managed to acknowledge after several more seconds of thinking about what might have happened outside the door of the presidential box, and what that might mean for us. With Mr. Lincoln's emotional intelligence, by this time I began to think that he may very well realize that in his timeline, something significant happened that Good Friday evening, which, for my guest in the control room, was the night before last.

"Okay," I said, coming back from my world of thought to the real world. "That's good to know," I repeated. "And do you happen to know how long it was after the play ended that you..."

"Suddenly traveled from there to here?" he suggested, coming up with the words more quickly than me.

"Yes," I smiled back.

"I do," he replied. "It was three minutes. After the conclusion of the play, and, as I said, I noted that it was 10:36, I spoke with Mary, and with Major Rathbone and Miss Harris. We all stood when the play ended, as the audience, including the four of us in the box, gave the performers a standing ovation. Major Rathbone and I then helped the ladies with their coats...he with Miss Harris and me with Mrs. Lincoln...and we began heading toward the back of the box.

"Major Rathbone stepped past me, Miss Harris, and Mrs. Lincoln, toward the door" he continued, "and was about to open the door when I noticed things around me suddenly getting dark. For an instant, I thought the lights of the theater were dimming. Then I realized that it was just a small space around me, and not 10 seconds later, I found myself on the very spot I'm standing in now."

"I can't imagine how disoriented you must have felt," I said. "On my end, I began walking through a space that I knew was dark...and unusual...before I started. In your case, you were there in the theater, doing nothing uncommon, and suddenly you're in a completely different time and place."

"Yes, I must admit that it was very unexpected," he replied. "Nothing that I've ever experienced. Perhaps nothing that anyone except the two of us and a few others have ever gone through. But my time with you, including our visit to Bronson Park and to

Springfield, has helped me to feel much better prepared for my journey home."

"Good," I said. "That's good, and I agree that it'll be helpful for your return trip.

"If you were in the process of leaving the presidential box at 10:39 p.m.," I continued, "and you were near the door at the back of the box, you were probably obscured, at least somewhat, from people in the rest of the theater. And if Mrs. Lincoln, Miss Harris, and Major Rathbone were ahead of you, they were most likely looking rearward, toward the door. In other words, if your watch indicated that you traveled here at 10:39 your time, and at that time the number of people looking in your direction was very small—maybe zero—that certainly seems to be the best time and location to target your destination: 10:39 p.m. near the back of the presidential box. Do you agree that that's the best solution?"

Mr. Lincoln remained silent for perhaps 10 seconds, and I could tell that he was deep in thought.

"Yes," he nodded. "That solution may not be completely without risk, but given all factors, returning me to the exact time and spot that I left—not before or after—is the best option given what we know."

"Good," I agreed. "Then let's set the controls for that point in time and space," I said, stepping around to the operators' side of the dashboard.

Leaving the date set where it was, I adjusted the time to 10:39 p.m. I then adjusted the destination, which was a little more complex, involving sighting down through a device that looked somewhat like the viewer on a stereoscopic microscope. The operator looked down at a physical representation of the destination point, and then used knobs on the sides of the scope, almost like using an Etch-a-Sketch, to move thin vertical and horizontal bars as crosshairs.

When I had the destination time and special coordinates set, I asked Mr. Lincoln to double-check them. It's always good to have a quality check done on scientific work, and in this case, my guest was doubling as the guinea pig. I asked him to go ahead and move the crosshairs if he felt they needed adjustment.

"I'm going to move the horizontal bar slightly toward what would be the front of the box," he said, after perhaps 20 seconds looking through the scope. When he was done, he invited me to double-check his adjustment, keeping with the second-pair-of-eyes paradigm.

"Yes, you would know the exact location better than I," I said, after looking through the scope. "That looks good to me."

Having said that, Mr. Lincoln and I stood and looked at each other for several seconds.

"I think we're ready to go," I said.

"Yes, I think we are," he replied.

Sending Him Home

"When I was a kid, my father used to say, 'Our greatest hopes and our worst fears are seldom realized.'"

- Jim McKay, September 6, 1972, Munich Olympics

We had been so busy for the last hour that I was struck by the sudden stillness, quiet, and lack of urgency. Everything was done, and we were ready to return Mr. Lincoln to his own time and space. Before walking toward the darkness of the Void, he took a step toward me and reached out his right hand.

"Albert, I cannot begin to tell you how much I appreciate your efforts, not only to return me back from whence I came, but also in letting me return to Kalamazoo and to my home in Springfield. Thank you for everything."

"Sir, the pleasure was mine. I grew up learning about you, your upbringing, your presidency, and especially how you did the right thing with emancipation. I'll never forget this experience."

"Nor will I," he replied. He then proclaimed, "Alright, here I go."

I pressed the green button on the dashboard to prepare the entire system for his travel. Dozens of lights on the control panel turned from yellow to green, the electronic buzzing sound increased, and the subtle smell of ozone became evident, as there had been when I first arrived the previous morning. He walked toward the edge of the Void, and then, just before taking his first steps into it, he turned over his shoulder and looked at me.

"Goodbye, Al."

"Goodbye, Mr. President."

He then stepped into the Void. I continued to see him for several seconds, and then his image became less clear, like a person walking into a dense, dark fog. I heard the light tapping of his leather soles on the hard floor at first, and those also diminished, coinciding with the disappearing of his visual image.

Then there was nothing but darkness and silence, and after several more seconds, the slightest of bluish-white flashes, and then again nothing.

After I'd stood there about 15 to 20 seconds, I determined that it would be a good idea for me to remain in the room, for at least a few minutes, in case anything happened for which he needed my help. I sat down in the chair farthest from the ladder. I placed my feet flat on the floor, folded my hands in my lap, and waited, quite still and quietly, keeping my ears tuned in for even the slightest sound.

After about five minutes, I glanced down at my watch. I smiled to myself as I did so, thinking about how diligent my guest had been in keeping his pocket watch accurate. I also enjoyed having a watch that showed me the exact time, but mine does that automatically, syncing with an app on my phone which in turn syncs with a server somewhere on the planet, on which a time that's within a tiny fraction of a second is stored.

I thought about what we'd done over the last two days. As Mr. Lincoln and I had discussed, given the knowledge that we had, I maintained that we had done the right thing. I had given him information about today's world, but with the understanding that if he ever found himself in a position to act on that information, he'd refrain from doing so. And without a better understanding of timelines and how they're changed, I continued to believe that sending the Abraham Lincoln I knew back to the exact minute he left on that Good Friday evening was the best thing to do.

I remained still and silent, but after a few more minutes, I began thinking in earnest about what my next steps would be. I determined that when I returned to my house, I'd browse the Internet looking for anything related to President Lincoln, his family, and the Civil War, and note if anything had changed because of our actions here.

I'd also spend a bit more time in this building before leaving the area, seeing if there were any clues about who had operated this station or who I might contact. In general, I continued to firmly believe that the knowledge about this facility should not be made public; if the decision were made to make it public, it would be made by someone in a far higher "pay grade" than me. I was retired and happy to be doing things that frequently require little planning.

After almost half an hour, I was satisfied that there would be nothing more I could do here.

When I first arrived two days earlier, all of the controls were as they are now, with the same switches left on, the only exception being the exact time and location of destination. I normally tend to turn switches off in rooms when nobody is using them, but in this instance, I thought it was a far better idea to leave things turned on.

I stood up and glanced at my watch again. It was now about 12:15 a.m. the next day; I'd be getting home late. That was fine, but I knew I'd sleep well.

I walked around the room looking for any additional clues. I didn't see any…just switches, dials, and other electronic components, and things like the tool cabinets I'd seen the previous day. Content that there was nothing more here to see, I turned toward the ladder and climbed upstairs, closing the hatch after I got to ground level. Before closing it, I turned on my iPhone flashlight again to provide enough light to see where I was going and to perform a very rudimentary inspection before leaving this station, probably for good.

As I noted when I first arrived, this room had very little in it. I systematically looked up at the ceiling, along all the walls, and down at the floors to see if there was anything I hadn't seen yet. Nothing. I walked around the back of the single, plain table that sat there.

I was taking my last look at the table and nearly ready to leave when I noticed a small drawer on the back side of the table. The drawer didn't run the entire span of the table back to front, so I couldn't have seen it from the other side.

I curled my fingers under the bottom edge of the drawer and pulled, very slowly. I wasn't keen on setting off an alarm, but if I did, I was just going to answer any questions that were asked. The chances were that if someone received an alert from this place, they knew what its function was.

I shined my flashlight down to see the drawer's contents. There was just a thin ledger with a leather and cloth binding and two old pens. I took the ledger out of the drawer, set it down on top of the table, and opened it.

At first quickly thumbing through the pages, I saw that all 30 pages were filled out, with printed names, signatures, and dates for a number of individuals. Several of the names appeared multiple times. A notation at the top of the first page said "Start of Log 1" and at the bottom of the last page it said "End of Log 1. Continued in Log 2."

The ledger was being used as a sign-in logbook, to be signed by personnel and/or visitors who had visited this site.

I looked more closely at the dates. The first pages had consecutive log-in signatures that were frequently several days or even weeks apart, and the frequency increased toward the end. My thought was that the first visitors came while the facility was first being planned and developed, and later signatures after it was in operation.

The first signatures were dated much earlier than I had expected: April 1942. America had become involved in World War II just four months earlier. I certainly didn't remember everything about April 1942, but I knew that after many after fearful and terrifying days for Americans after Pearl Harbor, our military planned and executed a successful attack on the Japanese homeland for the first time that month, when Lt. Col. James "Jimmy" Doolittle led a group of 16 B-25 Mitchell bombers, each carrying four bombs, that took off from the deck of the USS Hornet at sea and dropped their payloads on Tokyo, at the complete surprise of the leaders who had planned the Pearl Harbor attack.

The last signatures in this log were entered in December 1963. That date was less revealing because, presumably, there was a subsequent logbook somewhere with more recent signatures.

I didn't think the actual names in the book would tell me much, and I didn't want to stay in the shed for an extended period looking through them. But I took a quick scan in case they told me anything.

My eyes locked on two signatures in the book.

On the second page of the book, not quite halfway down, was a signature that caught my eye and wouldn't let go. On November 15, 1942, the facility in which I was sitting was visited by Nicola Tesla. For some reason, the Austrian-born American regarded by many as our nation's greatest inventor had been called in to visit this facility.

I continued browsing through the logbook to see if he had signed it again. I did not see his name again, but while looking for it, I found three entries on three separate days for another name I recognized. On at least three separate days between early 1958 and late 1963, the facility was visited by our nation's preeminent theoretical physicist.

"J. Robert Oppenheimer"

The entries answered a few questions but raised many more.

The fact that Nicola Tesla and J. Robert Oppenheimer were involved with—or at least knew about—this project at first told me that the project was managed by the federal government. But then I recalled the hot-and-cold relationships both of these brilliant men had with our government.

There has never been valid evidence that either of these men of science did not love the United States. Both of them loved the nation whose mission was spelled out in the Constitution and its laws, as well as its citizens. But both had histories of taking exception to much of the intervention by the United States into affairs of other countries.

I put the logbook back in the drawer, wondering where the second logbook might be, and why it wasn't still in the drawer. The appearance of the building when I first arrived less than 48 hours earlier suggested that it was abandoned years ago, but not formally: If it had been formally decommissioned, the power would have been turned off, the equipment would have been removed, and the facility would have been decommissioned, probably removed altogether and made to look like it had never been here.

But the door was unlocked and ajar, the power was left on, and evidently, I was on my way back to 1865 until my sojourn was interrupted by another son of the Midwest heading in my direction from the past. And that fellow Midwesterner happened to be Abraham Lincoln.

I realized that my head was down, my shoulders slumped, and that I was just flat-out tired. I had just experienced two days that I never could have imagined, that probably nobody else on the planet had ever experienced, and I wasn't even sure that I could talk about it with anyone.

I could make the decision to come back later if I chose. Or not. But for now, I had too much to think about, and I was too tired. I was going home.

That's My Story...For Now

That's about it.

I drove straight home from the facility in Mentha. I had a lot of thoughts going through my head when I got into bed, but did manage three or four hours of sleep. Most nights since then have been about the same. After I woke up the next morning, I got online and googled hundreds of key pieces of information, events, and people related to Lincoln and the Civil War. So far, I haven't seen anything that has changed as a result of President Lincoln being here. The history I knew before I ever saw the facility seems to be the same as it was after I got back. The Civil War turned out the same. In the history books of our timeline, Mr. Lincoln met the same sad fate that Good Friday evening as the one I learned about in elementary school, and then read about in a lot of books since. I even watched the entire *Civil War* series Ken Burns again to look for changes. There was absolutely nothing different that I could notice.

So without being an expert on timelines, it would seem to me that by returning Mr. Lincoln to that precise minute after the play ended at Ford's Theatre, it restored him to his proper timeline. The books I've read since I last saw him confirms that John Wilkes Booth did get inside the president's box during Asa Trenchard's humorous line in the third act, and carried out the deed he'd planned. And although Booth was successful in carrying out his role, his conspirators failed. Based on that, it does seem that a person's actions have the potential to take him or her in any of a number of timelines, which in turn later branch out into an additional number of them. It seems that there really were at least two versions of the exact same Abraham Lincoln and the people around him, just on different timelines that diverged sometime during the play.

So, it seems that despite the time Mr. Lincoln and I spent together, things turned out the way they were supposed to in our timeline, and I would imagine, in his, as well.

And, as I mentioned, the decision about what to do with the facility won't be mine. I haven't mentioned it to anybody, not Molly or our kids or anyone. This is the first I've told anybody about it.

My one remaining concern has to do with something that happened afterward, which may or may not be related to my involvement with Mr. Lincoln and the facility.

Just two days after I returned Mr. Lincoln to his time and place, I went to the Meijer store near our house to get a few groceries. After I'd loaded them in the trunk, started my car and was leaving the parking lot, I happened to glance over a couple rows of cars, and there was the man again…the one we had seen at the Culver's in Lincoln, Illinois. The one who looked like a young Christopher Walken. He was sitting in the driver's seat of a black Chevy Suburban, like the one we saw there. He acted nonchalant, but I could tell that he was watching me.

It was definitely him, but he had changed. Now, the guy I'd seen just a few days earlier with a buzzcut and stubble on his face had much longer hair and a full beard.

I had the experience of a lifetime getting to spend two days with Abraham Lincoln, and we did what we thought we needed to do. And I thought that when he returned home, I was done.

Now, who knows?

Abraham Lincoln's Speech in Kalamazoo, Michigan

Following is the actual text of the speech given in Kalamazoo by Illinois lawyer Abraham Lincoln on August 27, 1856. Of all the speakers that day, Lincoln was the only one whose speech was known to have been recorded. His speech was recorded using the phonography method by a reporter for the *Detroit Daily Advertiser*. The correspondent added annotations to indicate when the crowd reacted by laughing, applause, and cheering.

Although the stated purpose of the speech was to support the very first Republican nominee for president, John C. Frémont, Lincoln did not specifically mention Frémont's qualifications but instead centered his remarks on the Kansas-Nebraska Act of 1854, the pro-slavery nature of which led to the formation of the Republican Party to fight the proliferation of slavery.

> *"Fellow countrymen:*
>
> *Under the Constitution of the United States another Presidential contest approaches us. All over this land – that portion, at least, of which I know much – the people are assembling to consider the proper course to be adopted by them. One of the first considerations is to learn what the people differ about. If we ascertain what we differ about, we shall be better able to decide.*
>
> *The question of slavery, at the present day, should not only be the greatest question, but very nearly the sole question. Our opponents, however, prefer that this should not be the case. To get at this question, I will occupy your attention but a single moment.*

The question is simply this: Shall slavery be [allowed] into new territories, or not? This is the naked question. If we should support Frémont successfully in this, it may be charged that we will not be content with restricting slavery in the new territories. If we should charge that James Buchanan, by his platform, is bound to extend slavery into the territories, and that he is in favor of its being thus spread, we should be puzzled to prove it. We believe it, nevertheless.

By taking the issue as I present it, whether it shall be permitted as an issue, is made up between the parties. Each takes his own stand. This is the question: Shall the Government of the United States prohibit slavery in the [territories of the] United States?

We have been in the habit of deploring the fact that slavery exists among us. We have ever deplored it. Our forefathers did, and they declared, as we have done in later years, the blame rested upon the mother government of Great Britain. We constantly condemn Great Britain for not preventing slavery from coming amongst us. She would not interfere to prevent it, and so individuals were able to introduce the institution without opposition. I have alluded to this, to ask you if this is not exactly the policy of Buchanan and his friends, to place this government in the attitude then occupied by the government of Great Britain – placing the nation in the position to authorize the territories to reproach it, for refusing to allow them to hold slaves.

I would like to ask your attention, any gentlemen to tell me when the people of Kansas are going to decide. When are they to do it? I asked that question two years ago – when, and how are [they] to do it? Not many weeks ago, our new Senator from Illinois (Mr. Trumbull), asked Douglas how it could be done. Douglas is a great man – at keeping from answering questions he don't want to answer. He would not answer. He said it was a question for the Supreme Court to decide. In the North, his friends argue that the people can decide at any time.

The Southerners [Democrats] say there is no power in the people, whatever. We know that from the time white people have been allowed in the territory they have brought slaves with them. Suppose the people come up to vote as freely, and with as perfect protection as we could do it here. Will they be at liberty to vote their sentiments? If they can, then all that has ever been said about our provincial ancestors is untrue, and they could have done so, also. We know our Southern friends say that the General Government cannot interfere. They could as truly say, 'It is amongst us – we cannot get rid of it.'

But I am afraid I waste too much time on this point. I take it as an illustration of the principle, that slaves are admitted to the territories. And, while I am speaking of Kansas, how will that operate? Can men vote truly? We will suppose that there are ten men who go into Kansas to settle. Nine of these are opposed to slavery. One has ten slaves. The slaveholder is a good man in other respects; he is a good neighbor, and being a wealthy man, he is enabled to do the others many neighborly kindnesses. They like the man, although they don't like the system by which he holds his fellowmen in bondage. And here, let me say, that in intellectual and physical structure, our Southern brethren do not differ from us. They are, like us, subject to passions, and it is only their odious institution of slavery, that makes the breach between us.

These ten men of whom I was speaking, live together three or four years; they intermarry; their family ties are strengthened. And who wonders that in time, the people learn to look upon slavery with complacency? This is the way in which slavery is planted, and gains so firm a foothold. I think this is a strong card that the Nebraska party have played, and won upon, in this game.

I suppose that this crowd are opposed to the admission of slavery into Kansas, yet it is true that in all crowds there are some who differ from the majority. I want to ask the Buchanan men, who are against the spread of slavery, if there be any present, why not vote for the man who is against it? I understand that Mr. Fillmore's position is precisely like Buchanan's. I understand that, by the Nebraska bill, a door has been opened for the spread of slavery in [to] the territories. Examine, if you please, and see if they have ever done any such thing as try to shut the door.

It is true that Fillmore tickles a few of his friends with the notion that he is not the cause of the door being opened. Well; it brings him into this position: he tries to get both sides, one by denouncing those who opened the door, and the other by hinting that he doesn't care a fig for its being open. If he were President, he would have one side or the other – he would either restrict slavery or not. Of course, it would be so. There could be no middle way.

You who hate slavery and love freedom, why not, as Fillmore and Buchanan are on the same ground, vote for Frémont? Why not vote for the man who takes your side of the question? 'Well,' says Buchanan, 'it is none of our business.' But is it not our business? There are several reasons why I think it is our business. But let us see how it is. Others have urged these reasons before, but they are still of use. By our Constitution we are represented in Congress in proportion to our numbers, and in counting the numbers that give us our representatives, three slaves are counted as 2 people. The State of Maine has six representatives in the lower house of Congress. In strength South Carolina is equal to her. But stop! Maine has twice as many white people, and 32,000 to boot! And is that fair? I don't complain of it. This regulation was put in force when the exigencies of the times demanded it, and could not have been avoided. Now, one man in South Carolina is the same as two men here.

Maine should have twice as many men in Congress as South Carolina. It is a fact that any man in South Carolina has more influence and power in Congress today than any two now before me. The same thing is true of all slave States, though it may not be in the same proportion. It is a truth that cannot be denied, that in all the free States no white man is the equal of the white man of the slave States. But this is in the Constitution, and we must stand up to it. The question, then, is, 'Have we no interest as to whether the white man of the North shall be the equal of the white man of the South?'

Once when I used this argument in the presence of Douglas, he answered that in the North the black man was counted as a full man, and had an equal vote with the white, while at the South they were counted at but three-fifths. And Douglas, when he had made this reply, doubtless thought he had forever silenced the objection.

Have we no interest in the free Territories of the United States – that they should be kept open for the homes of free white people? As our Northern States are growing more and more in wealth and population, we are continually in want of an outlet, through which it may pass out to enrich our country. In this we have an interest – a deep and abiding interest. There is another thing, and that is the mature knowledge we have – the greatest interest of all. It is the doctrine, that the people are driven from the maxims of our free Government, that despises the spirit which for eighty years has celebrated the anniversary of our national independence.

We are a great empire. We are eighty years old. We stand at once the wonder and admiration of the whole world, and we must enquire what it is that has given us so much prosperity, and we shall understand that to give up that one thing, would be to give up all future prosperity. This cause is that every man can make himself. It has been said that such a race of prosperity has been run nowhere else. We find a people on the Northeast, who have a different government from ours, being ruled by a Queen. Turning to the South, we see a people who, while they boast of being free, keep their fellow beings in bondage. Compare our Free States with either, shall we say here that we have no interest in keeping that principle alive? Shall we say, 'Let it be'? No – we have an interest in the maintenance of the principles of the Government, and without this interest, it is worth nothing.

I have noticed in Southern newspapers, particularly the Richmond Enquirer, *the Southern view of the Free States. They insist that slavery has a right to spread. They defend it on principle. They insist that their slaves are far better off than Northern freemen. What a mistaken view do these men have of Northern laborers! They think that men are always to remain laborers here – but there is no such class. The man who labored for another last year, this year labors for himself, and next year he will hire others to labor for him.*

These men don't understand when they think in this manner of Northern free labor. When these reasons can be introduced, tell me not that we have no interest in keeping the territories free for the settlement of free laborers.

I pass, then, from this question. I think we have an ever-growing interest in maintaining the free institutions of our country.

It is said that our party is a sectional party. It has been said in high quarters that if Frémont and Dayton were elected the Union would be dissolved. I believe it [that the South does so think]! I believe it! It is a shameful thing that the subject is talked of so much. Did we not have a Southern President and Vice-President at one time? And yet the Union has not been dissolved. Why, at this very moment, there is a Northern President and Vice-President. Pierce and King were elected, and King died without ever taking his seat. The Senate elected a Northern man from their own numbers, to perform the duties of the Vice-President. He resigned his seat, however, as soon as he got the job of making a slave State out of Kansas. Was not that a great mistake?

(A voice: 'He didn't mean that!')

Then why didn't he speak what he did mean? Why did he not speak what he ought to have spoken? That was the very thing. He should have spoken manly, and we should then have known where to have found him. It is said we expect to elect Frémont by Northern votes. Certainly, we do not think the South will elect him. But let us ask the question differently. Does not Buchanan expect to be elected by Southern votes? Fillmore, however, will go out of this contest the most national man we have. He has no prospect of having

350

a single vote on either side of Mason and Dixon's line, to
trouble his poor soul about.

(Laughter and cheers)

We believe it is right that slavery should not be tolerated in
the new territories, yet we cannot get support for this
doctrine, except in one part of the country. Slavery is looked
upon by men in the light of dollars and cents. The estimated
worth of the slaves at the South is $1,000,000,000, and in a
very few years if the institution shall be admitted into the new
territories, they will have increased fifty percent in value.

Our adversaries charge Frémont with being an abolitionist.
When pressed to show proof, they frankly confess that they
can show no such thing. They run off upon the assertion that
his supporters are abolitionists. But this they have never
attempted to prove. I know of no word in the language that
has been used so much as that one, "abolitionist", having no
definition. It has no meaning unless taken as designated as a
person who is abolishing something. If that be its
signification, the supporters of Frémont are not abolitionists.

In Kansas all who come there are perfectly free to regulate
their own social relations. There has never been a man there
who was an abolitionist – for what was there to be
abolished? People there had perfect freedom to express what
they wished on the subject, when the Nebraska bill was first
passed.

Our friends in the South, who support Buchanan, have five
disunion men to one at the North. This disunion is a sectional
question. Who is to blame for it? Are we? I don't care how
you express it.

This government is sought to be put on a new track. Slavery is to be made a ruling element in our government. The question can be avoided in but two ways. By the one, we must submit, and allow slavery to triumph, or, by the other, we must triumph over the black demon. We have chosen the latter manner. If you of the North wish to get rid of this question, you must decide between these two ways – submit and vote for Buchanan, submit and vote that slavery is a just and good thing, and immediately get rid of the question; or unite with us, and help to triumph. We would all like to have the question done away with, but we cannot submit.

They tell us that we are in company with men who have long been known as abolitionists. What care we how many may feel disposed to labor for our cause? Why do not you, Buchanan men, come in and use your influence to make our party respectable?

(Laughter.)

How is the dissolution of the Union to be consummated? They tell us that the Union is in danger. Who will divide it? Is it those who make the charge? Are they themselves the persons who wish to see the result? A majority will never dissolve the Union. Can a minority do it?

When this Nebraska bill was first introduced into Congress, the sense of the Democratic party was outraged. That party has ever prided itself, that it was the friend of individual, universal freedom. It was that principle upon which they carried their measures. When the Kansas scheme was conceived, it was natural that this respect and sense should have been outraged.

Now I make this appeal to the Democratic citizens here. Don't you find yourself making arguments in support of these measures, which you never would have made before? Did you ever do it before this Nebraska bill compelled you to do it? If you answer this in the affirmative, see how a whole party has been turned away from their love of liberty!

And now, my Democratic friends, come forward. Throw off these things, and come to the rescue of the great principle of equality. Don't interfere with anything in the Constitution. That must be maintained, for it is the only safeguard of our liberties. And not to Democrats alone do I make this appeal, but to all who love these great and true principles. Come, and keep coming! Strike, and strike again! So sure as God lives, the victory shall be yours.

(Great Cheering)"

Epilogue

The Statue of Abraham Lincoln in Kalamazoo's Bronson Park was dedicated on August 27, 2023, on the 167th anniversary of Lincoln's speech there. Photo by the author.

Thank you for joining me for this story.

The story includes both fiction and fact. As I neared the end of writing it, I came to realize that between the two, fiction and fact, the facts related to the life of Abraham Lincoln and those around him were more fantastic than the meager literary device of time travel I incorporated.

I've tried to convey the character of Abraham Lincoln, without assigning him characteristics that he didn't possess during his relatively short life of 56 years. His "superpowers" were the desire to learn and better himself and to do what he thought was right, which included saving the Union and obtaining freedom for millions of people.

The story about our family's visit to Lincoln's tomb a few days after Liam Neeson is true. When our kids were growing up, we'd go to fun places such as Mount Rushmore, Washington, D.C., Boston, New York City, Beaver Island in Michigan, and one memorable family trip to Florida to visit Disney World, Cocoa Beach, and the Kennedy Space Center. And whenever we'd go, Molly, Katy, and Sam would always humor Dad (me) when I wanted to take little side trips along the way to visit museums and historic places. When we'd visit places like Jimmy Carter's boyhood home in Plains, Lincoln's boyhood home in Kentucky, or Ford's Theatre in Washington, I appreciated that they'd allow me to do my thing. But years later, it was not an isolated incident for one of the kids to say "Hey Dad, remember when we were at Ford's Theatre and we went downstairs to see John Wilkes Booth's diary, and the door to the presidential box...?" Without my knowing it, the little seeds of history were planted on those days, and we were able to do the fun stuff, too.

To me, in some ways 150+ years seems to be a very long time, but at the same time, it can seem not long ago at all. As William Faulkner wrote, "The past is not dead, in fact, it's not even past." If the life of Abraham Lincoln had not ended prematurely on Good Friday night of 1865 at Ford's Theatre, he may well have lived until after my father was born early in the 20th Century, not many generational degrees of separation for me.

At the very time I was writing this book, starting in 2018, a dedicated group of people was planning to memorialize Abraham Lincoln's visit to Kalamazoo. The group, the Kalamazoo Abraham Lincoln Institute, planned and raised funds to have a statue created and erected in Bronson Park. It was a long journey for many group members. As one example, for Cameron S. Brown, the institute's president and former Michigan state senator and representative, it was an 11-year journey.

But the group was successful, and on August 27, 2023—the 167th anniversary of Lincoln's speech in Kalamazoo—a seven-foot statue of him was unveiled near at the north side of Bronson Park. More than 1,000 people were on hand, and speakers paid tribute to the man from Springfield. A vintage band, the Dodsworth Saxhorn Band, played and a Texas-based singer, Alfrelynn Roberts, gave a spine-tingling a cappella rendition of "The Battle Hymn of the Republic." In addition to Cameron S. Brown, speakers included:

- Tom George, M.D., whose research was a major driver in the effort to install the statue
- Dr. Michael Rice, State Superintendent of Public Education and former superintendent of Kalamazoo Public Schools
- Kalamazoo Mayor David Anderson
- Gary Swain, State Commander of the Sons of Union Veterans of the Civil War

Mayor Anderson expressed a common thought, saying "A long, long time ago, a person we all know was at this very location and provided some words that continue to go down in history. We could not be prouder in Kalamazoo to be the only place in Michigan where this esteemed statesman came and provided the important words which were a precursor in which his legacy ended up being."

Mayor Anderson continued, "We care about Abraham Lincoln, and we'll remember that we were here on this day. Look around you, and ask 'How are we going to make sure that this is a place where we love, honor, and respect each other?'"

Tom George has described Abraham Lincoln as being "at the crux of American history." More than 150 years after his presidency, he remains the key figure between the period of the nation's founding and the current day.

Lincoln changed, and so did we. During much of his time as a politician and lawyer, many Americans, including a number of his friends and associates, were more adamant than Lincoln about ending slavery and ending it quickly. His position for many years was that "the peculiar institution of slavery" was a terrible thing, but that the U.S. Constitution did not allow the federal government to force the states to end it. But end it he did, with the Emancipation Proclamation, and with amendments that would be added to our Constitution. Those amendments were not ratified until after his death, but they exist largely because of him.

In turn, although popular sovereignty and Stephen Douglas won out twice, in 1854 and 1858, the People supported Lincoln instead of Douglas in 1860 or George B. McClellan in 1864. And citizens in the North and South alike who advocated seceding from the Union (including states in New England, New York and New Jersey in decades before the Civil War) now recognized the strength in numbers that could be realized by the *United* States of America.

The events of history changed Abraham Lincoln, and Lincoln in turn changed the country. He was, in fact, a man "of the People, for the People, and by the People."

Members of the Dodsworth Saxhorn Band played at the dedication of the Abraham Lincoln statue at Kalamazoo's Bronson Park on August 27, 2023. Photo by Fran Dwight.

Acknowledgements

Thanks to all of you who love history, trivia, and off-the-wall ideas. You know who you are.

Many thanks to my friends of many years, Jennifer Giles and David Martin, who reviewed this book. I appreciate their patience, attention to detail, and love of the English language. Jenn and David, I owe you big-time.

Thanks to Fran Dwight, a wonderful Kalamazoo-based photographer, who has such a great artistic eye for capturing important subject matter, like people and love. Your photos are an integral part of this book.

Appreciation to the Kalamazoo Abraham Lincoln Institute for keeping Mr. Lincoln's dreams alive, and for making his statue at Bronson Park a reality. In particular, thanks to Tom George for spending so much of his life to research the topic. He's the go-to guy for information about Abraham Lincoln's 1856 visit to Kalamazoo.

Thanks to all of my history teachers throughout grade school and college for inspiration, and to my friends at the Historical Society of Michigan for making a safe place for spreading the gospel of history.

And importantly, thanks to my family for encouraging me to complete this work. Researching and writing *Texting Lincoln* was a labor of love and a physical and emotional need, and I appreciate your support while I worked on it. To all three of you, thanks for your company and humor while we visited Springfield, Illinois; Hodgenville, Kentucky; Gettysburg, Pennsylvania; the White House, the Lincoln Memorial; Ford's Theatre; the Studebaker National Museum in South Bend; The Henry Ford in Dearborn, Michigan...

References

The following references were used in the creation of this book and/or provide interesting information about the life of Abraham Lincoln.

Wikipedia: Abraham Lincoln. Retrieved December 20, 2023 at Abraham Lincoln - Wikipedia

Wikipedia: Radio. Retrieved December 20, 2023 at Radio - Wikipedia

Eighmey, Rae Katherine. *Abraham Lincoln in the Kitchen: A Culinary View of Lincoln's Life and Times*. Smithsonian Books, 2017

Wikipedia: Bronson Park Historic District. Retrieved December 20, 2023 at Bronson Park Historic District - Wikipedia

Kalamazoo Public Library (online article). "Bronson Park: A Commons in the Center of the City." Retrieved December 20, 2023 at Bronson Park — Kalamazoo Public Library (kpl.gov)

Merrin, Doug. "Abraham Lincoln Used 'Michigander' as an Insult. *The Sun Times News*, Washtenaw County, Michigan, April 1, 2021. Retrieved January 1, 2024. Abraham Lincoln Used "Michigander" as an Insult | The Sun Times News

Witsil, Frank. "6 places in Michigan you can see President Abraham Lincoln letters, artifacts." *Detroit Free Press*, July 13, 2023. Retrieved January 5, 2023. https://www.freep.com/story/news/local/michigan/2023/07/13/michigan-abraham-lincoln-collectables/70403285007/

Wikipedia: Radio. Retrieved January 18, 2024. Radio - Wikipedia

Timmerman, Elizabeth. Bronson Park: "A Commons in the Center of the City." Kalamazoo Public Library website. Written 2000, updated May 2006, retrieved January 18, 2024. Bronson Park — Kalamazoo Public Library (kpl.gov)

Wikipedia: Kalamazoo, Michigan. Retrieved January 18, 2024. Kalamazoo, Michigan - Wikipedia

"Westnedge Avenue, S., 925: Octagon House - Allen Potter Residence." Kalamazoo Public Library website. Retrieved January 18, 2024. Westnedge Avenue, S., 925: Octagon House – Allen Potter Residence — Kalamazoo Public Library (kpl.gov)

"Sarah Lincoln Grigsby: Abraham Lincoln Birthplace National Historical Park, Lincoln Boyhood National Memorial." National Park Service website. Last updated January 12, 2022, retrieved January 20, 2024. Sarah Lincoln Grigsby (U.S. National Park Service) (nps.gov)

"Abraham Lincoln's First & Second ABC School Teachers; Zachariah Riney & Caleb Hazel Sr." Digital Research Library of Illinois and Chicago History. November 18, 2020, retrieved January 20, 2024. The Digital Research Library of Illinois History Journal™ : Abraham Lincoln's First & Second ABC School Teachers; Zachariah Riney & Caleb Hazel Sr. (drloihjournal.blogspot.com)

Wikipedia: Nancy Hanks Lincoln. Retrieved January 20, 2024. Nancy Lincoln - Wikipedia

"Lincoln's Home." National Park Service website. Last updated December 19, 2023, retrieved January 20, 2024. Lincoln Home National Historic Site (U.S. National Park Service) (nps.gov)

Wikipedia: William Herndon (lawyer). Retrieved January 20, 2024.
William Herndon (lawyer) - Wikipedia

Herndon, William H. and Weik, Jesse W. *Herndon's Lincoln.* Edited by Wilson, Douglas L. and Davis, Rodney O. Knox College Lincoln Studies Center and University of Illinois Press, Urbana and Chicago (2006).

Wilson, Douglas L. and Davis, Rodney O. "Editor Interview, Herndon's Lincoln." Abraham Lincoln Online website. Updated online 2020, retrieved January 20, 2024.

Zeitz, Josh. "The Man Who Created the Lincoln We Know." *Politico Magazine* online. April 14, 2015, retrieved January 20, 2024. The Man Who Created the Lincoln We Know - POLITICO Magazine

"Abraham Lincoln and William H. Herndon." *The Lehrman Institute Presents Abraham Lincoln's Classroom* online. Retrieved January 20, 2024. Abraham Lincoln and William H. Herndon – Abraham Lincoln's Classroom (abrahamlincolnsclassroom.org)

"Mary Lincoln's Trips to Europe." *Mary Todd Lincoln Research Site* online. Retrieved January 20, 2024. Mary Lincoln's Trips to Europe (rogerjnorton.com)

Geduld, Herb. *"Lincoln's last words: How I should like to visit Jerusalem."* Clevelandjewishnews.com. Updated Oct. 4, 2011, retrieved January 20, 2024. https://www.clevelandjewishnews.com/archives/lincolns-last-words-how-i-should-like-to-visit-jerusalem/article_4056423a-f7db-547b-9665-54d9a64170af.html

Borvick, Gedaliah. "Why is there a Lincoln Street in Jerusalem?" 5TJT.com website. January 6, 2021, retrieved January 20, 2024. https://www.5tjt.com/why-is-there-a-lincoln-street-in-jerusalem/

"Mary Lincoln." Online article by The White House Historical Association. Retrieved January 20, 2024. Mary Lincoln - White House Historical Association (whitehousehistory.org)

Wikipedia: Nicolay and Hay. Wikipedia article about the friendship and working relationship of Abraham Lincoln's personal secretaries, John G. Nikolay and John Hay. Retrieved January 22, 2024.: Nicolay and Hay - Wikipedia

Wikipedia: Nicolay and Hay's book: Abraham Lincoln: A History - Wikipedia

Wikipedia: John George Nicolay. Wikipedia article with references bout John G. Nicolay, President Lincoln's personal secretary.: John George Nicolay - Wikipedia

Wikipedia: John Hay: Wikipedia article about John Hay, President Lincoln's personal secretary John Hay - Wikipedia

Wikipedia: 30th United States Congress. Retrieved January 22, 2024. 30th United States Congress - Wikipedia

Wikipedia: 1864 Presidential Election. Retrieved January 22, 2024. 1864 United States presidential election - Wikipedia

"American Colony in Jerusalem, 1870 to 2006." Library of Congress website. Retrieved January 22, 2024. https://www.loc.gov/collections/american-colony-in-jerusalem/articles-and-essays/american-colony-in-jerusalem-timeline-1828-1980/1828-to-1873/

Jacoby, Jeff. "When Lincoln's Secretary of State Went to Jerusalem." Aish.com. August 3, 2022, retrieved January 22, 2024. https://aish.com/when-abraham-lincolns-secretary-of-state-went-to-jerusalem/

Burlingame, Michael. "Abraham Lincoln: Campaigns and Elections." The history of Abraham Lincoln's elections including his 1860 and 1864 presidential elections. University of Virginia Miller Center. Retrieved January 22, 2024. Abraham Lincoln: Campaigns and Elections | Miller Center

"The Boys: Abner Y. Ellis (1807-1878)." *Mr. Lincoln and Friends* website. Retrieved January 22, 2024. Abner Y. Ellis (1807-1878) - Mr. Lincoln and Friends (mrlincolnandfriends.org)

"Timeline of Our History." U.S. Secret Service website. Retrieved January 22, 2024. Timeline of Our History (secretservice.gov)

"Reminiscences of Stephen A. Douglas." *Atlantic Monthly*. August 1861. https://www.theatlantic.com/magazine/archive/1861/08/reminiscences-of-stephen-a-douglas/628340/

Miller, Tom. "Where Mary Todd Lincoln Shopped for China – No. 448 Broadway." *Daytonian in Manhattan* website. Article about Mary Todd Lincoln's purchase from NYC department store. Retrieved January 22, 2024. http://daytoninmanhattan.blogspot.com/2011/11/where-mary-todd-lincoln-shopped-for.html

"Virtual Tour of the Lincoln Home National Historic Site." Website created and maintained by National Park Service. Retrieved January 22, 2024. https://artsandculture.google.com/story/virtual-tour-of-the-lincoln-home-national-historic-site-lincoln-home-national-historic-site/AwUR7IXhfshLKg?hl=en

Wikipedia" Old State Capitol State Historic Site." Online page providing information about the Old State Capitol Building in Springfield, Illinois. Retrieved January 22, 2024. Old State Capitol State Historic Site - Wikipedia

"History Reborn: The Restoration of the Illinois Old State Capitol." Thirty-minute video describing the landmark restoration of the Old State Capitol Building in Springfield, Illinois. Retrieved January 22, 2024. History Reborn: The Restoration of the Illinois Old State Capitol - YouTube

"Lincoln-Herndon Law Offices." "Historic Places" page on *Abraham Lincoln Online* website. Retrieved January 22, 2024. https://www.abrahamlincolnonline.org/lincoln/sites/law.htm

"Mr. Lincoln's Office: Final Cabinet Meeting." *Mr. Lincoln's White House* website. Secretary of the Navy Gideon Welles' diary notes of the last cabinet meeting in the Executive Mansion, April 14, 1864. : https://www.mrlincolnswhitehouse.org/the-white-house/upstairs-at-the-white-house/upstairs-white-house-mr-lincolns-office/mr-lincolns-office-final-cabinet-meeting/

George, Tom M. "'Mechem' or 'Mack': How a One-Word Correction in the Collected Works of Abraham Lincoln Reveals the Truth about an 1856 Political Event." *Journal of the Abraham Lincoln Association*, a website hosted by Michigan Publishing, a division of the University of Michigan Library.Volume 33, Issue 2: Summer 2012. https://quod.lib.umich.edu/j/jala/2629860.0033.204/--mechem-or-mack-how-a-one-word-correction-in-the-collected?rgn=main;view=fulltext

"Deconstructing the Kalamazoo Paper Industry." Kalamazoo Public Library website. Retrieved December 3, 2023. https://www.deconstructingpaper.com/?page_id=27

Somers, Lucas R. "Lincoln's Dreams: An Analysis of the Sixteenth President's 'Night Terrors' and Other Chimeras." Western Kentucky University Masters Thesis, an analysis of Lincoln's dreams. (2025). https://digitalcommons.wku.edu/cgi/viewcontent.cgi?article=2528&context=theses

Kalamazoo Abraham Lincoln Institute website: Institute (kalamazoolincolninstitute.org).

Made in the USA
Middletown, DE
25 February 2024

49891757R00205